T5-AFK-943

The Lorette Wilmot Library
Nazareth College of Rochester

DEMCO

Home Material

Home Material:
Ohio's Nineteenth-Century Regional Women's Fiction

Sandra Parker

Bowling Green State University Popular Press
Bowling Green, OH 43403

LORETTE WILMOT LIBRARY
NAZARETH COLLEGE

Copyright 1998 © Bowling Green State University Popular Press

Library of Congress Cataloging-in-Publication Data
Home material : Ohio's nineteenth-century regional women's fiction /
    [compiled by] Parker, Sandra.
        p.   cm.
    Includes bibliographical references.
    Contents: The picture / Julia L. Dumont -- Aunt Hetty / Julia L.
Dumont -- A tale of early times / Pamilla W. Ball -- Maid of the
Muskingum / Pamilla W. Ball -- The Indian martyrs / Caroline Lee
Hentz -- The senator is but a man / Harriet Beecher Stowe -- Mrs.
Wetherbe's quilting party / Alice Cary -- The stirring off / Mary
Hartwell Catherwood -- Rose day / Mary Hartwell Catherwood --
Solomon / Constance Fenimore Woolson -- Wilhelmina / Constance
Fenimore Woolson -- Hillsbury folks -- the scalawag / Jessie Brown
Pounds -- Trouble at Craydocks Corners / Jessie Brown Pounds.
    ISBN 0-87972-765-9. -- ISBN 0-87972-766-7 (pbk.)
    1. Ohio--Social life and customs--Fiction. 2. Frontier and pioneer
life--Ohio--Fiction. 3. Domestic fiction, American--Ohio. 4. Ameri-
can fiction--Women authors. 5. American fiction--19th century.
6. Country life--Ohio--Fiction. 7. American fiction--Ohio.
I. Parker, Sandra (Sandra A.)
PS571.O3H66   1998
813'.30809287'09771--dc21   98-11977
                                                                     CIP

Cover design by Dumm Art

813. 3080
9287
Hom

Dedicated to Maxine Keene

and also to

Ada Throop Parker,

who went west in a covered wagon

What we have here in the Middle West, the particular, the fresh way, in which the ancient stream of life manifests itself, colored and shaped by local conditions, has never before been and will never be again. We must catch it, or its essence is eternally lost. (182)

—Ruth Suckow
"Middle Western Literature"

Contents

Acknowledgments

I would like to express my gratitude to the National Endowment of the Humanities for its 1982 grant to Hiram College, "Regionalism in the Humanities," which introduced me to the academic discipline of regional studies. I am especially indebted to the chief director of this workshop, namely my colleague David Anderson who has provided challenges, information, comradeship, and selfless support for my studies. I am also appreciative to Hiram College for its sabbaticals that allowed the pursuit of my scholarly interests, especially to the staff members of Hiram College's library who have aided research, acquired materials, and answered endless inquiries: Joanne Sawyer, archivist; Lisa Johnson, reference librarian; and Mary Lou Selander, interlibrary loan, many thanks for your loyal assistance.

For vital work compiling this manuscript, I am indebted to Mat Palmer. Most especially, I wish to thank Joyce Dyer, Hiram's writing director, for her staunch mentorship, first, in believing in this project, and second in providing guidelines for its refinement; her attention to details and sense of style have been invaluable. Beyond the campus, I am also grateful to Susan Koppelman, a fellow Ohio reader, for her insights and encouragement.

If uncovering *Home Material*'s tradition of Ohio's women writers has taught me anything, it is that none of us move ahead without such community support.

Introduction

This chronologically selected anthology of eight literary women provides an inclusive text that makes accessible an Ohio literary tradition that begins with lost aspects of frontier life in the 1830s written by contemporaries Julia L. Dumont and Pamilla W. Ball and ends with Jessie Brown Pounds's restrospective re-creation of the Western Reserve's frontier culture at the century's close. Ohio in 1803 became America's seventeenth state, and it (as well as New England and the South) was a region where self-conscious literary tradition was cultivated. The stories in this volume all preserve the original punctuation and spelling; they explore Ohio's places and contemporary idioms in a variety of styles, yet they all attempt to define the frontier experience from their particular perspectives as Ohio women.

In presenting a selection of literary texts about the experiences of nineteenth-century Ohioans, my aim is to add a dimension to our understanding of regional experiences. This collection will, I hope, offer insights into a variety of authors and a range of texts, many previously neglected, and amplify our understanding of women's role as regional writers during Ohio's premodern era. I suggest that until we recognize the significance of such early writers our picture of the region remains incomplete. Beyond its existence as an artifact of literary history, a complement to the excellent histories of Ohio's settlement and extant documentary material, regional fiction is a genre that allows readers unique access to pioneers' lives. Unfortunately, reprints of fiction about the Middle West have been out of print for over a century, are difficult to obtain, and have received less attention than the East, South, and West. So I hope that this collection will encourage the cultivation of a fuller understanding of middle-western culture.

The representative regional texts in this collection include the work of writers whose names have endured in the canon of Ohio's literary history, such as Harriet Beecher Stowe, Alice Cary, and Constance Fenimore Woolson, as well as several authors, Julia L. Dumont, Pamilla Ball, and Jessie Brown Pounds, who have essentially disappeared. Early tales, such as those of Dumont, Ball, and Hentz, deserve to be resurrected in order to remind modern students how early Ohio's "western" culture included women writers who were both mythmakers and social critics. H. B. Stowe is included to illustrate Ohio's undernoted function as an ideological keystone to the Abolition movement and the Civil War, as well as to provide more attention to Stowe's under read classic. Also included are magnificent works in the local color tradition that deserve reprinting because they offer superb, realistic insights into the village culture of rural Ohio, especially the stories of Cary, Catherwood, Woolson, and the unacknowledged Pounds. These Ohio authors illustrate Lillian S. Robinson's call for enlargement of the canon that must include the rediscovery and reappraisal of lost and undervalued women writers (109).

Considered as a continuing legacy, all of their texts are worthy objects of study that provide insights into our forebears' lives, represent a diverse range of women's narratives, and demonstrate the importance of Ohio as a site for the tradition of women's regional writing.

Indeed, literature is historically mediated, and like any significant region of America, Ohio has a history that helps to explain its evolving literary traditions. Following the Northwest Ordinance and subsequent statehood, Ohio's frontier reality lasted only a few decades and quickly altered, as Howard Mumford Jones points out, after 1830 when the wild "West" of Ohio's frontier transmuted into America's new "Middle West." In his words, "in three generations it passed from being a wilderness into a predominantly agrarian culture" (70). And during the following decades, a vast influx of immigrants joined the dominantly British middle-western settlers in Ohio, creating a complex, multicultural identity. Later migrants included such Germanic religious sects as Moravians and Mennonites who came to Ohio's remote hills, like Zoar. From such places as France, Germany, and Switzerland, settlers poured into Ohio's burgeoning urban centers—Cincinnati and, especially, Cleveland.

The evolution of women's writing in the Middle West has in some ways reflected regional changes over the nineteenth century. Women's writing moves away from imitative romantic treatments of pioneer crises in the early days of the era and toward sophisticated regional fiction that emphasizes how provincial environs shape or mirror characters who speak in vernacular and become products of their setting.

The humble beginnings of Ohio women's regional writing is found in a private journal, *Journey to 'Hio in 1810*. Here, Ohio's earliest woman writer describes the migration experience, a hardy trans-Appalachian trek from New Haven, Connecticut, to Warren, Ohio. However, this narrative by Margaret Van Horn Dwight, niece of Timothy Dwight, Yale University President between 1795 and 1817, remained out of print until 1912 when it appeared in the *Atlantic Monthly* and later in book form.

Ohio's nineteenth-century writers, therefore, did not know Dwight and were unable to read her or use her as a model. Instead, they were reading eighteenth-century fictional frontier narratives by eastern writers. Among these recreations of eastern settlement experiences are romances, such as the Indian-American narrative of Eliza Bleecker, *The History of Maria Kittle* (1793), and regionally-based stories, such as Susannah Rowson's *Reuben and Rachel; or Tales of Old Times* (1798). Many, as Richard Slotkin suggests, are captivity narratives or stories that depict the destruction of Indian Americans, if only for the purpose of acquiring their potentially valuable land (4). Through the opening decades of the nineteenth century, interest in indigenous materials continued in the works of men writers such as Washington Irving's *Sketch Book* (1819-20) and James Fenimore Cooper's *Leather Stocking Tales* (1823-1841), as well as the novels of popular women writers like Lydia Maria Child's *Hobomok* (1821) and Catharine Sedgewick's *Hope Leslie* (1827), which concerns New England's Pequod Indians.

In Ohio, romanticized pioneer stories about the "Vanished American" theme soon appeared in the works of middle-western regionalists. James Strange French, for example, published *Elkswatawa; or the Prophet of the West* (1836), which describes Tecumseh's brother. Julia L. Dumont also wrote an exculpatory biography of the charismatic Shawnee leader who attempted the creation of an intertribal alliance that would revitalize Indian-American culture and preserve their lands. He died in 1813 while fighting with the British the War of 1812, but his significance as a threatening symbol of indigenous resistance carried lasting potency on Ohio's western frontier.

Many other regional women writers, like Pamilla W. Ball, Julia L. Dumont, and Caroline Lee Hentz, also address the displacement and genocide of "noble savages." Their ambivalent attitudes toward America's indigenous peoples run the gamut from showing them as the massacring enemy, for example in Dumont's "The Picture," to defending them with a dubious kind of egalitarianism. Thus Dumont's version of America's frontier story includes both sympathy for Tecumseh and a description of bloody wars between his people and the Anglo-Americans who were destroyed at Fort Wayne, while romanticizing the "noble savage" characterizes the frontier tales of Pamilla W. Ball and Caroline Lee Hentz in "Maid of the Muskingum" and "The Indian Martyrs." The Native Americans of Ball and Hentz are pitied as victims of rapacious Euro-Americans whom the authors indict. These authors express sympathy for victimization and often connect that of pioneer white women and Native Americans. The authors, however, only celebrate indigenous peoples who have become powerless, natives who "cease thinking of exterminating" Caucasian settlers.

No Ohio captivity narrative is included in this anthology because the topic is only peripherally approached by Ohio's women regionalists.

Certainly Julia L. Dumont and Pamilla W. Ball knew many stories about regional captives who were kidnapped for slaughter, adoption, or barter by Native Americans. For instance, James Everett Seaver in 1824 wrote a popular account of the Ohio kidnapping of Mary Jemison who, captured by the Seneca tribe, preferred to live out her life in New York state as the "white woman of the Genesee." However, the captivity theme remains a subordinated issue in Ohio women's stories like Dumont's "Ashton Gray" and Ball's "Hugh Mason," neither included in this anthology, which focus upon the protagonists' postcaptivity experience. In general, Ohio's early women regionalists who treat the rigors of frontier life employ narrative strategies associated with their predecessor's romantic fiction; they approach the genocide of America's indigenous peoples with honest fear, sympathy, and regret.

All the writers in this anthology were influenced to one degree or another by their reading. But midcentury writers were more heavily influenced by the narratives of British authors who evolved the story of rustic places than by early Native American narratives. Thus, regional women authors contributed a vision of frontier civilization that was built upon modifications of established literary forms other than narratives of frontier violence; prominent models included romance, polemic, and realism. Among the most significant literary foremothers for midcentury writers were the British authors who evolved the story of rustic places, especially Mary Russell Mitford, Elizabeth Gaskell, and George Eliot, who respectively published *Our Village* (1826-32), *Cranford* (1853) and *Scenes of Clerical life* (1857), works that sold well and were excerpted in numerous American journals.

The state's first generation of writers, represented in this anthology by Julia L. Dumont, Pamilla W. Ball, and Caroline Lee Hentz, composed frontier stories that adapted the Native American theme, presented local history, cautioned new migrants, and praised the new homeland. However, their fiction is often marred by being didactic and naive in style.

The second generation reacted against the stringent conditions of frontier life. Alice Cary powerfully describes the post-frontier experience in Ohio with all of its grueling labor, loneliness, and hardship for women in Mount Healthy. In midcentury Harriet Beecher Stowe was also promoting the state as a rough-and-ready countryside that could be truly pacified by the extended warmth of the American hearth. Stowe and Cary in this anthology represent a transitional generation whose often sentimental stories are more realistic and skillful than frontier romances and emphasize the period's preoccupations with domesticity. The early impetus for this style came from national figures like Sarah

Josepha Hale, the celebrated and influential eastern editor of *Godey's Lady's Book* (1837-77), who in 1828 called for an American literature that would be characterized by a "record of conjugal and maternal love" (72). Women's domestic style continued for decades, and even after the Civil War, Harriet Beecher Stowe's *Hearth and Home* (1869) essays pleaded for literature about the "simple and homely scenes of every-day life." Following such injunctions, countless American women developed regional narratives connected to home management.

The third generation of writers, represented in this anthology by Constance Fenimore Woolson, Mary Hartwell Catherwood, and Jessie Brown Pounds, are characterized by the way they sought to preserve the vanishing mores of post-bellum Ohio. Their mature stories illustrate the standards applied by Judith Fetterly and Marjorie Pryse, who define regional writers as those who draw a culture from within, cherishing a locale and its people and avoiding condescension. As they say, such regional fiction, therefore, signals affection for place and a style where character, in a sense, becomes plot with subtle tone, feeling, and emotions conveyed through people and place, not action.

These late-century regional stories have been labeled "local color," a phrase somewhat less in favor among modern critics. Living from 1811 to 1896, Harriet Beecher Stowe's long career incarnates two significant approaches to women's writing; she both demonstrates midcentury domesticity and is a key influence in creating the style of short regional tales that became called local color. Ohio played an interesting role in the evolution of these sketches, which were first written while she was living in Cincinnati, which she called the "West," during the 1840s. Later published in *The Pearl of Orr's Island* (1862) and *Oldtown Folks* (1869), these New England stories helped to forge the new American style that Sarah Orne Jewett and Mary E. Wilkins Freeman are usually credited with perfecting. All three New Englanders, in turn, influenced other writers, including Ohio's regionalists, to adopt the style of the polished regional story.

Of the eight writers in this anthology, only Mary Hartwell Catherwood completed upper-level education, graduating from Granville Female College in Ohio. Jessie Brown Pounds attended two years at Hiram College; Constance Fenimore Woolson completed high school at the prestigious Madame Chegaray's in New York City. Harriet Beecher Stowe was educated at the Hartford Female Seminary by her famous sister, Catherine, educator and women's rights advocate, while informal education occurred for Pamilla W. Ball, Julia L. Dumont, Alice Cary, and Caroline Lee Hentz. Following the practice at the time, Dumont, Stowe, and Catherwood all earned their living as teachers.

Another interesting aspect of these regionalist writers' lives is how they fulfilled their culture's expectations for "womanly women." None were free-spirited bohemians who challenged rules of decorum. Only Alice Cary and Constance Fenimore Woolson never married, and each woman lived out her life caring for family members. Dumont, Ball, Hentz, and Stowe were widows with children; Catherwood was a wife and mother who chose to live apart from her husband. Pounds married in midlife, adopted two children, but never bore children of her own.

Though living in the Middle West for a significant part of their adult lives, these women were not physically isolated. In fact, most of them were remarkably well traveled. Even the most committed resident of the state, Pounds, lived for three years in Chicago and visited many out-of-state and Canadian church conferences. Ball happily migrated from Virginia westward to Ohio; Cary contentedly migrated eastward to New York City from Ohio, while Dumont, Catherwood, and Hentz moved among the middle-western states of Ohio, Indiana, and Illinois. The most well traveled were Harriet Beecher Stowe, the committed New Englander who left Ohio in 1850 for Maine and Massachusetts, where she largely stayed, except for holidays in the South and on the Continent, and Woolson, who departed from Ohio to visit the east coast and South, then became an international expatriate, living and dying in Europe.

Nor were these writers intellectually isolated. Alice Cary and Harriet Beecher Stowe chose to reside on the east coast, living in what modern readers would probably consider to be in an urban, literary milieu. Woolson traveled in international intellectual circles, and was friends with Henry James. In contrast, Pamilla W. Ball was isolated in Zanesville during the 1830s, but a contemporary writer Julia L. Dumont had many professional acquaintances, as did Caroline Lee Hentz, Mary Hartwell Catherwood, and Jessie Brown Pounds. Each woman was widely published, had a devoted readership, and knew many writers, editors, and intellectual friends.

During the century, from Ohio's earliest immigrant writers, like Ball and Dumont, to later settlers like Stowe, Hentz, and Woolson, to those "charter" writers who were born in the Buckeye state, Catherwood and Pounds, many similarities in viewpoints are evident; these women writers entertain with tears, romance, suspense, and pathos. Their narratives are influenced by readers' expectations, like the convention of predictable closure. For example, stories like "Rose Day" and "Wilhelmina" illustrate the popular nineteenth-century style as they respectively end with a marriage and a funeral.

Indeed, nearly all of these authors demonstrate the era's dominant cultural constructs and gender stereotypes as well as interesting areas of silence. Subjects that they downplay include female sexuality, passion—except within the approved context of marriage or spirituality—and childbearing. Other topics were approached only indirectly. For instance, from early frontier writing to writing at the century's end, women remained cautious about publicly criticizing the American social system that denied them personal and legal autonomy. When protesting disempowering cultural behaviors like alcoholism, for instance, the narrator may express overt complaint and present negative portrayals of fictional male characters, as Ball does in "Woman's Destiny." This approach repudiates men's rugged individualism, the masculine tolerance of drinking, gambling, and self-destruction—three themes demonstrated in Dumont's "Aunt Hetty" where the title character is left to grieve in silence after her son's death from such excesses. Ann Douglas Wood warns that this female revisionism could be dangerous, seen as an attack on "male preserves" (5). Other stories, in contrast, only imply a male critique because their emphasis is placed upon positive advocacy of woman's community. This approach is conveyed in the stories of Ball, Cary, and Catherwood whose ideology of female merit stresses women's values as a replacement for men's self-interest. Alice Cary's "Mrs. Wetherbe's Party" is a good example with its inclusion of a women's quilting bee, characterized by information sharing, companionship, and interpersonal support.

One of the most recurrent themes found in their writing throughout the century was temperance, not surprising as Cleveland, Ohio, was the birthplace of the WCTU, or Women's Christian Temperance Union, founded by Frances Willard in 1874. But temperance is an early subject for first-generation regionalists like Julia Dumont whose frontier stories such as "The Picture" and "Aunt Hetty" portray the awful consequences of alcoholism. Pamilla Ball's "Woman's Destiny" centers on the tragedy caused by "deleterious beverages." In the middle of the century, second-generation writers continued to indict alcoholism, a central concern in Alice Cary's mature story "Mrs. Wetherbe's Party" where an Ohio provincial "saves" an urban decadent. Late-century writers, like Jessie Brown Pounds, also continue the portrayal of wanton, self-indulgent intemperance in her sketches of "The Scalawag," the village drunk in the Western Reserve village of Hillsbury.

Other themes shared by these women writers include surviving isolation, such as was imposed by the eastern outmigration. This topic is depicted in Ball's "A Tale of Early Times" and Dumont's "The Picture." Among other related themes are the emerging identity of pioneer women, obstructions to romantic love, and challenges to boundaries—physical, psychological, social, and ideological. Frontier women and settlers were infrequently depicted as choosing the allure of adventure, which might, nonetheless, be imposed upon them, as in stories like "The Maid of the Muskingum."

Often several of these preoccupations are intermixed. For example, Pamilla Ball's story "A Tale of Early Times" dovetails romantic interests, women's frontier culture, and an example of how false values can be replaced by healthier "western" community. This story plots the confluence of two loving youths with contrasting educational, class, and regional backgrounds; their middle-western courtship overcomes all differences—threats from slavery, decadent wealth, and corrupt morality (imported from the South)—to forge a new, frontier egalitarianism. Thus Ball's regional "moral" demonstrates the transcendence of both social and geographical boundaries.

As these examples suggest, though diverse in political ideology, point of origin, and lifestyle, the region's women writers all appealed to justice, common sense, and patriotism. They admired middle-class values, such as sympathy, renunciation, and commitment to the institutions of family and church. Their lives, in fact, counter popular platitudes and myths about the deprivations of regional writers.

From early in the nineteenth century, America's literary centers were Boston and New York, where publishers showed a strong bias toward New England. Indeed, prominent eastern writers such as Margaret Fuller called for "compositions founded on regional history and relevant to pioneer experience" (130). Brahmin culture was led by intellectuals, such as Henry Wadsworth Longfellow, Ralph Waldo Emerson, Nathaniel Hawthorne, and Oliver Wendell Holmes, who endorsed regional writing, but their interests centered upon their own region, the east coast and New England.

Local interest in defining the Middle West became apparent as early as 1828 when Ohio editor Timothy Flint in his *Western Monthly Magazine* described American settlers as simple, vigorous, independent people who wanted to read about "the things by which we are surrounded" (14). Benjamin Drake, another Ohioan, in 1833 urged the fostering of western genius to "augment the number of Western readers and create a Western heart" (16). Eleven years later, in 1844, Julia Dumont, one of the region's hopeful authors, reflected the regional enthusiasm of her mentors when she expressed a loyal commitment to write "distinctly home material." Indeed, from the earliest days of the Ohio frontier, during the 1820s and 1830s, middle-western writing was supported by regional magazines and newspapers.

Eastern snobbishness toward provincial western pioneers was reinforced by distinguished British visitors such as Frances Trollope in her

Domestic Manners of the Americans (1832) and Charles Dickens in his *American Notes* (1842), who focused their anger and mockery on the state of Ohio. Their travel writings documented "western" faults and galvanized rebuttals from dozens of frontier writers who arose to defend and celebrate Ohio's rural trans-Appalachian identity. Reactions to these outsiders' attacks on the region led to increased self-consciousness and pride; for instance, William D. Gallagher, a prominent western literary editor of the *Cincinnati Mirror and Ladies' Parterre*, in 1834 named the region's best writers, including Julia L. Dumont, Pamilla W. Ball, Caroline Lee Hentz, and Harriet Beecher Stowe. He described them as "mothers" who were preparing Ohio youths for "active scenes of life" (229). Ten years later the eminent editor inaugurated the *Western Literary Journal and Monthly Review* with an essay challenging regional authors to diffuse a knowledge of the region's history and resources.

By midcentury, changes in American attitudes were appearing. The East spawned a new medium for publication—the literary magazine, which expanded readership and opened once hegemonic publications to a wider and more diverse group of writers that included many regional women. Perhaps the eastern literary establishment, recognizing that divisiveness among regions had torn the nation apart and also that the newly-leisured upper class who provided a market for travel literature, as Richard H. Brodhead points out, became more receptive in the 1870s and 1880s to middle-western writing. This midcentury widening of the "national" literary market created invitations to such Ohio authors as Harriet Beecher Stowe, Alice Cary, Mary Hartwell Catherwood, and Constance Fenimore Woolson.

As a consequence, middle-western women discovered expanded options for publishing beyond regional resources and moved onto the pages of such prestigious journals as the *New Harper's Monthly, Scribner's Monthly,* and the *Atlantic Monthly*, edited by Ohio-born William Dean Howells between 1871 and 1881, who emerged as America's arbiter of literary taste by liberating east-coast Brahmin provincialism that now began to recognize writers from all regions.

In 1889 Howells wrote in the opening issue of *Harper's New Monthly* that regional writing must be appreciated for its "honest observation." Twelve years later, after the turn of the century, Howells continued to praise regionalism which celebrated "manners and the codes of past and present" (*Literature and Life* 174). Another late-century advocate of regionalism, Hamlin Garland, similarly endorsed provincial life as the most appropriate subject for the American writer in his 1894 essay *Crumbling Idols*. Their critical support also encouraged twentieth-century writers to continue investigating regional themes, including many famous Ohioans, such as Sherwood Anderson and Toni Morrison, whose careers are still based upon the Buckeye state's home material.

By midcentury, Stowe and Cary appeared in Gamaliel Bailey's abolitionist Washington-based weekly, the *National Era*. Boston's *Atlantic Monthly* provided a vehicle for Cary, Catherwood, and Woolson. New York's *Harper's Monthly* published Cary and Woolson. At the same time, many women writers did not turn their back on regional publications; for example, Alice Cary was simultaneously publishing in religious and secular journals from the East, Middle West and West, like Bret Harte's expressly regional publication, *Overland Monthly*.

The one Ohio woman writer who did not find a national readership was Jessie Brown Pounds, who only published in her region's denominational publications, particularly Disciples of Christ's *Christian Standard* and *Christian Evangelist,* though at the end of her life in 1920 she became an editor and contributor to Chicago's nondenominational *Christian Century.*

Also noteworthy is that many authors, among them Dumont, Cary, Catherwood, Woolson, and Pounds, reached the public directly by publishing their own fiction anthologies. Julia L. Dumont published her definitive anthology, *Life Sketches from Common Paths,* the year before she died in 1856; it was published in New York by D. Appleton. Alice Cary had New York's Edgewood publish her two early anthologies about Ohio, *Recollections of Country life* (1851) and *Clovernook; or, Recollections of Our Neighborhood in the West* (1853), after she migrated east to New York City in 1850. Constance Fenimore Woolson published her regional middle-western stories, *Castle Nowhere: Lake-Country Sketches* (1875), after she moved to the East when she was thirty-five years old. And Pamilla W. Ball, driven by economics and a desire for recognition, edited her own newspaper, where her own work was prominently featured. Only Jessie Brown Pounds used a regional publisher, Cincinnati's Standard Publishing Company, for her two short-story anthologies, *A Woman's Doing and Other Stories* (1886) and *Runaway and Other Stories* (1889).

Why were so many readers suddenly interested in middle-western writing by women? They entertained and moralized, two popular and interrelated narrative goals at the time that determined stories' focus, structure, and form. The authors appealed to readers by employing a range of narrative techniques including the era's most popular genres: the romance of frontier narratives is illustrated by the earliest writers, Dumont, Ball, and Hentz; domesticity is embodied in a selection from Stowe's influential abolition polemic; and regional realism is developed by Catherwood, Cary, Woolson, and Pounds. The domestic novelists project a world that is child-centered and grounded in the values of liberal Protestantism. Their evangelical piety is morally pedagogic and by mid-century is directed toward redefining the Republic's understanding of slavery through Harriet Beecher Stowe's evangelical model of social action, the abolition polemic, *Uncle Tom's Cabin* (1852). Meanwhile, there were other contemporary women writers, like Caroline lee Hentz, who in works like *The Planter's Northern Bride* (1854) and *The Lost Daughter* (1857), use domestic arguments to serve apologists of slavery. Such politically motivated examples of women's domestic narration did not, as scholars like James Hart and Ann Douglas have noted (12), survive the Civil War era.

However, the theme of reconciliation remained enormously popular in postbellum regional writing that cultivated readership by assessing the cost of Ohio's Union role in the Civil War. For instance, Woolson's "Wilhelmina" provides a devastating description of a civilian postwar casualty. Covert treatments of the postbellum recovery appear in a number of stories that depict the region in an elegaic style that sustains the republic while memorializing its passing cultural order. In Ohio after the Civil War, Alice Cary, Mary Hartwell Catherwood, Constance Fenimore Woolson, and Jessie Brown Pounds wrote superb short regional stories that indirectly helped bind the region's wounds. They used narrative sophistication and consummate artistry to weave anew the diffuse threads of regional culture in their local color Ohio-based stories.

It seems ironic that as Ohio's regional women writers established national reputations and fame beyond the Alleghenies, such as Alice Cary did with her writing about Mount Healthy and Constance Fenimore Woolson with her riveting stories about Zoar, they simultaneously became estranged from their nourishing culture of origin. Both Alice Cary and Constance Fenimore Woolson, for example, left the region. Dumont and Catherwood moved west of Ohio; Cary, Stowe, and Woolson went east; and Hentz traveled south. Only Pounds chose to spend her whole life in the state. Readers may wonder whether regionalists write about their subject matter differently when they are in residence or in exile, an issue implied by Mary Austin when she provocatively suggests that regional writing could be described as being *about* a region, rather than *of* it (105).

Over a hundred years ago, regionalism was a literary style that encouraged fledgling authors to cultivate their talents. Today we can discern a variety of reasons for our ancestors' interest in regional short stories. Nineteenth-century readers had limited leisure and education; they appreciated narrative brevity, were chauvinistic, and eager to read about their own environs. Then by the close of the century Americans became preoccupied by the Gilded Age and World War I, and there was a decline in regionalism. Publishers' new enthusiasm was for realism, naturalism, modernism, and dark topics. Regardless of shifts in publishers' emphases, regional fiction has continued into the end of the twentieth century. Louise Erdrich, a famous practitioner of regional style, observes that "truly knowing a place provides the link between details and meaning" (23). These human links are seen in stories which describe the region's evolution from frontier, to farm, to village, with settlers cursing and defending Native Americans, clearing farmland, and boiling down maple sugar. Indeed, it might be said that nineteenth-century women writers helped invent Ohio's identity.

Despite the diversity of nineteenth-century narratives in this anthology, a retrospective of women middle-western regionalists reveals that their work is literary and worthy of inclusion in America's literary canon. Ohio's middle-western women's fiction deserves its place alongside that of the region's more acclaimed men authors like Zane Grey, Ambrose Bierce, Artemis Ward, and W. D. Howells.

Indeed, the work of our region's nineteenth-century foremothers provides clues to understanding the modern era's continuing regional preoccupation. The work of Ruth McKenney, Mary Deasy, Jo Sinclair, Dawn Powell, Joan Chase, Pulitzer Prize–winners Rita Dove, Mary Oliver, and Nobel laureate Toni Morrison all connects, even begins, in a mysterious way with the stories in this volume. In this anthology twentieth-century readers will encounter the strong sense of place in Ohio's earliest regional writing, that Eudora Welty calls "the ground conductor of all the currents of emotion and belief and moral conviction" (67).

Bibliography

Austin, Mary. "Regionalism in American Fiction." *English Journal* 21 (1932): 97-107.

Brodhead, Richard H. *Culture of Letters*. Chicago: University of Chicago Press, 1993.

Donovan, Josephine. *New England and Local Color Literature*. New York: Ungar, 1983.

Drake, Benjamin. "Remarks on the Importance of Promoting Literary and Social Concert . . . Delivered to the Literary Convention of Kentucky." November 8, 1822.

Dwight, Margaret Van Horn. *Journey to 'Hio in 1810*. New Haven: Yale University Press, 1912.

Emch, Lucille B. "Ohio in Short Stories, 1824-1839." *Ohio State Archaeological and Historical Society Quarterly* 53 (July-Sept. 1944): 209-50.

Erdrich, Louise. "Where I Ought to Be: A Writer's Sense of Place." *New York Times Book Review* 28 July 1985: 22-24.

Fetterly, Judith, ed. Introduction. *Clovernook Sketches and Other Stories.* New Brunswick: Rutgers University Press, 1987.

Fetterly, Judith, and Marjorie Pryse. "Alice Cary: 1820-1871." *Legacy* 1.1 (Spring 1984): 1-3.

Fetterly, Judith, and Marjorie Pryse, eds. *American Women Regionalists 1850-1910.* New York: Norton, 1992.

Flint, Timothy, ed. Editorial. *Western Monthly Magazine* 10 June 1828: 10, 12-13.

Fuller, Margaret. *Papers on Literature and Art.* New York: Wiley, 1846.

Gallagher, William D. "Brief Notices of Western Writers." *Cincinnati Mirror* 3 May 1834: 229.

——. "On Western Character." *Cincinnati Mirror* 16 Feb. 1833: 82.

Garland, Hamlin. "Local Color as the Vital Element of American Fiction." *Proceedings of the American Academy of Arts and Letters and the National Institute of Arts and Letters.* New York: American Academy of Arts and Letters, 1951-1976: 41-45.

Hale, Sarah Josepha. "The Frontier House." *The Legendary* 1. Ed. E. N. P. Willis. Boston: Goodrich, 1828. 269-89.

Hart, James D. *The Popular Book: A History of America's Taste.* New York: Oxford University Press, 1950.

Howells, W. D. *Literature and Life.* New York: Harper, 1902.

Jones, Howard Mumford. *The Age of Energy.* New York: Viking, 1970.

Knepper, George. "Early Migration to the Western Reserve." *Western Reserve Magazine* Nov.-Dec. 1977. Special insert: 37-44.

Martineau, Harriet. *Society in America.* Garden City: Anchor, 1962.

Morrison, Charles Clayton. Obituary. *Christian Century* 10 Mar. 1921: 6.

Person, Leland, Jr. "The American Eve: Miscegenation and a Feminist-Frontier Fiction." *American Quarterly* 37 (1985): 668-85.

Petry, Alice Hall. "Universals and Particular: The Local Color Phenomenon Reconsidered." *American Literary Realism* 12 (1979): 110-26.

Pounds, Jessie Brown. "Life and Modern Fiction." *Christian Century* 24 Feb. 1921: 9.

——. "Books of Yesteryear." *Christian Century* 3 March 1921: 7-8.

Richardson. Lyon. "Constance Fenimore Woolson." *Southern Atlantic Quarterly* Jan. 1940: 18-36.

Robinson, Lillian S. "Treason Our Text: Feminist Challenges to the Literary Canon." *The New Feminist Criticism.* Ed. Elaine Showalter. New York: Pantheon, 1985. 105-21.

Roosevelt, Theodore. "What Americanism Means." *Forum* 30 Apr. 1894: 198-99.

Slotkin, Richard. *Regeneration Through Violence*. Middletown: Wesleyan University Press, 1973.

Suckow, Ruth. "Middle Western Literature." *English Journal* 21.3 (1932): 175-81.

Venable, W. H. *Beginnings of Literary Culture in the Ohio Valley*. Cincinnati: Robert Clarke, 1891.

Welty, Eudora. "Place in Fiction." *South Atlantic Quarterly* 55 (1956): 57-72.

Wood, Ann Douglas. "The Literature of Impoverishment: The Women Local Colorists in America, 1865-1914. "*Women's Studies* 1.1 (1972): 3-45.

Julia L. Dumont

1794-1857

William Turner Coggeshall, our first promoter of "local literature" from the "great Central Valley of the United States," in his 1860 anthology, *Poets and Poetry of the West*, introduces Julia L. Dumont as one of the region's earliest woman writers to deserve preservation. The next literary historian interested in the Ohio Valley was W. H. Venable who in his 1891 study, *Pioneer Poets and Story-Writers,* also praises Dumont. Today Julia L. Dumont is virtually unknown, though for more than three decades she was popular for her inspiring narratives about westerners who were rugged individualists.

In a sense, Julia L. Dumont's life represents a paradigm of Ohio's early regional woman writer. Her parents were original Marietta settlers from Rhode Island who had migrated with the Ohio Company in 1788, and Julia Louise Cory was born in Waterford, Washington County, on the banks of the Muskingum in 1794. Then she was taken East as a child; her father died; her mother remarried; the family moved to Saratoga county, New York. In 1812 Julia Cory worked as a schoolteacher and married John Dumont. The following year they migrated to Cincinnati, an area then called the Athens of the West and center of middle-western literary activity.

Only a year later, in 1814, the Dumonts moved to Indiana where she gained renown as the teacher of Edward Eggleston, another regionalist writer who celebrated an Ohio Methodist preacher in his *The Circuit Rider* (1874). Years after her death, in 1879, Eggleston described the influence of his "preceptress," in *Scribner's Monthly*, praising Dumont for once occupying "no mean place as a writer of poetry and prose tales" (750).

During her prime, Dumont's contemporary literary reputation grew from publishing in a variety of early Cincinnati periodicals, among them: the *Western Literary Journal and Monthly Review*; the *Ladies' Repository; Saturday Evening Chronicle* in which "Theodore Harland" won an 1827 prize; the *Literary Gazette* (1824-25); the *Cincinnati Mirror and Ladies' Parterre*, which became the *Cincinnati Mirror and Western Gazette of Literature and Science* (1834-36) and published the romantic tale, "Ashton Grey," about an Ohio River boatman whom Gallagher praises as a contribution to the "stock of Western Literature."

Her principal concerns were with ethics and justice, **whether per-**sonal or institutional. For instance, as early as 1824 the *Literary Gazette* published Dumont's sympathetic biography of the Shawnee **chief** Tecumseh who is depicted as a child cruelly mistreated by **white men.** Though killed eleven years before in Canada when he was **fighting with** the British against "Americans" in the War of 1812, Tecumseh **was still a** terrible figure for settlers who had been frightened by his rebellious **for-**mation of a league of Indian tribes to check whites' westward expansion.

Julia Dumont's narratives were not usually so controversial, **but her** strength was often found in lively content. W. H. Venable praised **her** picturesque descriptions of pioneer customs along the Ohio River **in** western romances like "Ashton Grey" (1832), a story about the **conse-**quences of the Indian Wars. Grey is a "novitiate in wild-wood life," **a** Pottawatamie captive who grows into a knight errant of the "wild **unre-**claimed West" who speaks, reads, and writes standard English, **unlike** the frontier roustabouts who speak in dialect, saying such things as **"per-**tikeler," "truk," and "airth." The antagonists include an oddly villainous stepfather who "lived a wild Ingen life" and is hungry for his son **"as a** famished wolf" and eastern immigrants who learn the uselessness **of** "aristocratic hauteur." Gallagher says Grey represents the **"mundane** sphere" which touches "deeper springs of feeling" and places "a **claim** upon our regard"; he enthusiastically rates Dumont's western tale **along-**side eastern romances such as Washington Irving's "Rip Van Winkle" and "Sleepy Hollow."

Many of Julia Dumont's narrators mock eastern cultural **hegemony** as in "The Picture" (1836), for example, where the narrator asks for **a** "true" regional story, one that unfashionably rejects chivalry, tenderness, pathos. "The Picture" draws upon recent history—French and **English** claims led to the 1763 French and Indian War and a treaty which **forbid** settlement west of the Alleghenies. The American Revolution led **to** expansion and such confrontations as a bloody slaughter of innocent Delawares by the Tuscarawas River in 1782, known as the "bloody **year**" of Ohio history. Bellicose Shawnees raided settlers in the region **through** 1703 when President George Washington launched a punitive **campaign** by sending General Anthony Wayne and militia to Cincinnati. **They** erected a line of forts between Lake Erie and the Ohio River, a line **that** ended at the confluence of the Maumee and the Auglaize at Fort **Defi-**ance. "Mad Anthony," as the Revolutionary War hero was called, **and his** soldiers decisively battled the Indian warriors, which led to the **1795** Treaty of Greene Ville. Dumont's "The Picture" retrospectively **narrates** these military confrontations; for example, she describes **defensive** buildings like Fort Washington and Fort Recovery, which were **designed** to support the soldiers of St. Clair's army. "The Picture" views these historical events through the eyes of one backwoods hero, Roswell Carr Harman, a man who survives the defeat of St. Clair, the building of Fort Wayne, the War of 1812, and retires to a wonderful home near Cincinnati.

Other Dumont stories also commence with framing devices that reject Eastern "puffing" of the West and Old World calls for "grandeur in ruins," "classical associations," and "gorgeous pageants." Julia Dumont repudiates the dishonest hyperbole of romance, though both nineteenth and twentieth-century critics have been critical of her "romantic" style, which Lucille Emch calls "Lady's Book writing," a reflection of the popular "sentimental tale in the thirties" (233).

Yet, Julia L. Dumont's fiction rejects various aspects of popular romantic conventions as she strives for regional verisimilitude in post-frontier Ohio. She tempers romance's ideals with a powerful sense of domestic realism in such mature stories as "A Family History" and "Aunt Hetty." "A Family History" (1844) mocks "transcendental" literary styles, calls for preservation of Western "home material," and illustrates her viewpoint with a contemporary story about Cincinnati's urban development. This story, written seven years before Nathaniel Hawthorne's *House of the Seven Gables* (1851), exposes a house "bearing the impress of time" with its own tale to tell about Cincinnati, that "queen and queenly city."

Shortly before she died of tuberculosis in 1857, Julia L. Dumont collected "Ashton Grey" and a number of shorter narratives in *Life Sketches from Common Paths,* which is loosely organized as a story sequence about a typical middle-western village. Dumont's stories combine romance and realism in a descriptive sequence, as did precursors like: Englishwoman Mary Russell Mitford (*Our Village,* 1824-32), and Americans Catharine Sedgewick (*A New England Tale,* 1822), Emily Chubbuck [Judson], *Alderbrook,* 1846), and Charlotte A. Fillebrown Jerauld (*Chronicles and Sketches of Hazlehurst,* 1860). Julia Dumont's narratives are similarly designed to show how locality shapes character. For example, "Aunt Hetty" is labeled by the male narrator as being a "superior woman of her class." Her life illustrates domestic realism; it is a story about a German immigrant's isolation and disempowerment. Aunt Hetty buries her dissolute son who has died in a cholera epidemic. This story epitomizes Dumont's home material and life-long empathy with the downtrodden.

Julia L. Dumont was a teacher, wife, and mother who buried four sons, a daughter, and husband. With failing health she went south but returned to the family where she finished assembling *Life Sketches from*

Common Paths. As Coggeshall insightfully remarks, Dumont's "indomitable industry" did not lead to "high literary position" or fulfill her promise because household cares, feeble health, and low self-esteem all "prevented her from attempting more" (46).

Julia L. Dumont was an indigenous Ohio writer who rejected offers from eastern publishers so that she could give her narratives to "local press" and aid struggling village publications. Because of her dedication, Dumont became the first woman writer to distinguish herself in the Ohio region. She represents, as she said in the introduction to *Life Sketches*, the moral embodiment of Ohio's earliest tradition of women writers who set out to reify the "reality of goodness in our bad world" (9).

The Picture

Julia L. Dumont

The pangs
Tender and sweet of Love—the excitement high,
Of War and Chivalry

"It is impossible," said I. "I can make nothing of the picture!"
"What picture? what is impossible?" said my venerable friend. "In these
wonder-working days, I thought that word was expunged from our
vocabulary."

I had set down to write a story. All the exciting influences of an
early summer morning were around me. The very air that stole into my
room breathed of poetry; and the waving shadow that fell near me, from
the stirred foliage of my window, was full of sentiment. Annuals, and
monthlies, and Border Legends, were on my table. My brain was
thronged with brilliant fancies. I had made me a pen "gracefu' and
yieldin'" as Miss Gould's, and had written with a most imposing flourish: *For the Literary Journal and Monthly Review. A Western Sketch.*
Now what was this Sketch to be? Romantic it must certainly be, and
pathetic, and chivalrous, and tender, and glowing, and imaginative; and
above all, it must be *western*. It was for a western magazine—it was
intended for western readers—and the *writer*, said I, drawing myself up
with the thought, the writer is to all intents and purposes, western. I
dipped my pen in the ink. It is an easy matter to invent a story, said I;
and then one may throw *out* the dark lines that always chequer reality.—
So I leaned my head on my hand, and tried to grasp some of the visions,
that for the last half hour had been passing in such splendid review
before me. But they had somehow assumed a strange indistinctness.
Except a few bright forms, whom upon second glance I remembered to
have already met in some of the magazines above mentioned, they
seemed now to have neither form nor place. I struggled, but in vain, to
reduce them to anything tangible. They mingled—faded—melted—in
fine they were all evaporated. What could I do? It was obvious that I
could *not* get on without a beginning. I will appeal to memory, said I.
Some old legends will do, gathered from the early settler; and unfolding
the records, I ran hurridly over some twenty years, to the time of my first

19

crossing the mountains, when the West was all new to me, and my impressions were vivid. A few wild tales of border adventure marked the page, and among them a Picture of which my heart had kept the key as well as memory. It was accompanied with an incident or two of my own life; and as I paused to look at it, I went step by step over the events thus connected with it.

My first debut upon arriving here, though it was mid-summer, had been to knock shiveringly at a back-woods cabin, and, like Julius Caesar, "when he was in Spain," to faulter out "as a sick girl—give me some drink!" A fever common to the West in its early settlement,—*half ice, half fire,*—had fast hold of me, and I was not able to leave that cabin for weeks. My host was poor—and my own resources, like the last stream I had crossed. Still I was taken care of. The neighbors came in to proffer the little attentions so grateful to the sick; and one little delicacy after another, was brought in for the stranger. Among the mingled visions of reality and delirium, that flitted around me, there seemed one ministering Spirit whose presence always brought balm and healing. Without any distinct perception of aught else that passed, I soon learned to note her coming, and to attend anxiously to her directions. Her voice operated as a spell upon the waywardness of disease; and however perseveringly I rejected medicine from other hands, it was taken at once from hers. As the violence of my fever at last abated, and reason resumed her empire, I learned that she was the wife of Col. Harman; and his residence, some half mile distant, was pointed out to me. The Colonel himself had accompanied her; and now, that I was able to bear it, he proposed removing me to his own house. My scruples,—for delicacy suggested scruples, though the proposal was most welcome,—were at once over-ruled. There was a decision in the manner of Col. Harman that admitted no parley. His carriage was brought to the door; the phials on my table were tossed out, an action equivalent to "you will need no more of them;" and I was lifted from my couch and placed in the vehicle. It was all done as a thing of course; there was nothing to be said in the matter. My eye was at once cheered with the lovely domain before us, and we were driving leisurely up the long and deeply shaded avenue, that led to the house. Mrs. Harman met us at the door, and her smile was a thousand welcomes. That yearning anguish with which the invalid thinks of the far-off home with its associations of mother and sisters and familiar shades and remembered fountains, gradually left my heart, and the vague melancholy incident to a debilitated system, gave place to grateful feeling and renovated cheerfulness. How could it be otherwise in the dwelling of Colonel Harman? There was that peculiar and settled bright-ness over it, which is sometimes shed upon a human dwelling as if all *there* had an exemption from shadow or change, and just stood still amid the sunny lapse of life's summer day. Twenty years ago, the charming seats now scattered through every section of our own Ohio, were somewhat sparse; but *one* like Col. Harman's might arrest the eye of the traveler, even now. It was a large low building, jetting out into several ramifications, the effect of repeated additions to the original edifice, and rested in a profusion of shrubbery. The grounds were laid out in something of the style of the Kentucky planter. The fine old trees of other centuries were yet left standing upon a lawn in front chequering the golden light with deep shadow, and giving to the whole an air of repose, that seemed to say, the loveliness of the scene owed nothing to bustling industry; it had always just naturally been so. With this scenery mingled light and shade, beauty and strength; the family was in perfect keeping. Col. Harman was one of our native Backwoodsmen. You may find a portrait of the class in any of our Western Sketches. Something caricatured, perhaps considerably *more so* than the original, but the outlines have a similitude, and in Col. Harman you would have recognised them. There was a vigor, a racy freshness in his character that one could not have mistaken; an energy in his manner, a latitude of conception, an occasional display of animal force, that could not fail to identify him with backwoods characters. His wife, though something in the wane of female power, was yet a lovely woman, in whom the embellishments of fashionable life and of intellectual cultivation were evidently united. Her conversation, though perfectly free from all assumption of literature, yet bore its reflection—as a clear stream, whose sparkling flow her thoughts resembled, does the shadow of the foliage on its margin. Her character was made up of the attributes of woman, as originally formed; not for earth, but for Paradise; and the rich tone of her nature, like a crimsoned sky, gave a coloring of beauty to the common-places of life. With all this charm of mind, the refinement of soul and manner, she looked up to her husband with the unlimited devotion of woman's fondest love. There could be no mistake in it! Her eye darkened at his approach, her smile brightened, her voice had a deeper music. It is only love that calls for the thrilling chords of woman's nature,—and, despite of *contrast*, in the characters of husband and wife, the wreathing embrace of the ivy around the oak seemed not more fitting. Col. Harman, indeed, knew little of literary refinements or classic sentiment; but there was an original strength in his mind and character upon which her own gentle nature could wholly repose. His remarks were confined to men and things, but there was intellect in them—there were traits too about him, in his very character of a backwoodsman, that might have given him power over any woman's fancy; a high courtesy of manner, originating from a chivalrous disregard of self, and entirely apart from ceremony; an aspect as open as day, and a freedom of bearing bespeaking self-dependence and conscious power. With all this too, there was a depth in his nature, that gave a passionate strength to his affections. He appreciated *all* the loveliness of his wife. He might not perhaps have found terms for it; but he felt it, as one does the glow of a glorious sunset; and the expression that at times lighted up his singularly handsome face, told all that could have been said. Such were the inmates of that dwelling, and amid the continuous flow of rich and confiding hearts, there were all the adventitious aids of domestic charm—books—music—flowers—whatever taste could ask or wealth purchase.

A few brief days restored me to health. I passed on to another section of the country, and to more stirring scenes. Still the remembrance of that family accompanied me; it remained a *picture* on my memory, and here, on the page I had just turned—though the dust of twenty years had gathered on it, I found it still unfaded.

"What portraits for a story now?" said I, calling out every shade of expression from the well remembered lineaments. I could only draw them with the fidelity they are sketched here—romance herself affords no finer conceptions, and a little narrative flung round them, and it would be done! The thought was delightful, and again pressing my hand on my brow to stop all useless whirling there, I struggled to draw out a few threads that would answer as a woof for the figures.

It was no use any way I could fix it. My threads were all tangled and broken as I drew them, and at last flinging the whole concern impatiently from me, I broke out into the identical exclamation at the beginning of this chapter; to which point I have now got back.

"What picture!" said my old friend, at that moment entering my room. I was willing to turn all attention from myself, so I sketched the above draft all over to him. He seemed at first a little impatient of the detail, but as I went on the faded lines of his countenance gathered interest.

"Colonel Harman," he repeated, "aye, many is the hour of sunshine I have spent under his roof, and many a welcome have I had from his wife's swimming eyes." "You know him then?"—"Know him!—Yes, as I do the old English Primer—but come, away with this nonsense," continued he, glancing over my paper—"You are to go home with me you know, and I am this moment ready for riding. You may pick up matter for a dozen tales as we go along, for every foot of old Kentuck is rife with the memory of olden romance."

I sprang from my table. For long months had I been confined to the city, and never was summons more welcome. The whole phantasma of the morning vanished; and as I led my horse from the ferry-boat and vaulted into my saddle, I felt that my pulses already beat truer and more healthfully. Why not? There was an exhilaration at my heart that set my whole system to rights.

It was yet early morning, and the glory with which the new day touched the whole earth, had not yet all faded. Behind us lay the queen of the West, with her spires stretching to the skies, and before us was spreading out in continued perspective, the rich landscapes of Kentucky, blending cheerfulness and plenty, beauty and luxuriance. The sun had gone up gorgeously, and stem, leaf and flower, with their load of dew-drops, looked as if the stars, that had twinkled on through the night, instead of going out, had been showered down upon them. With this golden prospect of the West, the white-haired figure now riding at my side, afforded an impressive association. He had trodden its soil while yet a wilderness, and the memories of that age hung about him like green mistletoes upon a decayed tree. His, however, was that vigorous old age, that can scarcely be likened to decay. Though an early settler here, he was of a different class from the border hunter; he had left the classic halls of Virginia, for the paths of western enterprize, and had brought with him a mind of cultivated feeling. This was even yet unimpaired, and the legendary lore, with which it was stored, formed no inconsider-able part of his usually animated and spirit-stirring conversation. We were riding along the margin of a small tributary of the Licking, when my friend suddenly halted, and sent a kind of musing look over a planta-tion on the opposite side of the stream. "I told you," said he," that we would gather matter for a romance or two on our journey. This very spot is connected with circumstances, that partake in no small degree of the coloring of fiction. Somewhere *there*, on the other side of this creek—I think I could find the very place—I knew it for some years, by the black-ened hearth stones, but they are all scattered now I suppose; any how, there stood about opposite to us more than forty years ago, the cabin of one Isaac Carr. It was in the year eighty-four, I think. Yes, it must have been, for the Indians had then ceased to molest the settlements for a year or two, and the families in the stations had begun to scatter out. It was all a wilderness here then, except a little patch round that cabin. One can hardly realize that this *is* the same spot; so changed, and in so few years. Why, it seems as but yesterday; how well do I remember its appearance when I first passed through here. The heavy forest, silent and lonely, and seemingly eternal as the grave; the creek rolling darkly beneath its shad-ows—the dense tangled cane brake, and that cabin—it seems as if I could see the inside of it even now. On a clean, though poor bed, which was almost its only furniture, there lay an interesting meek eyed woman, dying of consumption; and seeming always to linger near it, though often busied in the little occupations of the humble household, there was a young girl just turning to womanhood, with a tall slight form, as much like those willows there, yielding so gracefully to every ripple of the stream, as anything I can think of. She had large hazel eyes; or perhaps you would have called them blue—fringed with long heavy lashes, through which their clouded hues seemed always shifting! You would not have thought her exactly handsome, for she was a little pale, and her features not altogether regular; but there was a strange sweetness in her smile, and her face had an expression of mingled seriousness and spirit, that gave it great interest. Her hair was very dark and glossy, lying in wavy masses round her forehead and falling over her shoulders, which were white and polished, in rich heavy curls.

She was not the daughter of Carr, but an orphan, who had been brought to Kentucky in its earlier settlement by her relations. This family was killed by the Indians, and Edith Lennox, that was her name, was carried off a prisoner. As was usual upon such occasions, the neighbors rallied immediately in pursuit. She was rescued, and on being brought back, was taken to Carr's cabin. Mrs. Carr was one of those meek quiet women, whom we sometimes come across in the roughest walks of life, with a gentleness of nature, one might almost say refinement, that no circumstance of poverty or position can destroy. They are about the same thing as the little delicate flowers that we find once in a while half hidden among rocks and coarser vegetation; too modest to attract much notice or to seem *out of place*, however greatly at variance with the objects round them. She undertook to raise the little friendless girl as her own, and never was trust more sacredly fulfilled. Edith proved a sweet tempered girl, with fine health, and pure, high-toned, rather than hoiden spirits.

Mrs. Carr's own habits were those of order and neatness, and quiet devotion, and in these Edith was carefully and steadily trained. As her friend's health gradually became broken and feeble, as she assumed the active charge of their little concern; and when the poor invalid at last yielded to the insidious inroads of a lingering disease, she was her nurse; too young indeed to be eminently skilful, but affection and unwearied zeal supplied the deficiency.

You need no sketch of Isaac Carr. His character is one too sadly familiar—a poor wretch, who had brutalized himself by intemperance, till his *human* nature had become extinct. But there is one other, belonging to that cabin, whose recollection comes over me with no ordinary feeling. There was a lad of some seventeen years—affording a fine specimen of a class, at that time growing up in our Kentucky forests. A youth whose form was expanded by forest breezes, and seasoned to action by border sports and perils. You could not have seen him without feeling the power of nature's chiseling. His whole frame breathed like that of a young war-horse in every muscle, with the superabundant floodtide of life. I had seen him while yet the family were confined to one of our 'Stations;' and at a time when he was a competitor in those exercises of border prowess, which formed the principal amusements of our youth at that day. Roswell Carr, as he was called, though that was not his real name, was a child of a former marriage of his mother; but as she had emigrated to Kentucky with her present husband, the boy usually went by his name; but as I was saying, or rather have already said, Roswell was but one of a *class* of backwoods heroes. Still among the proudest of the class, I saw him distinguished. As a runner, a wrestler, a marksman, he distanced all of his age. It required no great sagacity however, to see, boy as he was, that though the mould of circumstance had given his character a certain *cast*, the elements of which it was composed were of the first order. The habitudes of border life had touched it with a hue of wildness, but there was a ground-work of softer color. His kindling eye, as he stood on the arena of youthful strife, told that he felt the renown of personal prowess as no tame impulse; but the glad interest which every eye evinced in his success, from that of the stern veteran, to the prattlers at his knee, fully attested that other and better aspirations had their share of dominion. There were whole days when Roswell chose to sit beside his feeble and low-spirited mother, though the shouts of competing parties rang through the Station. Sometimes he ran great hazards to procure her some trifling comfort. After the family left the station, he became their sole dependence. He called Edith Lennox his sister, and from the moment she had come under his mother's care, seemed to consider her an object of his special protection. But for her, his home would have been a sad one. The weak and subdued tones of his mother, always fell heavily on his heart; but the very step if Edith Lennox, was associated with life, and all its most cheering impulses. The influence of a bright healthful aspect, in the abode of habitual ill health and sorrow, must be felt to be appreciated.

You noticed a mile or two back, a fine mansion house; that site at the time I speak of, was occupied by a family from Pennsylvania, of the name of Draper. Some pecuniary losses had induced them to emigrate, but they were still comparatively wealthy, and lived in a style very different from their neighbors. After all, they were dissatisfied, and at the last determined to return. Mrs. Draper was a benevolent woman. Roswell Carr had occasionally been employed by them, and had spoken of his mother's illness, and from that time she called frequently at their cabin. In one of these visits, she spoke of the preparations they were making for removal.

"And so you are going back to Pennsylvania?" said the invalid, with her usually quiet smile; "to your people, and to your old neighbors, and every thing you have left."

She was for some minutes silent, and it was evident that the memory of the meek sufferer had wandered back to her own home; to scenes of innocent enjoyment perhaps, and kindred tendernesses; but these feelings seemed not of long duration. She raised her emaciated arms and looked wistfully at her thin yellow hands. A glow, not of earth, passed over her thin features; and she said with that peculiar fervor with which religious faith imbues the most common minds—"But I am going to my Father's house also; and I shall meet them that loved me there, and there shall be no sorrow nor suffering there, nor any more parting, but all joy, joy that no man taketh from us."

For some moments the glow on her face remained, and she seemed lost in the contemplation of the glories faith had revealed; but gradually the chain was broken. The manly voice of her boy was heard at the door, and the shadows of life again came over her spirit.

"It will be hard for Roswell," she said, "he is a tender boy. To be sure it is little that I have been able to do for him in a long time, but it is something to him, to have one in the world who always looks kindly on him. But God will raise him friends," she continued with renewed confidence of manner; "besides, he is used to take care of himself, and has grown up one may say, in danger and hardship. But there is Edith Lennox," and her countenance again saddened; "I can't somehow look at her, with her sweet earnest face, without being distressed for her more than is right for me.—She is so young, to be left again without any one to depend on, and then she is so good conditioned and affectionate. How often she has said to me, when quite small, if I happened to make much of her, or talk of something I would like to get her, 'Oh! I don't want any thing in the world now I've got a mammy to love me'—And sometimes she would say, when she ran to meet me, if I was tired, 'but you don't kiss me hard.' Poor thing! the neighbours will do for her, I know, but she'll be lost so, when she has no one any more to pet her."

Mrs. Draper was affected. Her eyes instinctively turned upon Edith, who, all unconscious of being the subject of their remarks, was gliding round busied with her usual domestic occupations.

"She does not indeed look like one to be tossed like a ball through rough and careless hands," thought Mrs. Draper; and musing for a moment, she turned to the sick woman, and said—"Are you willing, my dear neighbour, that I should take Edith back to Pennsylvania. I will give you my promise that I will take your place in being kind to her, and will consider her just the same as my own."

"Am I willing?" repeated Mrs. Carr with great energy—"Oh, you don't know what a load you've took off of my heart. *You* will love her, I know you will, for you will see into her nature, and then you can't help it. I shall now die contented."

"I will then speak to her immediately," said Mrs. Draper, and Edith was called to the bedside of her friends.

"But what am I to leave you for dear mother," said Edith, gasping for breath as she heard the proposal. "Are you tired of me?" "Oh no, no!" said Mrs. Carr, winding her arms gently round the astonished girl. "But Edith, I told you that I had but a little while to stay with you, any way, and I shall die a great deal easier for knowing that you are left with somebody that will be kind to you. Mrs. Draper will learn to love you, as soon as I did, and"—"If God takes you away," exclaimed Edith, weeping bitterly, "I know that I must bear it, because you say *his* will is always right, but don't think I will leave you of myself ever—ever—and while you are sick too! You would not ask it of Roswell!"

Mrs. Carr was agitated, but she felt this was the last duty she could pay to the child of her adoption, and she was firm in it. Her reasons were soothingly given, and Edith's acquiescence was solemnly required, as the fulfillment of her last wish.

"What is the matter with Edith?" demanded Roswell, somewhat impetuously as entering the cabin at that moment, his rapid glance was fastened on the sobbing girl. "What ails her mother?" he said as with a flushed and anxious brow: he now stood at Edith's side.

"She is hurt to leave us, my child, and so will you be to hear of it. But it must be, Roswell."

"Leave us! Edith do you say? Mother, what do you mean?" It was explained to him.

"And do you mean to go Edith?" Roswell spoke calmly; but the accents were forced and measured.

"Oh brother Roswell, what will I do?" said Edith, wringing her hands, "what can I say?"

"You don't want to go then" exclaimed the youth passionately—"You had rather stay with us, Edith? Is this what you mean; say so, and let me see who is the one dare take you."

The strong frame of the boy trembled as he spoke.

"You are wrong my child, very wrong," said his mother. "It is a hard trial enough both for me and Edith—but only think for a minute, and you will see that it is all for the best. I don't want to hurt you Roswell; but you know that I can't last long, and then what will become of her. You are but a boy." "Well, and what of it? Has not my strength been enough dear mother, to keep you from much want? And while I have hands, think you, if you were gone"—Roswell's lip quivered— there was a hard struggle in his filial nature, but he mastered it. "Mother," resumed he, as flinging off the momentary weakness, his aspect assumed an expression of some singularly sustaining confidence—"Mother, there is such a thing, as having more strength than is just natural to one, when we need it for them we ought to take care of. I used to be tired of long jobs, and wanted my liberty; but since you've been sick, nothing is hard to me, any more, that I can turn to account for you; and so it has been with Edith. When we first came to this cabin, you remember she was lost for some days in the woods, and the neighbors were all out hunting her a long time, till they all got tired and gave it out. But you know I still looked on, and I never thought of being tired; and when I at last found her five miles off, and her feet were all so bruised and torn that she could hardly walk, I brought her all the worst of the way on my shoulder, just as easy as I could a fawn."

Edith looked up and smiled through her tears. "Yes, mother," she said, "and when I wanted him to stop and rest, he would say, 'Oh mother will be so glad to see you;' and he did not stop at all till there came on that dreadful thunder storm you remember, before we got home. Oh! how the lightning ran like red serpents all round the black sky. I had always been so 'fraid of it afore, but when I clung fast to brother, I thought I was safe—for you, know mother nothing ever harmed *him*, and so it was. The great trees rocked round us, for I could see them by the lightning, bending their high heads backwards and forwards; but nothing touched us, and the moon came out brighter than ever. And have you forgot mother the time you called the *hard* winter. There was nothing you know hardly to eat, and when anything was brought into the Station, it was but a little for any one; but Roswell always made me share his part. I ought to have been ashamed to, but I was not big enough, and for all this, when he must have been half starved. I remember that he was the liveliest boy in the Station; and when the little children was crying for hunger, he would run with them on his back, or toss them in the air for hours, to make them forget it."

Mrs. Carr's fading eye rested on her son for a moment, with a mother's pride.

"And what of it all, my dear Edith? she at last said, as the vivid recollection of the little events so simply narrated, again gave place to the trying present.

"Oh mother," said Edith; "only dear mother, don't talk to me now of a better home—Don't tell me of other friends who can provide fine things for me; only let me stay where I am, and I shall be happy."

Mrs. Carr sunk back on her pillow. Emotion and effort had entirely exhausted her strength, and for some moments she seemed to be dying. A cordial was administered, and she revived. Still however, she was unable to resume the subject, and lay with closed lids, and features more than usually sunken. Roswell leaned over her, and kissed her ashy brow with mournful passion.

"You are going to die mother," he exclaimed—"You will leave me, and who is there in the whole world to care for me now, but Edith."

The scene, simple as it was, had become painfully affecting.—Mrs. Draper rose, and leading Roswell from the bed, she said, "This conversation agitates your mother too much. We will say no more of Edith's going now. We are not yet ready ourselves, and I certainly shall not think of taking her without her consent."—She then turned back to the sick bed, and Mrs. Carr drew her towards her, and again spoke for some minutes in a low but earnest voice. Mrs. Draper took Edith's sun-bonnet, and putting it on her head, she said, "come, you have confined yourself so closely to the house for some days, it will make you sick. I was going to send a trifle to your mother, that she thinks she can eat, but the walk will do you good, and so you must come home with me. Roswell will stay by her till you return." Roswell turned suddenly round and looked Mrs. Draper almost fiercely in the face; but her open countenance quieted the awakened suspicion, and she and Edith left the cabin together. At the door they met the half senseless staggering Carr. The pure high-minded girl recoiled, as with drunken fondness he spoke to her. "Do you know," said Mrs. Draper, "that as you have been raised in his house, this man may still assume a sort of right over you my dear, that he may easily insist upon keeping you under his roof, after you have lost the protection of her who has been to you as a mother?"

Edith shuddered, and even some hours after she returned, that expression of recoil had not altogether left her countenance. She seemed unusually weary, and her voice as she spoke to Roswell, was low and tremulous.

"You have talked with Mrs. Draper now yourself, my dear Edith,' said Mrs. Carr, when they were at last left alone—"Tell me my child whether I may be at rest on your account."

"I have promised all you wish," said Edith, bursting into tears; and the arrangement was settled.

There was nothing said on the subject before Roswell. There was a kind of hurried watchfulness in his manner at times, as if he would have asked her purpose, but he seemed to want the courage, and his mother's rapid decay, now left little thought for aught else. The hour of her release at last came. A few neighbors had gathered round her bed, and a chapter had been read from the worn bible that lay on her pillow. Rosewell stood at her feet, gazing with a fixed look on the features that had always beamed on him with such tenderness; and Edith sat at her head watching to catch every sound of the voice she so well loved.

There is something of sublimity in the death scene of the poor and lowly, when brightened by the promises of faith. Religion is not *there* a mere matter of creed, but an *influence* mightier than the Spoiler. The dying one stretched upon a bed of straw—the neglected—the contemned—the forgotten—are then to realize her promises. It is their hour of triumph—Poverty, and toil, and suffering are fading forever from their vision, and the glories of Heaven are thrown open wide on their sight. So was Elizabeth Carr, dying—there was no conflict in the scene; nature itself was yielding up calmly her last powers. A little bustle was heard at the door of the cabin, and one of the neighbors who went to see what it was, returned and spoke in a low voice to Edith. She seemed at first scarcely to comprehend what was said to her, but the next moment, clasped her hands with a strong expression of agony.

Mrs. Carr looked up; her feelings were again called back to life. "They have come for Edith," she said, and a smile of love once more brightened the lineaments now fast settling in death.—Some one whispered to Edith, "They wait for you. The family starts before sun up tomorrow." "Oh not now, not now," she said, hiding her face in her hands. Mrs. Carr struggled to speak.

"Yes, now, now, dear Edith, it is the right time—it was all I asked to see finished," Her eyes again closed.

A neighbor, who seemed to have been apprised of the arrangement with regard to Edith, had tied up her little wardrobe, and now stood beside her holding her bonnet—"Come, dear—she wants to know that you go."

Edith looked at the calm face of the dying. Her eye had once more brightened—she again spoke, though in broken murmurs; "Remember your father who is in Heaven—we shall meet—Kiss me Edith."

The poor girl with a stifled sigh of agony, bent to her clammy lips—those lips whose kiss of love had so often soothed her childish sorrows—and then she was borne forcibly and forever from her.

Roswell had stood all this time motionless as a statue. Wholly absorbed in watching the changes of his mother's countenance, he had heeded nothing that passed around him, till her own question, "have they come for Edith," roused him. His eye was then turned to Edith with a look of wild, but still vague apprehension. He spoke not however, till she was borne past him. He then sprang to the door. She was already placed on her horse, and the neighbors stood round her taking their leave. Roswell only uttered her name. What is there in human tones to speak at times such an amount of agony? Not a soul was there but felt in that one sound, the weight of the boy's double bereavement. Edith, half spent with the passionate sobbings, looked up. She struggled for utterance— She would have said—"I *will* stay with you my brother! I will be your sister still," but the reins she unconsciously held, were drawn round by another arm—a spur was given to her horse—it sprang forward—the neighbors turned back into the house, and it was over.

Roswell turned back also. He took his place at his mother's head. He took her hand in his—"Mother, look on me once more;" that look was given—that hand returned his pressure, and a moment after he stood alone.

Roswell immediately left the neighborhood. A feeling of detestation for his step-father, suppressed while his mother yet lived, probably influenced him. For some years after, I do not know that he had any fixed residence; not that there was anything unsettled in his nature, but those were times of wild and active adventure; and Roswell Carr, without profession or patronage to call forth the energies of his character, or to task his ambition worthily in the tamer paths of life, was not one to be found there. Some five or six years after the little events I have detailed, the proud city we have left behind us was first laid out; but the Indian tribes, whose long suspension of hostilities had been but the sullen remission of an unspent storm, now commenced a new series of warfare on the northern side of Ohio. The settlement of the wilderness city was consequently measurably suspended. A fort was erected however, and troops were sent on by the government for the protection of the settlers. I had left Kentucky some time previous to this, but was now again on my way thither—business detained me some weeks at the fort, and here for the first time since his mother's death, I again met with Roswell Carr. Fort Washington, as the place itself was now generally designated, already presented a scene of rather lively interest. The settlers were indeed few, but the spirit, which in so few years has redeemed a vast territory from primitive wilderness, was even then awake there, and the influence of cheering hopes was felt as a vital spring by the infant community. The Governor of the territory, with its judicial officers, had arrived there with their families, and a small circle was already formed with the distinction of *caste*, and the important by-laws, and as many of the habits of fashionable life as circumstances, made the very best of, would admit. The pageant of an army too, had all due effect—feathers and uniforms contrasted finely with our forest scenery, and a famous sprinkling of Colonels and Captains, gave no little tone to the ephemeral society of the place. Among these, there was one by the name of Munson, who had brought with him a young and delicate bride, together with a lovely girl, whose countenance, as I had occasionally met her in their prescribed walks, had left an impression that haunted me. Some trifling service rendered in the course of casualties to Captain Munson, procured me an invitation to his house. I eagerly accepted it, and was presented to the ladies in question.

"Mrs. Munson—Miss Lennox," said my host.

"Miss Lennox," I repeated—is it possible—can it be?—I stopped, uncertain and confused.

"I am Edith Lennox," said the charming girl, with the same bright smile I have noticed"—"the same Edith whom you knew in a Kentucky cabin."

All reserve was at once banished, and in chattering familiarly over the circumstances of the past, I learned those that were more immediately connected with the present.

The losses which had brought Mrs. Draper to Kentucky, had it seems been unexpectedly restored, by events unconnected with my story, soon after his return. Mrs. Draper herself did not long survive, but the pledge that she had given of kindness to Edith was fully redeemed by her family, and the stranger orphan shared with Mr. Draper's own daughter, now the fair bride of Captain Munson, all the advantages of opulence and fashion. Miss Draper's marriage, unfortunately, was without paternal sanction, and this circumstance, unwilling as Captain Munson could but feel, to leave her exposed to the coldness of displeased friends, extorted his consent that she should accompany him thither. Edith was bound to the whole family; perhaps equally, by the strongest gratitude; but Mrs. Munson, as an outcast, had now the deepest claim on her feelings, and she was resolved at once to share the perils and difficulties her friend was likely to encounter, in so adventurous a step.

An interview like this, could hardly fail establishing me at Munson's upon the friendliest footing. Such a family circle within the environs of a border Fort, was the acme of social enjoyment. A young officer whom I also met there by the name of Armar, enhanced its cheerfulness, and the next evening, and the next, found me again there. Edith proposed a walk; little danger was at that time apprehended in the vicinity of the garrison, and even when there was, the impatience of confinement often got the better of prudence. Edith I saw at once, was like a caged bird, and the glances she threw upon the boundary of the forest that shut in our view, told me that she panted for its free range. We strolled along the margin of the river, and I found that Miss Lennox's presence was to be felt wherever she moved. The rich promise of her childhood, had been ripened by cultivation, and was now fully developed. In person she was but little altered, at least in detail. Her cheek, quite colorless formerly, had acquired a pale bloom, and her almost shadowy frame had rounded into more perfect symmetry; but there was no other change, save that which the airy witchery of tasteful drapery necessarily flung over a form that I had been used to see only in a frock of coarse striped cotton. In this respect, the change was indeed something like that which spring flings over his shrubs. Woman is a creature for the eye, let us say what we will; and Edith had lost nothing of the charm of nature, she was far lovelier than ever.

A young man, with his arm rested on his gun, stood leaning against a Sycamore that shadowed the stream. His dress, consisting of a dark linsey hunting shirt, fringed with white and belted closely round him, identified him as one of our border young men. Nevertheless, motionless as he stood, it was a figure to arrest the eye even beside the elegantly dressed officer upon whose arm Edith Lennox leaned. He started at our approach, and with a slight bow, and a look of acknowledged recognition directed to myself, passed us. What a face to disprove all aristocratical leanings in nature—calm—thoughtful—impressive, with dark deep eyes that were lifted upon us as he passed, full and almost proudly—one of those marble complexions without the color, but with all the polish of health, and a brow—the wind at that moment blew back the brown curls that shaded it—so still—so ample—such a brow might afford a subject for a painter. After all, it was but a backwoodsman! Such was the translation of the glance flung over him. What a revulsion of thought! What associations *could* a gay party like ours—we had been joined by some of the elite of the garrison—attach to a Kentucky hunter, but venison and Indian scalps? Major Armar was talking to Miss Lennox in his highest flow of polished eloquence. The young hunter; with that high freedom of movement evidencing the familiar exercise of strength and vigor, bounded over a ravine near us and disappeared; but Miss Lennox's eye had followed him. "Don't you know him, Miss Lennox," said I, unconsciously speaking, as if the perplexity of her feature had been audible— "that is Roswell Carr."

"Roswell Carr—good heaven!—My brother as I always called him. I should have known him indeed; and why did you suffer me to pass him thus?"

"I hardly knew—I thought perhaps other scenes"—

"Oh sir," said Edith, "you know not what I owe that young man— he does not know me, I see—will you be so good as to tell him where I am, and that I wish to see him."

"Roswell," said I, some hours after, seeking him up in pursuance of my commission. I had already met him upon my first arrival here, and laid claim to the familiarity of 'Auld lang Syne.' "Roswell, have you forgotten the fair girl who used to bound so gracefully along our Kentucky ravine? or have a few years changed her so, that you do not know her?"

"You mean Edith Lennox," said the young man very calmly; "no, I han't forgot her."

"Did you then know her, when you passed her to day? Did you know she was here?"

"Why should not I—she is not altered in *pertiklar?*"

"True," said I, "and I might have known that you had been too long in the same garrison not to have seen her—but Roswell, what the deuse has come over you? If you knew Edith Lennox was here, why have you kept yourself a stranger from her? She remembers you, and with gratitude, and wants to see you forthwith."

Roswell lifted his eyes to mine with a seriousness so settled, that he very depths of their calmness thrilled me.

"Edith Lennox," said he, flinging his gun on his shoulder, "had a kind heart, and I allow no common thing could work much change on it that way. But she is not a Kentuck girl now, and if I was to call on her, it would not be to meet one as I used to meet her."

"But stay Roswell," said I, grasping his arm, for he was already striding from me; "Miss Lennox has commissioned me to bring you to her—What! shall I tell her, that you do not wish to see her?"

"Well, well," said he, turning quietly round, "let us go then, 'tis no use talking, if the thing is to be done."

His manner was so cold, that I should not have dreamed of any effort in the decision, but I saw the veins on his forehead were filled for a moment almost to bursting. No trace of agitation was however visible when we reached Munson's door, and never had I felt the force of simple character more strongly than as we entered my friend's parlor. The conventional refinements and comparative elegancies of life throw a sort of glare over the social circle, always imposing to the unpracticed eye; and most of the little assemblage, over whom Roswell Carr now flung his survey, probably felt the distinction thus given them, in its utmost force. But the young hunter stood before them with an eye and limb as unembarrassed as when treading his own forest paths. His countenance was grave, and his bearing had nothing in it of assumption, but the expression of both look and manner was "that of a man to man was equal all the world over." Edith Lennox came forward to meet him. The same decision of thought and purpose that had characterised her childhood, now enabled her to act wholly for herself. Radiantly lovely in the light which her own rich feelings shed around her like a glory, she came forward to meet and welcome her childhood's friend. Roswell stood calm—almost cold—almost silent—but little as she herself regarded the artificial barriers now existing between them, she could but be aware of them, and though embarrassed, was not chilled. A half hour of somewhat unpleasant reserve succeeded. Any remark to the young man upon common topics, on the part of Edith's friends, was rendered almost out of the question, by a previous supposition, the semi-barbarianism of all his class; and his own brief replies were little calculated to promote the enquiries Miss Lennox would have made after all she had seen or known amid the scenes of her childhood. But Captain Munson, from feelings of delicate consideration for his fair friend, at last made an effort that was tolerably successful. He spoke of the country—of the peculiar situation of the settlers, and of their warfare with the savages. In these remarks too, Major Armar, as usual one of the family circle, gradually joined; but there was something in his tones sufficiently indicative of speaking to an inferior, and more than once, the young Kentuckian flung up a front of such startling power, that Edith's whole perceptions were carried back to past years. Thus she had been used to seeing him, a figure whose energies no one would have cared to call into action by idle insult. Major Armar's condescending notice was at last altogether withdrawn, and wholly divided between a favorite air and a favorite pointer. But Captain Munson's manner, was calculated to draw forth the manly freedom of Roswell's nature; and the inquiries which had at first been forced, gradually became those of interest.

It was easy to see, that upon all points connected with the general interests of the country, the young hunter had gathered a fund of positive information;—that he was so familiar with the measures of government, and had weighed their bearing upon the intended results, with a grasp embracing all the practical grounds of opinion. Captain Munson was at once surprised and gratified. Himself ardently interested in the critical aspect of affairs at that juncture; he drew the young man on with an eagerness of attention, even more flattering than the growing cordiality of his manners. But an hour passed, and Roswell's visit was done. Edith Lennox rose. The heightened color on her cheek evidenced something of effort. "Mr. Carr," she said in a low voice, "I have not forgotten—I can never forget what I owe to one whose cares we once equally shared. May I hope that you will also remember you have a right to any—to all sisterly kindness." The words died away upon her lips. Roswell Carr had for the first time lifted his eyes to hers—he seemed for one moment to have forgotten all other existence, and they were literally pouring upon her the hoarded tenderness of long years of passion. The pang that shot through Edith's frame, blanched her cheek to ashes. That moment of distant though mysterious intelligence, told the history of all his lonely musings. But she had been accustomed to self-control—she rallied herself—she finished the sentiment—"You have a right to every grateful office in my power."

Roswell recollected his position—he bowed—he was gone; and Edith turned to listen, once more, to the polished trifling and elegant flatteries of Major Armar.

Such a girl as Edith Lennox, under any circumstances, must have created a *sensation*; but situated as she now was, a solitary star for scores of epauletted idlers to gaze on, she was soon weary of the adulatory incense poured out at her feet. But the exclusive attentions of Major Armar, had at last distanced other aspirants—he was in high favor with the Munsons, and at the time of my introduction there, was considered as the successful candidate. Roswell Carr never called there again, nor did they again meet; but Edith knew that he had not left the fort. I have said, that she was impatient of confinement: she loved nature and the privilege of communicating with it alone. Her spirit was naturally fearless, and early habits had contributed to render her singularly regardless of danger. At those hours, when she knew Major Armar was engaged in official duties, she was in the habit of stealing from the fort, and strolling along the wild paths in its vicinity. In these walks, she had more than once seen Roswell Carr loitering near her. She at first supposed it accident, but upon its repeated recurrence, she was struck with the conviction, that he watched her steps, and thus lingered near her, only as a guard.—Her strolls were of course ended. Meanwhile, an army that had been organized for the chastisement of the savages, was at last in readiness; and the settlers in the fort, with the fair form of Edith Lennox and her friends, stood gazing at the proud array, as banners and plume disappeared beyond the dark outline of forest.

I need not follow the army upon their fearful path. The defeat of St. Clair, an epoch as familiar as it was disastrous. It was a tremendous harvest, and death held a glorious carnival over its piled up swarths. The battle was over, but the carnage was not finished. The remnant of the army was flying before their terrible enemy, and some one among the wounded and the weary, was momently adding one more to the stricken-out rolls. Among the wounded was Major Armar, and overcome with exhaustion he too had yielded himself up to die. The stern law of self-preservation in that hour of wild extremity, asserted its selfish mastery over the noblest heart. No one paused to heed the dying—friendship itself, had no ear for the shrieks with which life went out, or appealed for aid. Yet there was a pause. A form of strength had sprung past the fallen and bleeding Armar, but it suddenly turned. Roswell Carr, for it was he, had caught the pallid countenance of the officer, and he turned to ask "what can I do for you."

A pack horse, whose fallen rider had just yielded up life in the rear of the fleers, at that moment came up with them—Roswell caught the bridle, and raised Armar to his feet. The hope of life gave a new spring to his suspended powers. His wounds were slight, but his blood was ebbing profusely. Binding them up with a part of his dress, the young Kentuckian lifted him on his horse, and urged him forward. The war-whoop of the pursuers was on their ears.—The main body of the fugitives passed, and Major Armar was borne on in the rush, but not till he had heard a shot ring in his very ear, and seen his preserver fall.

Some miles after the pursuit ceased, better feelings had time to gain something of their usual ascendancy over personal fear, and the wounded and fallen were picked up and borne forward. Among these was Roswell Carr; he had risen after the shot he received, and had continued his flight some distance. Exhausted at length however with suffering, and the loss of blood, he had again fallen. With the close of that dreadful day, the survivors reached a place of safety. Fort Recovery was twenty-seven miles from the place of slaughter, and there, a bitter council was held by the few remaining officers. It was thought advisable to return to Fort Washington immediately, and some few days after, all that remained of our gallant army, was once more in view of our own fortress. What a spectacle! I am not going to moralize upon it; but pardon me—the return of that handful of men, war-torn and gloomy, emerging from those shadows where the hosts with whom they had gone forth had so lately passed from my view, rests even now on my memory like some dark painting—a painting that one cannot turn from without heaviness. Strong and wildly throbbed the heart of Edith Lennox and Mrs. Munson, as those soldier-men drew nigh. But one moment of suspense, and the latter was in the arms of her husband; and though he had been the sole survivor of countless multitudes, the world to her had undergone no change;—and Edith's lover was also at her side, pale indeed, and scarcely yet recovered from his wounds, but more devoted—more tender—more insinuating than ever. And yet there was a restlessness in her eye, that told of some still latent anxiety—some unsatisfied interest—What that interest was, was soon decided. Captain Munson was not one to forget the duties of humanity, even in the first outpourings of heart-felt tenderness. There were those in the garrison who needed attention. Most of the wounded had been left at Fort Recovery, but many who thought themselves able to march, had given out on the way, and he now went himself to see what measures had been taken for their comfort. He returned with a brow much saddened.

"Miss Lennox," he said, "Roswell Carr has been brought back wounded, and is now thought to be dying. He has asked to see you, and Major Armar will conduct you to him. He has lost his life probably in saving that of Major Armar, and if he had no claim—but my dear Edith, for heaven's sake what ails you? I thought you strong-hearted in scenes of distress—why Emily, she is fainting," —and in truth the color had gradually faded from her face, lip, brow and cheek, till every sign of life had gone out.—But she did not faint, and grasping Munson's arm, she instantly rose and moved as if instinctively towards the door. Mrs. Munson took her husband's arm also, and they passed on without speaking.

Carr lay in one of the block houses at the extremity of the garrison, and a crowd had gathered round him with that interest, which a noble-nature extorts from all classes. His wounds, though considered at first but slight, had early induced a fever, which the fatigues of their march had not tended to subdue. It had now reached its crisis, and the surgeon had explicitly informed him, that his hours were numbered. A wish to see Edith Lennox was all that he had expressed; and Edith, supported by her friends, now entered. The crowd gave back—Roswell was greatly changed. It is upon lineaments of beauty and strength that the work of disease is most appallingly traced. Edith looked on him without uttering a sound; there was a stillness as of death upon her yet pallid features. Major Armar stood upon the opposite side; he was embarrassed;—he felt that it was a moment of strong claim upon his better nature, and would fain have uttered something of acknowledgment; but the school of elegance in which he had been trained, gave no lessons for simple feeling. It was with difficulty he murmured some forced expression of obligation, and regret. Roswell was yet perfectly conscious, and his speech scarcely impaired.

"It is little," he said in reply to Major Armar, "for a man to die who leaves no one the worse for it, and as for kindness, it was not that I thought of. But your life was *valued* by Edith Lennox, and I would have flung away my own a hundred times if there had been need for her."

"And you have come, dear Edith," he continued some moments after, turning his face towards her, where she had sunk upon her knees beside his pallet—"you have come," he now murmured in the same tones in which he had been accustomed to address her in their childhood;—"but I knew you would, for you were always kind, and now I may once more call you sister."

A burst of convulsive weeping gave Edith utterance. "Oh my brother! my brother! she exclaimed, "why have you ever ceased to call me so? When, oh Roswell, did I disclaim to be your sister?"

"I mean not that Edith—you were always good—but I have loved you with a love, stronger than that of a brother's. It will not shame you now, dear Edith, and I may speak it out. I would have died for you in any way it might have come—I could have toiled for you, and watched for you, and cherished you as a mother does her child." Edith lifted her sunken head from his pillow with a wild expression of passionate hope.

"Oh live—live then," she exclaimed, "to love me still. What has the whole world to give me, dearest Roswell, to a love like yours—my brother—my friend—live but for my sake, and you shall find there is one heart, as faithful as your own."

Roswell's glazing eye, lighted up with a brilliance almost like the flashing up of a strong blaze. He looked in her face with a terrible earnestness, as if doubting what he heard, and then asked, "Edith, do you love me?" "Yes," she replied firmly, "in life for death."

His breath grew short—the light faded from his eye, and that heart so long unused to happiness—did *not* cease to beat, for Roswell did not die; but it became low, unconscious of the rich flood of joy which had been so suddenly poured over all its lonely depths. There was a long and fierce struggle, and many hours of agony did Edith pass before it was decided. Spasm after spasm succeeded, and then a long and deep torpor. But the singular strength of his nature prevailed. Whether the touch of joy assisted the springs of life in regaining their power, or that his hour was not come, 'tis no matter. From that stupor, he passed to a healthful perception of existence; and Edith was yet leaning over him to receive his first calm smile of waking bliss. One moment of agony had given Miss Lennox a perfect knowledge of her own heart; and the vague and dreaming interest of years, to which perhaps she could have assigned no definite term, was suddenly drawn out like concealed writing, in strongly defined characters. With these feelings once avowed, her purpose was as settled as if it had been the result of years of deliberation; she considered herself as consecrated, and whether to the living or dying, the world had no longer any claim upon her thought.

"I know all of you would say," she replied to the half frenzied remonstrances of her friends. "I can anticipate all that can be said, but I cannot revoke a vow that my heart acknowledges, and that Heaven has registered. Spare me then, unavailing reproaches; and when the time comes, for to hearts like yours, it must come, that you again think of me with kindly interest, do not think of me as one lost. I am not acting rashly—I know the path I have chosen. It will probably be one of humble hardship, and rough encounter.—What then?—It is a path with which I was early familiar, and I return to tread it with one who has already borne me over its rougher places, with an enduring watchfulness of love, that elsewhere I should look for vainly. You speak of Major Armar, but I have no engagements with him to forfeit. I was grateful for his attentions; I listened to his flatteries, but my heart required a kind of sentiment that belonged not to his character; and you will see Emily, he will return to the gay world to which he belongs, without a sigh for aught he may leave in Western wilds."

Edith was right. The affections of Major Armar were unclasped at once, by the proof she had given of perverted taste, and without any tragic violence to his nature. Upon the return of the army to the East, some few days after, there was no one perhaps, who took leave of Miss Lennox with less pain.

Roswell Carr rose from his pallet to a state of new impulse. The growth of the embryo city, was checked for two years by the continued hostilities of the Indians, but still new cabins went up, and new accessions of emigrants increased the hum of life and activity. Among those dwellings, there was *one* distinguished by those impalpable marks with which refinement invests the humblest residence; and from it you might have marked the steps of one whose quick, firm tread, bore evidence of an elastic and enterprising spirit. Had you traced him homeward, a bright form would have met you at the door, and she that was Edith Lennox, would have seemed more lovely in her then matronly character, than in her proudest hour of conquest. A splendid mansion now occupies the place where the cabin stood. We passed it but an hour since, and some fair fingers upon a piano there, were dispensing most sweet sounds; but I have been far more thrilled by the low warblings which at those times were not unfrequently heard floating upon the still evening air around that cabin. After the peace of Wayne, its tenants flung themselves back into the rich forests of Ohio, and plenty and beauty soon sprang up around them."

"Well, and what more?" I inquired, speaking for the first time, as for the first time in his long story the venerable narrator paused.

"Nothing, except what you were yourself busy with, when I called you from your room. I have told you *Carr* was not my hero's real name, and he had assumed it long before his second meeting with Edith—it was Harman;—he was a distinguished officer in our last war, and the picture you sketched to me this morning, is only the consummation of a 'romance in real life.'"

Aunt Hetty

Julia L. Dumont

Yet still she filled life's task, although a part
in its glad sunshine was no more her own,
Toiling with busyfeet—the while her heart
Gave out a voiceless but unceasing moan.

The instances in which I have been called, since journeying on your
western waters, to witness the mortal grasp of the Asiatic destroyer now
among us, has more than once made me sick at heart. But I have just
returned from the burial of one of its victims, with feelings so like the
music of Carroll, that I cannot resist the impulse of sitting down at once
to give you the story (for story it is) in detail.

I am *alone,* in the principal hotel of a village on the eastern bank of
your great highway of waters. It is September, and the day has been the
very blandest; but when I landed here, last evening, the weather seemed
to have the breezeless sultriness of a southern August.

On recognizing the place as the stopping-point of my voyage, I was
struck with its appearance. I had spent a night here some two months
previous, and it was then all astir with business life. Now there seemed
to hang over it a quiet like that of perfect desolation. I was not permitted,
however, to dwell on the matter, my attention being drawn to an object
of more immediate and most painful interest. Beside me, as I passed
from the boat, two or three of the hands were carrying from it the stal-
wart but convulsed form of a young man, who, knowing as I did that the
cholera was on board, I saw at once was struggling with the fierce ago-
nies of that terrible malady.

But what time was there to mind the death-throes of a mere fellow-
being? Action and emprise are the only influences to get a hearing on
our great highways. The poor fellow was tossed on the wharf, with evident satisfaction to the bearers at getting rid of their burden. The rush of
steam, the voice of command, the plash of waves, mingled in one stirring sound, and again the boat was ploughing on her way, as if the principle that impelled it were the very lord of destiny. I had myself
approached the sufferer with no light interest, but was unable to make
the least personal effort; being not only in great anguish at the moment,

but moving with extreme difficulty. A severe sprain in my only efficient foot, some few hours previous, and want of attention, had caused it to become violently inflamed. But some three or four men, of that well-known class that haunt the river purlieus, were lounging about the wharf, and to these I applied to have the sick man carried to the hotel, but a few rods distant. At my appeal one of them carelessly approached the sufferer, and stood looking with perfect unconcern at the face already distinctly marked with that peculiar seal which is perhaps the most appalling of death's many signets.

"Cholera, eh? Nothing to notice here, stranger," said he; "Come, brace up, old Ben," he added turning, without the least notice of my continued and urgent appeal, to a stout-looking personage, who was nevertheless availing himself of a post for support; "no rest for the wicked, man—another grave's to be dug to-night! No baby's neither," he added, touching the struggling form with his foot; "some long inches to cover when they're once fairly straitened."

Happily, I believe the brutal allusion did not reach its unconscious object; yet it was with some difficulty I kept myself calm.

"Suppose," said I, flinging him a small bill as the only argument that could at all avail, "suppose you are a little charier of your wit till the man is taken care of. Make some arrangements for taking him to the Eagle, and let a doctor be called without a moment's delay."

"Faith!" he replied, looking at the bill with a peculiar sort of meditative satisfaction, "doctors are getting scarce among us. Only one left, and he green as a frog-pond. But what do you want of one? You don't know much about the cholera, I reckon, stranger. Why, the fellow's caved in already."

"There's life yet," said I, "and therefore something to be done. Pray, don't waste any more words."

"Well, well," said the man, evidently one of those busy, bustling, officious spirits that are leaders in their class; "any thing in the way of trade. Dan Garnett is not one of them as turns his back to a job. Bear a hand, comrades," he called out to the others standing on the wharf; "best get a blanket—here's one the wharfman died on himself yesterday—good as any. Stir yourselves quickly! live men are lighter than dead ones, and he'll be heavier soon. We'll handle him kearfully enough," he added, in reply to my impulse; "but you see, stranger, we'd better by half let the council know there's another coffin wanted than to be troubling him now."

"Never mind—carry him steadily!" Alas! I too saw that a mightier hand than that of human strength was upon him; but I could not leave him thus.

"Bear ahead, then," said Dan Garnett; "hold up, old Ben—strike a bee-line, old rat! Aint got enough to steady you, eh? Well, the bar at the old Eagle aint drained out yet."

"You have the cholera badly in your village, I suppose," said I, remembering, as I hobbled on painfully beside the bearers, the dubious intimation of my new acquaintance.

"Not at all, stranger—not a case among us—wound up here, sir— closed the concern teetotally. Them as is left here now is hard subjects. You'll find poor entertainment, I'm thinking, at the Eagle. You've staid there afore now, havent you? Well, there's some little difference in things now. Them as was flying about there two weeks ago, ladies and boarders and waiters, and what not, have all took private lodgings. Boss and the old cook have come through, and that's all. Wife and three young daughters all gone—pretty girls, too! proud as Lucifer—though but small room have they for airs now. Them's the last we buried this very morning. Plenty of quiet room for travellers, you see.—Let down your load, boys; let's see if boss is stirring. I rather think, though, he's hanging by the graves yet. What do you think now, stranger?" he asked, as the burden was lowered, and he turned a look of careless scrutiny to the livid face; "short work it makes, and sure—gone off, though, very quietly," he continued, still looking at the darkened face with perfect complacency; "they don't all go that way. Do you mind, Ben, the screech that old Hughes fetched as the last breath went out of him? I never stir if it didn't go through me like an ague-shake. The old fellow," he added, turning to me, "was the richest man in the place—griping old land-holder—and you see he was bound not to die. But the grinning old skeleton held on to him jest as he would to a poor fellow that owed him; and now he's got but five feet of ground left.—One more hist, comrades! We must take the corpse round to old Judith; the Eagle, I 'low, will have to give it lodgings for to-night any how. It's going to be tremendous squally by appearance, and ther'll be poor chance likely to give it snugger quarters afore morning."

I had sunk, during these remarks, upon the steps of the portico, unable to stand from the fast increasing anguish of my limb; but connecting with the name of Judith (whom I remembered as the old black cook) the possibility of relief, I got up once more and hobbled eagerly after them. The old woman was sitting alone at the back of the silent and empty house, swaying herself to and fro with a leisure to which she was no doubt little accustomed. The approach of the ghastly burden borne towards her appeared to excite in her neither dismay, awe, revolt, nor surprise. Her mind was evidently already too full of the images of death to admit a single new impression.

"Come, Judith, bestir yourself," said Dan Garnett; "here's travellers ahead. One of 'em, though, don't want nothing but lodging. Where shall we stow him? in the porch here?"

"Well, I suppose," replied the old woman, her own stony aspect seeming more like the dead than the living, "you can lay him on that table thar; its whar they've all been laid out principally."

"Well, there he is! Straiten him out, boys. Aunt Hetty ought to be here now to close his eyes—rather stary, I think!—but you can do that, Judith. Fix up his jaws, too, while your hand is in. Stow away his plunder, Ben—enough in that big trunk, I judge, for decent fixing without his being beholden. But go one of you and see if the councilmen have any thing to say about it,—and stay! take 'em the measure for the coffin—six feet good; and mind, Ben, you get the grave started before sun-up."

I had at once appealed to old Judith for some effort in my own behalf, and I was now waiting, not without some impatience, upon her tardy movements in fulfilling the melancholy office pointed out to her.

"Aunt Hetty, now, *likes* to fix up dead folks," said Dan Garnett, returning from the bar where, as he said with a significant nod at old Judith, he had gone to see if the brandy was likely to hold out provided it should be needed in some new case.

"If it was not such a night now," he continued (and in truth the storm-spirits were by this time fairly up), "I'd go and bring Duchy to smooth him up a little. I ought to do it any how," he added, his visit at the bar already calling the amenities of his nature into high exercise; "the good soul has along been sent for when a corpse was to be rigged out in their last gear, and she seems to sort o 'look for it."

"And mighty well it was too, for them as had friends to bury," said Judith, seeming for the first time to reply in a tone of human interest; "she was not only willing, but she seemed to have a 'ticular strength like, when every body else was down, and them that wasn't weren't none too willing to lend a hand. But you'd be foolish enough to trouble her to-night, let the weather be fair or foul. I 'speck no body can hold out allays. She jist gone from dead to dead, and haint laid her head on a pillar a whole night since she first put her hand to it. Any how, what odds does it make to a stark body like that, whether you cover him up as he is, or in span clean rigging? He's got no friends, I 'low, to trouble themselves."

Judith's reasoning seemed for a time conclusive; and opening an inner door, she now pointed out to me a lounge, which she assured me was all fresh changed, and of which I was most thankful to avail myself. Dan Garnett meanwhile ensconced himself in an arm chair at my side, and whistled Dan Tucker with great self-complacency, and in strange dissonance to the dirge-like winds now shrieking without, which it required little effort of fancy to imagine were wailing for those they would wake no longer.

Meanwhile the preparations which the old woman had set herself earnestly about for my suffering limb proved of no avail. Specifics hitherto infallible in my case were vain. Even that of brandy—the one friend, Dan Garnett said, in all need, and which he insisted on pouring out more lavishly for my relief, failed. My distress was indeed extreme, and the inflammation was evidently assuming a rather serious character.

"Well, my good fellow," said I to Dan Garnett,—we got wonderfully meek when suffering forces home upon us our real dependence upon each other,—"it is storming fearfully, but if I wait on it long I shall be in a fair way to lose my leg. Bring your doctor to me if he is green; you are too old a stager to mind the weather."

"Of course," said my ready friend, his kindly mood having as yet had no chance to evaporate; "Dan Garnett aint sugar nor salt to mind a little thunder and lightning, and it aint a doctor's business to lie a-bed, no how. Get me a *numberil,* Judith; I don't want it for myself, but while I'm out I'll jist go round and fetch Aunt Hetty."

"I tell ye then again ye'd be mighty foolish, massa Garnett, that's sartain," she replied; "I s'pose though ye're not in earnest."

Dan, however, was not only in earnest, but with that maudlin pertinacity of purpose that was not to be overruled, terrible as the storm was,—bending the umbrella which he attempted to raise so roughly that he flung it back into the porch,—he started bravely ahead; and we had not long to wait the issue. A few minutes after the entrance of the physician, who came speedily at the summons, Dan returned himself, accompanied by Aunt Hetty. So at least she was addressed by Judith and the doctor—by the latter with great kindness and even respect; and despite my extremity of suffering, I could but look with something of curiosity at the person to whom such striking reference had been repeatedly made. All my preconceived ideas, however, of a weird old woman with an indurated and Meg Merrilies frame and spirit, was put aback by the quiet and quaint figure (for she was dressed in the peculiar garb of her countrywomen) that stood before me. She seemed scarcely forty, though the fair German complexion and the great length of soft brown hair, that could not have been so plainly arranged as to lose its grace, might make her seem much younger than she really was. Her features, too, small and perfectly regular, had a softness that it seemed no exposure could displace. But what rivetted my attention was the intense sorrow that was the fixed expression of every lineament and motion. The expression was unobtrusive—silent, but not to be mistaken. It lay a strange depth of gloom in the light blue eye. The features, that but for it one would have instinctively associated with health, and hope, and all genial affections, were fairly steeped in it. It startled me in the soft German accent with which she replied in broken English to the doctor's kind inquiries for her welfare. Even in the ready movement with which she set about assisting him in some preparation for my suffering limb (ready, but most saddened), it was yet an accompaniment.

The especial task for which she had been brought was not now to be thought of. The storm was rushing violently through the porch where the body lay, repeatedly extinguishing the light with which Aunt Hetty strove more than once to shield it from the beating elements, notwithstanding Judith's assurance that "the dead man didn't mind it, any how," together with occasional asseverations of Dan Garnett's foolishness in troubling her at all about the matter—a reprehension in which even the doctor, a young but amiable man, who evidently gave a full heart's sympathy where skill proved unavailing, seemed disposed fully to join.

"Our friend Dan has certainly shown more thought for the dead than the living," said he, "a rather questionable duty, as I take it. But Aunt Hetty," he said, turning to her with a serious interest in his manner, "owes something to herself; and as soon as the storm lulls, I move she go home and waive the unpleasant office for which she has been summoned."

I looked at Aunt Hetty. The answer came slowly, after some minutes, during which she seemed hesitating whether to reply. She said in the lowest tones,—and oh! how mournful—"I has dressed great many as had moder and sister."

Judith's previous argument had already reversed the inference, but the doctor bowed to it without reply. The night wore on. By degrees there fell a hush, both on the elemental turmoil and the human sounds of the hour. Dan Garnett lay stretched on the floor in a profound slumber. Judith had swayed herself to sleep in her chair, and my own plaints, rather loud and deep for the credit of my manhood, were subsiding rapidly in a growing sense of ease. Only the tones of the doctor, still drawn out by my eager questioning, and dwelling with infinite feelings upon the details of the visitation that had depopulated the place, were now to be heard. How heart-rending were those details! What a power of human suffering did they attest! "Facts," said the narrator, "that make medical science a mere dream; that called out, too, in the most vivid opposition, the darkest and brightest traits of our nature. Friend fled friend. Others took post beside strangers and enemies. Throughout all I have described to you," he added, with a look of gratified recollection, "there was one humble and quiet spirit, that was never for a moment idle. From the hour the scourge was among us, she was always to be found amid the scenes of its most terrible triumph. A watcher by the dying, their tire-woman for the grave, Aunt Hetty was at all hours devoted to tasks from which the nerve of manhood might have well shrunk."

"Aunt Hetty!" I repeated, looking round for her, at the mention thus of her name. Where was she? She had passed from the room without a sound, or I should have noticed her. "She has probably," said the doctor, glancing at the partly open door, "settled herself out there with the dead body; such place seems always to suit her feelings in preference to any other."

He was not mistaken. Amid the dim light breaking through the still struggling clouds, I discerned her sitting on a low stool, in attitude now as motionless as the outstretched form whose ghastly length lay before her.

"Some morbid feelings," continued the doctor, "have doubtless had some bearing upon her singular devotedness, but even these have to me something in them almost sacred. Poor Aunt Hetty! Sorrow has in truth raised her above life's common instincts."

"And what have been her sorrows?" said I; "you seem to know them. I had already fancied there was a history in her face—pray, what is it?"

"Well, it is a very brief one; a single fact, as it does that of many others, forming a sombre web to her whole life. She came a few years since with her husband and an only son, of some twenty years, from Germany. They settled here upon some rough grounds which they purchased upon the outskirts of the village, and which they soon converted into a pretty and pleasant home, alike marked by taste and toil. Industry and rural neatness with our German emigrants is rather a national than individual distinction; but Aunt Hetty's neighbors soon learned to distinguish her as a superior woman of her class—gentle, cheerful, active, self-sacrificing, true, and kind, with an ever-ready and open hand, and with her soft, broken English full of soul and sunshine.

"But occasional clouds were flitting over this usually happy spirit— an evil daily deepening, that could but wake in a mother's prescient heart many a boding fear. The son, who was evidently the very daylight of her soul, a handsome and manly-looking fellow, with an open and generous nature, as I am told, was adventurous and dissipated—the fine elements of his mother's nature, which he perhaps inherited, being robbed of their beauty in his, by excess and perversion. No amount of indulgent tenderness,—for both father and mother were devoted to their boy,—could keep him under the paternal roof. Returning thither only occasionally, and with tokens of reckless habitudes that made these visits but seasons of troubled misgivings, he spent most of his tie on the river, or at some of the various ports, but always it would seem in idle and profitless adventure.

"The father at last sickened. A painful disease fastened on him, with which his strong frame struggled for months; and all this time his son was wholly absent. Death finally released him; but ere he died, a rumor had come that the young man, having been engaged in an affray where one of the party fell a victim, was imprisoned in New Orleans. From what I know of Aunt Hetty's character, she would have gone to him at once; but she might not leave her dying husband to another's care. A few days after released her from this duty; but she returned from the grave to read a letter from one of her fellow-emigrants,—who could write a mother such things?—that her boy was to be hung—upon what day—and other horrible minutiae; though the terrible day was already past, for the letter had by some casualty been delayed. A young German girl at service in the place was with her when the dreadful missive was received. Long afterwards she was asked in my hearing, by some one more curious than feeling, how Aunt Hetty bore the news. She burst into tears, and wringing her hands bitterly, exclaimed, 'Mein Got! mein Got! may I never see such another agony!'"

"But from that hour nobody, I am told, has ever heard from Aunt Hetty herself the slightest allusion to her sorrows. Since that time, indeed, she has been rarely seen; going always when called for to the sick, but never otherwise leaving her own domicil voluntarily, till since our visitation from the cholera. Her little garden, however, was still worked and kept with its wonted neatness; being not only her means of livelihood, but, as my professional rounds among the destitute have led me to know, of many a little charity still extended to them through the medium of an orphan child in her service. But so carefully has she seemed to avoid all human eye, that even her out-door labors are done in the early morning ere her neighbors are astir, or when she can avail herself of moonlight hours, lengthened far into the night,—as are my yarns, I perceive," added the doctor, looking at his watch with a sudden and good-natured change of voice and manner. "We are getting, I see, into the small hours, and you are easy—thanks to Aunt Hetty's suggestions, I suspect, more than to my own skill. You can sleep now," he said, taking his hat, with a bland smile, quite as soothing as the opiate he had administered; "I am not sure, indeed, but you've been dozing already, fancying, no doubt, you were some prince with a pensioned storyteller at your bedside. But settle yourself now to bright dreams—a privilege I shall hasten to take myself, if it may be permitted me."

And so he left me—in a silence. And now I was at last permitted to think over all the gloomy images the last few hours had presented. What a night it had been! By what associations I was surrounded! and yet, thanks to our most concentrated human selfishness, I slept at once, profoundly forgetful of all the late anguish of the stricken household—of the many darkened habitations around me; awoke, too, after some hours of pleasant rest, to a sense of perfect satisfaction at finding myself still at ease. Some matin sounds indicated that the morning was breaking, but its cold gray obscurity afforded no incentive to shake off my slumber. A light, dim and feeble, I saw was burning in the porch, where Aunt Hetty had probably still kept her vigil, and I heard steps there; but my mind was as yet too inert to make any questioning in regard to them. I had again closed my eyes, and lay in the half dreamy state, when the outer sense receives what yet the thought takes no cognizance of. A low murmur of soft, sorrowful sounds had come fitfully upon my car for some time, ere I rallied sufficiently to distinguish them from the seeming sighs and the various sounds that followed the storm. But my perceptions cleared. It must be Aunt Hetty! and raising myself at last, with a strong feeling of interest, I looked through the glass panel of my door, which she must have closed while I slept, to see if I were right. She was still as when I last observed her, alone with the dreamless sleeper, but not, as then, motionless. She was bending over the body with a near but dim lamp-light flickering on the fixed lineaments, and was adjusting the hair and the position of the head with great care. But while thus busied she was from time to time uttering in her own language, which it chanced that I familiarly understood, expressions of wailing tenderness and implied despondence, that I find it impossible to translate. At times she paused in her task, and stood for a moment contemplating the features, doubtless so changed that even love could not have recalled the lineaments—such is the effacing touch of the cholera; and then again turning from the earnest gaze, and renewing the endeavor to soften the dark traces of the spoiler, she would break into renewed utterances of the most heartbreaking pathos.

"Ah! these thick black curls! so glossy yet. Some mother has been proud once,—smooth 'em out this way, and lay them round the great forehead. She will think this a sorrow—she will bow her head, when she should raise it and give thanks. Let the angels whisper it to her; let them bid her give praise by day and by night—her God has not hidden his face when her mother's heart cried to him."

So full of unimaginable sorrow were the tones, that in very pain of hearing, though I could but listen with my whole soul, I was glad when they were interrupted. The burly sleeper on the floor uproused himself, and the first sound of his voice drove back the broken wail to the sorrowing heart. She turned to him at once as he now stood beside her, with the same settledness of look she had previously worn.

"You said dere was tings to put on him?"

"Did I?" said Garnett, applying his hand to his head as if he would dig up the recollection; "well, I can't say exactly—sort o'foggy this morning. There's his trunk, though—remember bringing it along. Plenty in that, I reckon, by its heft," pushing it towards her, touching the lock too at the same time no ways gently with his foot; 'open, too, I guess—the boat-hands flung it on the wharf as if it burnt their fingers. There!" he continued, wrenching open the lid as Hetty looked at it somewhat hesitatingly, and now flinging from it a quantity of decent and most neatly arranged clothing; "plenty for scores of dead men, you see, and nicer lots than they need be for such an outfit; money, too, if more's wanted," he added, as a kerchief with a corner tied up fell heavily on the floor.

Aunt Hetty was evidently disturbed by the unwarranted freedom. "Oh, I want nothing but dese," she said, laying by a few articles, and putting the rest back anxiously in their previous order. "Can you no fix de lock? she said, examining it herself, and then assisting to tie a cord tightly around it. "Do you, Judy, put it away safe (for the old woman and myself were now part of the group) till de master may-be will be able to see no ting wrong is done."

She then turned back to the body. "Ah, yes! if you will be so good den," she continued, in reply to my proffer of the little assistance I was able to render, and putting in my hands the articles she had selected. Then raising the body herself—an effort of which, indeed, she looked incapable—she was reaching to me for some of the intended array, when a small volume fell from beneath the vest she had just loosened. Her eye fell on it with an intensity I can never forget. I stooped to pick it up. The binding had some marks of foreign style, and the leaves falling open as it fell, I saw it was a German Bible. The name "Henrique Van Ernstein" was written on a blank leaf, with the words in German, "Given me by my dear mother, April 27, 18—," and striking my eye as I raised it, I read them involuntarily aloud.

"Henrique Van Ernstein!" The sound was echoed back on my ear in a cry so startling, so strong, so thrilling, that months after I seemed occasionally to hear it. The body fell rather than was laid back from her hold, as she turned her head to clutch the book from my hand.

"My God! my God!"—again she spoke in her own language—"'tis his! 'tis my boy's! 'tis Henrique's!"—and then suddenly turning her gaze wildly, but with a fixed look, for a moment on the face of the dead, she uttered yet another cry, bearing in its prolonged tones the very extremity of human emotion, and then fell on the body, clasping it round in a hold in which all the vain yearnings of long years seemed concentrated. She was pouring out upon that dull, cold ear expressions and names of passionate fondness, with which a mother's heart only overflows. "Mine own! mine own! my boy! my Henrique! my beloved! my beautiful!"

Mightier indeed is Love than Death, said I mentally, as I would fain have drawn her from the ghastly embrace. The effort was all unheeded. Yet again and again, kissing the livid lips, she would raise herself to fix a lengthened gaze on the face, seeming with every moment, as she thus stood tracing the lineaments, to find some new line familiar to her heart,—all this while, too, continuing to pour out such a flood of the very agony of joy, of maternal passion in its utmost excess, as few of those whose lives reach the longest date can call to memory. "My boy! My Henrique! How was it I had forgot to know my own? A mother to look strangely on her boy! How should I think he had filled a grave of shame?—his mother?—but he comes himself—comes to tell her of the black falsehood. It is he—it is Henrique! Oh, thou great and merciful Lord God! thou art indeed a God of truth and justice and pity and forgiveness and loving-kindness!"

But these bursts of the many mingling passions of the poor woman's soul at last subsided. They were finally merged in one absorbing strength of prayer, or rather of thanksgiving, poured out upon her knees beside her dead, in His ear who has all power to tranquillize the surging billows. And from the outpouring of thanks and praise, how calm she at last arose. Calm, did I say? There was a radiance in the serenity of that now still face, bespeaking a peace that the poor estimate of our more human feelings may not measure. With this look she now turned to the making arrangements for the burial of her boy. Again with kisses—oh! how fond, but now scarcely mournful—she arranged the curls of such unchanged beauty round the capacious brow, and once more, as she had been wont in other days, she folded the snowy shirt over the bosom, icy and unconscious now, but whose last pulse she knew had been true to her and to the teachings of those happier days. And there, too, she again placed the treasured volume that had been her last gift of love. That it had been the stay and solace of her wandering Henrique, there could be no doubt. It was much worn. Upon a second blank leaf, bearing a date of her most awful memory, he had written some brief expressions of intense thankfulness, seeming to imply an unexpected deliverance from some dark impending fate; and throughout the whole volume, many of whose pages were now scarcely legible, there were leaves turned down, marking those especial passages in which the soul of penitence finds utterance for its own emotions.

There are still tokens in our debased nature of better elements that were once a part of it. They who had, the preceding evening, looked with such reckless faces on the dying man, were again present. They had come with the hearse that had been sent round for the body. But their countenances now had taken a touch of feeling. Aunt Hetty's dissolute but open-handed boy had, it seemed, been well known to them, and of this her simple expression denoted her aware. Pointing to the body, she said quietly, "Look at him—it is Henrique!" Some others, too, were there. Despite the desolation of the place, a half dozen persons gathered around the mourner and her dead. They were perhaps of those who knew her only as a late tender of the bedside of her own dying. Among them, with his hat drawn over his brow, was the master of the house, whose steps, through my long waking hours the preceding night, I had heard traversing the empty chambers. All were at last ready and waiting to attend Aunt Hetty with the remains back to her cottage—for there where the father slept, the son was also to be laid. I had feared my kind doctor, who had also joined us (grasping my hand with a smile not at variance with the tears he struggled to suppress), might veto my attempt to accompany them; but he gave me his arm to help me to the little vehicle he had in waiting, without a syllable.

It was one of those mornings of soft brightness that so often follow a night of storms. The glad ministrants of nature, revivified by it, were pouring out balm, and beauty, and fragrance, and melody, on every hand. But these bright influences awake no thought of jarring dissonance with earth's tenderer sorrows. They have too much of holiness. The sound of bird and bee, and the stir of "young leaves," as we passed, seemed to melt into the deep funeral hush that was upon our sense. We reached the grave, as yet scarcely completed by those who had gone forward with the first dawn for that purpose. It was in a deeply shaded and grassy nook of a little enclosure pertaining to the cottage, and planted by him on whose grave their blossoms were yearly shed, with orchard trees. Even the face of Dan Garnett, now speedily completing the task in which he had voluntarily engaged, attested, as he at last stood leaning on his spade, the spell and power of some sanctifying presence. One of Aunt Hetty's German neighbors, who had been early an assist sharer in the scenes of the morning, read the burial service in their own language. The mother's hands were clasped, but seemingly in prayer—not in anguish. A few sobs and murmurs met my car—not bitter, but low and tender—evidently Love's last farewell—and then her voice, singularly musical and deep, went up through the stillness of the secluded spot in an anthem of mingled faith and thanksgiving. Deeper and clearer the strain arose, as strengthening the soul that breathed it. The doctor whisperingly admonished me of the prudence of returning, but it was the reluctance that I turned from the spot. The triumphant tones were yet floating away to the still heavens, beyond which, no doubt, the angels were also hymning the safe housing of the erring Henrique.

Bibliography

Coggeshall, William Turner. *The Poets and Poetry of the West.* Columbus: Follett, Foster, 1860: 43-46.

Coyle, William. "Julia Louise Corry Dumont." *Ohio Authors and Their Books.* Cleveland: World, 1962. 181.

Dumont, Julia L. "Aunt Hetty." *Life Sketches from Common Paths.* New York: Appleton, 1856: 227-44.

——. "The Picture." *Western Literary Journal and Monthly Review* 1.5 (1836): 37, 290-309.

Eggleston, Edward. "Some Western School Masters." *Scribner's Monthly* Mar. 1879: 750-53.

Emch, Lucille B. "Ohio in Short Stories, 1824-1839." *Ohio State Archaeological and Historical Society Quarterly* 53 (July-Sept. 1944): 230-33.

Gallagher, William D. "Brief Notices of Western Writers . . . No. 4. Mrs. Julia Dumont." *Cincinnati Mirror and Western Gazette of Literature and Science* 3 May 1834: 129.

Venable, W. H. *Beginnings of Literary Culture in the Ohio Valley.* Cincinnati: Robert Clarke, 1891.

LORETTE WILMOT LIBRARY
NAZARETH COLLEGE

Pamilla W. Ball

There is no biographical evidence to provide birth or death dates for this early Ohio author. From her writing a reader learns that she migrated from Virginia to Zanesville, Ohio. in the early 1830s. She was an educated widow from Virginia with two children to support, and the distinguished frontier editor W. D. Gallagher encouraged her to write fiction based on her experiences. Early in the decade she published a series of regional stories in Gallagher's *Cincinnati Mirror, and Ladies' Parterre* and in 1837 launched her own Zanesville periodical.

The writing of Pamilla W. Ball or Mrs. Phillippa W. Ball, the two spellings she utilized as author and editor, was polemical and demonstrates early regional women's concerns. For example, in August 1833, Ball published a story called "Woman's Destiny," a temperance tale that epitomized the victimization of frontier women. The author shows that migration increases, rather than decreases, women's vulnerability to a treacherous husband because the frontier removes such eastern supports as family, religion, and culture. "Woman's Destiny" is a cautionary tale that begins with a dead man, moves to his wife's decline, and provides an extended narrative flashback. The New England-bred woman who disobeys her stepfather and marries a lieutenant who was disbanded from the War of 1812 finds that the man was lured by her fortune and beauty. He becomes an "emaciated victim of idle and intemperate habits" whose alcoholism and gambling continue after their westward migration to Ohio.

Other stories by Ball are more sanguine. Her "A Tale of Early Times" (1835) is original, a comic tale that challenges Frances Trollope's uncomplimentary view of Ohio in her *Domestic Manners of the Americans* (1833), which was excerpted a year earlier in the *Cincinnati Chronicle and Literary Gazette*. The peripatetic Trollope sailed from England in 1827 and spent twenty-six months in Ohio, a state she criticized for its topography, domestic economy, manners, gender relationships, and lack of "old World romance." Ball cleverly challenges Trollope's generalizations about the provinces by approaching her indictments through an indirect route; she addresses the complaint that Americans are bad "domestic servants." "A Tale of Early Times" foregrounds a story about Republican "help" against a background story about Virginia migrants; this scenario includes an abused Virginia slave,

55

Uncle Sip, and a plantation owners's upper-class daughter, Margaret Balling, who is hopelessly dependent. Ohio counterbalances their sloth with a wholesome Buckeye family, the Steeles, who treat "help" like family and even lend "help" to the pathetic Margaret.

Domestic realism also provides Pamilla Ball with the opportunity in "A Tale of Early Times" to repudiate a number of specific complaints which had been made by Frances Trollope, "the old Englishwoman," as Cincinnatians called her. For instance, Trollope had accused frontier women of being thin, haggard, and isolated. In contrast, Ball shows them to be "Diana-like" at a quilting party, which dramatizes women's happy community life. Furthermore, the defense of "America's peasant laborers" (117), as Trollope called them, is extended by the story's narrator, an old man who supports quiet, rather than loquacious, dinners. He explains, "Mrs. Trollope has sneered at us for engaging in little conversation during our meals," and continues, "I once heard an Ohio worky give an excellent reason for his alleged taciturnity at dinner. We have," said he, "so many good dishes to discuss and so few causes of complaint that we eat. The foreigner has so meager a bill of fare that he ekes out his scanty meal with political discussion and sulky grumbling at the existing state of things."

After publishing for several years in the *Cincinnati Mirror and Western Gazette,* in April 1837 Pamilla Ball began publishing her own weekly newspaper, Zanesville's *Evening Visiter*, which appeared every Saturday for sixteen months. Regional publications were important; the first newspaper in the Cincinnati region appeared in 1783; following 1810 other newspapers appeared in small towns like Chillicothe, Marietta, Lebanon, St. Clairsvillle, Steubenville, Dayton, and Lisbon. Among the earliest women editors to initiate a western literary periodical, Pamilla W. Ball followed the era's editorial conventions; the *Evening Visiter* included excerpts from famous writers and eastern publications, as well as Ball's own regional material.

Among the stories she published were several that were popular and dealt with white people's treatment of Ohio's indigenous peoples. In earlier stories like "The Recluse of the Bluff" (1831), she presented an idealized white girl who leaves her misanthropic father and marries a "noble" savage. Three years later, in "The Haunted Tree" Ball approached racial genocide; in this brief story an eighty-year-old chief named Onaloosa muses on the "painful yet exhaustless theme": "who are they for whom the red man must be swept from the earth?" Onaloosa abandons his Muskingum River tribe, which has needlessly murdered a white woman. Ball's most elaborated Indian story appears in the first edition of the *Evening Visiter.* "The Maid of the Muskingum" is a vehicle in which Ball compares several aspects of victimization; there is the genocide of the Native Americans, abused white womanhood, and corrupting Europeans. The prescient Indian chief Big Beaver twice visits Virginia, once rescuing a pregnant white woman and later discovering her imprisoned cousin. At the end of the tale, the young white couple coexists with two aged, bachelor Indians, Big Beaver and Watomako on the banks of the Muskingum.

Injustice and abusive families are also exhibited in tales like her Virginia story "The Wrecker's Daughter" (1834), as well as an untitled *Evening Visiter* sketch where alcoholism, domestic violence, and patriarchal chauvinism destroy family life. Throughout her literary career in the 1830s, Pamilla W. Ball continued to write cautionary tales that implored males to reform and women to survive. The editor W. D. Gallagher, her mentor, encouraged these themes, which were characteristic of the period's domestic fiction. Only in Ball's sketches where personal experiences or comic wit are allowed to intrude does the reader catch a glimpse of the author's more complicated and delightful character.

After 1838 when the *Evening Visiter* ceased publication, Pamilla Ball disappears from the region's written records. In her editorials there is some autobiographical information, which reinforces her fictional themes of female victimization. Ball's autobiographical exposition emphasizes the pathetic—she is a "comparative stranger—without money—without one supporting relation to cheer" her on. She complains about her "extremely unpleasant circumstances" and the challenges of poverty, ill health, and single parenthood. Earning a living was crucial, and in December of 1837 Pamilla Ball asked Zanesville residents not just to buy her newspaper, but to patronize a one-night theatrical performance for her benefit. It would dramatize Caspar Karlinski, the Patriot Father; readers were promised that propriety would be observed, but the fund raiser was unsuccessful. The village's 4,000 population was apparently unable or unwilling to support her journalism, and Pamilla W. Ball's pleas for subscriptions that would prevent her "family from suffering" were ignored.

One of Ball's last personal essays in her newspaper is called "Home Again" and describes a roundtrip stagecoach journey she undertook from Zanesville to Somerset, Rushville, Columbus, Circleville, Chillicothe, and back to Zanesville. For this July 1837 trip, Pamilla W. Ball calls herself an "uninitiated traveller," a woman "of a certain age," who grew up in Virginia mountains, and finds joy in Ohio's "beautiful rural scenery," including Indian mounds and fortifications. Ball is social; she contacts a "friend of my childhood," meets the young editor of the Chillicothe paper, and in Columbus, visits with William D. Gallagher, her editor friend, "a gentleman to whom I owe the small share of literary merit I may possess—for his encouraging patronage was the first stimulus to exertion and self-confidence." At the end of her wearying stagecoach trip, Ball turns to calling herself "elderly," "homesick" and "a very bad traveller." At one point, an "old negress" on the stagecoach accuses Ball of having "an eye look like you was used to oderin" and says Ball resembles someone whose "conscience is always hurtin 'um." Ball responds that she was, indeed, from "Vaginny" and once "owned slaves."

A year later, her newspaper ceased publication and Pamilla, or Philippa W. Ball, disappears from Ohio's cultural records. All that remains are her frontier tales and the assurance that in the summer of 1837 when the mature Pamilla W. Ball returned to Zanesville from her mid-Ohio stagecoach journey, she was profoundly satisfied to be "at home again with real satisfaction" in "Buckeye-land."

A Tale of Early Times

Pamilla W. Ball

A word may become local as easily as a prejudice; and in that case, always conveys a totally different set of associations to the mind from its original signification.—Thus, the word *ordinary*, in Ohio, implies a novel meaning to one reared south of the Potomac; and *servant* is an unknown phrase to the middling classes of our free community—the tidy, pretty girls who scrub, and cook, and wash for us, disdaining the degrading epithet. Help, therefore, means in Virginia, assistance—and in Ohio, becomes another part of speech, signifying maid of all work. But to my story.

What booted it the storm raged and howled around the hospitable dwelling of the Ballings? *Uncle Sip*, a gray-haired, erect old negro servant, had piled the ash and hickory upon the burnished andirons, until the top of the pile lay level with the marble mantle under which it blazed and sparkled. Sperm candles, in massive silver candlesticks, were reflected from a splendid gilt-framed mirror above, and the well-kept family plate, looked from its variety and lightness as if just from Massy's hands, as it glittered on the polished sideboard. A sofa was wheeled before the fire, and a splendidly inlaid lady's work-table was placed before it, on which lay books and music and the implements of embroidery. Luxuriously curtained and carpeted, the apartment bade defiance to the inroads of the howling storm. A poor man who had toiled all day in the cold, and then retired to his half-warmed, half-lighted cabin, would have exclaimed, how comfortable.—A poor woman who had plied her needle all day, in a little cold garret, would have thought, how delightful. No such thing; there was neither comfort nor delight in that mansion. Its master was one of the decayed aristocracy of his state, whom an overgrown slave *force*, another locality, together with the popular faults of his state, high living and losses on the turf, had reduced to almost beggary. The slaves he had reared had been sold; his paternal home must go next, and his sons seek in a new state the standing in society and wealth he had fondly hoped to bequeath them in his own.

In the middle of the sofa sat an elderly spinster; and a pretty fashionable looking girl, was engaged in working muslin on her left. On her right sat two fine looking young men—and sorrow, if not gloom, over-

59

spread the countenances of the whole party. Even Uncle Sip, as he stood with one foot advanced and his arms folded at a respectful distance, seemed to partake in the general melancholy!

"I fear," said Horatio, the younger of the two gentlemen, "that my father will forget to come; and I should be sorry to go without telling him, farewell."

"Hark," said their sister, bending her head in an attitude of listening, "to the dogs whine."

"It is my master," said Sip, advancing to the door.

"You must not be surprised, Mr. Morton," said Charles Balling gravely, "if my father is rather violent to night. He has had some tough trials lately, and he is old."

I bowed, and drew my cushioned arm-chair from the hearth. In a few minutes a fine tall old man, with bleached locks and sinewy frame, entered the room. All rose to receive him; and Margaret, his daughter, placing a stool before the sofa, assisted in drawing off his drab greatcoat, which she gave to Sip, who quickly returned with slippers; and drawing first one boot and then another, his master thrust his relieved limbs into the warm furred slippers.

"Are you not very cold, papa?" timidly inquired Margaret.

"No, child," he exclaimed; "there has been too much to arouse hot blood in me, to feel cold. I failed," he said, turning to his sons, "in procuring a loan from Clinch; and you must go to the backwoods penniless. Ho! Sip, bring me some brandy and water."

"I believe, father, you did not perceive Mr. Morton," said Charles.

"No really," he said, rising and shaking me cordially by the hand. "You must pardon me, sir; my mind was so pre-occupied by parting with my boys."

I assured him I sympathized with his feelings, but hoped the separation would be temporary.

"It will be eternal, sir," he exclaimed violently; "think you I will survive my respectability long enough to see them return?"

The old lady gave me an admonitory shake of the head, and I remained silent while he declaimed with such vehemence upon the political condition of the state, and a dozen local subjects, as to produce almost exhaustion.

"And now, sir," he concluded, "I who have maintained the dignity of a long line of most respectable ancestors—I who have reared a fine family around me, must submit to see my great-grandfather's estate brought to the hammer, and pass, probably, into my tobacco factor's hands—my slaves sold at New Orleans, and my sons go to the West. It is the yankees, sir, the yankees who do this. But where," he interrupted himself, "is that rascal Sip, with the brandy and water?—how dare you, sir, keep me waiting so long?"—and he aimed a blow at the almost venerable looking servant, which, however, only took effect on the silver salver on which he presented the deleterious beverage, sweeping therefrom the cut-glass decanters, and strewing the rug with the sparkling fragments. A summons to supper relieved us all. The old gentleman was by turns affectionate and severe; but when the meal ended, father awoke in his heart, and he wept aloud. A strong man's tears are sternly impressive. He folded his sons in his arms—there was a pause, in which he seemed to collect his thoughts and strive to subdue his emotion.

"I bless God," he said, solemnly, "that your mother is in Heaven and spared this hour.—Never marry until you can support a wife; and then, my sons, remember your mother, and never disgrace her in a choice. Be men—and may God bless you!"

He hurried from the room—and Margaret and her aunt fell sobbing on their necks. "I trust, my dear boys," said Miss Balling, "you will not forget your poor father's last injunction. I do not fear for Charles; but my darling Horace, never disgrace us by a marriage in an upstart family."

Horatio promised obedience, and urging them to retire, as it was late, and the stage which started from the nearest town at day-break would be gone if they did not reach there in time to secure seats. Our horses were at the door—and Uncle Sip knelt to buckle his young master's spurs for the last time. Tears were in the old servant's eyes, and they fell upon the polished boot.

"Farewell, my dear old friend," said Horatio, taking hastily from his pocket-book a note, and placing it in Uncle Sip's hand. The faithful negro, who from youth had identified his own affections and interests with his master's, drew back. "No, no, master Horace, my dear young master, Sip would rather give than take from you. God knows, I grieve enough to think master's sons should have to leave home in a manner bare, and go to them nasty backwoods without a *fortin*, and not even a servant to wait on them. What will they do! what will they do!" and the old man shook his gray head in sorrow. "Be comforted Uncle Sip," said Horatio; "we will work and make a fortune."

"Work!" exclaimed the astonished slave—"work!—that I should ever live to hear a son of Col. Balling say so!"

"Farewell, Sip," said Charles, placing a silver watch in the old servant's hand—"farewell; there is a keepsake; and take care of my father, Sip, and never desert him."

The young men turned from the halls of their ancestors—the home of their childhood—and we commenced our journey westward. Our adventures would occupy too large a space to relate; suffice it that, in the course of a few months, the brothers were settled as clerks in mercantile in Ohio. They had received letters from home, and learned with regret that their father's long inherited estate was indeed sold, and the old man almost beggared in his old age. Charles Balling was grave and proud, and unless he turned local politician, there was little hope of his rising in the West, either to wealth or eminence. Horatio, on the contrary, was lively, communicative, and apprehensive; and I soon foresaw that he was destined to retrieve his father's fallen fortunes. Old habits were with him discarded without regret when put in competition with modes of greater utility; and old prejudices were sedulously kept in the back ground until they were forgotten.

Business called me up the river during the second year of our residence in Ohio; and Horatio accompanied me. Night overtook us curiously spying round an old mound on the banks of the river.

"Bless me!" said Horatio, drawing out his watch, "it is almost six, and no clearing I suppose within half a dozen miles." We mounted our horses, and after riding some time, began to conclude Horatio would prove a true prophet, when the barking of a dog made welcome intrusion on our cogitations, and a few minutes after a bluff looking young man, in a blue linsey huntingshirt, and low round crowned hat, came towards us from an angle in the road.

"Stop friend," cried Horatio; "how far to the nearest public house?"

"About five miles," said the stranger, thrusting his hands in his pockets, and looking at our horses who seemed fatigued and spiritless. "Five miles," said Horatio despondingly. "Why, if you don't mind close stowing, and ain't very nice," said he, "just go ahead (and he pointed his thumb over his shoulder) about a quarter of a mile, until you come to some wild-cherry trees, and turn off down a path, and you will come to my shanty. Turn in and tell Nanse I sent you. I'll be back presently;" and so saying, he resumed the rapid walk in which we had interrupted him.

"Come on," exclaimed Horatio, "for I am devilish hungry, and may be *Nanse* can give us something to eat." It was now quite dark; but our horses soon pricked up their ears, and very readily turned down the wild-cherry path. As we rode under the branches of the trees, we seemed to give unwonted discomfiture to sundry species of poultry who, by cackling, crowing, and gobbling, evinced a latent uneasiness as much as to say, humph! here are hungry travelers. Dismounting, we tied our horses to a fence and entered the door.

A large fire of logs was blazing up the chimney, over which hung the tea-kettle together with sundry pots, skillets, and stewpans, all emitting a most promising vapor. A fine tall girl, dressed in dark stuff, which tightly fitted her beautiful bust, was setting the supper table, and another, whose bright laughing eyes seemed full of mischief, was assisting her. Two or three others were at the other end of the cabin, ripping a quilt from the frame; but their gay silvery voices were hushed, and they suspended their employment to gaze upon Horatio and myself as we entered beneath the rude doorway. We briefly informed them that we had been *forwarded* by a gentleman whom we had met. The tall girl, about whom there was an air of much natural dignity, placed chairs and invited us to be seated, and remarked that Mrs. Steel, glancing towards the blushing young woman at her side, had sent *her man* to invite some boys to play with the girls upon quilting out her first quilt; and she imagined it was he whom we had met. In a very short time Steel returned accompanied by five or six good looking, stout young men, mostly dressed in hunting shirts, variously trimmed and fringed according to the fancy of the wearer. The boys looked shy and the girls reserved, while discussing the good things with which the young wife had loaded her table. Shylock it was, I believe, who paid so flattering a tribute to Scotch breakfasts; he should have lived long enough to have supped in Ohio among the farmers, in the luxurious season of Autumn. Washington Irving has immortalized a Dutch tea table; would I had his graphic powers to do justice to our Ohio farmer's supper. Woe to the yellow dyspeptic who ventures to sit at such a board; his rye toast will begin to lose its imaginary virtues. Mrs. Steele's guests certainly did credit to her cooking, if not by empty compliments, by rapid appropriation of its productions. Mrs. Trollope has sneered at us for engaging little in conversation during our meals. I once heard an Ohio *worky* give an excellent reason for his alleged taciturnity at dinner. "We have," said he, "so many good dishes to discuss and so few causes of complaint that we eat. The foreigner has so meager a bill of fare that he ekes out his scanty meal with political discussion and sulky grumbling at the existing state of things, which denies him even the guerdon of substantial food for his daily labor." Be that as it may, Mrs. Steele's excellent tea seemed to have given the required excitement, for no sooner had the fair hostess, assisted by the tall girl whom they all familiarly called Nanse, removed the table, than a scene of playful hubbub ensued which defies description. For myself (be it known to the reader), who am "in the sere and yellow leaf," I retired to one corner, and,to use a common phrase, made myself scarce. Not so Horatio. I had noticed from our first entrance his dark and animated eye following every movement of the Diana-like figure of the handsome Nanse, and he entered with youthful spirit into all their local plays, much to the annoyance of a thin, pale, and genteel looking young man, the district schoolmaster, who had hitherto been considered Nanse's beau. His sallow cheek grew paler, and he retired to the corner by my side. "Who is that fine looking girl?" enquired I. "She is," he replied, "the daughter of a neighboring farmer, who is well to do, but his girls always go out before they are married, and Nancy is now hired to Mrs. Steel, although she is much more like a lady than the little witch of a wife." I turned round; Horatio was standing on the floor beside the hired girl; his fine, animated face glowing with admiration as she bent her blushing cheek while she was listening to something he was whispering in her ear. She was certainly a very beautiful woman; and one naturally wondered whence came that majestic swan-like grace with which she moved among her young companions. I had forgotten that among the untutored daughters of the Aborigines, I had often made the same observation. Nature molded her a nymph and exercise in the open air had given her grace and elasticity. Her eyes were dark and liquid, and her beautifully penciled brows laid low upon the lids. Her cheek was rather clear than rich, but sometimes the eloquent blood came rushing beneath its transparent surface, dying it the richest damask. When she spake, her parted lips showed a treasury of pearls a queen might envy; while the tender, pensive smile, told there was in her uncultured intellect a rich mine of mental treasures. As I looked upon her, and marked the kindling glance in Horatio's eye, Colonel Balling's injunction flashed over my mind. Horatio will become a real Buckeye, I foresee, thought I.—The guests departed. Mr. Steel invited us to walk forth and see if our horses had eaten their corn. And now first came the startling conviction to the young traveler, that he must sleep in the same apartment with the lovely girl with whom he had been romping for the last three hours.

"How the devil, Morton, do you do when you are scouting across the country and have to sleep in the same apartment with women."

"I always," replied I, "walk out, as we do now, and the girls are always safely stowed away before I return; and I quietly take possession of the bed or pallet my host offers me, where I sleep soundly till day, when I dress and go out again."

"Dress," said Horatio; "I should suppose undressing out of the question."

"Not with me," I replied. "I always undress while travelling, and feel it a great relief."

We now returned, and found the apartment in profound quiet. Mrs. Steel and Nanse we perceived to be in bed, for we saw no more of them; and Steel covering the fire, only left the glow of the embers to lighten the room. Horatio drew off his boots and coat, and disappeared beneath the bedclothes as rapidly as if the eyes of a city belle had been on him. For myself, I leisurely disrobed to my drawers and shirt, and blessed my good fortune in having but one bed-fellow in a good comfortable bed. Those only who have traveled in the West, some years back, can appreciate my grounds for thankfulness upon this point. Steel was piling logs upon the glowing coals of the last night's fire, when I awoke in the morning; and rousing Horatio from his morning dreams, we dressed, and walked out to look after our horses. While dispensing to them a plentiful breakfast from the farmer's corncrib, Nanse tripped lightly past us, and filling a large bucket from a spring that bubbled up among the grove of poplars, returned with it as unembarrassed in her gait, and with us as elastic a step as a wood nymph. Horatio looked after her, and a train of new reflections seemed awakening in his mind. Steel now came out, and insisting on dressing our horses himself, sent us to the house, where his wife and Nanse were getting breakfast.

"Pray what did you dream last night," she said, raising her laughing blue eyes to Horatio.

"Really, I cannot remember," he replied.

"Ah, but you must remember; for I threw the new quilt over you, and whatever you dreamed will come true."

Horatio colored deeply and turned a quick, involuntary glance towards Nanse, who was leaning against the wall, and surveying him with a pensive, abstracted air. Their eyes met, and she blushed, while the little mischievous wife ran gaily on with her everlasting chatter. I reminded Horatio twice it was time to ride before he could understand, and then he rose with evident reluctance. Drawing out my purse, I enquired what the farmer charged for our lodgings.

"Oh, you were no trouble to me," he said, laughing; "I am only sorry we could accommodate you no better; if you are a mind, you may give the women something."

I drew forth a pocket testament, and adding to it fifty cents, gave it to his wife, leaving Horace to settle with the hired girl. He bit his lip, and hesitated; then taking from his bosom a beautiful little ruby, set with pearl, he presented it to Nanse. The bright carmine flushed over neck and brow as she said, almost haughtily, "I cannot accept a gift from a strange gentleman."

"Won't you oblige me," said Horace, with a supplicating tone as he sunk into a chair, and raised his eyes to hers.

"No, No, I ought not—that is—I do not wish to remember you."

"And why not, Nanse," said Horatio, taking her hand.

"Because," replied she, gravely, "you are I dare say a great gentleman, and I am a poor girl; and you would not remember *me* as your equal, and therefore it would not be right to remember you."

"The blood flashed into Horatio's face.

"You are right; but I shall always remember you with respect and—and admiration."

We shook hands, and bade them farewell.

"How odd." said Horace, after riding two whole hours without speaking, "how odd that the farmers wife, who certainly was above want, should accept remuneration, and the hired girl refuse it."

"Upon my word," replied I, laughing, I am glad to find you have not lost your tongue as well as your heart. I really thought it had gone on a pilgrimage to the moon after your wits; heaven forfend our meeting any more such pretty servant girls as yonder queenly maid, or I may be tempted to renounce my own bachelorship."

Our journey ultimately proved successful in its object, and in a month or two afterwards I opened a large mercantile establishment in a western town with Horatio as joint partner. He had received letters from home informing him of the death of his father and aunt, and as his sister Margaret was left unprotected, I proposed that we should keep house and send for Margaret to superintend our establishment. Horace gladly acceeded to the proposition, and during his absence I took care to secure the services of a famous hired girl, and a boy besides, well knowing that I should find the pretty Margaret accomplished, *not educated*.

The first three months of our house-keeping showed that we were greatly behind our neighbors in the article of comfort, and greatly exceeded them in expense.

"Bless me," said Horace, at breakfast one morning, "what bread! I wish Margaret you would learn to make bread yourself, and not depend on hired girls."

Margaret colored, but she was good tempered, and when her brother kissed her cheek as he passed her chair to go out, she forgave him for the indignity of wishing her a cook.

"Good gracious Mag, do you call this coffee," said he another morning as he observed me slowly pouring the thick mixture back into my cup. "It is a waste of cream and sugar; you really, Mag, must make us better coffee."

"Indeed brother I would if I knew how," said the confused girl; "but you know I never went to the kitchen at home," and the tears swelled in her eyes.

"Forgive me dear sister, I know it."

"You will have to bring Nanse yet," said I, giving him an arch look, "and she will teach Miss Balling housewifery and in return will easily learn polish and fashion."

Horatio's face turned crimson. "Pshaw! Mr. Morton." Margaret looked up surprised, and I took my hat and walked to the store.

It was a fine spring evening, and I proposed to Horatio, who seemed spiritless and unwell, to take a ride in the country. We passed several farm houses; before the door of one sat a pretty looking woman milking a cow. "Does not that tall girl remind you of *Nanse*," said I laughingly, "she who had so delicate a sense of propriety." I always remarked that Horatio colored when I spoke of our adventure, and now the allusion seemed more annoying than usual. "Now" said I, "I am not jesting, Horace; I am going the same route for goods this summer, and I design to call and enquire if Nance is yet unmarried; and if so, and her character and connections are decent and respectable, I shall—

"What," said Horace, breathlessly.

"What, why I'm tired of bad bread and bad soup, and bad coffee; and, in short, I believe Nanse would make an excellent housewife, and"—Horace turned deadly pale—"and I believe if you won't marry, or can't marry a hired girl, because of your gentility; why, in that case, I will be tempted to commit the sin of matrimony myself rather than have such bad coffee.

"Mr. Morton," said Horatio, "I owe you a deep debt of gratitude; but permit me, sir, to say I will allow no man to trifle with my feelings. Charles would certainly reproach me; and Margaret—what would she say?"

"As for Charles," said I dryly, "I suppose you will allow him to choose his own wife! and he need know nothing of yours, except that she is a virtuous female. For Margaret, permit me to say, she is so deplorably ignorant of the necessary business of life, as to make her grateful to a sister-in-law who would teach her to perform the requisite duties of a western man's wife; and she, in return, I have no doubt from her amiable temper, will take pleasure in polishing and refining her handsome sister."

"Are you really in earnest?" enquired Horatio, eagerly.

"Never more so," I replied.—We returned in good spirits;—and the autumn found Horatio Balling a happy married man, and a successful trader; and I—why, I never complain now of the coffee.

The Maid of the Muskingum

Pamilla W. Ball

Above Zanesville, or rather between Cox's paper mill and the town, is a beautiful level green, and the bold declivities which surround it, render it more remarkable. Here, years ago, the warrior WATOMAKO built his wigwam, and claimed as his hunting ground the land now called Hamline's away over the beautifully rounded hills, and back through Billy Lee's orchard, to the river. Deer abounded in the forest, and the bold hunter kept a plentiful supply in the birch-bark hut where he reigned sole lord—for no wife or child shared his solitude. Seldom he joined the war parties his tribes sent forth; and when he fought, it seemed only to exhibit his prowess; not to win spoil or captives. He lived entirely alone, and none save the wandering hunter crossed the threshold of his wigwam. It had been a bright morning in June; the sycamores which lined the river bank, had scarcely yet permitted the dewy moisture all to exhale from the fragrant sweet briar, which clung round their stems like blushing feminine love embracing manhood in its fold. The deep blue river—the tall forest—the pure unclouded sky, and the brilliantly carpeted earth, formed a scene which might have disarmed misanthropy of half its bitterness; yet the warrior reclined in the shade of his wigwam, and gazed with listless and unadmiring eyes on the fair landscape. His eye was dull, for his faculties were lethargised; his ear was closed to the winged choristers—and in that state of savage indolence which ignorance induces, a slumberous apathy sealed his senses. Presently, however, the splashing of an oar caught his ear; and raising from his recumbent posture he beheld an ornamented canoe rapidly approaching, rowed by a single warrior. The water flashed like molten silver to the vigorous dash of his oar, and in a minute more the frail boat shot under the spreading shade of a maple, and the tall muscular savage, stooping to the bottom, raised a little girl in his arms and sprung on shore. The hair of the maiden was as black, her eye as dark, as that of her protector; but the skin, through which the youthful blood flushed eloquently, was pure as Parian marble, and its delicate texture told of tender nursing and habitual seclusion. The child might be ten years old, perhaps; but her figure was so slight, her lip so fresh and dimpled, and her eyes so dewy in their lustrous brightness, that they created the impression of infancy. Watomako recognized in him the chief of his own tribe, and he gazed in surprised silence upon the beautiful child, as it nestled close to the bosom of the renowned warrior chief. But in a moment he had obeyed the requisitions of hospitality, and the softest skins were spread and the pipe lighted for his unlooked for guest.

"My brother has caught a beautiful dove, and its color is not that of the red man," he remarked.

"Go down, Nora, and play in the shade of those trees," said the chief, gently placing her on the velvet turf—and the little girl gaily bounded off.

"No my brother she is of another race—the pale faces who crossed the wide waters owned her, but now she is mine."

"I never saw a pale face before;" remarked Watomako, as his eye followed the child as she chased the yellow butterfly from flower to flower."

"Listen! Watomako, and give heed to my word; for when did the BIG BEAVER speak without cause? I never quailed in battle, nor spoke foolish in council; yet now my red children are angry with me, and they grow like the distant thunder, that foretells a storm. You rest here in peace, Watomako; your sky is clear—your arrow is sharp, and you doze away your life, and none says—Watomako does wrong; he is like the forest oak—there are many of them, all strong and beautiful, and they all flourish, and are alike; and none finds fault—but I am the lofty pine that strikes my root into the interstices of the barren rock, and no eye looks upward to heaven but its glance rests on me; and no storm rages but its fury is spent on my head; no flower flourishes beneath my shade—no tender vine encircles my rugged stem; and my branches form no bower befitting yon gentle dove. Take her then, Watomako, to they spreading shade, and the choicest gifts a chief can give, shall be thine."

Watomako continued smoking even when his chief ceased speaking; yet, the working of his features did not escape his observation.

"And has the dove," he said, "no parent bird that will mourn for her? Watomako is true.

The wily chieftain shot a glance of strange import on the heavy features of the Indian: "Would Watomako know more of the little pale face? Listen then. Moons ago I called my tribe, and Watomako came among the rest. They were like the leaves of the forest, and their war-clubs were knotted to strike death to the foe. I told my people of the white race, who live at the foot of the mountain. I reminded them how few and weak they were, when they first came—and also told them that they had spread over the land, even to the very mountain foot, and soon the swelling wave would roll over the barrier, and even the mighty father of waters would not check their course. I proposed that now while we were strong and many, we should descend into the valley and sweep them away, even from the Alleghenies to the wide sea over which they came!—but my warriors had heard of the whites, and said, "they offered peace: they had been told, too, that they called fire from the clouds to consume their enemies, and they feared them; they would not be led to battle against the strangers, and they returned to their hunting ground. I mused on all I heard, and the fire still burned in my heart. I dressed myself like a hunter; I tied a bundle of skins on my back, and filling my pouch with parched corn, I started on my journey. Long I travelled towards the rising sun, before I saw one of the strangers I so desired to meet. Thought I our scouts have deceived us; they are few and far off, and my brother did right not to follow so distant and small a foe. But warrior, I saw them at last, and I felt that the red race would quickly be gone before them. Their knowledge far exceeds the red man's knowledge, and they are far more subtle. I came in peace, and they taught me many things, and I lingered long among them. But Watomako, it was neither their wonderful knowledge, nor their power, that detained me so long. My brother is true, and I put my life in his hand.—Among the pale face squaws, was one whose dark eyes and sweet smiles caused a strange influence over my heart. I used to stand for hours before her door, and listen to her as she sang the sweet songs of her country, to the frolic child that flitted like a bird around her. Woman's eye is quick to spy love, and Nora smiled tenderly on me, when she met my eye. At last I saw her no more. She did not live in the cabin with her father. I then learned much of their tongue, and the little girl often talked to me. But even she I could not see, except at a distance; and I wandered through the fort of the white man, like the restless spirit that allures the wandering hunter into the dank morass. One day I retired to the woods to indulge my moody feelings. I will go home, I thought; the Great Beaver is little, very little, among the strangers! He is but a dog to the white man, and the beautiful squaw is gone. I hung my head, and I was ashamed to think that a woman had so nearly made me forget my brethren and my tribe. I will return I said; I will again meet my warriors! I raised my head and Nora stood before me. The little girl held her hand. Surprise, pleasure, joy, held me mute.

"You are not glad to see me then?" said Nora, and she burst into tears.

Every tear fell on my heart like a drop of fire. "Tell me, lady, who has injured you, and my best heart's blood will be spilt in your revenge!" I took her beautiful soft hand and she sunk down on the ground at my feet. I sat beside her. Country, tribe, rank, all were forgotten! I could not make you, warrior, understand her surpassing fascination;—it must be felt to be told. I gave myself, heart, body and soul, to her service."

"Hear me," she said, "I have been a victim to a heartless man; will you take me to your country! away in the depths of the forest I would live and rear this little girl."

"I am chief of a powerful tribe, lady. I am yet young, and in full strength: my tribe reaches from the great waters of the north, far to the south, and bands of brave warriors obey my word. Our maidens will make garments of the otter and beaver, and our young men will bring you the choicest game; come and be mine!" I said, proudly, "and you shall be the chief's counsellor and wife." Nora gazed on me, a strange light awoke in her eyes, and the bright blood crimsoned her cheek, as laying her hand on the girl's head, she said "and my child?" "shall be mine!" She gave herself to me, and we journeyed on to my home; but the weather was too unsettled for so delicate a being to travel; and though I bore her in my arms across every stream, and over much of the mountain path, still she drooped like the delicate lily surcharged with rain; and—and I only reached my home in time for her to die."

A strong convulsion passed over the features of the handsome savage, and he covered his face with his hands.

"My people were displeased at my long absence; a neighboring tribe had taken advantage of it, to insult and inure some of them; and the very night of my arrival home was appointed for the march of a strong band to revenge the aggression. They sullenly demanded that I should lead them, though I saw they did not wish it. I refused. I could not leave HER, and they threatened, and scowled on me. I buried her in darkness and anguish, and placing the gentle dove in a boat, I sailed down the river to my brother. He is wise; I leave her to nestle in his bower, and go to fight the battles of my kinsmen; to wash out in the gore of the enemies of my tribe, the calumnies of my foes. They say I am under the spell of a sorceress; but never man fought as I will fight to prove it false."

Watomako rose; he gave the calumet of peace to his chief. "My root strikes deep; my branches spread so wide and deer reposes in my shade; the game is plenty around me; the fishes sport in my waters; the poor white dove shall shelter in my branches, and the tempest shall not harm her. Fear not for her, for Watomako's arm is strong and his arrow sharp, and death will reach him who tries to ensnare her."

The chief tried to partake of the plentiful repast the warrior hermit spread before him, but grief checked him, and he could only gaze upon the lovely little blossom he was to leave so soon in the wild solitude of nature. The unconscious maiden kissed the compressed lips of her protector, and then, at his bidding, ran forth to the wild dingles to seek the berries that abounded, and the warriors parted.

Time rolled on. Watomako had sunk the warrior in the hermit—for her went no more to the battle-field, but lived in his own undisturbed domain. Nora had become "life of his life," and to listen to her wild warblings, or to the stories, a thousand times repeated, of her far-off home across the wide waters, beguiled many a weary hour, and furnished speculation for many a fanciful day-dream. The lovely girl had grown almost to womanhood; and the raven tresses, that clung in close curls around her snowy forehead, had grown into luxuriant ringlets, that shaded her white neck and shoulders from the sun's "too ardent frown." Health and exercise had developed the fragile figure, and though too slight to compare with the muscular daughters of the forest, yet grace and beauty lingered in every curve-line of her sylph-like form. Her bird-like voice came ringing in clear melody on the morning breeze, and Watomako loved to listen to its silvery music, better than aught else on earth. For her he hunted, when before he remained idle; and for her he had made many contrivances for domestic purposes, the remembrance of which clung to the poor child. But year succeeded year, and the chief claimed not his charge; and Watomako rejoiced that it was so.

Meantime the whites had spread over the face of the whole eastern country, and news came that they had boldly sailed down the western waters.

"Our chief was wise!" thought Watomako; when the evil was small, it might have been crushed; but now it is grown too powerful. Once we might have driven them into the seas, and rid us of them altogether; but now"—and his eye rested on Nora, and he ceased to think of extermination.

But where was the chieftain? The battlefield became his home, and war his sport. Wherever danger invited, or honor was to be won, he was foremost at the contest; yet he spoke no more of exterminating the whites; though bitter thoughts would follow every new account of their increasing numbers and prosperity. But war, like every thing else, will have its intervals of cessation; and then, the chief throwing his bloody warclub, leaned gloomily along his cabin floor, musing on the lost fair being in whom he had centered all his hopes of happiness. Success had won its usual meed of homage from the multitude, and the chief was almost adored for his courage and fortitude; yet he bitterly remembered their once rebellious conduct, and despised the honors they so lavishly heaped on him. His heart was alienated from his tribe and people, and his thoughts were often wandering away to the civilized white men, who seemed destined to supersede the savage indian. In one of these moods, after rescuing from the stake a victim to the barbarous custom of immolating an enemy to appease the cravings of revenge, he resigned the symbols of his rank and authority, and taking leave of the savage tribe over whom he had long exercised the rights of chieftainship, he equipped himself for travel; and turning towards the rising sun, determined to seek the countrymen of her who had engrossed all the affections of his nature.

The chief found that the whites had indeed widened their boarders, since his first visit among them. He rambled from fort to fort—from settlement to settlement—until at last, wearied that he found none like her he had so worshipped, and curious to see the first permanent settlement they had effected, he turned his steps toward James-Town. At that period, our colonies received yearly accessions in convicts (as they were termed;) and many persons, innocent of every stain, save some supposed state crime, were hurried to America, and sold into servitude amid felons and criminals. A Dutch ship lay at anchor in the James river, and on board her were an hundred convicts, who, the morning after her arrival, were exposed to sale for a term of years. The chief, following the multitude who surrounded the beach, found himself near the long line drawn up to be exposed to public examination. He walked before them, and anxiously gazed upon the countenances of the victims.—There a hardened felon boldly returned his glance;—and here, a degraded female declared her shame in her countenance; few, very few, seemed to feel that dejection of spirits which one would naturally look for in persons in their situation;—and the chief had nearly finished his walk of observation, when a youth, shrinking back from the withering gaze of the multitude, behind his neighbor, and endeavoring to hide his convulsed features beneath the ruff of the once handsome Spanish cloak he wore, caught his eye. A costly beaver, from which the jewelled buttons had been torn, flapped over his young fair face. There was something in the slight glance the chief caught, that arrested his attention, and he stopped before the boy. At that moment a planter came up, accompanied by the officer who had the superintendence of the sale.

"And is this slight fair thing, the one?" asked the planter, rudely grasping the right arm of the youth.

For an instant, the brilliant dark eyes were lighted up, and a gleam of fiery scorn rested on the face of the speaker, as his hand grappled the handle of a dagger that peered beneath the folds of his full short cloak; but the flash died away—the hand sank down powerless—and a momentary quiver shook the muscles of his nether lip.

"Yes," replied the officer, "that is he—he is consigned to your care, and a good riddance to England he is likely to prove; for so rash and hot-blooded a boy never lived since Hotspur's day."

"And said his right royal highness nothing else?" enquired the planter; "surely, Barley—step hither—surely that is the duke's own eye and lip! When you and I first waited on him, dost remember the poor Scotch girl Nora?"

"Hist! strangers may hear thee," replied the officer in an under tone. "To-morrow night, I will tell thee more atrocious acts of him you wot of, than saving thy rascally neck from the gallows, to send thee to be eaten by savages. Meantime, take the boy home with thee; and the sooner our royal master hears of his being scalped, the pleasanter to his royal ear. Hardin," he continued, addressing the boy, "here is an old retainer and friend of your patron, and you are to live with him:"—and so saying, he turned to the crowd, who were pressing on him and importuning him with questions.

The planter, rudely accosting the boy, led him away to his clapboard cabin. The chief had heard the whole conversation, and the name of Nora had awakened a sensitive chord in his bosom. He had never ceased to gaze upon the fluctuating countenance and beautiful face of the apparently high-souled boy; and the strong living likeness to her who was so treasured in his memory, called up a thousand conflicting emotions. He readily understood that some foul play was intended, and he determined to watch the planter, who was a man of notoriously bad character. For the two succeeding days he saw nothing of the youth: though he walked as near the house he saw him enter, as he well could without exciting suspicion; but on the evening of the second, he saw the officer and planter enter together; and as the night was very dark, he crept close beneath the casement, at the back of the house. Here he listened to a tale of guilt and murder, which, though but half understood, yet taught him to feel that it was no ordinary misery that had driven Nora to leave her race, and seek the alliance of the wild savage of nature.

"And you really think the boy recognized Buckingham for the one who did the deed?" enquired the planter, as the other rose to depart.

"Ay did he, and he sprung at his throat, even in the royal presence, like one of your wild-cats."

"The devil!" responded the other, "I wish his highness would give his dirty jobs to some one else, and let me turn an honest man."

"Why, if your conscience, Dick, begins to hurt you, I can give these broad angels to that swarthy devil of an indian that gives me such loving looks as I pass him, as if he would rather take a sip of my blood, than at the red wine-cup!"

"No, no, give 'em to me; I have served him long, and it shall not be said Dick flinched at the last."

Accordingly, the officer counted twenty broad pieces of gold, and taking a cross, drawn with the point of a dagger, tinged with some coloring matter, on a piece of parchment, from the planter, by way of receipt, the friends and confidants in iniquity parted.

The chief felt no time was to be lost; and a strange, indefinable interest arose in his heart for the child, as he believed him to be, of Nora.

The next morning the planter left the house—and the chief, sauntering round, kept his eye upon the door. Presently the youth, pale and thin, with a look of melancholy languor, came out, and threw himself along the grass that grew before the door. The chief courteously approached, and speaking in low subdued tones, said—

"The arrow sometimes pierces the tender dove, and it seeks the shade of the gushing fountain. One such lives far to the setting sun, and the branches are too thick for the arrow to enter. Would she not be a fairer mate for the heart-sick boy, than the rough men here?"

"I do not understand you," said the boy, the vivacity of youth awakening in his fine face at the address of the chief.

"I mean plain and fair, and none ever trusted the Beaver and repented. Yon man is paid to kill you. Fly with me, and I will bear you safely to Nora's other child."

"To whom?" exclaimed the youth, springing to his feat, and grasping the arm of the muscular indian.

"To your mother's grave!—to little Nora!—but be quiet, and do not awaken suspicion."

"I am ready this moment—lead on!" and the chief, folding his robe of skins around his fine majestic form, walked on past the sentinel, who knew him well, and supposed him merely going out to kill game for the use of the fort, and scarcely thought it worth while to challenge the boy, whom he supposed was idly loitering round.

The youth followed the chief sometimes in silence, until at length they reached the recesses of the forest. Here the chief paused, and gazing long and tenderly on Hardin, at last asked "child of a beloved one, dost thou remember thy mother?"

"Remember her—aye! Indian, better ask if I can forget her.—If I could have forgotten her—forgotten her wrongs and injuries, the abhorred Buckingham would have been saved the crime of exiling me from my native land. But how," he abruptly asked, "came you to know her?"

The chief related to him what he had before confided to Watomako.

"Aye" he bitterly exclaimed, as the sad warrior paused; "aye she was lovely, was beautiful enough to inspire even savages with love, and yet she fell a victim to the most atrocious villain on earth, and her own countryman too. Oh! Scotland—Scotland! woe for thee, when even thy matrons are torn from thy bosom, to become the lemans of a king's minion, and then at his bidding, sold into slavery."

"And did none of thy warriors avenge her wrongs?" inquired the chief?

"Avenge her, no, they bent the knee to the haughty favorite and forgot her wrongs. But I live yet," he said, as the proud fire flashed from his eyes.

"And that thou mayest live long, even to avenge her," said the chief, "follow me,—the journey is long and laborious, but I will lead thee to they mother's other child, far from all danger from the treacherous whites."

On a beautiful calm evening, Nora, wearied of solitude, had rambled forth to the banks of the Muskingum. It was the fall of the leaf, and a thousand gaudy dies had replaced the grateful green that in summer robed the forest. The flowing tendrils of the sweet briar overhung the banks of the river, like tattered banners, that swayed to the breeze, in strong contrast with the sombre mistletoe. A slight whirlwind swept a cloud of brilliant leaves from a maple, against which she leaned, into the bosom of the river, and Nora stood watching them float down with the current. "Ah! she thought, I shall be like one of those leaves. I shall live alone until I fall to the earth with age, and none will know or enquire what became of me. Watomako is very old and feeble, and the chief will never—never come any more," and the tears swelled beneath the white lids as her eyes rested unconsciously on the rippling waves at her feet. Old memories were stirring in her heart, and she thought of the days when they journeyed to Watomako's, and the chief used to call her his gentle dove, and carry her like an infant in his strong muscular arms. And then her thoughts wandered away, over the "dark blue sea," to her baby home; and an old grey haired venerable man, who used to kiss her, and her own beautiful mama, and a wild, yellow haired boy, who played with her, and gathered gowans on the green, to stick among her black curls.—

Nora dashed the tears from her dark eyes and looked up. A birch canoe, propelled by the lazy dash on an oar, came slowly floating on the current, and as it gradually swept around the bend of the bank, a tall majestic form arose in it, and stood with folded arms, gazing around. In another minute he pointed to the landing below, and the rower raised to his feet, and drew from his head the hat that flapped over his features. Nora, "in act to fly," stood fixed in astonishment. The brow of the oarsman was as fair as her own, and sunny curls were clustering around his blue veined temples—his clothes were not those of the Indian, and though torn and soiled, were yet of rich materials, such as she remembered to have seen among the whites. She gazed unconsciously, until the boat came opposite where she stood, when the eye of the chief caught a glance of her figure. In a moment his arm was raised. The boat turned to the bank, and speaking a few words to the youth he sprang on shore. "Nora," exclaimed Hardin, as he followed the chief, who had folded her to his bosom in a strong embrace, "Nora do you remember me?"

The bright crimson of shame and surprise were glowing in her sun burned cheek, as she faintly replied, "I have dreamed I saw some one just like you, but I cannot remember you."

"Not remember Hardin?—Hardin, who loved you like a brother?"

"Not brother!—not brother!" said Nora, musing, as she repeated the words slowly, as if trying to recollect the language of her childhood.

"Cousin, then, if you will," said Hardin, gaily laughing. "Ah! that is the word—that is it, cousin Hardin!" "And are you cousin Hardin? he was a little boy, and my aunt Nora loved him—Oh! how she used to cry for him, when we came to that ugly Virginia; and she told me to call her mama, to put her in mind of you."

"Hardin, said the chief, looking from one to the other, "are you sure Nora is not your sister?"

"Yes indeed, I am sure," he gaily replied, "for her parents are now mourning for her on the banks of the Clyde, and I am sure no parent lives to mourn for me. The wretches who conveyed my mother to Buckingham, found Nora with her, and carried her off."

"And will you try to convey her back?—There is much danger in the path."

"No! I return no more to my country, shamed and dishonored! Is not this a paradise to live in, and is not your gentle dove a fit inhabitant? No, chief, here let us remain and we will be your children! What say you, Nora—think you that you could live contented on the banks of the Muskingum?"

Nora's fair neck was glowing, as if the crimson sun-light of evening was casting its shadows over it, as she whispered "Yes! with YOU I am content to stay!"

Bibliography

Ball, Pamela. "Home Again." *Evening Visiter* 2 Aug. 1837: 129-30.

——. "The Maid of the Muskingum." *Evening Visiter* 1 Apr. 1837: 1-4.

"A Tale of Early Times." *Cincinnati Mirror, and Western Gazette of Literature and Science* 23 Mar. 1835: 173-74.

Caroline Lee Hentz

1800-1856

Caroline Lee Whiting Hentz was a native of Lancaster, Massachusetts, and daughter of a Revolutionary War general. As a girl she began writing as "Mob Cap" for the *American Courier* and in 1824 married Nicholas M. Hentz who had fled from France when Louis Philippe was restored to the throne. His unsteady academic career led the family from Northampton to Chapel Hill, North Carolina, and later to Covington, Kentucky, where he ran a girls' school.

Her husband, Nicholas Marcellus Hentz, was the author of *Tadeuskund, the Last King of the Lenape*, 1825, a melodramatic tale of the Delaware indians. He writes within the conventions popularized by James Fenimore Cooper's *Leather-Stocking Tales*. Hentz's regional interests were shared by his wife who similarly used the frontier setting and historical tales to structure her own romanticized regional sketches, including ones that drew upon Ohio. The romantic novels *Lovell's Folly* and *Ernest Linwood* were set in this area, as well as her play, *Lamorah or the Western Wild* (1832). These works were written during her two years in the Ohio region, as were some poems and short western stories which appeared, for example, in *Hall's Western Magazine* (1833-37). Typical of this phase of Hentz's regional career is the romanticized use of Ohio's frontier traditions she employs in her idealized short story "The Indian Martyrs" which was published in the *Cincinnati Mirror, and Ladies' Parterre* in 1832.

Set in 1777 during the Northwest Territory's bloody Indian wars, the story presents undisciplined white soldiers in a fort garrison who murder an innocent Indian ally and his wife because of the white men's anger over another tribe's depredations. Hentz presents Captain Stuart, the commander who is compelled to protect the "children of the forest" by adopting Sakamaw's and Lehella's son, Adario. He adopts the boy and eventually marries him off to his daughter, creating a Christian "entwining in heart and soul" of the "band that should unite these descendants of their sundered tribes."

After the Hentz family moved to Cincinnati in 1832 they became members of the Semi-Colon Club, a literary society frequented by regional intellectuals like the Beechers and the Stowes, which ended its activities in 1837 because of a financial crisis. While in Cincinnati, Caroline Lee Hentz wrote short fiction, a play, and also a novel; in 1832 the play, *Lamorah or the Western Wild*, was produced in the city. Her first novel, *Lovell's Folly,* remained unpublished for years because its theme was based upon a controversial personal experience; her husband suppressed the novel, calling its subject matter libelous and the reason for their forced departure from Ohio. In the novel there are characters who closely resemble persons in Dr. Daniel Drake's Semi-Colon Club where Nicholas Hentz had made a jealous scene over attentions his wife received from a man she calls in her novel "Colonel King." The resulting scandal and Hentz's insistence that his family leave Ohio limited Caroline Hentz's stay in the region to two years. This traumatic episode had several consequences for her literary career; she was removed from the Middle West and the intellectual circles of America's "Athens"; her southward move made her more culturally isolated; and new subject matter presented itself. At the end of her career, Cincinnati's Semi-Colon Club episode also reappeared in her fiction as the source of another novel's plot and self-justifications. *Ernest Linwood, or the Inner Life of the Author*, was published posthumously in 1856.

For fourteen years after leaving Cincinnati's literary world, the Hentz family moved among a variety of frontier towns in the deep South. During this time, Caroline Lee Hentz continued to write and publish, she said, in spare half hours and even among a throng. In 1842 her husband became an invalid; by 1846 she established a reputation with *Aunt Patty's Scrap Bag*, in which an exceptionally unattractive heroine is featured who later reappears in Hentz's *The Lost Daughter* (1857) and *Linda . . . A Tale of Southern Life* (1850), an antiabolitionist best-seller, in which Linda escapes from a tyrannous family and receives succor from black slaves and Indians.

After 1851 Caroline Lee Hentz was successfully supporting the family by turning out popular romantic novels about the South. This included her most famous publication, *The Planter's Northern Bride* (1854). Thus, Caroline Lee Hentz became a leading writer of the plantation romance and literary champion of the southern social and economic system. Her novels were weakly plotted but supported by vivid sense descriptions and what her generation called "elegant style." Their tone was Christian, humorless, and ennoblingly moral. Hentz glorified piety, purity, separate gender spheres, and the ideal of self-sacrificing womanhood.

Her regional "plantation" novel partly evolved as a response and rebuttal to Abolitionists, especially Harriet Beecher Stowe's vastly influential *Uncle Tom's Cabin,* which preceded *The Planter's Northern Bride* in 1852. Whereas Stowe believed that "woman's sphere" included the responsibility of confronting Abolition and standing up for slaves' Christian rights to freedom, Hentz was a conservative who wanted women to extend the moral leadership of their feminine experience only in the restricted sense of conserving the status quo. Thus, Caroline Lee Hentz represents the "pink and white" tyranny that Harriet Beecher Stowe castigated.

Hentz's conservative gender and political viewpoints restricted her writing to derivative formulas that limited her content and enforced a style that disallowed such facets as humor. Today Hentz's role as southern apologist is largely forgotten, as are her romantic melodramas and formulaic use of the regional tale. She remains in the shadow of Harriet Beecher Stowe, her rival who forged ahead after leaving Cincinnati by letting her regional literary instincts expand toward innovative domestic realism.

The Indian Martyrs

Caroline Lee Hentz

It was verging toward the evening of an autumnal day, in the year 1777. The forests began to assume the varied and magnificent tints, peculiar to this season, in an American clime; those rich, brilliant dyes, which, like the hectic glow on the cheek of consumption, while it deepens the charm and the interest of beauty, is yet the herald of decay. The prevailing hue was still of a deep, unfaded green, but the woods were girdled by a band of mingled scarlet, green and yellow, whose gorgeous colors might well be compared to the wampum belt of the Indian, tracing its hues against the darker ground-work of the aboriginal forest. These inimitable tints were reflected as in a mirror, which the children of the forest denominated the "silver wave," known to us by the more familiar, but not less euphonious name of the "Ohio"; but its bosom was not then covered with those floating palaces, which now winged by vapor, glide in beauty and power over the conscious stream. The bark canoe of the savage, or the ruder craft of the boatman, alone disturbed the silence of the solitary water. On the opposite bank, a rude fortification constructed of fallen trees, rocks and earth, over which the American flag displayed its waving stripes, denoted the existence of a military band, in a region as yet uncultivated and but partially explored. Towards this fort, a canoe was rapidly gliding, whose motions were watched by the young commander as he traversed the summit of the parapet, with a step which had long been regulated by the measured music of the "ear-piercing fife and spirit-stirring drum." The canoe approached the shore, and as Captain Stuart descended to receive his forest visitor, his eye, accustomed as it had been to the majestic lineaments of the savage chief, could not withhold its tribute of involuntary admiration, as they were now unfolded to him, invested with all the pomp which marked his warlike tribe. He was indeed a noble representative of that interesting, but now degenerate race, once the sole possessors and lordly dwellers of the wilderness, now despoiled and wandering fugitives, from the land, chartered to them by the direct bounty of heaven. The gallant tuft of feathers which surmounted his swarthy brow, the wampum girdle which belted his waist, his deerskin robe, ornamented with the stained ivory of the porcupine, corresponded well with the expression of his glittering eye, and the proportions of his martial limbs. From the lofty glance of that eye, he had received the appellation of the Eagle; but the commander of the fort now hailed him by the name of Sakamaw, which simply signifies chief.

"Brother," said Sakamaw, as he leaned with stately grace on his unquivered bow, "brother, will the pale man dwell in peace and friendship with the tribe of the Shawnees, or shall the eagle spread its wings to the shore, that lies nearer the setting sun? The Mengwe have sworn to obey the white father, who lives far beyond the great Salt Lake. The wolf and the turtle have given their allegiance to him, and the serpent and the buffalo rise up against the pale tribe that are dwelling in our wilderness. Sakamaw, the friend of the white man, comes to warn him of the threat, to know if the Eagle shall curl his talons underneath his folded plumes, or arm them with the war bolt that shall find the heart of his enemy."

It was not without the deepest emotion that Capt. Stuart heard this intelligence, that the British army had received such powerful and dreaded allies, as these fierce and vindictive tribes. He felt that he occupied a perilous station, and not withstanding the high trust he had always placed in Sakamaw, who was emphatically called the friend of the white man, as he looked upon the dark brow and giant frame of the Indian warrior, all that he had heard of the treachery and revenge of the sable race, flashed upon his excited imagination. Capt. Stuart was brave, but he was in arms against a foreign foe, who had stooped to the baseness of strengthening its power, by an alliance with the children of the wilderness, arming in its cause their wild, undisciplined passion, and adding to all the horrors of border warfare to the desolation that hangs over the embattled field. He may be forgiven by the bravest, if for one moment, his generous blood was chilled at the tidings, and suspicion darkened the glance which he turned on the imperturbable features of the eagle chief.

"Young man," said the savage, pointing towards the river, whose current was there quickened and swollen by the tributary waters of the Kenawha, "as the silver wave rolls troubled there by the stream that murmurs in its bosom, so does my blood chafe and foam, when its course is ruffled by passion and revenge. Feel of my veins—they are calm. Look on my bosom—it rises and falls, uncovered to the eye of the Master of life. Were Sakamaw about to do a treacherous deed, he would fold his blanket over his breast, that he might hide from the Great Spirit's view, the dark workings of his soul."

"Forgive me, noble chief!" exclaimed Stuart, extending his hand with military frankness and warmth. "I do not distrust you; you have come to me unweaponed, and we are armed; you are alone and we have the strength of a garrison, and more than all, you warn me of treachery and hostility on the part of other tribes, and bring us offers of continued peace from your own. I cannot, I do not doubt 'your' faith, but as the rules of war require some pledge as a safeguard for honor, you will consent to remain awhile as hostage here, secure of all the respect which brave soldiers can tender to one, whose valor and worth has made the fame of this forest region."

Sakamaw assented to this proposal with proud, unhesitating dignity, and turned to follow the young officer, whose cheek burned through its soldierly brown, as he made the proposition, which military discipline required, but which he feared might be deemed an insult by the high-minded savage. Sakamaw cast his eye for a moment on the opposite shore, where it was immediately arrested, and his foot stayed in its ascent by the objects which there met his gaze. An Indian woman, leading by the hand a young boy, of the same tawny hue, approached to the water's side, and by impressive and appealing gestures, seemed to solicit his attention and compassion.

"Why does the doe and the fawn follow the panther's path?" muttered he to himself, "why do they come where the dart of the hunter may pierce them, and leave the shelter of their own shady bowers?"

He hesitated, as if resolving some doubts in his own mind, then springing into the canoe that lay beneath the bank on which he stood, he pushed it rapidly over the waters to the spot where they awaited him. Whether the dark shadow of future events cast its prophetic gloom before him, softening his heart, for the reception of conjugal and parental love, I know not; but there was something mysteriously tender in the manner in which he departed from the coldness and reserve peculiar to his race, and embracing his wife and son, placed them in the light bark he had just quitted, and introduced them in the presence of Stuart, who had witnessed with surprised sensibility, the unwonted scene. The sensations which then moved and interested him, have been since embodied in lines, whose truth the poet most eloquently felt:

> Think not the heart in desert bred,
> To passion's softer touch is dead—
> Or that the shadowy skin contains
> No bright or animated veins—
> Where, though no blush its course betrays,
> The blood in all its wildness plays.

"Sakamaw," said he, "you have decided well. Bring them to my cabin and see how warm and true a welcome a soldier's wife can offer. The walls are rough, but they who share the warrior's and the hunter's lot must not look for downy beds or dainty fare."

It was a novel and interesting scene, when the wife and son of the Indian chief were presented to the youthful bride of Stuart, who with generous, uncalculating ardor, had bound herself to a soldier's destiny and followed him to a camp, where she was exposed to all the privations and danger of a remote and isolated station. As she proffered her frank, yet bashful welcome, she could not withdraw her pleased and wondering gaze from the dark, but beautiful features of the savage: clothed in the peculiar costume of her people, the symmetry of her figure, and the grace of her movements gave a singular charm to the wild and gaudy attire. The refined eye of August Stuart shrunk intuitively, for a moment, from the naked arms and uncovered neck of the Indian; but there was such an expression of redeeming modesty in her countenance, and her strait, glossy hair, falling in shining folds over her bosom, formed so rich a veil, the transient disgust was lost in undisguised admiration at the beauties of a form which a sculptor might have selected as a model for his art. The dark-haired daughter of the forest, to whose untutored sight, the soldier's bride appeared fair and celestial as the inhabitant of a brighter sphere, returned her scrutinizing gaze with one of delighted awe. Her fair looks, which art had formed into waving curls on her brow, her snowy complexion and eyes of heavenly blue, beamed upon her with such transcendent loveliness, her feelings were constrained to utter themselves in words as she had learned from her husband the language of the whites.

"Thou art fairer than the sun, when he shines upon the silver wave," exclaimed Lehella, such the name of the beautiful savage, "I have seen the moon in her brightness, the flowers in their bloom, but neither the moon when she walks over the hills of night, or the flowers when they open their leaves to the south wind are so fair and lovely as thou, daughter of the land of snow."

The fair cheek of Augusta mantled with carnation, as the low sweet voice of Lehella breathed forth this spontaneous tribute to her surpassing loveliness. Accustomed to restrain the expression of her own feelings, she dared not avow the admiration, which had however passed from her heart into her eyes, but she knew that praise to a child was most acceptable to a mother's ear and passing her white hand over the jetty locks of the Indian boy, she directed the attention of her husband to the deep hazel of his sparkling eye, and the symmetrical outlines of a figure, which bore a marked similitude to the chiselled representations of the infant Apollo. The young Adario, however, seemed not to appreciate the favors of his lovely hostess, and shrinking from her caressing hand, accompanied his father, who was conducted by Captain Stuart, to the place where he was to make his temporary abode. The romance which gave a kind of exciting charm to the character of Augusta, had now found a legitimate object for its enthusiasm and warmth. By romance, I do not mean that sickly, morbid sensibility, which turns from the realities of life with indifference or disgust, yearning after strange and hair-breadth events,—which looks on cold and unmoved, while real misery pipes and weeps and melts into liquid pearl at the image of fictitious woe—I mean the elevation of feeling, which lifts one above the weeds of the valley and the dust and soil of earth,—that sunny brightness of soul, which gilds the mist and the cloud, while it deepens the glory and bloom of existence,—that all-pervading, life-giving, yet self-annihilating principle, which imparts its own light and energy to every thing around and about it, and animating all nature with its warmth and vitality, receives the indiscriminate bounties of heaven, the sunbeam, the gale, the dew, and the flower, as ministers of individual joy and delight. Augusta had already begun to weave a fair vision for the future, in which the gentle Lehella was her pupil as well as her companion, learning from her the elegances and refinements of civilized life, and imparting to her, something of her own wild and graceful originality. She witnessed with delight the artless expression of wonder at the simple decorations of her rude apartment elicited from her untaught lips, for though in the bosom of the wilderness, and dwelling in a cabin constructed of the roughest materials, the hand of feminine taste had left its embellishing races wherever it had touched. Wild, autumnal flowers mingled their bloom and fragrance over the rustic window frame; sketches of forest scenery adorned the unplastered walls, and a guitar lying on the table, showed that the fair mistress of this humble mansion had been accustomed to a more luxurious home and more polished scenes. I cannot but linger for a moment here, for to me it is enchanted ground—a beautiful and accomplished woman, isolated from all the allurements of the world, far from the incense of adulation, and the seductions of pleasure, shedding the light of her loveliness on the bosom of wedded love, and offering the fresh and stainless blossoms of her affection on that shrine, which next to the altar of her God, is holiest in her eyes. But I must turn to a darker spot, one which has left an ineffable stain in the annals of our domestic history, but which is associated with so many interesting events I would fain rescue it from oblivion.

The next morning the garrison was a scene of confusion and horror. A party of soldiers had been absent during the evening on a hunting expedition, being a favorite recreation in the bright moonlighted nights. When the morning drum rolled its warning thunder, and the hunters came not as wont to perform their military duties, a general feeling of surprise and alarm pervaded the fort. Gilmore, the next officer in rank to

Stuart had a very young brother in this expedition, and filled with frater-nal anxiety, he collected another party, and endeavored to follow the steps of the fugitives. After hours of fruitless search, they discovered a fatal signal, which guided their path, a blood staining the herbage on which they trod, and plunging deeper into the forest, they found the mur-dered bodies of the victims, all bearing recent traces of the deadly scalp-ing-knife. The soldiers gazed on the mangled and disfigured remains of their late gallant comrades with consternation and dismay, when Gilmore, rousing from their stunning influence, rushed forward, and raising the body of his youthful brother in his arms, defaced and bleed-ing as it was, he swore a terrible oath, that for every drop of blood that had been spilled, heaven should give him vengeance. The other soldiers, who had neither brother nor kindred among the ghastly slain, shrunk with instinctive loathing from their gory clay, but breathing imprecations against the savage murderers, they followed the steps of Gilmore, who weighed as he was by his lifeless burden, with rapid and unfaltering course approached the fort.

"Behold!" cried he, to Stuart, who recoiled in sudden horror at the spectacle thus offered to his view, "behold!" and his voice was fearful in its deep and smothered tones, "had he been a man—but a boy, commit-ted to my charge with the prayers and tears of a doting father—the Benjamin of his age—Oh! by the shed blood of innocence and youth—by the white locks of age, I swear—to avenge his death, on the whole of that vindictive race, who thus dare to deface the image of their Maker—my poor, poor brother!"—And then the soldier was overcome by dismay and deposited the mangled body in the ground, and throwing himself prostrate by its side, lifted up his voice and wept aloud. The manly hulk of Stuart was deeply affected by this awful catastrophe, and the violent emotion it had excited in one of the most intrepid of their band. That the treacherous deed had been committed by members of those tribes, of whose hostility Sakamaw had warned him, he could not doubt; and he looked forward with dark forebodings to the stormy warfare that must ensue such bold and daring outrage. He turned towards Augusta, who white with terror stood with her Indian friend, somewhat near the dark-browed group that surrounded the mourner and the mournered, and the thought that even the arm of Jove, "stronger than death," might not be able to shield 'her' from the ravages of such an enemy, froze for a moment the very life blood in his veins. Sakamaw was no unmoved spectator of the scene we have described; but whatever were his internal emotions, his features remained cold and calm as the chiselled bronze they resembled. He saw many a fierce and lowering glance directed towards him, but like lightning on the same impassive surface, neither kindling nor impassive, they played around the stately form of the eagle chief.

"White warrior," said he, advancing up to Stuart, in the midst of the excited soldiers. "The Serpent has coiled himself in the brake, to the midnight hour. The wolf has lurked and his fangs are dripping with the blood of the young. But the Eagle soars in the noontime beams and hurtles the thunderbolt in the face of his foe. His children are guiltless of the innocent blood."

While Sakamaw was speaking, there was a sullen murmur of discontent among the soldiers—the low groan that harbingers the tempest's wrath—Gilmore too, rose from his recumbent position, and stood with clenched hands, shut teeth, ashy lips, and eyes that burned red through tears that the heat of revenge was now drying ere they fell. There is nothing so exasperating to one inflamed by hot and contending passions, as the sight of stoic indifference of perfect self-control. As the waters chafe and foam about the moveless cliff, that stands in "unblanched majesty," in the midst of the raving element, the tide of human passion rages most violently, when most calmly opposed.

"Dog of an Indian!" muttered Gilmore, "painted hypocrite! fiend of subtlety and guile! How dare you come hither with your vain-boasting words, honey on your lips, and gall and bitterness in your heart? By the all beholding heavens! you shall answer for every drop of blood spilled last night by your own hand, or by the hands of your hellish tribe."

"Gilmore, Gilmore!" exclaimed Stuart in a tone of deep command, "you are worse than mad.—Respect the laws of military honor, nor dare to insult one, who has voluntarily surrendered himself, as a hostage for his tribe. This chief is under my protection, under the guard and protection of every noble and honorable heart. Look upon him, he is unarmed, yet with generous trust and confidence he has entered the white man's camp, to warn him of the very outrageous acts which we now mourn. Gilmore, be a man, be a soldier and command our sympathy—not our indignation."

The voice of the young commander, which had been wont to suppress every expression of mutiny or discontent, by its slightest tones, now made an appeal as vain as it was just. "Down with the red-dog! down with him, Gilmore!" burst forth and echoed on every side. Again did Stuart raise his commanding voice, "till it rose high and clear as the sound of a bugle's blast. He was answered by the same rebellious and daring shouts. Lehella, who had looked on in wild, undefinable alarm, now comprehended the full extent of the danger which hung over the devoted Sakamaw, and rushing through the lawless band, she wreathed her slender arms around his majestic frame in the unavailing hope of shielding him from their rage.

"Fly, Sakamaw, fly!" she exclaimed, "the deer is not swifter than the foot of the hunter. Fly with Adario from the home of the pale man—There is death in his gleaming eye."

"Sakamaw will never fly from the face of his foe. The Great Spirit is looking down upon my heart, and sees that it is white of the blood of the brave." As the noble savage uttered those words, he looked up into the deep-blue heavens and drew back the deer-skin robe from his breast, as if inviting the scrutiny of the All-seeing to the recesses of his naked heart. It would seem that

"If Heaven had not some hand in this dark deed,"

such magnanimous sentiments would have arrested the course of their revenge, but they were blind, and deaf and infuriated. Gilmore felt in his bosom for the pistol, which he carried for his own safeguard. Augusta saw the motion, which was unperceived by Stuart, who was endeavoring to stem the torrent swelling around him; with an irresistible impulse she pressed forward, and seized his arm at the very moment it was extended toward his victim. The motion and the report of the pistol were simultaneous. The angel of mercy was too late—the death shot pierced the bosom of Sakamaw, and the fond and faithful breast that had vainly interposed itself between him and the impending blow. They fell—the forest oak and the caressing vine—blasted by the same avenging stroke, and the pause that succeeds the thunder's crash, is more awful than that which followed the deadly deed.

"Great God!" exclaimed Stuart, "what have you done? all the rivers of the West cannot wash out this foul stain." With feeling of bitter agony he knelt by the side of the dying chieftain and his martyred wife.

"Sakamaw," he cried, "friend, brother of the white man, speak, if you have breath to utter, and may you believe me guiltless of this crime—would I have died ere I had beheld this hour."

The expiring Indian opened for the last time, that eye which had been to his tribe, a lamp in peace and a torch in war, but the eagle glance was quashed in the midst of death. Twice he endeavored to speak, but the word "Adario" was all he could articulate.

"Yes, Sakamaw," he cried, " I will be a father to thy boy, through life, in death I will cherish him."

Who can fathom the depth, the strength of a mother's love? Lehella, who had lain apparently lifeless on the bosom of Sakamaw, while Augusta with bloodless cheeks and lips hung weeping over her, seemed to arouse from the lethargy of death, at the name of her son. She raised her cold cheek from its bloody pillow, and joining together her hands, already damp with the dews of dissolution, exclaimed in a voice unutterably solemn, while she lifted her dim and wavering glance to heaven—"Oh! thou Every Where, protect my son."

With this sublime adjuration to the Omnipotent Spirit of the universe, her soul made its transit. An impressive prayer was in reality breathed by the dying Indian mother. Stuart and Virginia were left kneeling on either side of the dead bodies of the martyred Indians.

It is painful to record a deed which must forever stain the annals of American history; but now while we glow with indignation at the tale of Indian barbarities on the frontiers of the West, let us remember the story of their past wrongs—let us think of the fate of the magnanimous Sakamaw, whose memory,

"In long after years,
Should kindle our blushes and waken our tears."

Years rolled on. The wilderness began to blossom "like the rose," and the solitary places to look joyous with life, and bright with promise; while on the fair banks of the Ohio, the inhabited village, the busy town, or the prouder city, rise in beauty, and imitative splendor. It was where the father of ancient waters flows on in all the opulence of its waves, still in the bosom of the wilderness an isolated cabin reared its head through thick clusters of overshadowing vines and perennial trees. The moon showered down its virgin rays on the woods, the waters, the peaceful cottage, the rustling trees—and lingered in brightness round two solitary figures reclining on the bank, watching the course of the swelling stream. Its pallid beams revealed the features of a man, who had passed life's vernal season, and was verging towards the autumnal grey; but though the lines of deep thought or sorrow were distinctly marked on his pale brow, there was an air of military dignity and command investing his figure, which showed at once that his youth had been passed in the tented field. The other figure was that of a young man, in all the vigor of earliest manhood, in the simple dress of a forester, with the swarthy cheek, and glittering eye, and jet-black locks of the Indian race. As we do not aim at mystery in the development of this simple story, we will gather up in a few words the events of years, in whose silent flight, the young and gallant Stuart had become the subdued and pensive moralist who sat gazing on the brim of the stream; and Adario, the orphan boy of the murdered Sakamaw, the manly youth, whose ardent yet civilized glance, reflected the gleams that shown fitfully round them. The young, the beautiful Augusta, was now the dweller of "the dark and narrow house," and the widowed husband, disgusted with the world, retired still deeper into the shades of the West, with the child of his adoption, and one sweet inheritor of her mother's charms, who had been baptized by the soft name of Lehella, in memory of the mother of Adario. This only daughter, accompanied by a maternal friend, had for the first time, visited the scene of her parents' nativity, and it was to watch the boat which was to bring back the rose of the wilderness to its solitary bower, that the father and Indian youth, night after night, lingered on the banks, catching the faintest sound, which anticipation might convert into the ripple caused by the dipping oar. Restless and stormy, unuttered feelings agitated the breast of Adario. Bred under the same roof, educated by the same enlightened and gifted mind, these children of the forest grew up together, entwined in heart and soul, like two plants whose roots are wreathed, and whose leaves and tendrils interlace each other in indissoluble wedlock. The son of Sakamaw, the daughter of Augusta—the dark and the fair—the eagle and the dove; it seemed to the sad and imaginative Stuart that the that the spirit of the injured Sakamaw would rejoice in the band of ghosts, at the bond that should unite these descendants of their sundered tribes. "Adario, tortured by jealousy and fear, awaited the return of Lehella with all the very impatience peculiar to the dark nation from which he derived his existence. Though at her presence he was gentle and mild as the gentlest of his sex, and all the harsher traits of the aboriginal character were softened and subdued, retaining only that dignity and elevation, we can never deny is their own legitimate dower.

Though they had usually retired before the midnight hour, they remained this night longer by a kind of mysterious sympathy and indefinable apprehension. Clouds gathered over the calm and silvered heavens, and gradually deepening its darkness wrapt the woods and waters in their solemn shadows. A low, sullen growl broke at intervals on the silence of the night, and they looked up anxiously for the flash which was to be the herald of another peal of the yet distant thunder. All was gloom above, and around, still the same sullen, murmuring sound came more distinctly on the air, which was now damp with the laboring storm. At last a light gleamed on the waters—bright, but still remote—and sent a long stream of radiance down the channel of the river, far as the spot where they were seated, gazing in a kind of fascination on the unwonted splendor. Louder and louder were those sullen murmurs, and deeper and brighter grew the ominous and lightning-like flashes that illumined the darkness of the wilderness. Onward it came, as if containing the principle of vitality in the fiery element that spread broader and fiercer around it—howling forth as it came those unearthly sounds which to the ear of an untutored savage, would have seemed the angry thunders of the Maniton. Standing on the very brink of the river, with breathless suspense, they watched the approach of the blazing phantom, when the father, whose perceptions became clearer as it neared, and who had heard of those wondrous fabric, one of the noblest inventions of human genius, that propelled by vapor, triumph in speed over the majestic ship or the lighter barque, believed he now for the first time he beheld one of these wonders of the waves, enveloped in a glory which was only the herald of its destruction. The thought of his daughter, that she might be exposed to the awful fate, wrapped in those volumed flames, came over him like a death-blast. At this moment wild shrieks and tumultuous cries were heard confusedly mingling with the hoarse thunders and plunging sound of the waters—figures became visible through the sheets of flame, wreathed with blackening smoke that reflected now their lurid brightness on the whole face of the sky. Suddenly a form burst through the blazing curtain, like an angel of light mid the regions of despair—it was but a glimpse of loveliness; but that one glimpse discovered the far, far-waving locks, the snow white brow, and beauteous outlines of the daughter of Stuart. They saw her stretch forth her virgin arms to the pitiless heavens—then plunge through one devouring element into the cold embraces of another still as deadly. With one long, loud shriek of agony—the father and the lover sprang from the shelving bank, and disappeared in the ignited waves!

The morning sun shone bright and clear on the blackened wreck of the Evening Star, the name of the devoted boat, and the waters flowed on calmly and majestically, as if they had never echoed to the shrieks of the dying, or closed over the relics of human tenderness and love. The solitary cottage—was still the abode of life, and youth, and hope. Adario and Lehella redeemed from a fiery or watery grave, were once more embosomed in its peaceful shades; but they were orphans. The river of the West was now the sepulchre of the gallant soldier. Lehella wept for their father—but she wept on the bosom of her lover; and she felt she was not alone.

It was a mysterious destiny, that thus united the offspring of two hostile nations in the loneliness of nature, the sacredness of love, and the holiness of religion—for Adario had learned to worship the Christian's God. The memory of Sakamaw, the friend of the white man, is still hallowed in the traditions of the West; but many a traveller passes by the cottage of the wilderness, and gazes on its shaded image in the current that bears him along, unconscious that the son of the eagle chief and the daughter of his brave defender dwell within its secluded walls.

Bibliography

Brown, Lynda W. "Caroline Lee Hentz." *American Women Writers 2*. Ed. Lina Maineiro. New York: Ungar: 1979: 285-86.

Ellison, Rhoda C. "Introduction," *The Planter's Northern Bride*. Chapel Hill: University of North Carolina Press, 1970: vii-xxxii.

Ellison, Rhoda Coleman. "Mrs. Hentz and the Green-Eyed Monster." *American Literature* 22 (Nov. 1950): 345-50.

Hentz, Caroline Lee. "The Indian Martyrs." *Cincinnati Mirror, and Ladies' Parterre* 1 Sept. 1832: 193-95.

Labadidi, Iman. *A Study in Domesticity: The Life and Literary Works of Caroline Lee Hentz, 1800-1856.* University of Nottingham dissertation, 1989.

Shillingsburg, Mariam J. "The Ascent of Woman, Southern Style: Hentz, King, Chopin." *Southern Literature in Transition.* Ed. Philip Castille and William Osborne. Memphis: Memphis State University Press, 1983. 127-39.

Harriet Beecher Stowe

1811-1896

Harriet Beecher Stowe was a native of Litchfield, Massachusetts, who moved with her family to Cincinnati in 1832, which was then known as Porkopolis, a hog-packing center of 30,000 people, a rough frontier town. In the eighteen years until she left in 1850, Harriet Beecher lived in Ohio with her father, Lyman Beecher, a Congregationalist minister who had been appointed to the presidency of the newly established Lane Theological Seminary; he hoped to bring New England enlightenment to the "benighted West." Harriet, who had been self-supporting from the age of fourteen, continued to teach with her famous sister, Catharine Esther Beecher, who opened the Western Female Seminary in Cincinnati. In 1834, Harriet's literary career took off after she submitted "A New England Sketch" to Judge Hall's *Western Monthly Magazine*, where it won first prize and $50. The western journal continued to publish her New England regional sketches, which were built around memories of her northeastern home.

At the Semi-Colon Club she met one of her father's professors, Calvin Ellis Stowe, and his wife, Eliza, who became her fast friend. After Eliza's death, in 1836 Harriet Beecher married Stowe, who was an unprepossessing Biblical scholar of precarious means; between 1836 and 1850 they had seven children. In 1850 when he was offered a post at Bowdoin College in Brunswick, Maine, his wife, Harriet, was 39, pregnant, and thoroughly disgusted with Cincinnati where the Semi-Colon Club had closed and regional culture tolerated "fleshpots," wandering pigs, violence and cholera, which had recently killed one of her sons.

Other disappointments from the area cascaded upon her. There was in 1833 a painful visit to Kentucky where she observed slavery and an inspiring visit to Ripley, Ohio, where Rev. John Ranklin's house (today a state memorial) had provided refuge to an escaping slave and her son. Stowe learned that hounds, the Ohio River, and slave catchers had failed to stop the woman or her husband who later followed her on the underground railroad to Canada. Stowe's narrative version later became the keystone scene in Chapter 7, "The Mother's Struggle": "Eliza made her desperate retreat across the river just in the dusk of twilight. The gray mist of evening rising slowly from the river, enveloped her as she disappeared up the bank, and the swollen current and floundering masses of ice presented a hopeless barrier between her and her pursuer."

Another ugly Ohio memory came to Harriet Beecher Stowe from Cincinnati's rowdy lawlessness that caused her to abandon her conservatism on the question of women's silence on public issues. Stowe had gone to Cincinnati convinced that men should handle public affairs, while women should follow St. Paul's injunction and refrain from speaking out about political questions. But in 1836 she saw the lawless destruction of James G. Birney's abolitionist print shop; the mob destroyed a black section of Cincinnati and threw Birney's printing press into the Ohio River. The angry Stowe wrote a letter of protest to a local newspaper, but was not yet prepared to do so except under a male pseudonym.

She also remembered how the following year, 1837, she had urged Calvin Ellis Stowe to aid an escaping slave girl by driving her out Montgomery Pike to the Springdale home of Quaker John Van Sandt. This event became the fictionalized episode about Ohio's underground railroad in Chapter 9 of *Uncle Tom's Cabin,* "In Which It Appears That the Senator Is But a Man."

So Harriet Beecher Stowe was motivated to accomplish her own escape from Cincinnati in 1850. Later that year in Maine, she had a vision of an elderly black man being beaten to death; it was the catalyst for the story that became *Uncle Tom's Cabin*, which protested Ohio's recent passage of the Fugitive Slave Act that supported slaveholders' property rights, even if the slaves were in a non-slave state. Earlier her family had watched the consequences of events like America's 1808 prohibition against further importation of slaves and, though they admired William Lloyd Garrison's rhetoric and Frederick Douglass, they had not quickly supported abolition. But her Ohio experiences persuaded Harriet Beecher Stowe to oppose chattel slavery.

For some years she had contributed to Gamaliel Bailey's weekly abolitionist paper, the *National Era,* and he agreed to pay her $300 for several sketches about slavery which would be based on her Ohio experiences. In 1851 she began writing *Uncle Tom's Cabin,* subtitled by her husband "Life Among the Lowly," which was first serialized and then in 1852 was published as a book. An immediate sensation, it sold 300,000 copies in one year. The book was translated into over twenty languages and became the nineteenth-century's most famous and best-selling novel. In fact, the sale of the book at home and abroad exceeded that of any other book except the Bible.

One caveat to her domestic success came from the blame placed upon Stowe by many nineteenth-century readers who accused the writer of unfairness in her depiction of America's regions; she was accused of blindly praising the North (at least New England) and vilifying the South. Stowe believed that the story gave credit to southern characters, like Augustine St. Clare, and berated northern ones, like Miss Ophelia St. Clare and Simon Legree who was from Vermont. These debates emphasize how the success of *Uncle Tom's Cabin* was impelled by its regional subjects, each of which is depicted as imperfect.

Stowe was interested in showing how men and women are significantly shaped by the region where they live, knowledge perhaps gained from her own youthful migration that wrenched her away from New England's culture. Even Stowe's first regional sketch, "A New England Story," later renamed "Uncle Lot," was built upon perspectives imposed by distance. "A New England Sketch" opens in Newbury, Connecticut, and apostrophizes "my own New England—the land of bright and strong hearts: the land of deeds and not of words." Stowe adds that New England's merit is not intrinsic, but personal, because an author will always feel this way about "the land of our early years," even if it were "Kentuck."

Thus Stowe's nearly two decades in the "West" taught her more than simple contempt for "corduroy roads," as *Uncle Tom's Cabin* reveals. In this great novel and in her regional sketches that were collected in her 1843 collection, *The Mayflower*, published by Harper's and dedicated to Cincinnati's Semi-Colon Club, Stowe uses rural regional subject matter to project the significance of environment. Through the years that followed, Stowe wrote prolifically with a shrewd sense of audience and a gift for capturing the vanished culture of her childhood New England. Today many critics prefer her short sketches to her novels like *Dred; A Tale of the Great Dismal Swamp*, her 1856 slave novel about Nat Turner, or the historical satire on Calvinism, *The Minister's Wooing* (1859). Her regional sketches and stories, from those written while in Ohio to the Massachusetts volumes, like *The Pearl of Orr's Island* (1862) or *Oldtown Folks* (1869) influenced other regionalist writers, such as Sarah Orne Jewett, another New Englander credited with perfecting America's local color style.

After *Uncle Tom's Cabin*, Harriet Beecher Stowe's career flourished; for example, in 1853 she was hired by the *New York Independent* as a weekly contributor of sketches, stories, poems, and essays. This made her America's first woman columnist; she also wrote regularly for the *Christian Union*. Her writing made Harriet Beecher Stowe one of the most widely known women in the world; she was even invited to tour the British Isles, France, and Italy. Calvin Stowe had joined the faculty of the Andover Theological Seminary in Massachusetts, but Harriet's wealth provided for the family during the rest of their lives, and she built them two homes, one in Andover and another in Hartford.

All of this success was built upon the remarkable popularity of *Uncle Tom's Cabin,* a simple tale and basically a domestic polemic. This novel draws attention to changing conceptions of women's sphere and their potential source of moral energy. It uses domestic experiences that resonate with symbolic importance and is strongly colored by Stowe's view of females' moral imperative. As Mrs. Bird says to her husband, Senator Bird, your "heart is better than your head." His theoretical political position is overturned when reality substitutes a bloody Eliza and child at the kitchen door; Senator Bird becomes a hero by civil disobedience. The slave Uncle Tom is innately morally superior but is led to Christian martyrdom. As Tom says before he dies, heaven "is better than Kentuck" (41).

Thus throughout this long novel Stowe's regional eye and ear undergirds subtle but sweeping redefinitions of gender and race. She appeals to higher law to justify undercutting the Constitution's right to private property. The novelist creates themes of matrifocal domesticity and extended familial love; God meant the human race to be one family, Harriet Beecher Stowe believed, but at the end of *Uncle Tom's Cabin* she nonetheless advocates sending ex-slaves back to Africa because her radical abolitionism demanded emancipation and colonialization for slaves, rather than integration. In this sense, she relied upon the era's racist assumptions of human difference. But her broad human vision was based on community, a world where no children should ever be taken from their mothers or mothers should tolerate such social injustice, as Eliza says, "jest for havin' natural feelins."

Harriet Beecher Stowe adapts her family's Cincinnati experiences in this interesting novel which in its epilogue specifically addresses the "farmers of rich and joyous Ohio." But the text more typically refers to the region as "benighted," and offers descriptions like the following: "the soft, rich earth of Ohio, as everyone knows, is admirably suited to the manufacture of mud." In fact, among the eight Ohio chapters of the novel are several scenes tracing Eliza, her baby and husband as they escape from Cincinnati, to Sandusky, and toward Canada's shores. There are also a series of characters based on Ohioans she knew—real-life counterparts to John Van Sandt (John Van Trompe), the Quaker family, Levi and Catharine Coffin, and two black characters, Aunt Chloe and Cassy, who are drawn from Harriet's cook and friend, Eliza Buck.

Stowe's great Ohio-based novel may not be frequently read today, but it dignified its author and remains, as W. H. Venable said at the end of the nineteenth century, "in a true sense, a Western product" (297).

In Which It Appears That the Senator Is But a Man

Harriet Beecher Stowe

The light of the cheerful fire shone on the rug and carpet of a cozy parlor, and glittered on the sides of the tea cups and well-brightened teapot, as Senator bird was drawing off his boots, preparatory to inserting his feet into a pair of new handsome slippers, which his wife had been working for him while away on his senatorial tour. Mrs. Bird, looking the very picture of delight, was superintending the arrangements of the table, ever and anon mingling admonitory remarks to a number of frolicsome juveniles, who were effervescing in all those modes of untold gambol and mischief that have astonished mothers ever since the flood.

"Tom, let the door-knob alone—there's a man! Mary! Mary! don't pull the cat's tail—poor pussy! Jim, you mustn't climb on that table—no, no! You don't know, my dear, what a surprise it is to us all to see you here to-night!" said she, at last, when she found a space to say something to her husband.

"Yes, yes; I thought I'd just make a run down, spend the night, and have a little comfort at home. I'm tired to death, and my head aches!"

Mrs. Bird cast a glance at a camphor-bottle, which stood in the half-open closet, and appeared to meditate an approach to it, but her husband interposed.

"No, no, Mary, no doctoring! a cup of your good hot tea, and some of our good home living, is what I want. It's a tiresome business, this legislating!"

And the senator smiled, as if he rather liked the idea of considering himself a sacrifice to his country.

"Well," said his wife after the business of the tea-table was getting rather slack, "and what have they been doing in the Senate?"

Now, it was a very unusual thing for gentle little Mrs. Bird to ever trouble her head with what was going on in the house of the state, very wisely considering that she had enough to do to mind her own. Mr. Bird, therefore, opened his eyes in surprise, and said,

"Not very much of importance."

"Well; but is it true that they have been passing a law forbidding people to give meat and drink to those poor colored folks who come along? I heard they were talking of some such law, but I didn't think any Christian legislature would pass it!"

"Why, Mary, you are getting to be a politician, all at once."

"No, nonsense! I wouldn't give a fip for all your politics, generally, but I think this is something downright cruel and unchristian. I hope, my dear, no such law has been passed."

"There has been a law passed forbidding people to help off the slaves that come over from Kentucky, my dear; so much of that thing has been done by these reckless Abolitionists, that our brethren in Kentucky are very strongly excited, and it seems necessary, and no more than Christian and kind, that something should be done by our state to quiet the excitement."

"And what is the law? It don't forbid us to shelter these poor creatures a night, does it, and to give 'em something comfortable to eat, and a few old clothes, and send them quietly about their business?"

"Why, yes, my dear; that would be aiding and abetting, you know."

Mrs. Bird was a timid, blushing little woman, of about four feet in height, and with mild blue eyes, and a peach-blow complexion, and the gentlest, sweetest voice in the world;—as for courage, a moderate-sized cock-turkey had been known to put her to rout at the very first gobble, and a stout house-dog, of moderate capacity, would bring her into subjection merely by a show of his teeth. Her husband and children were her entire world, and these she ruled more by entreaty and persuasion than by command or argument. There was only one thing that was capable of arousing her, and that provocation came in on the side of her unusually gentle and sympathetic nature;—anything in the shape of cruelty would throw her into a passion, which was the more alarming and inexplicable in proportion to the general softens of her nature. Generally the most indulgent and easy to be entreated of all mothers, still her boys had a very reverent remembrance of a most vehement chastisement she once bestowed upon them, because she found them leagued with several graceless boys of the neighborhood, stoning a defenseless kitten.

"I'll tell you what," Master Bill used to say, "I was scared that time. Mother came to me so that I thought she was crazy, and I was whipped and tumbled off to bed, without any supper, before I could get over wondering what had come about; and, after that I heard mother crying outside the door, which made me feel worse than all the rest. I'll tell you what," he'd say, "we boys never stoned another kitten!"

On the present occasion, Mrs. Bird rose quickly, with very red cheeks, which quite improved her general appearance, and walked up to her husband, with quite a resolute air, and said, in a determined tone.

"Now, John, I want to know if you think such a law as that is right and Christian?"

"You won't shoot me, now, Mary, if I say I do!"

"I never could have thought it of you, John; you didn't vote for it?"

"Even so, my fair politician."

"You ought to be ashamed, John! Poor, homeless, houseless creatures! It's a shameful, wicked, abominable law, and I'll break it, for one, the first time I get a chance; and I hope I *shall* have a chance, I do! Things have got to a pretty pass, if a woman can't give a warm supper and a bed to poor, starving creatures, just because they are slaves, and have been abused and oppressed all their lives, poor things!"

"But, Mary, just listen to me. Your feelings are all quite right, dear, and interesting, and I love you for them; but, then, dear, we mustn't suffer our feelings to run away with our judgement; you must consider it's not a matter of private feeling,—there are great public interests involved,—there is such a state of public agitation rising, that we must put aside our private feelings."

"Now, John, I don't know anything about politics, but I can read my Bible; and there I see that I must feed the hungry, clothe the naked, and comfort the desolate; and the Bible I mean to follow."

"But in cases where your doing so would involve a great public evil—"

"Obeying God never brings on public evils. I know it can't It's always safest, all round to *do* as *He* bids us."

"Now, listen to me, Mary, and I can state to you a very clear argument, to show—"

"Oh, nonsense, John! you can talk all night, but you wouldn't do it. I put it to you, John—would *you* now turn away a poor, shivering, hungry creature from your door because he was a runaway? *Would* you, now?"

Now if the truth must be told, our senator had the misfortune to be a man who had a particularly humane and accessible nature, and turning away anybody had never been his forte; and what was worse for him in this particular pinch of the argument was, that his wife knew it, and, of course, was making an assault on rather an indefensible point. So he had recourse to the usual means of gaining time for such cases made and provided; he said "ahem," and coughed several times, took out his pocket-handkerchief, and began to wipe his glasses. Mrs. Bird, seeing the defenceless condition of the enemy's territory, had no more conscience than to push her advantage.

"I should like to see you doing that, John—I really should! Turning a woman out of doors in a snow-storm, for instance; or may be you'd take her up and put her in jail, wouldn't you? You would make a great hand at that!"

"Of course, it would be a very painful duty," began Mr. Bird in a moderate tone.

"Duty, John! don't use that word. You know it isn't a duty—it can't be a duty! If folks want to keep slaves from running away, let 'em treat 'em well,—that's my doctrine. If I had slaves (as I hope I never shall have), I'd risk their wanting to run away from me, or you either, John. I tell you folks don't run away when they are happy; and when they do run, poor creatures! they suffer enough with cold and hunger and fear, without everybody's turning against them; and, law or no law, I never will, so help me God!"

"Mary! Mary! My dear, let me reason with you."

"I hate reasoning, John—especially reasoning on such subjects. There's a way you political folks have of coming round and round a plain right thing; and you don't believe in it yourselves, when it comes to practice. I know *you* well enough, John. You don't believe it's right any more than I do; and you wouldn't do it any sooner than I."

At this critical juncture, old Cudjoe, the black man-of-all-work, put his head in at the door, and wished "Missis would come into the kitchen;" and our senator, tolerably relieved, looked after his little wife with a whimsical mixture of amusement and vexation, and, seating himself in the arm-chair, began to read the papers.

After a moment, his wife's voice was heard at the door, in a quick, earnest, tone—"John, John! I do wish you'd come here a moment."

He laid down his paper, and went into the kitchen, and startled, quite amazed at the sight that presented itself:—A young and slender woman, with garments torn and frozen, with one shoe gone, and the stocking torn away from the cut and bleeding foot, was laid back in a deadly swoon upon two chairs. There was the impress of the despised race upon her face, yet none could help feeling its mournful and pathetic beauty, while its stony sharpness, its cold, fixed, deathly aspect, struck a solemn chill over him. He drew his breath short, and stood in silence. His wife, and their only colored domestic, old Aunt Dinah, were busily engaged in restorative measures; while old Cudjoe had got the boy on his knee, and was busy pulling off his shoes and stockings, and chafing his little cold feet.

"Sure now, if she ain't a sight to behold!" said old Dinah, compassionately; "'pears like 'twas the heat that made her faint. She was tol'able peart when she cum in, and asked if she couldn't warm herself a spell; and I was just a' askin' her where she cum from, and she fainted right down. Never done much hard work, guess, by the looks of her hands."

"Poor creature!" said Mrs. Bird compassionately, as the woman slowly unclosed her large, dark eyes, and looked vacantly at her. Suddenly an expression of agony crossed her face, and she sprang up, saying, "Oh, my Harry! Have they got him?"

The boy, at this, jumped from Cudjoe's knee, and running to her side, put up his arms. "Oh, he's here! he's here!" she exclaimed.

"O ma'am!" said she wildly to Mrs. Bird, "do protect us! Don't let them get him!"

"Nobody shall hurt you here, poor woman," said Mrs. Bird encouragingly. "You are safe; don't be afraid."

"God bless you!" said the woman, covering her face and sobbing; while the little boy, seeing her crying, tried to get into her lap.

With many gentle and womanly offices, which none knew better how to render than Mrs. Bird, the poor woman was, in time, rendered more calm. A temporary bed was provided for her on the settle, near the fire; and after a short time she fell into a heavy slumber, with the child, who seemed no less weary, soundly sleeping on her arm; for the mother resisted, with nervous anxiety, the kindest attempts to take him from her; and, even in sleep, her arm encircled him with an unrelaxing clasp, as if she could not even then be beguiled of her vigilant hold.

Mr. and Mrs. Bird had gone back to the parlor, where, strange as it may appear, no reference was made, on either side, to the preceding conversation; but Mrs. Bird busied herself with her knitting-work, and Mr. Bird pretended to be reading the paper.

"I wonder who and what she is!" said Mr. Bird, at last, as he laid it down.

"When she wakes up and feel a little rested, we will see," said Mrs. Bird.

"I say, wife!" said Mr. Bird, after musing in silence over his newspaper.

"Well, dear!"

"She couldn't wear one of your gowns, could she, by any letting down, or such matter? She seems to be rather larger than you are."

A quite perceptible smile glimmered on Mrs. Bird's face, as she answered, "We'll see."

Another pause, and Mr. Bird again broke out,

"I say, wife!"

"Well! what now?"

"Why, there's that old bombazine cloak, that you keep on purpose to put over me when I take my afternoon's nap; you might as well give her that,—she needs clothes."

At this instant, Dinah looked in to say that the woman was awake, and wanted to see Missis.

Mr. and Mrs. Bird went into the kitchen, followed by the two eldest boys, the smaller fry having, by this time, been safely disposed of in bed.

The woman was now sitting up on the settle by the fire. She was looking steadily into the blaze, with a calm, heartbroken expression, very different from her former agitated wildness.

"Did you want me?" said Mrs. Bird, in gentle tones. "I hope you feel better now, poor woman!"

A long-drawn, shivering sigh was the only answer; but she lifted her dark eyes and fixed them on her with such a forlorn and imploring expression, that the tears came into the little woman's eyes.

"You needn't be afraid of anything; we are friends here, poor woman! Tell me where you came from, and what you want," said she.

"I came from Kentucky," said the woman.

"When?" said Mr. bird, taking up the interrogatory.

"To-night."

"How did you come?"

"I crossed on the ice."

"Crossed on the ice!" said everyone present.

"Yes," said the woman slowly, "I did. God helping me, I crossed on the ice; for they were behind me—right behind—and there was no other way!"

"Law, Missis," said Cudjoe, "the ice is all in broken-up blocks, a-swinging and a-teetering up and down in the water!"

"I know it was—I know it!" said she wildly; "but I did it! I wouldn't have thought I could,—I didn't think I should get over, but I didn't care! I could but die, if I didn't. The Lord helped me; nobody knows how much the Lord can help 'em, till they try," said the woman, with a flashing eye.

"Were you a slave?" asked Mr. Bird.

"Yes, sir; I belonged to a man in Kentucky."

"Was he unkind to you?"

"No, he was a good master."

"And was your mistress unkind to you?"

"No, sir—no! my mistress was always good to me."

"What could induce you to leave a good home, then, and run away, and go through such dangers?"

The woman looked at Mrs. Bird with a keen, scrutinizing glance, and it did not escape her that she was dressed in deep mourning.

"Ma'am," she said suddenly, "have you ever lost a child?"

The question was unexpected, and it was a thrust on a new wound; for it was only a month since a darling child of the family had been laid in the grave.

Mr. Bird turned and walked to the window, and Mrs. Bird burst into tears; but, recovering her voice, she said,

"Why do you ask that? I have lost a little one."

"Then you will feel for me. I have lost two, one after another,—left 'em buried there when I came away; and I had only this one left. I never slept a night without him; he was all I had. He was my comfort and pride, day and night; and, ma'am, they were going to take him away from me—to *sell* him,—sell him down south, ma'am, to go all alone,—a baby that had never been away from his mother in his life! I couldn't stand it, ma'am. I knew I never should be good for anything, if they did; and when I knew the papers were signed, and he was sold, I took him and came away in the night; and they chased me,—the man that bought him, and some Mas'r's folks,—and they were coming down right behind me, and I heard 'em. I jumped right on to the ice; and how I got across I don't know,—but, first I knew, a man was helping me up the bank.

The woman did not sob nor weep. She had gone to a place where tears are dry; but every one around her way, in some way characteristic of themselves, showing signs of hearty sympathy.

The two little boys, after a desperate rummaging in their pockets, in search of the handkerchiefs which mothers know are never to be found there, had thrown themselves disconsolately into the skirts of their mother's gown, where they were sobbing, and wiping their eyes and noses, to their hearts' content;—Mrs. Bird had her face fairly hidden in her pocket-handkerchief; and old Dinah, with tears streaming down her black, honest, fact, was ejaculating, "Lord, have mercy on us!" with all the fervor of a camp-meeting;—while old Cudjoe, rubbing his eyes very hard with his cuffs, and making a most uncommon variety of wry faces, occasionally responded in the same key, with great fervor. Our senator was a statesman, and of course could not be expected to cry. like other mortals; and so he turned his back to the company, and looked out of the window, and seemed particularly busy in clearing his throat and wiping his spectacle-glasses, occasionally blowing his nose in a manner that was calculate to excite suspicion, had anyone been in a state to observe critically.

"How come you do tell me you had a kind master?" he suddenly exclaimed, gulping down very resolutely some kind of rising in his throat, and turning suddenly round upon the woman.

"Because he I *was* a kind master;—I'll say that of him, any way— and my mistress was kind; but they couldn't help themselves. They were owing money; and there was some way, I can't tell how, that a man had a hold on them, and they were obliged to give him his will. I listened, and heard him telling my mistress that, and she begging and pleading for me,—and then he told her that he couldn't help himself, and that the papers were all drawn;—and then it was I took him and left my home, and came away. I knew 'twas no use of my trying to live, if they did it; for't 'pears like this child is all I have."

"Have you no husband?"

"Yes, but he belongs to another man. His master is real hard to him, and won't let him come to see me, hardly ever; and he's grown harder and harder upon us, and he threatens to sell him down south;—it's like I'll never see *him* again!"

The quiet tone in which the woman pronounced these words might have led a superficial observer to think that she was entirely apathetic; but there was a calm, settled depth of anguish in her large, dark eyes that spoke of something far otherwise.

"And where do you mean to go, my poor woman?" said Mrs. Bird.

"To Canada, if I only knew where that was. Is it very far off, is Canada?" said she, looking up, with a simple, confiding air, to Mrs. Bird's face.

"Poor thing!" said Mrs. Bird, involuntarily.

"Is't a very great way off, think?" said the woman earnestly.

"Much further than you think, poor child!" said Mrs. Bird; "but we will try to think what can be done for you. Here, Dinah, make her up a bed in your own room, close by the kitchen, and I'll think what to do for her in the morning. Meanwhile, never fear, poor woman; put your trust in God; he will protect you."

Mrs. Bird and her husband reentered the parlor. She sat down in her little rocking-chair before the fire, swaying thoughtfully to and fro. Mr. Bird strode up and down the room, grumbling to himself, "Pish! pshaw! confounded awkward business!" At length, striding up to his wife, he said,

"I say, wife, she'll have to get away from here, this very night. That fellow will be down on the scent bright and early to-morrow morning; if 'twas only the woman, she could lie quiet till it was over; but that little chap can't be kept still by a troop of horse and foot, I'll warrant me; he'll bring it all out, popping his head out of some window or door. A pretty kettle of fish it would be for me, too, to be caught with them both here, just now! No; they'll have to be got off to-night."

"To-night! How is it possible?—where to?"

"Well, I know pretty well where to," said the senator, beginning to put on his boots, with a reflective air; and stopping when his leg was half in, he embraced his knee with both hands, and seemed to go off in deep meditation.

"It's a confounded, awkward, ugly business," said he, at last, beginning to tug at his boot-straps again, "and that's a fact!" After one boot was fairly on, the senator sat with the other in his hand, profoundly studying the figure of the carpet. "It will have to be done, though, for aught I see,—hang it all!" and he drew the other boot anxiously on, and looked out of the window.

Now, little Mrs. Bird was a discreet woman,—a woman who never in her life said, "I told you so!" and, on the present occasion, though pretty well aware of the shape her husband's meditations were taking, she very prudently forbore to meddle with them, only sat very quietly in her chair, and looked quite ready to hear her liege lord's intentions, when he should think proper to utter them.

"You see," he said, "there's my old client, Van Trompe, has come over from Kentucky, and set all his slaves free; and he has bought a place seven miles up the creek here, back in the woods, where nobody goes, unless they go on purpose; and it's a place that isn't found in a hurry. There she'd be safe enough; but the plague of the thing is, nobody could drive a carriage there to-night but *me*."

"Why not? Cudjoe is an excellent driver."

"Ay, ay, but here it is. The creek has to be crossed twice; and the second crossing is quite dangerous, unless one knows it as I do. I have crossed it a hundred times on horseback, and know exactly the turns to take. And so, you see, there's no help for it. Cudjoe must put in the horses, as quietly as may be, about twelve o'clock, and I'll take her over; and then, to give color to the matter, he must carry me on to the nearest tavern, to take the stage for Columbus, that comes by about three or four, and so it will look as if I had had the carriage only for that. I shall get into business bright and early in the morning. But I'm thinking I shall feel rather cheap there, after all that's been said and done; but hang it, I can't help it!"

"Your heart is better than your head, in this case, John," said the wife, laying her little white hand on his. "Could I ever have loved you, had I not known you better than you know yourself?" And the little woman looked so handsome, with the tears sparkling in her eyes, that the senator thought he must be a decidedly clever fellow, to get such a pretty creature into such a passionate admiration of him; and so, what could he do but walk off soberly to see about the carriage. At the door, however, he stopped a moment, and then coming back, he said, with some hesitation,

"Mary, I don't know how you'd feel about it, but there's that drawer full of things—of—of—poor little Henry's." So saying, he turned quickly on his heel, and shut the door after him.

His wife opened the little bed-room door adjoining her room, and taking the candle, set it down on the top of a bureau there; then from a small recess she took a key, and put it thoughtfully in the lock of a drawer, and made a sudden pause, while the two boys, who, boy like, had followed close upon her heels, stood looking, with silent, significant glances at their mother. And oh! mother that reads this, has there never been in your house a drawer, or a closet, the opening of which has been to you like the opening again of a little grave? Ah! happy mother that you are, if this has not been so.

Mrs. Bird slowly opened the drawer. There were little coats of many a form and pattern, piles of aprons, and rows of small stockings; and even a pair of little shoes, worn and rubbed at the toes, were peeping from the folds of the paper. There was a toy horse and wagon, a top, a ball,—memorials gathered with many tear and many a heartbreak! She sat down by the drawer, and, leaning her head on her hands over it, wept till the tears fell through her fingers into the drawer; then suddenly raising her head, she began, with nervous haste, selecting the plainest and most substantial articles, and gathering them into a bundle.

"Mamma," said one of the boys, gently touching her arm, "are you going to give away *those* things?"

"My dear boys," she said, softly and earnestly, "if poor dear, loving little Henry looks down from heaven, he would be glad to have us do this. I could not find it in my heart to give them away to any common person—to anybody that was happy; but I give them to a mother more heartbroken and sorrowful than I am; and I hope God will send his blessings with them!"

There are in this world blessed should, whose sorrow shall spring up into joys for others; whose earthly hopes, laid in the grave with many tears, are the seed from which spring healing flowers and balm for the desolate and the distressed. Among such was the delicate woman who sits there by the lamp, dropping slow tears, while she prepares the memorials of her own lost one for the outcast wanderer.

After a while, Mrs. Bird opened a wardrobe, and, taking from there a plain, serviceable dress or two, she sat busily at her work-table, and, with needle, scissors, and thimble at hand, quietly commenced the "letting down" process which her husband had recommended, and continued busily at it till the old clock in the corner struck twelve, and she heard the low rattling of wheels at the door.

"Mary," said her husband, coming in, with his overcoat in his hand, "you must wake her up now; we must be off."

Mrs. Bird hastily deposited the various articles she had collected into a small plain trunk, and, locking it, desired her husband to see it in the carriage, and then proceeded to call the woman. Soon, arrayed in a cloak, bonnet, and shawl, that had belonged to her benefactress, she appeared at the door with her child in her arms. Mr. Bird hurried her into the carriage, and Mrs. Bird pressed on after her to the carriage steps. Eliza leaned out of the carriage, and put out her hand—a hand as soft and beautiful as was given in return. She fixed her large, dark eyes, full of earnest meaning, on Mrs. Bird's face, and seemed going to speak. Her lips moved,—she tried once or twice, but there was no sound,—and pointing upward, with a look never to be forgotten, she fell back into the seat, and covered her face. The door was shut, and the carriage drove on.

What a situation, now, for a patriotic senator, that had been all the week before spurring up the legislature of his native state to pass more stringent resolutions against escaping fugitives, their harborers and abettors!

Our good senator in his native state had not been exceeded by any of his brethren in Washington, in the sort of eloquence which has won for them immortal renown! How sublimely he had sat with his hands in his pockets, and scouted all sentimental weaknesses of those who would put the welfare of a few miserable fugitives before great state interests!

He was as bold as a lion about it, and "mightily convinced," not only himself, but everybody that heard him;—but then his idea of a fugitive was only an idea of the letters that spell the word,—or, at most, the image of a little newspaper picture of a man with a stick and bundle, with "Ran away from the subscriber" under it. The magic of the real presence of distress,—the imploring human eye, the frail, trembling human hand, the despairing appeal of helpless agony,—these he had never tried. He had never thought that a fugitive might be hapless mother, a defenseless child,—like the one which was now wearing his lost boy's little, well-known cap; and so, as our poor senator was not stone or steel,—as he was a man, and a downright noble-hearted one, too—he was, as everybody must see, in a sad case for his patriotism. And you need not exult over him, good brother of the Southern States; for we have some inklings that many of you, under similar circumstances, would not do much better. We have reason to know, in Kentucky, as in Mississippi, are noble and generous hearts, to whom never was tale of suffering told in vain. Ah, good brother! is it fair for you to expect of us services which your own brave, honorable heart would not allow you to render, were you in our place?

Be that as it may, if our good senator was a political sinner, he was in a fair way to expiate it by his night's penance. There had been a long continuous period of rainy weather, and the soft, rich earth of Ohio, as every one knows, is admirably suited to the manufacture of mud,—and the road was an Ohio railroad of the good old times.

"And pray, what sort of road may that be?" says some eastern traveler, who has been accustomed to connect no ideas with a railroad, but those of smoothness or speed.

Know, then, innocent eastern friend, that in benighted regions of the west, where the mud is of unfathomable and sublime depth, roads are made of round rough logs, arranged transversely side by side, and coated over in their pristine freshness with earth, turf, and whatsoever may come to hand, and then the rejoicing native calleth it a road, and straightway essayeth to ride thereupon. In process of time, the rains wash off all the turf and grass aforesaid, move the logs hither and thither, in picturesque positions, up, down and crosswise, with divers chasms and ruts of black mud intervening.

Over such a road as this our senator went stumbling along, making moral reflections as continually as under the circumstances could be expected,—the carriage proceeding along pretty much as follows,— bump! bump! bump! slush! down in the mud!—the senator, woman and child reversing their positions so suddenly as to come, without any very accurate adjustment, against the windows of the down-hill side. Carriage sticks fast, while Cudjoe on the outside is heard making a great muster among the horses. After various ineffectual pullings and twitchings, just as the senator is losing all patience, the carriage suddenly rights itself with a bounce,—the two front wheels go down into another abyss, and senator, woman, and child all tumble promiscuously on to the front seat,—senator's hat is jammed over his eyes and nose quite unceremoniously, and he considers himself fairly extinguished;—child cries; and Cudjoe on the outside delivers animated addresses to the horses, who are kicking, and floundering, and straining, under repeated cracks of the whip. Carriage springs up, with another bounce,—down go the hind wheels,—senator, woman, and child fly over on to the back seat, his elbows encountering her bonnet, and both her feet being jammed into his hat, which flies off in the concussion. After a few moments, the "slough" is passed, and the horses stop, panting;—the senator finds his hat, the woman straightens her bonnet and hushes her child, and they brace themselves firmly for what is yet to come.

For a while only the continuous bump! bump! intermingled, just by way of variety, with divers side plunges and compound shakes; and they begin to flatter themselves that they were not so badly off, after all. At last, with a square plunge, which puts all on to their feet and then down into their seats with incredible quickness, the carriage stops,—and, after much outside commotion, Cudjoe appears at the door.

"Please sir, it's a powerful bad spot, this yer, I don't know how we's to get clar out. I'm a thinkin' we'll have to be gettin' rails.

The senator despairingly steps out, picking gingerly for some firm foothold; down goes one foot in an immeasurable depth,—he tries to pull it up, loses his balance, and tumbles over into the mud, and is fished out, in a very despairing condition, by Cudjoe.

But we forbear, out of sympathy to our readers' bones. Western travelers, who have beguiled the midnight hour in the interesting process of pulling down rail fences, to pry their carriages out of mud holes, will have respectful and mournful sympathy with our unfortunate hero. We beg them to drop a silent tear, and pass on.

It was full late in the night when the carriage emerged, dripping and bespattered, out of the creek, and stood at the door of a large farm-house.

It took no inconsiderable perseverence to arouse the inmates; but at last the respectable proprietor appeared, and undid the door. He was a great, tall, bristling Orson of a fellow, full six feet and some inches in his stockings, and arrayed in a red flannel hunting-shirt. A very heavy *mat* of sandy hair, in a decidedly tousled condition, and a beard of some days' growth, gave the worthy man an appearance, to say the least, not particularly prepossessing. He stood for a few minutes holding the candle aloft, and blinking on our travelers with a dismal and mystified expression that was truly ludicrous. It cost some effort of our senator to induce him to comprehend the case fully; and while he is doing his best at that, we shall give him a little introduction to our readers.

Honest old Jan Van Trompe was once quite a considerable land-holder and slave-owner in the state of Kentucky. Having "nothing of the bear about him but the skin," and being gifted by nature with a great, honest, just heart, quite equal to his giant frame, he had been for some years witnessing with repressed uneasiness the workings of a system equally bad for oppressor and oppressed. At last, one day John's great heart had swelled altogether too big to wear his bonds any longer; so he just took his pocket-book out of his desk, and went over to Ohio, and bought a quarter of a township of good, rich land, made out free papers for all his people,—men, women, and children,—packed them up in wagons, and sent them off to settle down; and then honest John turned his face up the creek, and sat quietly down on a snug, retired farm, to enjoy his conscience and his reflections.

"Are you the man that will shelter a poor woman and child from slave-catchers?" said the senator, explicitly.

"I rather think I am," said honest John, with some considerable emphasis.

"I thought so," said the senator.

"If there's anybody comes," said the good man, stretching his tall, muscular form upward, "why, here I'm ready for him; and I've got seven sons, each six foot high, and they'll be ready for 'em. Give our respects to 'em," said John; "tell 'em it's no matter how soon they call,—make no kinder difference to us," said John, running his fingers through the shock of hair that thatched his head, and bursting out into a great laugh.

Weary, jaded, and spiritless, Eliza dragged herself up to the door, with her child lying in a heavy sleep on her arm. The rough man held a candle to her face, and uttering a kind of compassionate grunt, opened the door of a small bedroom adjoining to the large kitchen where they were standing, and motioned her to go in. He took down a candle, and lighting it, set it upon the table, and then addressed himself to Eliza.

"Now, I say, gal, you needn't be a bit afeard, let who will come here. I'm up to all that sort o' thing," said he, pointing to two or three goodly rifles over the mantelpiece; "and most people that know me know that 't wouldn't be healthy to try and get anybody out o' my house when I'm agin it. So now you jist go to sleep now, quiet as if yer mother was a-rockin' ye," said he, as he shut the door.

"Why, this is an uncommon handsome un," he said to the senator. "Ah, well; handsome uns has the greatest cause to run, sometimes, if they has any kind o' feelin, such as decent women should. I know all about that."

The senator, in a few words, briefly explained Eliza's history.

"Oh! ou! aw! now, I want to know!" said the good man pitifully; "sho! now sho! That's natur now, poor crittur hunted down like a deer,— jest for havin' natural feelin's, and doin' what no kind of" mother could help a doin'! I tell ye what, these yer things make me come the nighest to swearin', now, o' most anything." said honest John, as he wiped his eyes with the back of a great, freckled, yellow hand. "I tell yer what, stranger, it was years and years before I'd jine the church, 'cause the ministers round in our parts used to preach that the Bible went in for there ere cuttings up,—and I couldn't be up to 'em with their Greek and Hebrew, and so I took up agin 'em, Bible and all. I never jined the church till I found a minister that was up to 'em all in Greek and all that, and he said right the contrary; and then I took right hold, and jined the church,—I did, now, fact," said John, who had been all this time uncorking some very frisky bottled cider, which at this juncture he presented.

"Ye'd better jest put up here, now, till daylight," said he heartily; "and I'll call up the old woman, and have a bed got ready for you in no time."

"Thank you, my good friend," said the senator; "I must be along, to take the night stage for Columbus."

"Ah! well, then, if you must, I'll go a piece with you, and show you a cross road that will take you there better than the road you came on. That road's mighty bad."

John equipped himself, and, with a lantern in hand, was soon guiding the senator's carriage towards a road that ran down in a hollow, back of his dwelling. When they parted, the senator put into his hand a ten-dollar bill.

"It's for her," he said, briefly.

"Ay, ay," said John with equal conciseness.

They shook hands, and parted.

Bibliography

Cox, James M. "Harriet Beecher Stowe: From Sectionalism to Regionalism." *Nineteenth-Century Literature* 38 (Mar. 1984): 444-66.

Hedrick, Joan. "'Peaceable Fruits'" The Ministry of Harriet Beecher Stowe." *American Quarterly* 40 (Sept. 1988): 307-32.

Kelley, Mary. *Private Woman, Public Stage: Literary Domesticity in Nineteenth Century America.* New York: Oxford University Press, 1984.

Moers, Ellen. *Harriet Beecher Stowe and American Literature.* Hartford: Stowe-Day Foundation, 1978.

Stowe, Harriet Beecher. *Uncle Tom's Cabin.* Serialized in *National Era.* 1851-52. Boston: John P. Jewett, 1852.

Tompkins, Jane. *Sensational Designs: The Cultural Work of American Fiction.* New York: Oxford University Press, 1985.

Wagenknecht, Edward. *Harriet Beecher Stowe: The Known and the Unknown.* New York: Oxford University Press, 1965.

Alice Cary

1820-1871

Probably the most famous delineations of Ohio in regional writing during the nineteenth century came from the pen of a woman named Alice Cary, who for her first three decades lived in Ohio's Mount Healthy in Hamilton County and then at the age of thirty migrated from the Middle West to New York City. Despite Alice Cary's two decades of mature residence on the east coast, her lifelong subject matter as a writer remained the formative years experienced in her native Ohio. Even at the time of her death in 1871, Alice Cary's manuscript in process, *The Born Thrall,* describes the wrenching sufferings of a regional pioneer mother, a theme that preoccupied Cary throughout her life. This regional story was intended for publication in a radical feminist journal, the Washington, D.C. based abolitionist newspaper the *Revolution*, edited by suffragist Susan B. Anthony.

Alice Cary first published under the pseudonym Patty Lee. This early prose consisted of short sketches and stories about women's straitened sphere and social injustice and was placed in Cary's childhood environs. These tales were published as the introductory ten chapters of *Recollections of Country Life,* her first collection of sketches and short stories. In 1852, Cary issued *Clovernook; or, Recollections of Our Neighborhood in the West* and followed with a second volume in 1853. Cary's collections of short fiction concluded with *Pictures of Country Life* (1859). Alice Cary also turned her hand to three regional novels, *Hagar, A Story of To-Day* (1852), *The Bishop's Son* (1854), and *Married, Not Mated; or, How They Lived at Woodside* (1856). However, it was the two *Clovernook* volumes set in Mount Healthy, Ohio, that earned Alice Cary both her contemporaneous fame and continuing literary reputation.

Certain themes preoccupied Alice Cary throughout her career, whether appearing in her poetry or prose; these themes were characteristic of women writers of her era and reflect, for example, the influence of Susannah Rowson's 1791 romance *Charlotte Temple.* Cary similarly wrote cautionary tales about seduction as a threat to women's fragile autonomy, but her dominant focus remained the melancholy circumstances of growing up on the old western frontier. Alice Cary's stories exhibit major advances beyond the style of Ohio's earliest regionalists. Her characteristic style employs a female narrator who uses standard English and is empathetic toward the lives of the regional characters she observes. Her sketches and stories are strongest in characterization, minimize plot, and provide interest from the region's "exhibition of rural life," complete with dialect, realistic local details, and the consequent effect upon characters' minds and spirits, Alice Cary's theme is the psychic exploration of careworn westerners. In the words of Annette Kolodny, Alice Cary articulated the "nation's thwarted fantasies" (184) following the Civil War when sectionalism was being reevaluated and the glamour of the pioneers was fading.

Alice Cary was a product of that first, inspired pioneer tradition. Her family came to Ohio in 1803 after her paternal grandfather, a native of Lyme, New Hampshire, was given land in return for his service in the Continental Army; father and son, Robert Cary, crossed the mountains by wagon train and floated on a flatboat down the Ohio to Fort Washington. Thus Alice Cary was a second generation Ohioan, far removed from the pioneer struggles of her grandfather's generation, yet this Buckeye native knew poverty and rural hardship, as she was raised without education or encouragement in a poor farmhouse near Cincinnati.

From one point of view, Alice Cary's life has a Cinderella story ring to it: early deaths marked her temperament, a wicked stepmother darkened her days, but after she and a sibling joined in sisterly camaraderie and began publishing poetry in the Cincinnati *Sentinal* (Alice was eighteen), male mentors recognized their talent, and fame followed after 1850 when Alice eventually left Ohio for a more congenial and intellectual climate in New York.

In fact, Alice Cary was an indefatigable writer who in youth benefited from the self-conscious intellectual milieu of Cincinnati, the "Athens of the West" a mere eight miles south of Mount Healthy. During their twenties, Alice and her sister Phoebe submitted poetry to both western and eastern journals and newspapers, and their unpaid juvenalia was published in the Cincinnati's journals and religious periodicals, such as the Cincinnati *Ladies' Repository*, a Methodist monthly magazine published between 1841 and 1876. Here she also published prose pieces that later were collected into the *Clovernook* volumes and a variety of personal essays, including some that describe travel experiences between Ohio and New York. After 1847 Alice Cary was paid for poems and sketches. Between 1851 and 1855, Cary regularly contributed to such publications as the *National Magazine, Graham's, Sartain's Union Magazine,* edited briefly by fellow western regionalist Caroline Kirkland; and *Overland Monthly*, edited by Bret Harte.

Alice Cary's national success came from nonwesterner readers who appreciated the point of view she offered; of course, regional readers enjoyed her work, especially her romantic poems, but it took outsiders who were not immersed in the Middle West to really appreciate the unique and often dour viewpoint that she originated toward regional experience. Even after Alice Cary moved to the East, her career continued to be built upon the midwestern theme of impoverishment; her prose appeared in many prestigious national periodicals: Boston's Methodist monthly, the *National Magazine*; after 1856, in the weekly *New York Ledger*; between 1858 and 1870, in the *Atlantic Monthly*, and in the 1860s in *Harper's Monthly*.

Her evolving reputation was achieved through invaluable contacts with a series of eastern male mentors, beginning with the distinguished anthologist Rufus W. Griswold, whom she met in 1848; he included Alice and her sister Phoebe in his *Female Poets of America* and in 1849 published an edition of the sisters' poems. In his introduction, Griswold makes it clear that he had first read their poems in a western newspaper and attributes their inspiration to the region. In his words, "In the west, song gushes and flows, like the springs and rivers, more imperially than elsewhere. . . . minds seem to be elevated, by the glorious nature there, into the atmosphere where all thought takes a shape of beauty and harmony" (372).

It was Griswold's publications and friendship that began the process of channeling Alice Cary's work to a national audience. But he was not the only intellectual mentor to sponsor Alice Cary's entrance into the eastern literary establishment. Similarly acquaintance with her distant cousin, the influential Cincinnati editor William D. Gallagher who encouraged Julia L. Dumont and Pamilla W. Ball, led to Alice Cary's "first impression of a poet" which she describes in her sketch "Dreams and Tokens." Here "Bill Gallagher" is presented from the Hamilton county farmers' viewpoint as being distracted by aesthetics away from their comradeship. But in 1847 he introduced Alice Cary to fellow Cincinnatian Gamaliel Bailey, who soon moved to Washington to establish his abolitionist weekly, the *National Era*. Bailey invited Alice Cary to submit prose to his new paper, which in 1851-52 was soon serializing another Ohio-connected woman author, Harriet Beecher Stowe's *Uncle Tom's Cabin*.

Another of Alice Cary's valuable mentors was the famous regionalist John Greenleaf Whittier, a contributing editor of the *National Era* whose admiration for her prose led in 1851 to the following praise of her first collection of western sketches and short stories; they were, he wrote, "simple, natural truthful [with] a keen sense of humor and pathos of the comedy and tragedy of life in the country." Throughout the century, male critics continued to admire the prose of Alice Cary. Edward Eggleston called Alice Cary "the founder of the tradition of honest interpretation of the West" (Smith 268). In 1891 W. H. Venable's "Pioneer Poets and Story-Writers" praised Cary's stories for their "exact truthfulness and felicitous local coloring . . . [which must be] appreciated by every reader who has seen or studied farm-life in the Ohio Valley." He also notes the book's pervading sadness and rather depressing effect upon readers (490).

In the twentieth century, Henry Nash Smith calls Alice Cary "the first native of the Ohio Valley who attempted to interpret the region in fiction" (168). While that judgment ignores the work of earlier regionalists, like Julia Dumont, it does call attention to Cary's interpretative stance as a second-generation inheritor of pioneer traditions. As the pictorial frontispiece to *Clovernook* shows, Cary's self-perceived subject matter was agrarian or pastoral life for pioneer women; the engraving represents two women conversing in front of a rude cabin, while the illustration overlain with the word "Clovernook" is foregrounded by a Conestoga wagon and resting oxen; in the background shadows, pioneers gather around the campfire. In the introduction to this collection, Cary explains that it is her second-generation status in Ohio that provides the ideal opportunity for a writer: "[T]here is surely as much in the simple manners, and the little histories every day revealed, to interest us in humanity," she says; and adds that it is better to write about the era when people are no longer in the wilderness and concerned with "felling the opposing trees." Alice Cary's stories are described as "reed's music" designed to appeal to eastern, urban readers who should feel pity and sympathy for the "poor and humble" westerners who also have fine feelings. Cary defends her dark realism, saying that she is a "competent witness" who can "instruct readers" by creating a "true" exhibition of rural life. This theme is continued in her 1854 conclusion of *Clovernook; or, Recollections of Our Neighborhood in the West*, second series, where Alice Cary further defends her dark vision of rural life by emphasizing the realism of her stories' "pathos and tenderness in love, a bravery in adversity."

Alice Cary has been called by modern critics, led by Judith Fetterly, the "inaugurator of the regional short story as a fictional genre" ("Alice" 3); moreover, Alice Cary is credited with innovating a particular strain of short story which came to be known as Local Color, a subgenre of regional tale which is told from an outsider's ironic viewpoint. In Fetterly's words, Cary became "one of the earliest regional writers to fictionalize what the Eastern magazines would call 'local color,' and which, twenty years later would begin to define a new genre in the short story" ("Alice" 2).

The key to Cary's approach was memory. Her fiction's viewpoint is strained through distance and time. Throughout her two decades in the East, Alice Cary's imaginative resource continued to be the traditions and ambiance of her remembered life in southern Ohio. Each of her short story collections depicts Mount Healthy as it evolved from an isolated rural village to a Cincinnati suburb, a transformation Cary witnessed during the first three decades of her life.

"Mrs. Wetherbe's Party" superbly delineates three different environs in midcentury, postpioneer, rural Ohio, outside Cincinnati, its "Western Queen." The story is skillfully told by a mature community woman who recalls her participation in a domestic drama—a local quilting party which sheds light on conflicting family dynamics. Mrs. Wetherbe acts as a foster parent to her niece's son, Helph, whose crude, citified family mistreats him, ex-slaves, and immigrant-born servants. In contrast to the nurturance of the Ohio farm, there is a smug, nouveau rich, urban home and an impoverished slum tenement, both vitiated by masculine alcoholism. It is the clash of the values represented by these three settings that allows Cary to demonstrate the countryside's superior values.

Attacking the dual antagonists of alcoholism and snobbishness, Cary's delightful portraiture of rural life and manners repudiates Frances Trollope's accusations of western unsociability. Mrs. Wetherbe's home is the scene of humble but fervent good fellowship. The "personification of old-fashioned country hospitality" the author calls it, as the quilters and wood splitters indulge in excellent food and enthusiastic games like hunting the key, selling of pawns, paying penalties, blindman's buff, hold fast all I give you, and love and war. However, the story also illustrates the evanescent satisfactions of such revelry; individuals who negotiate compromises with urban life must pay the darkening costs of the transition into worldly maturity, as Helph and Jenny do at the end of the story when they finally allow themselves to marry. Thus the middle-western setting creates a complex and disillusioning background against which Ohio's foreground transcendence is framed within an unsentimental perspective.

Many believe that it is in her Ohio regionalist sketches and stories that Alice Cary truly triumphs over her material, one "particular neighborhood in the West" (Fetterly, *Clovernook* xxiii). Rural regional observations thus became Cary's supreme literary theme, what at the end of her Clovernook stories the author calls "the pulsations of surrounding hearts."

Mrs. Wetherbe's Party

Alice Cary

Longer than I can remember, my father, who is an old man now, has been in the habit of driving every Friday morning from his home, seven miles away, to this goodly city in which I now live. I may well say goodly city, from the view which presents itself as I look out from the window under which I have placed my table for the writing of this history, for my home is in the "hilly country" that overlooks this Western Queen, whose gracious sovereignty I am proud to acknowledge, and within whose fair dominions this hilly country lies.

I cannot choose but pause and survey the picture: the Kentucky shore is all hidden with mist, so that I try in vain to see the young cities of which the sloping suburbs are washed by the Ohio, river of beauty! Except here and there the gleam of a white wall, or a dense column of smoke that rises through the silver mist from hot furnaces where swart labor drives the thrifty trades, speeding the march to elegance and wealth. I cannot see the blue green nor the golden green of the oat and wheat fields, that lie beyond these infant cities, nor the dark ridge of woods that folds its hem of shadows along their borders, for all day yesterday fell one of those rains that would seem to exhaust the clouds of the deepest skies, and the soaked earth this morning sends up its coal-scented and unwholesome fogs, obscuring the lovely picture that would else present itself.

I can only guess where the garrison is. I could not hear.

"The sullen cry of the sentinal," even if the time of challenge were not passed—though long before the sunrise I woke to the music of the reveille, that comes morn after morn floating over the waters and through the crimson daybreak, to chase the dream from my pillow. Faintly I discern the observatory crowning the summit of the mount above me, and see more distinctly at its base the red bricks of St. Philomena, and more plainly still the brown iron and glittering brass of its uplifted spire, with the sorrowful beauty of the cross over all; while midway between me and the white shining of the tower of the cathedral, away toward the evening star, I catch the dark outline of St. Xavier.

Beautiful! As I said, I cannot choose but pause and gaze. And now, the mists are lifting more and more, and the sunshine comes dropping down through their sombre folds to the damp ground.

Growing, on the view, into familiar shapes, comes out point after point of the landscape—towers and temples, and forest and orchard trees, and meadow-land—the marts of traffic and the homes of men; and among these last there is one, very pretty, and whose inmates as you guess from the cream-white walls, overrun with clematis and jasmine, and the clambering walks of roses, are not devoid of some simple refinement of taste from which an inference of their happiness may be drawn —for the things we feel are exhibited in the things we do.

The white-pebbled walk, leading from the gate to the door-way, is edged with close miniature pyramids of box, and the smoothly-shaven sward is shadowed by various bushes and flowers, and the gold velvet of the dandelion shines wherever it will, from the fence close beneath the window sending up its bitter fragrance out of dew, while sheaves of green phlox stand here and there, which in their time will be topped with crimson blossoms.

The windows are hung with snowy curtains, and in one that fronts the sun, is hung a bird-cage, with an inmate chattering as wildly as though his wings were free. A blue wreath of smoke, pleasantly suggestive, is curling upward just now, and drifting southward from the tall kitchen chimney, and Jenny Mitchel, the young housewife, as I guess, is baking pies. Nothing becomes her chubby hands so well as the molding of pastry, and her cheerful singing, if we were near enough to hear it, would attest to nothing makes her more happy. And well may she sing and be happy, for the rosy-faced baby sits up in his white willow cradle, and crows back to her lullaby; and by and by the honest husband will come from healthful labor, and her handiwork in flour and fruit and sugar and spice, will be sure of due appreciation and praise.

Nowhere among all the suburban gardens of this basic rimmed with hills, peeps from beneath its sheltering trees a cozier home. They are plain and common-sense people who dwell here, vexed with no indistinct yearnings for the far off and the unattained—weighted down with no false appreciation, blind to all good that is not best—oppressed with no misanthropic fancies about the world—nor yet affected with spasmodic decisions that their great enemy should not wholly baffle them; no! The great world cares nothing about them, and they as little for the great world, which has no power by its indifference to wound the heart of either, even for a moment. Helph Randall, the sturdy blacksmith, whose forge is aglow before the sunrise, and rosy-cheeked Jenny, his blue-eyed wife, though she sometimes remembers the shamrock and sighs, have no such pains concealed.

But were they always thus contented? Did they cross that mysterious river, whose course never yet run smooth, without any trial and tribulation, such as most voyagers on its bosom have encountered since the world began—certainly since Jacob served seven years for Rachel and was then put off with Leah, and obliged to serve other seven for his first love? We shall see: and this brings me back to one of those many Fridays I have spoken of. I am not sure but I must turn another leaf and begin with Thursday—yes, I have the time now, it was a Thursday. It was as bright an afternoon as ever turned the green swaths into gray, or twinkled against the shadows stretching eastward from the thick-rising haycocks.

II.

It was early in July, when the bitter of the apples began to grow sweet, and their sunward sides a little russet; when the chickens ceased from peeping and followed the parent hen, and began to scratch hollows in garden beds, and to fly suddenly upon fences or into trees, and to crow and cackle with unpractised throats, as though they were well used to it, and cared not who heard them, for which disagreeable habits their heads were now and then brought to the block. Blackberries were ripening in the hedges, and the soft silk was swaying beneath the tassels of the corn.

Such was the season when, one day, just after dinner, Mrs. Wetherbe came to pass the afternoon, and, as she said, to kill tow birds with one stone, by securing a passage to the city on the morrow in my father's wagon—for many were the old ladies, and young ones too, who availed themselves of a like privilege. Of course it was a pleasure for us to accommodate here, and not the less, perhaps, that it was a favor we had never asked before, and was not likely to ask again.

She was a plain old lady, whom to look at was to know—good and simple-hearted as a child. She was born and had been bred in the country, and was thoroughly a country woman; her high heeled and creaking calf-skin shoes had never trodden beyond the grass of her own door-yard more than once or twice, for even a friendly tea-drinking with a neighbor was to her a matter of not more than biennial occurrence. And on the day I speak of she seemed to feel mortified that she should spend two consecutive days in a gad-about—in view of which necessity feeling bound in all self-respect to offer apologies.

In the first place, she had not for six years been to visit her niece, Mrs. Emeline Randall, who came to her house more or less every summer, and really felt slighted and grieved that her visits were never returned. So Mrs. Randall expressed herself, and so Mrs. Wetherbe thought, honest old lady as she was! And so it seemed now as though she must go and see Emeline, notwithstanding she would just as soon, she said, put her head in a hornet's nest, anytime, as to town; for she regarded its gayeties and fashions—and all city people, in her opinion, were gay and fashionable—as leading directly toward the kingdom of the Evil One. Therefore it was, as I conceive quite doubtful, whether for the mere pleasure of visiting her amiable niece, Mrs. Wetherbe would have entered the city limits.

She wanted some cap stuff and some home-made lines, if such things were to be procured in these degenerate days, though if she only had the flax she could spin and weave the linen herself, old as she was, and would not be caught running about town to buy it; for, if she did say it, she was worth more than half the girls now at work; and no one who saw how fast her brown withered fingers flew around the stocking she was knitting, would have doubted it at all.

"Nothing is fit for the harvest-field but home spun linen," said Mrs. Wetherbe, "and if Wetherbe don't have it he'll be nigh about sick, and I may jest as well go fust as last, for he won't hear to my spinning sence I am sixty odd; he says he don't like the buz of the wheel, but to me there's no nicer music."

The last trowsers of her own making were worn out, and along for several days past her good man had then been obliged to wear cloth ones; which fact was real scandalous in the good woman's estimation, and in this view it certainly was time she should bestir herself, as she proposed.

Moreover, she had one or two other errands that especially induced her to go to town. A black calico dress she must have, as she had worn the old one five years, and now wanted to cut it up and put it in a quilt, for she had always intended it to jine some patchwork she'd had on hand a long time, and now she was going to do it, and make a quilting party, and have the work all done at once. I, of course, received then and there the earliest invitation.

This was years ago, and fashion of such parties has long since passed away, but in due time I will tell you about this, as you may never have an opportunity of participating in such a proceeding.

Perhaps you may have seen persons, certainly I have, who seem to feel called on, from some feeling of obligation I do not understand, to offer continual apologies for whatever they do, or propose to do. It was so with good Mrs. Wetherbe, and after the announcement of this prospective frolic, she talked a long chapter of whys and wherefores, after this wise.

William Helphenstein Randall, Evangeline's oldest son, had been living at her house three or four years, and he had teased month in and month out, to have a wood-chopping and quilting, some afternoon, and a regular play party in the evening; and he had done so many good turns for her, that it seemed as if a body could hardly get round it without seeming reel disobleegin'; and though she didn't approve much of such worldly carryings on, she thought for once she would humor Helph; and then, too, they would get wood prepared for winter, more or less quilting done—for "though on pleasure she was bent, she was of frugal mind."

I remarked that I was under an impression that Mr. Randall was a man of property, and asked if Helph was out of college. "Why, bless your heart, no," said Mrs. Wetherbe, "he was never in a college, more'n I be this minute; his father is as rich as Cresus, but his children got all their larnin' in free schools, pretty much; Helph hasn't been to school this ten years a'most, I guess. Let me see: he was in a blacksmith's shop sartainly tow or three years before he come to my house, and he isn't but nineteen now, so he must have been tuck from school airly. The long and short on't is," continued the old lady, making her knitting-needles fly again, "Emeline, poor gal, has got a man that is reel clos't, and the last time I was there I most thought he begrudged me my victuals; but I was keerful to take butter and garden-sass, and so on, enough to pay for all I got." And she dropped her work, she was so exasperated, for though economical and savings in all ways, she was not meanly stingy. She had chanced to glide into a communicative mood, by no means habitual for her, and the perspiration stood in drops on her forehand and her little black eyes winked with great rapidity for a minute, before she added, "And that ain't the worst on't neither, he is often in drink, and sich times he gits the Old Clooty in him as big as a yearlin heifer!"

"Ay, I understand," I said," and that is why Helph happens to live with you."

"Yes," said Mrs. Wetherbe, resuming her knitting, "That's why, and it's the why of a good many other things; I don't know as I ought to talk of things that are none of my business, as you may say, but my temper gits riled and a'most biles over the pot, when I think of some things Jinny Mitchel has tell me: she's their adopted darter, you know; but that speaking of the pot reminds me that I broke my little dinner pot last week, and if there will be room for it I may want to kerry it along, and het a new leg put in. And so you see," she concluded," I have arrants enough to take me to down:" and she wiped her spectacles, preparatory to going home, saying the glasses were too young for her, and she must get older ones tomorrow, and that was one of the most urgent things, in fact, that took her to the city. Having promised that I would accompany her, to select the new dress, and dine with Mrs. Randall, she took leave, with an assurance of being ready at six o'clock in the morning, so as not to detain us a gain or morsel.

III.

When morning began to redden the eastern stars, our household was astir, and while we partook of an early breakfast, the light wagon, which was drawn by two smart young bays, was brought to the door. Baskets, jugs, and other things, were imbedded among the straw, with which our carriage was plentifully supplied, and a chair was placed behind the one seat, for my accommodation, as Mrs. Wetherbe was to occupy the place beside my father. I have always regarded the occupancy of the chair, on that occasion, as an example of self-sacrifice which I should not like to repeat, however beautiful in theory may be the idea of self-abnegation. But I cannot hope that others will appreciate this little benevolence of mine, unless they have ridden eight or more miles, in an open wagon, and on a chair slipping from side to side, and jolting up and down, behind two coltish trotters, and over roads that for a part of the time kept one wheel in the gutter and one in the air.

But I must leave to the imagination the ups and downs of this particular epoch of my life. Still one star stood, large and white, above the hills, but the ground of crimson began to be dashed with gold when we set forward.

Notwithstanding the "rough, uneven ways, which drew out the miles, and made them wearisome," these goings to the city are among the most delightful recollections of my life. They were to my young vision openings of the brightness of the world; and after the passage of a few years, with their experiences, the new sensations that freshen and widen the atmosphere of thought are very few and never so bright as I had then.

Distinctly fixed in my mind is every house—its color and size, and the garden walks and trees with which it was surrounded, and by which the roadsides between our homestead and that dim speck we called the city, were adorned; and nothing would probably seem to me now so fine as did the white walls, the smooth lawns, and round-headed gate-posts, which then astonished my unpractised eyes.

Early as we were, we found Mrs. Wetherbe in waiting at her gate, long before reaching which the fluttering of her scarlet merino shawl, looking like the rising of another morning, apprised us of our approach to it.

She had been nigh for about an hour watching for us, she said, and was just going into the house to take off ther things, when she saw the heads of the horses before a great cloud of dust; and though she couldn't see the color of the wagon, nor a sign of the critters, to tell whether they were black or white, she knew right-a-way that it was our team, for no body else druv such fine horses.

"Here, Mrs. Witherbe, get right in," said my father, who was fond of horses, and felt the compliment as much as if it had been to himself: and it was owing entirely to this that he said Mrs. Witherbe instead of Mrs. Wetherbe, though I am not sufficiently a metaphysician to explain why such cause should have produced such an effect.

Helphenstein, who was chopping wood at the door, called out, as we were leaving, "Don't forget to ask Jenny to come to the quilting;" and Mr. Wetherbe paused from his churning beneath a cherry-tree, to say, "Good-bye, mother; be careful, and not lose any money, for it's a hard thing to slip into a pus, and it's easy to slip out."

* * *

[Remainder of chapter 3 and most of chapter 4 depict the Randall family's rude treatment of Mrs. Weatherbe, and their servants, Jenny Mitchel and the ex-slave, Aunt Kitty.]

We were a long time in getting through our many errands, for Mrs. Wetherbe was detained not a little in surprise or admiration at this or that novelty. When a funeral passed, she could not think who could be dead, and essayed all her powers to get a glimpse of the coffin, that she might know whether it were a child or an adult; or if a horseman cantered past, she gazed after him, wondering if he was not going for the doctor, and if he was, who in the world could be sick; and then, she selected little samples of goods she wished to purchase, and carried them up to Emeline's, to determine whether they would wash well; but notwithstanding her frugality and cautiousness, she was not mean; and she lightened her purse on Jenny's behalf to the amount of the stuff for a pretty new dress. But she could not be spared for a week, and it was agrees that Helph should be sent to bring her on the day of the quilting; and so, between smiles and tears, we left her.

Alas for Aunt Kitty! nothing could alleviate her disappointment: she had prepared dinner with a special reference to us, and we had not been there to partake of it, or to praise her. "Poor souls! de Lord help you," she said; you will be starved a'most!"

Mrs. Randall was sorry dinner was over, but she never thought of getting hungry when she was busy.

It was long after nightfall when, having left our friend and her various luggage at her own homes, we arrived at ours; and we had earned excellent appetites for the supper that waited us.

V.

That going to town by Mrs. Wetherbe, as I have intimated, was chiefly with a view to purchases in preparation for the proposed quilting party and wood-chopping. Not only did we select calico for the border of the quilt, with cotton batting and spool thread, but we also procured sundry niceties for the supper, among which I remember a jug of Orleans molasses, half a pound of ground ginger, five pounds of cheese, and as many pounds of raisins. Mrs. Wetherbe had never made a "frolic" before, she said, and now she wouldn't have the name of being *near* about it, let it cost what it would. And great excitement ran through all the neighborhood so soon as it was known what she had been about, and rumor speedily exaggerated the gallon of molasses into a dozen gallons, the raisins into a keg, and so on. Many thought it was not very credible in a "professor" to have such carryings on; some wondered where she would find any body in Clovernook good enough to ask; others supposed she would have all her company from the city; and all agreed that if she was going to have her "big-bug" relations, and do her "great gaul," she might, for all of them. The wonder was that she didn't make a party of "whole cloth," and not stick her quilt in at all.

There was a great deal of surmising and debating likewise as to the quilt itself; and some hoped it was a little nicer than any patchwork they had seen of Mrs. Wetherbe's making. But this unamiable disposition gradually gave way when it was known that the frolic would embrace a wood-chopping as well as a quilting—"for surely," said they, "she don't expect chaps from town to cut wood!"

The speculation concerning the quilt began to decline; what matter whether it were to be composed of stars or stripes; "rising suns," or "crescents?" Mrs. Wetherbe knew her own business of course, and those who had at first hoped they would not be invited, because they were sure they would not go if they were, wavered visibly in their stout resolves.

From one of two families in which the greatest curiosity reigned, were sent little girls and boys, whose ostensible objects were the borrowing of a darning-needle or a peck measure from the harmless family who had become the centre of interest, but their real errands were to see what they could see. So the feeling of asperity was gradually mollified, as reports thus obtained circulation favoring the neighborly and democratic character hitherto borne by the Wetherbes. At one time the good old lady was found with her sleeves rolled back, mixing bread, as she used to do; and invariably she inquired of the little spies how affairs were going forward at their homes. After all, the neighbors began to think the quilting was not going to be any such great things more than other quiltings. For myself, I understood the whole subject pretty well from the beginning.

One morning as I looked up from the window where I sat, I saw Helphenstein Randall approaching, and at once divined his errand. He was mounted on Mr. Wetherbe's old roan mare, and riding a side-saddle; and he was in excellent spirits too, as I judged from his having the ragged rim of his hat turned up jauntily in front, and from his goading the beast with heels and bridle-rein; but not a whit cared the ancient mare; with youth she had lost her ambition, and now she moved in slow and graceless way, her neck bent downward, and her nose greatly in advance of her ears. Half an hour afterwards I was on the way to assist in preparations for the approaching festivities. But I was only a kind of secondary maid of honor, for foremost on all occasions of this kind was Ellen Blake, and in this present instance she had preceded me, and with hair in papers, and sleeves and skirt tucked up, she came forth in an at-home-attire, mistress-of-the-house fashion, to welcome me —a privilege she always assumed toward every guest on such occasions.

In truth, Ellen really had a genius for managing the affairs of other people, and for the time being she felt almost always the same interest in whatever was being done as though it were altogether an affair of her own. She was also thought, in her neighborhood, which was sort of a suburb of Clovernook, a full quarter of the way to the city, to be very good company, and it is no wonder that her services were much in demand. Very ambitious about her work was Ellen, and few persons could get through with more in a day than she; in fact there are few more faultless in nearly every respect; nevertheless, the was one objection which some of the most old-fashioned people urged against her— she was dressy, and it was rumored just now that she had got a new "hat," trimmed as full as it could stick of blue ribbons and red artificial flowers, and also a white dress, flounced half way up to the skirt.

Already the quilt was in the frames and laid out, as the marking was called, the chamber was ready for the guests, and Ellen said she thought she had been pretty smart—if she did say it herself.

"I wanted to take the bed out of my front room and have the quilting there, "Mrs. Wetherbe observed, "but this head-strong piece (pointing to Ellen) wouldn't hear of it."

"No, indeed," replied the girl; "it would have been the greatest piece of presumption in the world; la, me! If we young folks cut up as we do sometimes, we'd have that nice carpet in doll-rags, and then the work of taking down and putting up the bedstead—all for nothing, as you may say."

I fully agreed that Ellen had made the wisest arrangement. The chamber was large, covering an area occupied by three rooms on the ground floor; and being next to the roof, the quilt could be conveniently attached to the rafters by ropes, and thus drawn up out of the way in case it were not finished before nightfall. The ceilings were unplastered, and on either side sloped within a few feet of the floor, but the gable windows admitted a sufficiency of light, and there was neither carpet nor furniture in the way, except, indeed, the furnishing which Ellen had contrived for the occasion, consisting chiefly of divans, formed of boards and blocks, which were cushioned with quilts and the like. Besides these, there were two or three barrels covered over with table-cloths, and designed to serve as hat-stands. There was no other furniture, unless the draperies, formed of petticoats and trowsers, here and there suspended from pegs, might be regarded as entitled to be so distinguished.

The rafter were variously garnished, with bags of seeds, bunches of dried herbs, and hanks of yarn, with some fine specimens of extra large corn, having the husks turned back from the yellow ears and twisted into braids, by which it was hung for preservation and exhibition. One more touch our combined ingenuity gave the place, on the morning of the day guests were expected, and this consisted of festoons of green boughs and of flowers.

While we were busy with preparations in the kitchen, the day following my arrival, Mrs. Randall suddenly made her appearance, wearing a faded dress, an old straw bonnet, and bearing in one hand a satchel, and in the other an empty basket.

"Hi ho! what brought you, mother?" exclaimed Helph, who was watching our progress in beating eggs, weighing sugar, crushing spices, &c,; and this question was followed with "Where is Jenny?" and "How did you come?"

We soon learned that she had arrived in a market wagon, for the sake of economy; the her basket was to carry home eggs, butter, apples, and whatever she could get; and that, though she proposed to assist us, she would in fact disconcert our arrangements, and mar our happiness. Jenny was left at home to attend the house, while she herself recruited and enjoyed a little pleasuring.

No sooner had she tied on one of Mrs. Wetherbe's checked aprons and turned back her sleeves, than our troubles began; of course she knew better than we how to manage every thing, and the supper would not do at all, unless prepared under her direction. We were glad when Mrs. Wetherbe said, "Too many cooks spoil the broth, and I guess the girls better have it their own way." But Mrs. Randall was not to be dissuaded; she had come to help, and she was sure she would rather be doing a little than not. She gave accounts of all the balls, dinners, and suppers, at which she had been, and tried to impress us with the necessity of having our country quilting as much in the style of them as we could.

"We must graduate our ginger-cakes," she said, "and so form a pyramid for the central ornament of the table; the butter must be in the shape of pineapples, and we must either have no meats, or else call it a dinner, and after it was eaten, serve round coffee, on little salvers, for which purpose we should have pretty china cups."

I knew right well how ludicrous it would be to attempt the twisting of Aunt Wetherbe's quilting and wood-chopping into a fashionable party, but I had little eloquence or argument at command with which to combat the city dame's positive assertions and impertinent suggestions.

"Have you sent your notes of invitation yet?" she asked.

"No, nor I don't mean to send no notes nor nothing," said the aunt, a little indignant; "it ain't like as if the queen was going to make a quilting, I reckon."

But without heeding this pretty decisive answer Mrs. Randall proceeded to remark that she had brought out some gilt-edged paper and several specimen cards, among which she thought perhaps the most elegant would be, "Mr. and Mrs. Wetherbe at home," specifying the time, and addressed to whoever should be invited. But in vain this point was urged; the old-fashioned aunt said she would have no such mess written; that Helph might get on his horse and ride through the neighborhood and ask the young people to come to the quilting and wood-chopping, and that was enough.

There was but one thing more to vex us, while anticipating the result of our efforts—a rumor the Mrs. Wetherbe had hired a "nigger waiter" for a week. Many did not and could not believe it, but others testified to the fact of having seen the said waiter with their own eyes.

With all our combined forced, preparations went actively forward, and before the appointed day every thing was in readiness—coffee ground, tea ready for steeping, chickens prepared for broiling, cakes and puddings baked, and all the extra saucers filled with custards or preserves.

Ellen stoutly maintained her office as mistress of the ceremonies; and Mrs. Randall took her place as assistant, so that mine became quite a subordinate position, for which I was not sorry, as I did not feel competent to grace the elevated position at first assigned me.

Helph had once or twice been warned by his mother that Jenny would not come, and that he need not trouble himself to go for her; but he persisted in a determination to bring her; in fact his heart was set on it; and the aunt seconded his decision in the matter, as it was chiefly for Helph and Jenny she had designed the merry-making, and she could not and would not be cheated of her darling purpose.

"Well, have your own way and live the longer, "said the mother; to which the son answered that such was his intention; and accordingly, having procured the best buggy the neighborhood afforded, and brushed his coat and hat with extra care, he set out for the city, before sunrise, on the long anticipated day. Dinner was served earlier than usual, and at one o'clock we were all prepared—Mrs. Wetherbe in the black silk she had had for twenty years, and Ellen in her white flounced dress, with a comb of enormous size, and a wreath of flowers above her curls; but when "Emeline" made her appearance, neither our surprise nor a feeling of indignant disappointment could be concealed: she had appropriated to her own use Jenny's new dress, which Mrs. Wetherbe had bought expressly for this occasion.

"Now you needn't scold, Aunt Wetherbe," she said: "it was really too pretty a thing for that child; and besides, I intend to get her another before long."

"Humph!" said the old lady, "every bit and grain of my comfort's gone," and removing her spectacles she continued silently rubbing them with her apron, till Ellen, who was standing at the window, on tip toe, announced that Jane Stillman was coming "with her changeable silk on."

And Jane Stillman had scarcely taken off her things when Polly Harris was announced. She wore a thin white muslin, and a broad-rimmed Leghorn hat, set off with a profusion of gay ribbons and flowers, though she had ridden on horseback; but in those days riding-dresses were not much in vogues, at least in the neighborhood of Clovernook.

Amid jesting and laughter we took our places at the quilt, while Ellen kept watch at the window and brought up the new comers—sometimes two or three at once.

Mrs. Wetherbe had not been at all exclusive, and her invitations included all, rich and poor, maid and mistress, as far as she was acquainted. So, while some came in calico gowns, with handkerchiefs tied over their heads, walking across the fields, others were attired in silks and satins, and rode on horseback, or were brought in market wagons by their fathers or brothers.

Along the yard fence hung rows of side-saddles, and old work horses and sleek fillies were here and there tied to the branches of the trees, to enjoy the shade, and nibble the grass, while the long-legged colts responded to calls of their dams, capering as they would.

Nimbly ran fingers up and down and across the quilt, and tongues moved no less nimbly; and though now and then glances strayed away from the work to the fields, and suppressed titters broke into loud laughter, as, one after another, the young men were seen with axes over their shoulders wending towards the woods, the work went on bravely, and

Polly Harris soon called out, clapping her hands in triumph, "Our side is ready to 'roll.'"

Ellen was very busy and very happy, now overseeing the rolling of the quilt, now examining the stitching of some young quilter, and now serving round cakes and cider, and giving to every one kind words and smiles.

"Oh, Ellen," called a young mischief-loving girl, "please let me and Susan Milford go out and play;" and forthwith they ran down stairs, and it was not till they were presently seen skipping across the field with a basket of cakes and a jug of cider, that their motive was suspected, and then, for the first time that day, gossip found a vent.

"I'd be sorry," said Mehitable Worthington, a tall, oldish girl, "to be seen running after the boys, as some do."

"La, me, Mehitable," answered Ellen, who always had a good word for everybody, "it ain't every one who is exemplary like you, but they are just in fun, you know; young wild girls, you know."

"I don't know how young they be," answered the spinster, tartly, not much relishing any allusion to age, "but 'birds of a feather flock together,' and them that likes the boys can talk in favor of others that likes them."

"Why, don't you like them?" asked Hetty Martin, looking up archly.

"Yes, I like them out of my sight," answered Mehitable, stitching fast.

Upon hearing this, the dimples deepened in Hetty's cheeks, and the smile was as visible in her black eyes as on her lips.

"I suppose you wish you had gone along," said Mehitable maliciously, "but I can tell you the young doctor is not there; he was called away to the country about twelve o'clock, to a man that took sick yesterday." Hetty's face crimsoned a little, but otherwise she manifested no annoyance, and she replied, laughingly, that she hoped he would get back before night.

Mehitable was not thus to be baffled, however; her heard was overflowing with bitterness, for he whom she called the *young* doctor was, in her estimation, old enough to be a more fitting mate for herself than for Hetty, her successful rival; and no sooner was she foiled in one direction than she turned in another, revolving still in her mind such sweet and bitter fancies. "I guess he is no such great things of a doctor after all," she said; and elevating her voice and addressing a maiden on the opposite side of the quilt, she continued, "Did you hear, Elizabeth, about his going to visit Mrs. Mercer, and supposing her attacked with cholera, when in a day or two the disease fell in her arms?"

This effervescence was followed by a general laughter, during with Hetty went to the window, apparently to disentangle her thread; but

Ellen speedily relieved her by inviting her to go with her below and see about the supper.

"I should think," said Elizabeth, who cordially sympathized with her friend, "the little upstart would be glad to get out of sight;" and then came a long account of the miserable way in which Hetty's family lived; "every one knows, "they said, "her father drinks up every thing, and for all she looks so fine in her white dress, most likely her mother has earned it by washing or sewing; they say she wants to marry off her young beauty, but I guess it will be hard to do."

When Hetty returned to the garret, her eyes were no so bright as they had been, but her subdued manner made her only the prettier, and all, save the two ancient maidens alluded to, were ready to say or do something for her pleasure. Those uncomfortable persons, however, were not yet satisfied, and tipping their tongues with the unkindest venom of all, they began to talk of a wealthy and accomplished young lady, somewhere, whom it was rumored the doctor was shortly to marry, in spite of little flirtations at home, that some people thought meant something. Very coolly they talked of the mysterious belle's superior position and advantages, as though no humble and loving heart shook under their words as under a storm of arrows.

The young girls came back from the woods, and hearing their reports of the number of choppers, and how many trees were felled, and cut and corded, the interrupted mirthfulness was restored, though Hetty laughed less joyously, and her elderly rivals maintained a dignified reserve.

Aside from this little episode, all went merry, and from the west window a golden streak of sunshine stretched further and further, till it began to climb the opposite wall, when the quilt was rolled to so narrow a width that but few could work on it to advantage, and Ellen, selecting the most expeditious to complete the task, took with her the rest to assist in preparing the supper, which was done to the music of vigorous strokes echoing and re-echoing from the adjacent woods.

VI.

Beneath the glimmer of more candles than Mrs. Wetherbe had previously burned at once, the supper was spread, and it was very nice and plentiful; for, more mindful of propriety, there were at least a dozen broiled chickens, besides other substantial dishes, on the table. I need not attempt a full enumeration of the preserves, cakes, pies, puddings, and other such luxuries, displayed on Mrs. Wetherbe's table, and which it is usual for country housewifes to provide with liberal hands on occasions of this sort.

Ellen was very proud, as she took the last survey before sound the horn for the men-folks; and well she might be so, for it was chiefly through her ingenuity and active agency that every thing was so tastefully and successfully prepared.

Mrs. Randall still made herself officious, but with less assurance than at first. Ellen was in nowise inclined to yield her authority, and indeed almost the entire responsibility rested on her, for poor Mrs. Wetherbe was sadly out of spirits in consequence of the non-appearance of Helph and Jenny. All possible chances of evil were exaggerated by her, and in her simple apprehension there were a thousand dangers which did not in reality exist. In spite of the festivities about her, she sometimes found it impossible to restrain her tears. Likely enough, she said, the dear boy had got into the canal, or the river, and was drownded, or his critter might have become frightened—there were so many skerry things in town—and so run away with him, and broke everything to pieces.

Once or twice she walked to the neighboring hill, in the hope of seeing him in the distance, but in vain—he did not come; the supper could be delayed no longer, and sitting by the window that overlooked the highway, she continued her anxious watching. No so the mother; she gave herself little trouble as to whether any accident had befallen her son; perhaps she guessed the cause of his delay, but, so or not, none were gayer than she.

Her beauty had once been of a showy order; she was not yet very much faded; and on this occasion, though her gown was of calico, her hair was tastefully arranged, and she was really the best dressed woman in the assembly. Of this she seemed aware, and she glided into flirtations with the country beaux, in a free and easy way which greatly surprised some of us unsophisticated girls; in fact, one or two elderly bachelors were sorely disappointed, as well as amazed, when they understood that the lady from town was none other than Helph's mother! I cannot remember a time when my spirits had much of the careless buoyancy which makes youth so blessed, and at this time I was little more than a passive observer, for which reason, perhaps, I remember more correctly the incidents of the evening.

The table was spread among the trees in the door-yard, which was illuminated with tallow candles, in very simple paper lanterns; the snowy linen waved in the breeze, and the fragrance of tea and coffee was, for the time, pleasanter than that of the flowers; but flowers were in requisition, and such as were in bloom, large or small, bright or pale, were gathered to adorn tresses of every hue, curled and braided with the most elaborate care. At a later hour, some of them were transferred to the buttonholes of favored admirers.

What an outbreak of merriment there was, when, at twilight, down the hill that sloped against the woods, came the gay band of choppers, with coats swung on their arms, and axes gleaming over their shoulders. Every thing became irresistibly, provocative of enjoyment, and from every window and every nook that could be occupied by the quilters, went mingled jests and laughter.

The quilt was finished, but Mehitable and Elizabeth remained close within the chamber, whether to contemplate the completed work, or to regale themselves with each other's accumulations of scandal, I shall not attempt to guess.

A large tin lantern was placed on the top of the pump, and beside it was a wash-tub filled with water, which was intended as a general resort for the ablutions of the young men. Besides the usual roller-towel, which hung by the kitchen door, there were two or three extra ones attached to the boughs of the apple-tree, by the well; and the bar of yellow soap, procured for the occasion, lay on a shingle, conveniently near, while a paper comb-case dangled from a bough betwixt the towels.

These toilet facilities were deemed by some of the party altogether superfluous, and their wooden pocket-combs and handkerchiefs were modestly preferred. During the fixing up the general gayety found vent in a liberal plashing and dashing of water on each other, as also in wrestling bouts, and contests of mere words, at the conclusion of which the more aristocratic of the gentlemen resumed their coats, while others, disdaining ceremony, remained, not only at the supper but during the entire evening, in their shirt sleeves, and with silk handkerchiefs bound around their waists, as is the custom with reapers.

"Come, boys!" called Ellen, who assumed a sort of motherly tone and manner toward all the company, "what *does* make you stay away so?"

The laughter among the girls subsided, as they arranged themselves in a demure row along one side of the table, and the jests fell at once to a murmur as the boys found their places opposite. "Now, don't all speak at once," said Ellen: "How will you have your coffee, Quincy?"

Mr. Quincy Adams Claverel said he was not particular: he would take a little sugar and a little cream if she had them handy, if not, it made no difference.

"Tea or coffee, Mehitable?" she said next; but the young woman addressed did not drink either—coffee made her drowsy like, and if she should drink a cup of tea, she should not sleep a wink all night.

Elizabeth said, Mehitt was just like herself—she drank a great deal, and strong. The jesting caused much laughter, and indeed the mirth was quite irrepressible—on the part of the girls, because of the joyous occasion, and their greater excitability, and on that of the young men, because of the green and yellow twisted bottles that had glistened that afternoon in the ivy which grew along the woods: even more for this, perhaps, than for the bright eyes before them.

One said she drank her tea "naked;'" another, that Ellen might give her half a cup first rate—she would rather have a little and have it good, than have a great deal and not have it good. And in this she meant not the slightest offence or insinuation.

"I hope," said Mr. Wetherbe, speaking in a diffident voice, and pushing back his thin gray hair, "I hope you will none of you think hard of my woman for not coming to sarve you her self—she is in the shadder of trouble, but she as well as myself thanks you all for the good turn you have done us, and wishes you to make yourselves at home, and frolic as long as you are a mind to;" and the good man retired to the house to give his wife such comfort as he could.

*　　*　　*

[Chapter continues the party scene.]

VII.

We will now return to Helphenstein, and give some particulars of the night as it passed with him. It was near noon when he drew the reins before the house of his father, with a heart full of happy anticipations for the afternoon and evening; but his bright dream was destined quickly to darken away to the soberest reality of his life. His father met him in the hall with a flushed face, and taking his hand with some pretense of cordiality, said in an irritable tone, as though he had not the slightest idea of the nature of his errand, "Why, my son, what in the devil's name has brought you home?"

He then gave a doleful narrative of the discomforts and privations he had endured in the few days of the absence of Mrs. Randall, for whom he felt, or affected to feel, the greatest love and admiration, whenever she was separated from him; though his manner towards her, except during these spasmodic affectations, was extremely neglectful and harsh.

"What is a man to do, my son Helph?" he said; "your poor father hasn't had a meal of victuals fit for a dog to eat, since your mother went into the country: how is she, poor woman? I think I'll just get into your buggy, and run out and bring your mother home; things will all go to ruin in two days more—old black Kitty aint worth a cuss, and Jenny aint worth another."

And this last hit he seemed to regard as most especially happy, in its bearing upon Helph, whose opinions of Jenny by no means coincided with his own; but his coarse allusion to her, so far from warping his judgment against the poor girl, made him for the time oblivious of everything else, and he hastened in search of her.

"Lord, honey, I is glad to see you!: exclaimed Aunt Kitty, looking up from her work in the kitchen: for she was kneading bread, with the tray in her lap, in consequence of rheumatic pains which prevented her from standing much on her feet.

"What in the world is the matter?" asked Helph, anxiously, as he saw her disability.

"Noffin much," she said, smiling; "my feet are like to bust wid the inflammatious rheumatis—dat's all. But I's a poor sinful critter," she continued, "and de flesh pulls mighty hard on de sperrit, sometimes, when I ought to be thinkin' ob de mornin' ober Jordan."

And having assured him that she would move her old bones as fast as she could, and prepare the dinner, she directed him where to find Jenny, saying, "Go 'long wid you, and you'll find her a seamsterin' up stairs, and never mind de 'stress of an old darkie like me."

As he obeyed, he heard her calling on the Lord to bless him, for that he was the best young master of them all. Poor kind-hearted creature! she did not then or ever, as others heard, ask any blessing for herself.

In one end of the long low garret, unplastered, and comfortless, from the heat in summer and the cold in winter, there was a cot bed, a dilapidated old trunk, a broken work-stand, a small cracked looking-glass, and a strip of faded carpet. By courtesy, this was called Jenny's room; and here, seated on a chair without any back, sat the maiden, stitching shirts for her adopted brothers, when the one who, from some cause or other, never called her sister, appeared suddenly before her. Smiling, she ran forward to meet him, but suddenly checking herself, she blushed deeply, and the exclamation, "Dear Helph!: that rose to her lips, was subdued and formalized to a simple "Helphenstein." The cheek that was smooth when she saw him last, was darkened into manhood now, and her arm remained passive, that had always been thrown lovingly about his neck; but in this new timidity she appeared only the more beautiful, in the eyes of her admirer, and if she declined the old expressions of fondness, he did not.

The first feeling of pleasure and surprise quickly subsided, on her part, into one of pain and embarrassment, when she remembered her torn and faded dress, and the disappointment that awaited him.

"Well, Jenny," he said, when the first greeting was over, "I have come for you—and you must get ready as soon as possible."

Poor child! she turned away her face to hide the tears that would not be kept down, as she answered, "I cannot go—I have nothing to get ready."

And then inquiries were made about the new dress of which he had been informed, and though for a time Jenny hesitated, he drew from her at the last the confession that it had been appropriated by his mother, under a promise of procuring for her another when she should have made a dozen shirts to pay for it. An exclamation that evinced little filial reverence fell from his lips, and then as he soothed her grief, and sympathized with her, his boyish affection was deepened more and more by pity.

"Never mind, Jenny," he said, in tones of simple and truthful earnestness, "wear any thing to-day, but go—for my sake go; I like you just as well in an old dress as in a new one."

Jenny had been little used to kindness, and from her lonely and sad heart, gratitude found expression in hot and thick-coming tears.

Certainly, she would like of all things to go to the quilting, and the more, perhaps, that Helph was come for her; but in no time of her life had poverty seemed so painful a thing. During the past week she had examined her scanty wardrobe repeatedly; her shoes, too, were down at the heels, and out at the toes; to go decently was quite impossible, and yet, she could not suppress the desire, nor refrain from thinking, over and over, if this dress were not quite so much faded, or if that were not so short and outgrown—and then, if she had money to buy a pair of shoes, and could borrow a neck-ribbon and collar!—in short, if things were a little better than they were she might go, and perhaps, in the night, her deficiencies would be less noticeable.

But in the way of all her thinking and planning lay the forbidding *if*; and in answer to the young man's entreaties, she could only cry and shake her head.

She half wished he would go away, and at the same time feared he would go; she avoided looking at the old run-down slippers she was wearing, as well as at her patched gown, in the vain hope that thus he would be prevented from seeing them; and so, half sorry and half glad, half ashamed and half honestly indignant, she sat—the work fallen into her lap, and the tears now and then dropping, despite her frequent winking, and vain efforts to smile.

At length Helph remembered that his horse had not been cared for; and looking down from the little window, he found, to his further annoyance, that both horse and buggy were gone, and so his return home indefinitely delayed.

"I wish to Heaven," he angrily said, turning towards Jenny, "you and I had a home somewhere beyond the reach of the impositions practised on us by Mr. and Mrs. Randall!"

The last words were in a bitter but subdued tone; and it was thus, in resentment and sorrow, that the love-making of Helph and Jenny began.

*   *   *

[Chapter VIII is a brief twilight suburban scene.]

IX.

They were sitting together, Helph and Jenny, with the twilight deepening around them, speaking little, thinking much, and gazing through the long vistas open to the sunshine, and brighter than the western clouds. But they did not think of the night that was falling, they did not hear the wind soughing among the hot walls and roofs, and prophesying storm and darkness.

Suddenly appeared before them a miserably clad little boy, the one mentioned in a previous chapter as coming for money, and now, after a moment's hesitation, on seeing a stranger, he laid his head in the lap of Jenny, and cried aloud. Stooping over him, she smoothed back his hair and kissed his forehead; and in choked and broken utterances he made known his mournful errant: little Willie was very sick, and Jenny was wanted at home.

Few preparations were required. Helph would not hear of her going alone; and in the new and terrible fear awakened by the message of the child, all her pride vanished, and she did not remonstrate, though she knew the wretchedness of poverty that would be bared before him. Folding close in hers the hand of her little brother, and with tears dimming her eyes, she silently led the way to the miserable place occupied by her family.

It was night, and the light of a hundred windows shone down upon them, when, turning to her young protector, she said, in a voice trembling with both shame and sorrow, perhaps "This is the place." It was a large dingy building, five stories high and nearly a hundred feet long, very roughly but substantially built of brick. It was situated in the meanest suburb of the city, on an unpaved alley, and opposite a ruinous graveyard, and it had been erected on the cheapest possible plan, with especial reference to the poorest class of the community. Scarcely had the wealthy proprietor an opportunity of posting bills announcing rooms to let, before it was all occupied; and with its miserable accommodations, and crowded with people who were almost paupers, it was a perfect hive of misery. Porch above porch, opening out on the alley, served as dooryards to the different apartments—places for the drying of miserable rags—play-grounds for the children—and look-outs, for the decrepit old women, on sunny afternoons.

Dish-water, washing suds, and every thing else, from tea and coffee grounds to all manner of picked bones and other refuse, were dashed down from these tiers of balconies to the ground below, so that a more filthy and in all ways unendurable spectacle can scarcely be imagined, than was presented in the vicinity of this money-making device, this miserable house refuge.

Leaning against the balusters, smoking and jesting, or quarreling and swearing, were groups of men, who might be counted by tens and twenties; and the feeble and querulous tones of woman, now and then, were heard among them, or from within the wretched chambers. A little apart from one of these groups of ignorant disputants sat an old crone combing her gray hair by the light of a tallow candle, other females were ironing or washing dishes, while others lolled listlessly and gracelessly about, listening to, and sometimes taking part in, the vile or savage or pitiable conversations.

Children, half naked, were playing in pools of stagnant water, and now and then pelting each other with heads of fishes, and with slimy bones, caught up at random; and one group, more vicious than the others, were diverting themselves by throwing stones at an old cat that lay half in and half out of a puddle, responding, by feeble struggles, as the rough missiles struck against her, and here and there were going on such fierce contests of brutish force as every day illustrate the melancholy truth that the poor owe so much of their misery to the indulgence of their basest passions, rather than to any causes necessarily connected with poverty.

Depravity, as well as poverty, had joined itself to that miserable congregation. Smoke issued thick from some of the chimneys, full of the odors of mutton and coffee, and as these mixed with the vile stenches that thickened the atmosphere near the scene, Helph, who had been accustomed to the free air of the country, fresh with the scents of the hay-fields and orchards, found it hard to suppress the exclamation of disgust and loathing that rose to his lips, when he turned with Jenny into the alley, and his senses apprehended in a twinkling what I have been so long in describing.

Up the steep and narrow wooden stairs, flight after flight, they passed, catching through the open doors of the different apartments glimpses of the same squalid character—greasy smoking stoves, dirty beds, ragged women and children, with here and there dozing dogs, or men prostrate on the bare floors—either from weariness or drunkenness—and meagerly-spread tables, and cradles, and creeping, and crying, and sleeping babies, all in close proximity.

From the third landing they turned into a side door, and such a picture presented itself as the young man had never seen hitherto: the windows were open, but the atmosphere was close, and had a disagreeable smell of herbs and medicines; a single candle was lighted, and though the shapes of things were not distinctly brought out, enough was visible to indicate the extreme poverty and wretchedness of the family.

It was very still in the room, for the children, with instinctive fear, were huddled together in the darkest corner, and spoke in whispers when they spoke at all; and the mother, patient and pale and wan, sat silent by the bed, holding the chubby sunburned hands of her dying little boy.

"Oh, mother," said Jenny, treading softly and speaking low. Tears filled the poor woman's mild blue eyes, and her lips trembled as she answered, "It is almost over—he does not know me any more."

And forgetting, in the blind fondness of the mother, the darkness and the sorrow and the pain, and worst of all, the contagion of evil example, from which he was about to be set free, she buried her face in her hands, and shook with convulsive agony. All the deprivation and weariness and despair, that had sometimes made her, with scarce a con- sciousness of what she was doing, implore the coming of death, or anni- hilation, were in this new sorrow as nothing: with her baby laughing in her arms, as he had been but the last week, she would be strong to front the most miserable fate.

Tie after tie may be unbound from the heart, while our steps climb the rough steep that goes up to power, for the sweet household affections unwind themselves more and more as the distance widens between aspi- ration and contentment, and over the tide that sweeps into the shining haven of ambition there is no crossing back. The brow that has felt the shadow of the laurel, will not be comforted by the familiar kisses of love; and struggling to the heights of fame, the rumble of clods against the coffin of some mate of long ago, comes softened of its awfulest terror; but where the heart, unwarped from its natural yearnings, presses close, till its throbbings bring up echoes from the stony bottom of the grave, and when, from the heaped mound, reaches a shadow that darkens the world fro the humbles eyes that may never look up any more—these keep the bleeding affections, these stay the mourning that the great cannot understand. Where the wave is narrow, the dropping of even a pebble of hope sends up the swelling circles till the whole bosom of the stream is agitated; but in the broader sea, they lessen and lessen till they lose themselves in a border of light. And over that little life, moaning itself away in the dim obscurity of its birth-chamber, fell bitterer tears, and bowed hearts aching with sharper pains, than they may ever know whose joys are not alike as simple and as few. "Oh, Willie, dear little Willie," sobbed Jenny, folding her arms about him and kissing him over and over," speak to me once, only once more!: Her tears were hot on his whitening face, but he did not life his heavily-drooping eyes, nor turn towards her on the pillow. The children fell asleep, one on another, where they sat. In the presence of the strong healthy man they were less afraid, and nestling close together, gradually forgot that little Willie was not among them—and so came the good gift which God giveth his beloved in nights of sorrow.

In some chink of the wall the cricket chirped to itself the same quick short sound, over and over, and about the candle circled and fluttered the gray-winged moths, heedless of their perished fellows, and on the table stood a painted bucket half filled with tepid water, and beside it a brown jug and broken glass.

Now and then the mother and daughter exchanged anxious looks, as a footstep was heard on the stairs, but when it turned aside to some one of the adjoining chambers, they resumed their watching, not speaking their hopes or fears, if either had been awakened.

From the white dome of St. Peters' sounded the silvery chime of the midnight; the sick child had fallen asleep an hour before, but now his eye opened full on his mother, and his white lips worked faintly; "Jenny," she said, in a tone of low but fearful distinctness—for with her head on the bedside she was fast dozing into forgetfulness—"he is going—going home."

"Home," he repeated sweetly, and that was the last word he ever said.

The young man came forward hastily—the soft light of a setting star drifted across the pillow, and in its pale radiance he lad the hands together, and smoothed the death-dampened curls.

*   *   *

X.
[Jenny Mitchel's brother is dying in a Cincinnati tenament.]

XI.-XII.
[Continues consequences of boy's death and his drunken father's drowning.]

XIII.
All the boyish habits of Helph were at once thrown aside, and much Aunt Wetherbe marveled when she saw him a day or two after his return from the city, bring forth from the cellar a little sled on which, in all previous winters, he had been accustomed (out of the view of the highway, it is true), to ride down hill.

"What on airth now?" she said, placing her hands on either hip, and eyeing him in sorrowful amazement. A great deal of pains had been lavished on the making of the sled, the runners were shod with iron, and it was nicely painted; indeed, Helph had considered it a specimen of the best art, in its way, and now as he dragged it forth to the light, dusting it with his handkerchief, and brushing the spider-webs from among its slender beams, he found it hard to suppress the old admiration for his beautiful handiwork. Nevertheless, when he found himeself observed, he gave it a rough throw, which lodged it, broken and ruined, among some rubbish, and drawing his hat over his eyes to conceal from them the wreck, he strode away without at all noticing his aunt, who immediately went in search of her good man, who, in her estimation at least, knew almost every thing, to ask an explanation of the boy's unaccountable conduct.

But the strange freaks of the young man were not yet at an end, and on returning to the house he took from a nail beneath the looking-glass, where they had long hung, the admiration of all visitors, a string of speckled birds' eggs and the long silvery skin of a snake, and threw them carelessly into the fire, thereby sending a sharp pang through the heart of Aunt Wetherbe, if not through his own. He next took from the joist a bundle of arrows and darts, the latter cut in fanciful shapes, which he had made at various times to amuse his leisure, and crushed them together in a box of kindlings, saying, in answer to the remonstrance of his relations, that was all they were good for.

From the pockets of coats and trowsers he was observed at various times to make sundry ejectments, embracing all such trinkets as one is apt to accumulate during boyish years, together with bits of twine, brass-headed nails, and other treasures that are prized by youths disposed to be industrious and provident. But when he brought from an out-house a squirrel's cage, where many a captive had been civilized into tricks never dreamed of in his wild swingings from bough to bough, Aunt Wetherbe took it from his hands, just as she would have done when he was a wayward child, exclaiming with read displeasure, "Lord-a-mercy, child! has the old boy himself got into you?" But Helph soon proved that he was not possessed of the evil one, by the manliness with which he talked of the coming election, discussing shrewdly the merits of candidates and parties, and of such other subjects as he seemed to think deserving of a manly consideration. All the implements necessary to shaving operations were shortly procured, and Helph was observed to spend much of his time in their examination and careful preparation, though no special necessity for their use was observable, and hitherto the old razor o his uncle had only now and then been brought into requisition by him.

When the first flush of conscious manhood had subsided, a thought-ful and almost sorrowful feeling pervaded the dreams of the young man; he was much alone, knit his brows, and answered vaguely when ques-tioned. At last he abruptly announced his intention of beginning the world for himself. He would sell his horse, and the various farming implements he possessed, together with the pair of young oxen which he had played with and petted, and taught to plow and draw the cart, and with the means thus acquired he would procure a small shop in the vicin-ity of the city, and there resume his blacksmithing.

"Tut, tut," said the aunt, "I'd rather you would steal away from the splitting of oven-wood and the churning of a morning, just as you used to do, to set quail traps and shoot at a mark, than to be talking in this way. Your uncle and me can't get along without you: no, no, my child, you mustn't think of going.

Helph brushed his hand across his eyes, appealing to the authority which had always been absolute; and removing his spectacles, the good old man rubbed them carefully through the corner of his handkerchief as he said, sadly but decidedly, "Yes, my son, you have made a wise resolve: you are almost a man now (here the youth's face colored), and it's time you were beginning to work for yourself and be a man amongst men;" and approaching an old-fashioned walnut desk in which he kept all manner of yellow and musty receipts and letters, he unlocked it slowly, and pouring from a stout linen bag a quantity of silver, counted the dollars to the number of a hundred, and placing them in the hand of the young man, he said, "A little present to help you on in the world; make good use of it, my boy; but above all things, continue in the honest, straight path in which you have always kept, and my word for it, prosperity will come to you, even though you have but a small begin-ning. I have lived to be an old man," he continued, "and I have never seen the righteous forsaken, nor his seed begging bread."

Boyishly, Helph began drawing figures rapidly on the table with his finger, for he felt the tears coming, but it would not do, and looking rather than speaking his thanks, he hurried from the house, and for an hour chopped vigorously at the wood-pile.

It was soon concluded to hurry the preparations for his departure, so that he might get fairly settled before the coming on of cold weather, and a list of goods and chattels to be sold at public vendue, on a specified day, was made out, and bills posted on the school-house, at the cross-roads, and in the barroom of the tavern, stating the time and place of sale. Ellen Black was sent for in haste to come right away and make up half a dozen shirts, and the provident old lady briskly plied the knitting-needles, that her nephew might lack for nothing. All talked gayly of the new project, but the gayety was assumed, and Ellen herself, with all her powers of making sombre things take cheerful aspects, felt that in this instance she did not succeed.

Now that he was about to part with them, the gay young horse that had eaten so often from his hand, and the two gentle steers that had bowed their necks beneath the heavy yoke at his bidding, seemed to the young master almost humanly endeared, and he fed and caressed them morning and evening with unusual solicitude, tossing them oat sheaves and emptying measures of corn very liberally.

"Any calves or beef cattle to sell," called a coarse, loud voice to Helph, as he lingered near the stall of his oxen, the evening preceding the day of sale.

"No," answered the young man, seeing that it was a butcher who asked the question.

"I saw an advertisement of oxen to be sold here tom-morrow," said the man, striking his spurred heel against his horse, and reining him in with a jerk.

"I prefer selling to a farmer," said Helph, as he leaned against the broad shoulders of one of the steers, and took in his hands its horn of greenish white.

"My money is as good as any man's," said the butcher, and throwing himself from the saddle he approached the stall, and after walking once or twice around the unconsciously doomed animals, and pinching their hides with his fingers, he offered for them a larger sum than Helph expected; he however shut his eyes to the proposed advantage, saying he hoped to sell them to the neighbor who would keep them and be kind to them.

A half contemptuous laugh answered, in part, as the butcher turned away, saying he was going further into the country, and would call on his return—they might not be sold.

Thus far, Helph had not advised with Jenny relative to the new movement he was about making, but when all arrangements were made, and it was quite too late to retract, he resolved to ask her advice; and I suspect in this conduct he was not acting without a precedent.

From among a bunch of quills that had remained in the old desk from time immemorial, he selected one, with great care, and having rubbed his pocket-knife across the end of his boot for an hour or more, next began a search for ink, of which his uncle told him there was a good bottle full on the upper shelf of the cupboard. But the said bottle was not to be found, and after a good deal of rummaging and some questioning of Aunt Wetherbe, it was finally ascertained that the ink alluded to must have been bought ten or twelve years previously, and that only some dry powder remained of it now in the bottom of a broken inkstand: yet to this a little vinegar was added, and having shaken it thoroughly, the young man concluded it would answer. More than once during all this preparation, he had been asked what he was going to do, for writing was not done in the family except on eventful occasions; but the question elicited no response more direct than "Nothing much," and so, at last, with a sheet of foolscap, ink, and a quill, he retired to his own room— Aunt Wetherbe having first stuck a pin the candle, indicating the portion he was privileged to burn.

Whether more or less candle were consumed, I am not advised but that letter was written, I have good authority for believing. Murder will out, there is no doubt about that, and the day following the writing, Aunt Wetherbe chanced to have occasion to untie a bundle of herbs that, in a pillow-case, had been suspended from the ceiling of Helph's room for a long time, and what should she find but a letter addressed to Jenny Mitchel, fantastically folded and sealed with four red wafers; it has evidently been placed there to await a secret opportunity of conveyance to the post-office. Long was the whispered conference between the old lady and Ellen, that followed this discovery; very indignant was the aunt, at first, for old people are apt to think of love and marriage in the young as highly improper; but Ellen, whose regard for matrimony was certainly more lenient, exerted her liveliest influence in behalf of the young people, nor were her efforts unsuccessful, and an unobtrusive silence on the subject was resolved upon.

During this little excitement in doors, there was much noise and bustle without; Helph's young horse was gayly caparisoned, and bearing proudly various riders up and down the space, where among plows, harrows, scythes, and other agricultural implements, a number of farmers were gathered, discussing politics, smoking, and shrewdly calculating how much they could afford to bid for this or that article. Yoked together, and chewing their cuds very contentedly, stood the plumb young oxen, but no one admired them with a design of purchasing. The vendue was soon over, and all else had been sold, readily and well. The sleek bay was gone, proudly arching his neck to the hand of a new master, and the neighbors brought their teams to carry home whatever they had purchased, and Helph half sighed as one after another put into his hand the money for which he had bargained away the familiar treasures which had been a part of his existence.

As he lingered at the style, he saw approaching a large flock of sheep, closely huddled together, and with red chalk marks on their sides indicating their destiny; while behind came a mingled group of oxen cows and calves, all driven by the sanguinary butcher with whom he had refused to treat for his favorites.

"Well, neighbor," he said, thrusting his hand in his pocket and drawing thence a greasy leathern pouch, "I see you have kept the cattle for me after all."

At first Helph positively declined selling them, but he did not want them; it was very uncertain when there would be an opportunity of disposing of them as he wished, and when the butcher added something to his first liberal offer, he replied, "I suppose, sir, you will have to take hem." Riding into the yard, he drove them roughly forth with whip and voice, from the manger of hay and the deep bed of straw. They were free from the yoke, and yet they came side by side, and with their heads bowed close together, just as they had been accustomed to work. Passing their young master, they turned toward him their great mournful eyes, reproachfully, he thought, and crushing the price of them in his hand, he walked hastily in the direction of the house.

"The bad, old wretch," exclaimed Ellen, looking after the butcher, as she stood on the porch, wiping her eyes with the sleeve of the shirt she was making; and just within the door sat Aunt Wetherbe, her face half concealed with a towel, and crying like a child.

A week more, and Helph was gone, Ellen still remaining with the old people, till they should get a little accustomed to their desolate home. The tears shed over his departure were not yet dry, for he had left in the morning and it was now dusky evening, when as the little family assembled round the tea table, he entered, with a hurried and anxious manner that seemed to preface some dismal tidings.

Poor youth! His heart was almost breaking. He had no concealments now, and very frankly told the story of his love, and what had been his purposes for the future. Mr. and Mrs. Randall had suddenly given up their house, gone abroad, and taken Jenny with them, under the pretext of giving her a thorough education in England. But the young lover felt instinctively that she was separated from him for a widely different purpose. And poor faithful Aunt Kitty, she had been dismissed without a shilling above her scanty earnings, to work, old and disabled as she was, or die like a beggar. After much inquiry, he had learned that she had obtained an engagement at an asylum as an attendant on the sick.

"Dear old soul!" said Aunt Wetherbe, "you must go right away in the morning and bring her here; she shan't be left to suffer, and I know of it."

"Never mind—all will come out bright," said Ellen as Helph sat the night on the porch, alone and sorrowful.

But he would not be comforted: Jenny had not left a single line to give him assurance and hope, and even if she thought of him now, she would forget him in the new life that was before her. All this was plausible, but Ellen's efforts were not entirely without effect; and when she offered to go with him to the city and see Aunt Kitty, who perhaps might throw some light on the sudden movement, he began to feel hopeful and cheerful almost: for of all eyes, those of a lover are the quickest to see light or darkness.

Some chance prevented the fulfilment of Ellen's promise, and I was commissioned by her to perform the task she had proposed for herself. "It will help to keep him up, like," she said, "if you go along." A day or two intervened before I could conveniently leave home, but a last we set out, on a clear frosty morning of the late autumn. Behind the one seat of the little wagon in which we rode, was placed an easy chair for Aunt Kitty. A brisk drive of an hour brought us to the hospital; and pleasing ourselves with thoughts of the happy surprise we were bringing to the poor forlorn creature, we entered the parlor, and on inquiry were told we had come too late—she had died half an hour before our arrival, in consequences of a fall received the previous evening in returning from the dead-house, whither she had assisted in conveying a body. "I have ordered here to be decently dressed," said the superintendent, "from my own things; she was so good, I thought that little enough to do for her:" and she led the way to the sick ward, where Aunt Kitty awaited to be claimed and buried by her friends. It was a room fifty or sixty feet long, and twenty perhaps in width, lined on either side with a long row of narrow dirty beds, some of them empty, but most of which were filled with pale and miserable wretches—some near dying, some groaning, some propped on pillows and seeming stolidly to regard the fate of others and of themselves. The sun streamed hot through the uncurtained windows, and the atmosphere was pervaded with offensive smells.

As my eye glanced down the long tiers of beds where there was so much suffering, it was arrested by the corpse of the poor old woman—gone at last to that land where there are no more masters, no more servants. I shuddered and stood still as the two shriveled and haglike women wrapped and pinned the sheet about the stiffening limbs, with as much glee, imbecile almost, but frightful, as they apparently were capable of feeling or expressing. "What in Heaven's name are you laughing at?" said Helph, approaching them. "Just to think of sarving a dead nigger!" said one, with a revolting simper; but looking in his face, she grew respectful with a sudden recollection, and drew from her pocket a sealed letter, saying "May you can tell who this is for—we found it in her bosom when we went to dress her." It was a letter from Jenny to himself: poor Aunt Kitty had been faithful to the last.

Not till I was turning from that terriblest shelter of woe I ever saw, did I notice a young and pale-cheeked girl, sitting near the door, on a low and rude rocking-chair, and holding close to her bosom an infant but a few days old: not with a mother's pride, I fancied, for her eyes drooped before the glance of mine, and a blush burned in her cheek, as though shame and not honor covered her young maternity. I paused a moment, praised the baby, and spoke some kindly words to her; but she bowed her head lower and lower on her bosom, speaking not a word; and seeing that I only gave her pain, I passed on with a spirit more saddened for the living than for the dead, who had died in such wretchedness.

Jenny's letter proved a wonderful comfort to Helph, and cheerfulness and elasticity gradually came back to him; but when, at the expiration of a year, his parents returned without her, and bringing a report of her marriage, all courage, all ambition, deserted him, and many a summer and winter went by, during which he lived in melancholy isolation.

I shall not attempt to write the history of Jenny Mitchel, except this much, which had some relation to our life at Clovernook; and therefore pass abruptly into the future of my good friend Randall. Nearly fifteen years were gone since his sweetheart crossed the sea, and country belles had bloomed and faded before his eyes, without winning from him special regard: when, as he sat before a blazing hickory fire one evening, waiting for Aunt Wetherbe, who still enjoyed a green old age, to bring to the table the tea and short-cake, there was a quick, lively tap on the door, and the next moment, in the full maturity of womanhood, but blushing and laughing like the girl of years ago, Jenny stood in the midst of the startled group—Jenny Mitchel still! Helph had become a prosperous man of the world, and had been envied for the good fortune which his patient bravery so much deserved. The waves of the sea of human life had reached out gradually from the city until they surrounded his blacksmith's shop, and covered all his lots as if with silver; and he had been building, all the previous year, a house so beautiful, and with such fair accessories, as to astonish all the neighborhood acquainted in any degree with his habits or reputed temper. "What does the anchorite man to do with such a place? he never speaks to a woman more than he would to a ghost," they said; "so he won't get married; and nobody is so particular about a house to sell, and it can't be he's going to stay in it all alone." But Helph knew very well what he was about, and was content to keep his own counsel. If he had mailed certain letters out at Clovernook, our postmaster would have guessed at once his secret; but though Mr. Helphenstein Randall was very well known in town, there were so many objects there to interest the common attention that it was never observed when, every once in a while, he bought a small draft on England, nor that he more frequently sent letters east for the Atlantic steamers, nor that he received as frequently as there was foreign news in the papers, missives, every month more neatly folded and with finer superscriptions. He had been thought something of a philosopher, by Ellen Blake and I, and others were convinced perhaps by justifying reasons, that he was as little impressible by woman's charms as the cattle in his stalls. But there are not so many philosophers in the world as some pretend, and his heart was all aglow with pictures of one on whom he looked in dreams and in the distant perfumed gardens of his hope. Jenny, deserted, and struggling with all the adversities that throng the way of a poor girl alone in so great a city, had written at length from London all the story of her treatment by her lover's parents, and having time for reflection before he could answer her letter—provoking all his nature to joy and scorn—he had decided that she should not come back until she could do so with such graces and accomplishments as should make here the wonder and him the envy of all who had contrived or wished their separation. He had trusted her, educated her, and at last had all the happiness of which his generous capable.

Ellen Blake of course presided at the wedding, and the quilts quilted that night at Aunt Wetherbe's had been kept unused for a present to Helph's wife on her bridal night. When I am down in the city I always visit the Randalls, and there is not in the Valley of the West another home so pleasant, so harmonious, so much like what I trust to share in heaven.

Bibliography

Cary, Alice. "Mrs. Wetherbe's Party." *Clovernook; or, Recollections of Our Neighborhood in the West.* 2nd series. New York: Edgewood, 1853: 13-79.

Fetterly, Judith. Introduction. *Clovernook Sketches and Other Stories.* New Brunswick: Rutgers University Press, 1987.

Fetterly, Judith, and Marjorie Pryse. "Alice Cary: 1820-1871." *Legacy* 1.1 (Spring 1984): 1-3.

Griswold, Rufus W. *The Female Poets of America.* Philadelphia: Carey and Hart, 1894.

Kolodny, Annette. *The Land Before Her.* Chapel Hill: University of North Carolina Press, 1984.

Pattee, Fred L. *The Feminine Fifties.* Port Washington: Kennikat, 1966.

Smith, Henry Nash. *Virgin Land.* New York: Vintage, 1957.

Venable, W. H. *Beginnings of Literary Culture in the Ohio Valley.* Cincinnati: Clarke, 1891.

Mary Hartwell Catherwood

1847-1902

Mary Hartwell Catherwood was an educated, middle-western regionalist who dedicated her professional life to the written word. She contentedly remained in her native heartlands and spent most of her lifetime writing about the region in different genres, including regional poetry, essays, novels, short stories, and historical fiction.

In 1875, while still experimenting with her craft, the youthful Mary Hartwell codified her ideas about nineteenth-century women writers' sanctified duty when she concluded her first novel, *A Woman in Armor,* with this clarion call: "[W]oman is no helpless, weakling species of the genus man, but an independent, a cherishing, a strong, a daring nature, who in the armor of her own uprightness can fight the battles of the world and win them" (166).

Of course, Catherwood began life humbly in Luray, Licking County, Ohio, and at the age of nine Mary Hartwell moved with her parents and two younger siblings to Milford, Illinois. During the next year, 1857, her father died, followed shortly by her mother, and the orphaned Hartwell children were sent to their maternal grandparents in Hebron, Ohio. She looked after her younger siblings and ambivalently yearned toward the nearby Hebron-Buckeye Lake-Kirkersville swamp area, which Robert Price calls "a land of idyllic escape" (105).

At the age of fourteen, Mary Hartwell began teaching school in Licking County and publishing poems and sketches in the Newark, Ohio, *North American,* whose editor, M. L. Wilson, in 1864 assisted her admission to Granville Female College. After college, she continued her work as a free-lance writer, particularly serving as a regular contributor to *Wood's Household Magazine.* In 1874 she went for a year to Newburgh, New York, to work at the home of this magazine and become self-supporting. Soon she returned to Cincinnati, Ohio, where she wrote for a series of publications, among them *Ladies' Repository* and *Golden Hours.* In 1875, while living in the Queen City, her first novel, *A Woman in Armor*, was serialized in *Hearth and Home*; it articulated her polemical call to arms for America's middle-western women.

In the following year financial depression forced Mary Hartwell to return to relatives in Illinois where she married James Steel Catherwood in 1877, continued to write, and became friends with such regionalists as the Hoosier poet, James Whitcomb Riley. While living in Illinois and Indiana, four years later Catherwood published her second "Ohio" novel, *Craque-O'Doom* (1881), serialized in *Lippincott's Magazine*, which satirizes the provincial barrenness of Hebron, the enforced home of her teenage years. This narrative introduces a loving dwarf whose romantic interest is a local girl named Tamsin, who must learn how to love. *Craque-O'Doom's* treatment of middle-American spiritual shallowness has been cited as a forerunner of Sherwood Anderson's famous *Winesburg, Ohio*.

Though Fred Lewis Pattee calls Mary Hartwell Catherwood the "first American woman novelist of the period to be born west of the Alleghenies" (258), it is doubtful she will be remembered for her novels. While regionally and historically interesting to the scholar, her two Ohio-based novels could not be called skillfully written. Catherwood was the first prominent Ohio woman writer to be college educated at Ohio's new Granville Female College, which provides the setting for *A Woman in Armor*. In this short novel Granville is described as "Little Boston," a typical Ohio farmland village, deprived of its vegetation by pioneer hunters and farmers who had decimated the region's Native Americans, as well as its wildlife, bison, elk, beaver. Granville's agricultural culture remains unchanged by such developments as the 1870s appearance of the Ohio Central Railroad, the state's recent Constitutional Convention, or the Women's Temperance Crusade that had succeeded in taxing liquor.

Granville provides Catherwood with a liberal fictional enclave surrounded by midwestern farm fields. This weakly plotted romantic novel draws upon her youthful interest in women's rights and other contemporary issues, including religious movements, the "children's rights" issue, known contemporaneously as the child's crusade, and revisions to Ohio's legal system, which failed to protect women's financial resources from ne'er-do-well husbands. The theme of expeditious divorce culminates with a German immigrant's dialectal advice: "Den I lock der door ven der man ist gone!" The novel's overarching preoccupation with justice shows the twenty-three-year-old Mary Hartwell regarding authorship above all, but it is a male character who voices the novel's thesis: middle-western women writers must be committed to the moral power of the written word: "Pens are moving all over the world. Some of them will sweep like strong fingers across the harp of a whole people, and waken renown. And others will touch only a few strings, but make a sweet undertone. While a few will strike only a swift, strong note—the song or proverb of a century—and be heard no more" (136).

Mary Hartwell Catherwood's pen did eventually strike a strong note but not in the form of polemical novels. It was her realistic short fiction of the early 1880s that showed, depending upon choice of metaphor, how the mature Catherwood could make music or fight for a serious place as a middle-western regional writer.

During this decade, Mary Hartwell Catherwood used keen verisimilitude in her short tales about Ohio's corn belt, a prime subject that allowed her to focus realistically upon "plain Americans" remembered from her youth in central Ohio's "Pigeon Swamp" flats in Licking and Fairfield counties. This area remained a setting where New England migrants' way of thinking, speaking, and living intersected with those from the South, pioneers from Virginia, Maryland, and Kentucky, as well as "poor whites" from the Carolinas and Tennessee. Catherwood's mature reconstructions of the region's speech, manners, personalities, appearances, and community relationships are empathetic and vivid. Recreating the world she knew in the 1850s and 1860s, Catherwood's novels, children's tales, and short stories embody what Ruth Suckow calls "middlewestishness" (178). This expression was given apt expression in Catherwood's 1899 introductory note to her regional short story collection, *The Queen of the Swamp*, when she explained her intention to honestly preserve middle-western experience. Her motivation was the need to "embody phases of American life which have entirely passed away" (n.p.).

As early as June 1882, when William Dean Howells published Mary Hartwell Catherwood's "Serena" in the *Atlantic Monthly*, her regional fiction set in the 1860s introduced eastern readers to central Ohio's Hebron neighborhood. "Serena" recreates the mixed intimacy and bitter sordidness of the manners, customs, and folk beliefs that she remembered. In fact, the places and personal names in the story are mostly real: Serena is a favorite cousin; Moses and Jesse Jeffries are named after her grandfather and great uncle, Moses and Jesse Thompson; Jeffries is a neighbor; and Jimmy Holmes, the undertaker, lies buried in the graveyard of Fletcher's Chapel, the Methodist circuit church in Baltimore, Ohio, which serves as "George's Chapel" in the "Swamp" stories.

Setting in a dramatic sense embodies the story for Catherwood; for example, in "Serena" an outside narrator empathizes with a widowed, apparently disinherited farmer's daughter who has returned to the patriarch on his deathbed. Mean-spirited relatives uncharitably gloat over their imagined acquisition of wealth, but the wholesome setting triumphs and justice prevails. Catherwood's domestic story conveys keen verisimilitude of time, place, and dialect. The shrewd narrator comments to the reader about how provincial isolation shapes character, especially castigating Serena's rapacious, contemptuous male cousin, whom the narrator imagines thinking that women are "sort of cattle he had no fancy for" (197).

Originally many of these regional stories appeared in regional journals such as the *Ladies' Repository* and eastern publications, such as *Lippincott's Magazine* and *Harper's Bazaar*, which published "The Queen of the Swamp" and "Rose Day." Then in 1899 the local color short stories were anthologized in Catherwood's *The Queen of the Swamp and Other Plain Americans* according to their states of origin, starting with her birthplace, Ohio, and including nearby Kentucky, Indiana, and Illinois. The five Ohio stories are set in 1846, 1850, 1855, 1860, and 1875, effectively recreating the Hebron-Buckeye-Lake-Kirkersville swamp country of Hartwell's youth.

Thematically her protagonists are defined by matrimony; "Serena" traces the consequences of challenging parental mate approval, while in "The Queen of the Swamp," "The Stirring Off," "Rose Day," and "Sweetness," the female characters choose their own husbands. Male courtship is studied in these stories, especially in "Sweetness," which melds a mature lover's courtship of a devoted daughter and her invalided mother.

In the preface to her anthology, Catherwood comments upon her goals of being empathetic toward the difficulties of swamp country people and celebrating a time when "neighborhoods were intensely local." She speaks of the significance of such figures as the regional Methodist evangelists, horseback visitors who inspired Buckeye farmers to admiration or derision, but courted, married, and buried them. Then in "The Stirring Off," set in 1850, she demonstrates the influence of the outsider evangelist upon the Davis family, social leaders in the George's Chapel neighborhood of the Fairfield County Swamp. The nubile Jane Davis is courted by four neighborhood men, who are told at the maple sugar stirring off party that she is marrying Brother Gurley, the Methodist circuit rider. Catherwood's theme is the group's social affirmation through the enduring friendships that Jane Davis cultivates. It provides a negative answer to the text's question: "Is she light-minded?" The story ends on a comic note with the rejected suitors like Dr. Miller refusing further Davis hospitality because he feels "stirred off."

Set a quarter of a century later, "Rose Day" offers a complex psychological vision. In this story dissimilar forty-year-old twins—Marilla Victoria Baldwin, who has a "deadly acid added to her nature," and the pleasant Infanta Isabella Baldwin—are in conflict over Marilla's plans for a soap-making "orgy." Infanta, the happy Rose Day celebrant, defies her sister after receiving a revelation from an old beau and accepts his proposal to leave Ohio. Rilla, who has never appreciated the "feedom, ease, and escape of mature unmarried womanhood," also marries a man who is willing to remain on the farm and obey her domestic injunctions.

During the 1890s Mary Hartwell Catherwood organized the Western Association of Writers, which for two decades was an important conservative literary force in the Middle West. At a time when literary debates raged over "new realism," Mary Hartwell Catherwood assumed the role of spokesperson for middle-western conservatism. In 1893 she debated at the Chicago World's Fair with the famous regionalist Hamlin Garland, but by this point Catherwood's search for fresh material had led her toward French-inspired romances and away from middle-western realism. Indeed, Mary Hartwell Catherwood's historical romances such as *Lazarre* (1901), were contemporaneously popular, and her fame grew from these historical romances which, as Beverly Seaton points out, became the "best-selling genre at the turn of the century" (320).

Today Mary Hartwell Catherwood's place in regional literary history is again based upon her evocative short stories about middle-western village life. Catherwood's depictions of Ohio's cornlands culture are as fascinating today as they were in the late nineteenth century and remain among the state's best local color stories. Moreover, it was the mantle of literary respectability cast by these short stories that finally gave Catherwood the sort of respect she sought. Today serious readers continue to share her comic and empathetic view of the residue left behind the pioneers, the "dreary cultural wastelands peopled with squalid characters whose little dramas often illustrate such basic beauties of human nature as parental love" (Seaton 322). This was the meaningful contribution of Ohio's self-conscious woman in armor.

The Stirring-Off

Mary Hartwell Catherwood

Davis's boys said to all the young men at singing-school, "Come over to 'r sugar-camp Saturday night; we're goin' to stir off."

The young men, sitting on the fence to which horses were tied in dusky rows, playfully imitated the preacher when he gave out appointments, and replied they would be there, no preventing Providence, at early candle-lighting.

June Davis, attended by her cousin, also circulated among the girls in the schoolhouse during that interval in singing-school called recess, and invited them to the stirring-off.

The Davises, though by no means the richest, were the most hospitable family in the Swamp. They came from Virginia. Their stable swarmed with fine horses, each son and daughter owning a colt; and the steeds of visiting neighbors often crowded the stalls until these looked like a horse-fair.

The Davises entertained every day in the year. Their house was unpretending even for those times, being of unpainted wood, with a bedroom at each side of the porch, a sitting-room where guns and powder-horns hung over the fireplace, a kitchen, and a loft. Yet here sojourned relations from other countries, and even from over the mountains. Here on Christmas and New Year's days were made great turkey-roasts. Out of it issued Jane Davis to the dances and parties where she was a belle, and her brothers, ruddy, huge-limbed, black-eyed, and dignified as any young men in Fairfield County.

They kept bees, and raised what were called noble turnips. Their farm appeared to produce solely for the use of guests. In watermelon season they kept what might be termed open field. Their cookery was celebrated, and their cordiality as free as sunshine. No unwelcome guest could alight at Davis's. The head of the family, Uncle Davis was a "general," and this title carried as much social weight as that of judge. About their premises hung an atmosphere of unending good times. On Sunday afternoons late in November all the raw young men of the neighborhood drew in a circle to Davis's fireplace, scraping turnips or apples. Now the steel knives moved in concert, and now they jarred; the hollow wall of a turnip protested against the scrape, and Aunt Davis passed the heaping pan again. Or cracked walnuts and hickory nuts were the offerings. Then every youth sat with an overflowing handkerchief in his lap, and the small blade of his knife busy with the kernels,—backlog and forestick being bombarded with shells which burned in blue and crimson.

So when the Davises were ready to stir off in their sugar-camp, it was the most natural thing in the world for them to invite their neighbors to come and et the sugar, and for their neighbors to come and do so.

The camp threw its shine far among leafless trees. Three or four iron kettles steamed on a pole over the fire. In a bark lodge near by, Aunt Davis had put a lunch of pies and cakes before she went home, to be handed around at the stirring-off. It was a clear starry night, the withered sod crisp underfoot with the stiffness of ice. Any group approaching silently could hear the tapped maples dripping a liquid nocturne into trough or pan.

But scarcely any groups approached silently. They were heard chatting in the open places, and their calls raised echoes.

John and Eck Davis had collected logs and chunks and spread robes an blankets until the seating capacity of the camp was nearly equal to that of George's Chapel. Some of the girls took off their wraps and hung them in the bark house. One couple carried away a bucket for more sugar-water to cool a kettle, and other couples sauntered after them. There were races on the spongy dead leaves, and sudden squally of remonstrance.

Jane Davis stood in the midst of her company, moving a long wooden stirrer in the kettle about to sugar-off. Though her beauty was neither brown nor white, nor, in fact, positive beauty of any kind, it cajoled everybody. Her hair was folded close to her cheeks. There was innocent audacity in the curving line of every motion she made. The young men were so taken by the spell of her grace that she was accused of being unrighteously engaged to three at once, and about to add her cousin Tom Randall to the list.

Tom Randall was a Virginian, spending the winter in Ohio. He was handsome, merry as Mercutio, and so easy in his manners that the Swamp youths watched him with varying emotions. He brought his songs over the mountains: one celebrated the swiftness of the electric telegraph in flashing news from Baltimore to Wheeling; another was about a Quaker courtship, and set all the Swamp girls to rattling the lady's brisk response,—

> "What care I for your rings or money,—
> Faddle-a-ding, a-ding, a-day;

I want a man that will call me honey,—
Faddle-a-ding, a-ding, a-day!"

Tom Randall sat close to the fire, hanging his delicate hands, which had never done a day's chopping, over his knees. He looked much of a gentleman, Nora Waddell remarked aside to Philip Welchammer. To all the girls he was a central figure, as Jane was a central figure to the young men.

But Philip claimed that Virginians were no nearer perfection than out-and-out Swamp fellows.

"I didn't say he was a perfect gentleman," said Nora, with cautious moderation, "for I wouldn't say so of any man."

"He ain't proud," admitted Philip. "He's free to talk with everybody."

"Humph!" remarked Mary Thompson, sitting at the other side of Philip; "he ought to be. Folks in Georger Chapel neighborhood is just as good as anybody."

"Well, anyhow, I know he ain't a prettier dancer than Jane," sighed Nora, whose folks would not allow her to indulge in the godless motion which the music of a fiddle inspires. While Jane stirred and chatted, she was swaying and taking dance-steps, as if unable to refrain from spinning away through the trees. In this great woods drawing-room, where so many were gathered, it was impossible for her to hear any comment that went on.

"Jane makes a good appearance on the floor," responded Philip, who, being male, could withstand the general denunciations of the preacher and his mother's praying at him in meeting. "I like to lead her out to dance."

"Uncle and Aunt Davis are just as easy with Jane as if they wasn't perfessors of religion," sighed Nora Waddell.

"And their boys thinks so much of her," added Mary Thompson. "John can't go anywhere unless she ties his neck-han'ketcher for him. I've knowed him, when Jane was sick, to come and lean over her to get it fixed."

"If she's to leave them," said Philip, "I wonder how they'd do without her?"

"She's goin' to marry Cousin Jimmy Thompson, that I know," said Mary.

"She's engaged to Dr. Miller in Lancaster," insisted Nora. "I've saw volunties he's sent her."

"Dick Hanks thinks he's goin' to get her," laughed Philip. "He told me she's as good as promised him. And Dick's a good feller, if he wasn't such a coward."

"I don't believe Jane wants anybody," said Nora Waddell. "She's light-minded, and likes to enjoy herself."

Dick Hanks stood by Jane and insisted on helping her to move the stirrer. His hair inclosed his head in the shape of a thatch, leaving but narrow eaves of forehead above his eyebrows, though his expression was open and amiable. He looked like one of Bewick's cuts of an English cater. The Hankses, however, were a rich family, and, in spite of their eccentricities, a power in the county. Old Jimmy Hanks so dreaded the grave that he had a marble vault hewed, watching its progress for years, and getting himself ready to occupy it a few weeks after its completion. Lest he should be buried alive, his will decreed that the vault should be unlocked and the coffin examined at intervals. The sight of a face floating in alcohol and spotted with drops from the metal casket not proving grateful to his heirs, the key was soon conveniently lost.

His son Dick, hearty in love and friendship and noble in brawn, so feared the dark that he would not go into an unlighted room. When left by himself at the parting of roads after a night's frolic, he galloped his horse through brush and mire, and it was told that he had more than once reached home without a whole stitch to his back.

But in spite of the powers of darkness, Dick was anxious to take Jane Davis under his protection. The fire and the noisy company kept him from lifting his eyes to the treetops swaying slowly overhead, and the lonesome stars. All through the woods winter-night sounds and sudden twig cracklings could be heard. Dick, however, meant to take Jane Davis home, whether he could persuade one of the Davis boys to go home with him afterward or not.

In those days neighborhoods were intensely local. The people knew what historians have not yet learned about the value of isolated bits of human life. These young folks in the sugar-camp knew nothing of the events and complications of the great world, but they all felt more or less interested in the politics of Jane Davis's entanglements.

Her brother kept dipping a long spoon into the kettle she stirred, and dropping the liquid into a tin cup of cold sugar-water. As long as the hot stuff twined about in ropy arms, it was syrup; but as soon as it settled to the bottom in a clear mass, it was wax, and the change from wax to the grain of sugar is sudden one.

When Eck Davis announced, "It's waxed," the kettle was slung off in haste, and everybody left the tree which had propped his back, or the robe on which he had leaned, and the graining sugar was served in saucers and handed around. It could be eaten with spoons or "worked" into crackling ropes. Davis's boys took off the syrup kettles and covered them up in the bark lodge. They would be emptied into stone jars when the more important business of entertaining company was over. The fire now shone redder. Jane was cutting up pies and cakes in the bark house, all this warm light focused on her lowered eyelids, when more of her suitors arrived.

"I knowed the entire posse would be out," said Philip Welchammer in a laughing undertone to the girls sitting beside him. "Davises never misses invitin' anybody."

"You're too late, Jimmy Thompson," called Jane's elder brother before he noticed the preacher was in the party. "Your sheer's e't." When, however, Dr. Miller from Lancaster also came forward, John stood up stiffly and put on his company grandeur. He held the town-man in some awe, and was bound to be constrained by the preacher.

Jimmy Thompson, having met Jane with awkward heartiness, said he would make the young folks acquainted with Brother Gurley. They all knew Brother Gurley; but Jimmy was a wild young man, and his audacity in "brother"-ing the preacher was more delicious than home-made sugar. He afterward explained that the preacher had been turned onto the old folks for Sunday, and he asked him along to the frolic without suspicionin' he's come, but the preacher, he took a-holt as if that was the understandin'.

Jane met Brother Gurley and Dr. Miller with equal ease. A hush fell upon the company, and they ate and watched her serve the newcomers and appear to balance such formidable individuals in her hands. Affection was in that region the deadliest sin a girl could commit against her own popularity, and Jane's manner was always beautifully simple.

The preacher had a clean-shaven, large face, huge blue eyes, and laughing white teeth, and a sprinkling of fine, indefinitely tinted hair. His figure was vigorous, and well made to bear the hardships of a Methodist circuit-rider. His presence had the grasp of good-fellowship and power, and rather dwarfed Dr. Miller, whom all the girls thought a very pretty man. Dr. Miller wore side-whiskers, and a Lancaster suit of clothes finished by a fine round cloak hooked under his chin. When he took off his hat to bow, two curls fell over his forehead. The woman who would not take Dr. Miller if he wanted her must expect to have the pick of creation, and maybe she would miss is after all. He talked to Jane and ate maple sugar with the greatest of Lancaster ease, telling her he had put up with his cousin in Millersport and borrowed a horse to ride to camp. John Davis at once said the folks at home expected him to put up with them over Sunday, and the other young men resented the doctor's prompt acceptance of Davis's hospitality.

The preacher, holding his saucer of sugar in his left hand, was going around and giving the right hand of fellowship to every young person in camp. This was the proper and customary thing for him to do. A preacher who went into company anywhere on the circuit without shaking hands and pushing and strengthening his acquaintance would be a worse stumbling-block than a backslider given up to superfluous clothing and all kinds of sinful levity, or a new convert with artificials in her bonnet. But there was a tingling quality in Brother Gurley's grasp which stirred the blood; and his heavy voice was as prevailing in its ordinary tones as in the thunders of the pulpit.

"Did you bring your wife with you, Brother Gurley?" simpered Tabitha Gill, a dwarfish, dark old maid, devout in church and esteemed for her ability to make a good prayer.

Mary Thompson whispered behind her back, "Tabitha Gill's always for findin' out whether a preacher's married or not before anybody else does."

"Not this time," replied Brother Gurley, warming Sister Gill's heart with a broad, class-meeting smile. "But I expect to bring her with me when I come around again."

"Do," said Tabitha; "and stop at our house."

"I'm obliged to you, Sister Gill," replied the preacher. "You have a fine community of young people here."

"But they ain't none of 'em converted. There's a good deal of levity in Georger Chapel neighborhood. Now, Jane, now,—Jane Davis,—she's a girl nobody can help likin', but many's the night that she's danced away in sinful amusement. I wish you'd do somethin' for her soul, Brother Gurley."

"I'll try," responded the preacher heartily. He looked with a tender and indulgent eye at Jane, who was dividing her company into two parts, to play one innocent play before the camp broke up.

"Come away from here," whispered Philip Welchammer to the girl beside him, seceding from the preacher's group and adding himself to Jane's. "Tabitha Gill will be haulin' us all up to the mourners' bench pretty soon."

They played "clap-out," the girls sitting in their wraps all ready to depart, and the young men turning up their collars and tying on their comforters while waiting a summons. Jane was leader, and with much tittering and secrecy each young lady imparted to Jane the name of the youth she wished to have sit beside her. Dick Hanks was called first, and he stood looking at the array from which he could take but one choice, his lips dropping apart and his expression like that he used to display under the dunce-cap at Gum College. During this interval of silence the drip of sugar-water into troughs played a musical phrase or two, and the stirring and whinnying of the horses could be heard where they were tied to saplings. No rural Ohioan ever walked a quarter of a mile if he had any kind of beast or conveyance to carry him.

Then Dick of course sat down by the wrong girl, and was clapped out, and Dr. Miller was called. Dr. Miller made a pleasing impression by hesitating all along the line, and when he sat down by Mary Thompson her murmur of assent was a tribute to his sagacity. Cousin Tom Randall was summoned, and sung two or three lines of the "Quaker's courtship" before throwing himself on the mercy of Nora Waddell. He was clapped out, and said he always expected it. West of the Alleghanies was no place for him; they were even goin' to clap him out up at uncle's. Then the preacher came smiling joyfully, and placed himself by Tabitha Gill, where he was tittered over and allowed to remain; and one by one the seats were filled, the less fortunate men making a second trial with more success when their range was narrowed.

Everybody rose up to go home. But a great many "good-nights," and reproaches for social neglect, and promises of future devotion to each other, had first to be exchanged. Then Jimmy Thompson, who had driven in his buggy expressly to take Jane Davis home, and was wondering what he should do with the preacher, saw with astonishment that Brother Gurley had Jane upon his own arm and was tucking her shawl close to her chin. Her black eyes sparkled with a scarlet hood. She turned about with Brother Gurley, facing all the young associates of her life, and said, "We want you all to come to our house after preachin' tomorrow. The presidin' elder will be there."

"I don't care nothin' about the presidin' elder," muttered Jimmy Thompson.

"Goin' to be a weddin', you know," explained John Davis, turning from assisting his brother Eck to empty the syrup kettles, and beaming warmly over such a general occasion. "The folks at meeting will all be invited, but Jane said she wanted to ask he young people separate tonight."

"And next time I come around the circuit," said Brother Gurley, gathering Jane's hand in his before the company, "I'll bring my wife with me."

They walked away from the campfire, Jane turning her head once or twice to call "Good-night, all," as if she still clung to every companionable hand. The party watched her an instant in silence. Perhaps some were fanciful enough to see her walking away from the high estate of a doctor's wife in Lancaster, from the Hanks money, and Jimmy Thompson's thrift, into the constant change and unfailing hardships of Methodist itinerancy. The dancing motion would disappear from her gait, and she who had tittered irreverently at her good mother's labors with backsliders at the mourners' bench would come to feel an interest in such sinners herself.

"Dog'd if I thought Jane Davis would ever marry a preacher!" burst out Jimmy Thompson, in sudden and hot disapproval.

"Don't it beat all!" murmured Tabitha Gill. "And her an unconverted woman in the error of her ways! Jane's too young for a preacher's wife."

"Jane's fooled us all," owned Philip Welchammer heartily. To keep intended nuptials before the appointed time was as much a custom of the country as was prying into and spying out such affairs. Surprising her friends by her wedding was, therefore, adding to Jane's social successes; but only Dr. Miller could perceive her true reason for assembling her suitors at the last moment. While discarding them all, her hospitable nature clung to their friendship; she wished to tell them in a group the change she contemplated, so that no one could accuse her of superior kindness to another. Her very cruelties were intended mercies.

"That's the way the pretty girls go," sighed Cousin Tom Randall, seizing hold of Jane's younger brother: "the preachers get 'em. come on, Eck; I have to be helped home."

"I don't see when he courted her," breathed Dick Hanks, closing his lips after many efforts.

"Preachers is chain-lightnin'," laughed Jimmy Thompson. "He's been around often enough, and always stoppin' there."

"To-morrow after preaching'," said John impressively, as he came forward after hastily covering the jars. "We're goin' to have a turkey-dinner, and we want you all to be sure to come. And next time Brother Gurley and Jane makes the circuit, we'll have the infair at our house, too."

"That's just like Davises," exclaimed one of the dispersing group in the midst of their eager promises; "they wouldn't be satisfied unless they give the weddin' and the infair both, and invited all quarterly meetin' to set down to the table. I thought there was doin's over at their house; but then they're always bakin' and fussin'."

They could all picture a turkey-roast at Davis's: the crisp, brown turkeys rising from their own dripping, squares of pone as yellow as buttercups, and biscuits calculated to melt whitely with honey from glass dishes of sweet-smelling combs. There would be every kind of vegetable grown in the Swamp, and game from the banks of the Feeder and Reservoir, pies and cakes and coffee, and at least eight kinds of preserves. Jane Davis and the preacher would stand up in front of the fireplace, and after the ceremony there would be a constant rattle of jokes from the presiding elder and his assistants. And over the whole house would hang that happy atmosphere which makes one think of corn ripening on a sunny hillside in still September weather. A dozen times the long tables would be replenished and supplied with plates, all the usual features of a turkey-roast at Davis's being exaggerated by the importance of the occasion; and Aunt Davis would now and then forget to urge a guest, while she hurriedly wiped her eyes and replied to some expression of neighborly sympathy, that they had to lose Jane some time, and it was a good thing for a girl to get a religious man. Than about dusk the preachers and their congregation would start again to chapel, and Jane, in Millersport clothes, would shine on the front nseats as a bride, certain of an ovation when the after-meeting handshaking came. It would be a spite if she sat where tallow candles could drip on her from one of the wooden chandeliers, but she would enjoy hearing her bridegroom exhort, and he would feel like exhorting with all his might.

"Well, Doc," said John Davis, turning from the deserted camp and sinking fire to place himself by the bridle of the young man from Lancaster.

"No," answered Dr. Miller, "I'm obliged to you, John; but I'll ride back to Millersport to-night."

"You don't feel put out?" urged John, conscious of a pang because all the good fellows who courted Jane could not become his brothers-in-law.

"No; oh, no," protested Dr. Miller with chagrin. "She'd a right to suit herself. I'll be around some other day."

"We'd take it hard if you didn't," said John.

"But just now," concluded the doctor, "I feel what a body might call—stirred-off."

Dick Hanks was riding up close to Jimmy Thompson, while Jimmy unblanketed his mare and prepared for a deliberate departure.

"John, no," remarked Jimmy,—"he brothered the preacher right up, didn't he? They'll be makin' a class-leader o'John yet, if they can git him to quit racin' horses."

"Which way you goin' home, Jimmy?" inquired Dick Hanks anxiously.

"The long way, round by Georger Chapel, where I can look at the tombstones for company. Want to go along? We can talk over the weddin', and you're only two mile from home at our woods' gate."

"I guess I'll take the short cut through the brush," said Dick.

Jimmy drove through the clearing and fence-gap, where John Davis was waiting to lay up the rails again.

"What's that?" said John, and they both paused to listen.

It was sound of crashing and scampering, of smothered exclamation and the rasping and tearing of garments. Dick Hanks was whipping his steed through the woods, against trees, logs, and branches, as if George's Chapel graveyard, containing the ghastly vault of his father, and George's Chapel preacher, waving Jane Davis in one victorious hand, were both in merciless pursuit of him.

Rose Day

Mary Hartwell Catherwood

"I do believe this is rose day," said Infant, standing on the top step of the veranda in delight.

"I know it's soap-boiling day," asserted her twin sister, who had been baptized Marilla Victoria when she was baptized Infanta Isabella, quite forty years before. These twins entered the world at a period when flowery, daring names were the extreme of fashion, and previous to a rebound to plain and strong Ann, Elizabeth, Mary, Hannah, Jane, and their various combinations. Infant came very near being labeled Lovey Lucilla, and she felt thankful for her escape, and even attached to her diminutive.

Belle would never have suited her (she was not belle), while Infant did not shame her (she was more or less an infant at any age). She was slender, blue-eyed, and smooth-skinned, so smooth that wrinkles could scarcely make their indentation. And it never ceased to be appropriate for her to wear her hair in a braid down her back, tied with ribbons the color of the dress she wore. Infant herself could not separate the gray hair from the blond or all gray. She scampered over a fence and swung in the cherry-trees. Her long tranced girlhood never ended; and the slow life of the farm, simple as grass and wholesome as new milk, kept up the illusion that time was eternity. In their neighborhood these twins had been the Baldwin girls when they first toddled into meeting, when they went off to be educated at an expensive school, when they came back to paint and to play on a grand piano, when their parents died and they took charge of the farm; and the Baldwin girls would probably be their title when they become contemporary with all living grandmothers.

Occasionally Infant received a shock from the growth of young children. It was so astonishing to see a creature who was a baby but a short time ago, shooting aloft, long-armed and long-legged, and announcing itself in the teens. Such phenomena did not astonish Rilla, however. She resented them. Though she had the same fair complexion and comely make as her sister, a deadly drop of acid had been added to her nature. Her shoulders were bent. She loved to hear people talked about, and to lift the corners of her nose with scorn. She felt abused by much that had happened to her on this planet, and yet too insignificant in her own personality to take it out of the human race as she desired to do. The freedom, ease, and scope of mature unmarried womanhood were in no wise appreciated by her. These traits made Rilla an uncomfortable housemate, especially in winter, when the twins were snowed in with their books and trim housekeeping. Still, Infant loved Rilla's sourness along with Rilla. There was strong diversion in being scolded, and she always felt such a delicious warmth around her heart when she made it up with Rilla and gave her a handsome present, or took double turns at the cooking.

Rilla was very parsimonious, and felt bound to distort herself with aged gowns and long-hoarded hats. But Infant felt unhappy in any color except that tint of gray which has the thought of win in it. On this very rose day, though it was early in the morning, she wore a clinging gray challie dress. And a good background it would be for the roses Infant could hang upon it.

Nothing made Rilla lift the corners of her nose higher than Infant's flower days. But as Rilla would be lifting her nose anyhow, and could really scent no harm in these silent festivals, Infant continued to observe them year after year, and to afford her sister that triumphant sense of superiority which we all have upon beholding others' absurdities.

There was crocus day, when the first flowers broke the sod and made heavenly beauty in the spring. Infant decked herself with them, and put them on the dinner-table. More abundantly satisfactory, however, was lilac day. It took a critical eye to discern the exact date. If the lilacs browned about the edges, then, alas! lilac day had slipped past. They were not to be gathered too soon, either, if their full soul of fragrance was to be enjoyed. On lilac day Infant walked under burdens of lavender bloom. The walls, the pictures, breathed lilacs. And at night she went to sleep crushing her face into a nest of bunches, so that she had lilac dreams, and drew the sweetness into herself, like an Eastern woman absorbing roses.

But the best day of all was rose day. Before it arrived she had always ready a posy of poems from Keats, Wordsworth, Jean Ingelow, and Whittier, and read them in the morning while the dew was on the world. The Baldwin girls cultivated a great many roses. Rilla could hardly miss from her rose-water and home-made attar and rose preserves the heaps which Infant cut for her nonsense.

There was not a nicer day in the year than rose day, if Rilla would only abstain from boiling soap on that date. The sisters had inherited seventy-five thousand dollars apiece, but they made their own soap every spring of refuse fats and the lye of wood ashes. It could have been made cold in the cellar, if that way had not been too easy for Rilla. She held it a moveable festival, like rose day, and no one will ever gauge the degree of satisfaction she felt in haling her flower-wreathed sister up to the vile-smelling caldron to keep the stirrer going while she set about other duties. Rilla honored pioneer custom and her grandmother's memory by performing her soap incantations in the oldest, mouldiest, more completely shattered garment she possessed. This was a red wool delaine, so abased from its ruby tone that the drippings of the lye gourd could find little remaining space to burn or spot.

They boiled soap in a huge iron kettle in the chip yard. The blue wood smoke would envelop Rilla and her tarnished tatters as she ladled and tested, until she looked witch-like to passers along the road. her unhappy victim,the slim woman in gray, with a rope of roses would spirally around her from head to foot, a burden of roses on her bosom, and roses studded thickly along the band of her had, sat on the corded nwood as far as Rilla would allow from the soap, alternately inhaling their odor and rejecting the alkali steam. If Infant had to stir the soap, she would have a long-handled stirrer. The hot sun, beating on the chip yard and her huge hat, smote also the roses, and amidst their dying fragrance she had sad thought on the disappointments of life. So there was nothing but the morning of rose day which Rilla did not spoil.

But this anniversary Infant felt a sudden uplifting of courage within herself when her twin announced the soap orgy. "My soap-boiling will not come any more on rose day," she put forth strongly. "And I think I will pay Enos Robb's wife to make up my share of the fat and lye after this, Rilla."

"I would," said Rilla sarcastically, "particularly as Enos Robb and his wife and children don't batten on us already. Give them the piano and the best parlor chairs and the solid coffee service while you are about it."

"Why, Rilla, I didn't propose to give her my share of the soap. But it would be cheaply got rid of that way. Yes," exclaimed Infant, with sudden recklessness, "I would rather buy soap, and pay out money to have this dirty stuff carted off, than ever small it again while I live. Let us make a new rule, and give our fat and ashes to the Robbs. They have farmed for us ever since father died," Infant pleaded, "and whatever you say, Rilla, I know you have the greatest confidence in them."

"The poorhouse wagon is never going to call for me," said Rilla decidedly. "You can go and build a fire under the kettle, while I carry some more water to pour on the ash hopper. That lye is strong enough to bear up a setting of eggs, but we may need some more a little weaker."

"Rilla, I am as firm as the ash hopper itself. You can't shake me any more than you could our brick smoke-house. I won't help make any more soap—especially on rose day," added Infant to herself. "I don't see any sense in it."

"But you can see sense in spoiling dozens of good roses to load yourself up with like a mad Ophelia. You feel above all the associations of wash day, though the Princess Nausicaa didn't."

"Oh, Rilla, I don't feel above anything. I merely feel under that soap kettle, and as if it would crush my soul out, as the shields crushed Tarpeia, if I didn't throw it off."

"Well, I am going to make soap," said Rilla, whitening with intense disapproval of the liberty her twin proposed to grasp. "You are not a minor, and if you were, I'm not your guardian. But if you propose to go to yourself and leave me to myself, we both know what belongs to us, and it is easily done."

This time-worn hint, which in her girlhood used to startle and distress Infant so much, made but the slightest impression on her hearing now, as she leaned over the veranda railing to look at the roses. There were such abundant stacks of them: she might cut and pile them into a pyramid almost as tall as herself. Such smooth, sweet tea-roses, such crimson velvet-petaled Jacqueminots, blush and white so fragrant you would be willing to drown yourself in a sea of their scent; yellow roses piercingly delightful, Prairie Queens creeping all over the front of the house, old hundred-leaved varieties, having always in their depths a reminder of grandmother's chests and long, long past days. There were eighteen distinct families of roses, each family a mighty tribe, marshaled before Infant on lawn and dewy stretch of garden. It was rose day. She would not let herself think of anything else.

Rilla would not come to the embowered dinner-table which Infant prepared so carefully, and to which she called her sister exactly as the clock struck twelve.

Rose day never interfered with Infant's duties. Her conscience acquitted her of shirking. Often in dead winter-time, when the snow piled up, and Enos Robb's family settled down to the enjoyment of colds and rheumatism, she fed all the stock herself.

Rilla turned her back on Infant's several approaches, and dipped lye with a savagely noisy gourd to quench Infant's voice. Slugs and ants in the roses, and even mildew, were no drawback at all to rose day compared to Rilla. Habits of endurance become proof armor to one's sensibilities in the course of life, however; so Infant wandered off and absorbed the beauty of that day almost as completely as if she did so with Rilla's approval. There was tremulous heat over the meadows. The huge and strictly tended garden was a world by itself. Beyond that stretched their orchard, having a run of clear water winding through it, all thickly tufted along the margins with mint.

Infant stepped upon the spongy lichens of the fence and rested her arms on the top rail, while she looked along the narrow country thoroughfare. The sweet green world was dear enough to be pressed in her arms. Mingled mint and rose scents were satisfying. The noble strength of their Norman colts pasturing in the stock meadow was beautiful to the eye. Infant loved to hear the pounding of those tufted feet, and to note the brilliant blackness or gray dappling of the young creatures' coats glistening in the sun. She did not expect anything more unusual to happen on this rose day than her rebellion against Rilla and the splendor of the weather.

But who should come suddenly riding along the road, as if he an appointment with Infant, and meant to keep it the moment she set her foot on the rail, but the Honorable Truman Condit, who many years before rode as instantaneously out of her sight! She knew him in a flash, although his hair showed gray around the ears, and much experience had added unspeakably to his personality. He was on a Condit horse, evidently riding around to look at his old neighborhood. There was a great tribe of the Condits, all well-to-do, high-headed people. The Honorable Truman had been the local bright young man of his generation. He went west, where, Infant heard, he became a Senator and did tremendous things.

She was suddenly conscious that her rose-studded braid was not wound up in a decent lump as she wore it before her class of young ladies in Sunday-school. She felt contemptible and out of her place in the human process, although the Honorable Truman turned his horse straight into the fence corner to shake hands with her.

"Pretty nearly the same Infant Baldwin," he remarked. "But I do see some lines on your face."

"I suppose I've vegetated instead of lived all the time you have been doing so much," said Infant.

"Oh, I haven't been doing so much."

"We heard you had."

"We means Rilla and you. And you didn't marry?"

"No," said Infant, feeling it a stinging indignity that he should mention it, after that courtship so long ago buried. He had married, and raised a family out west. Rilla was probably right when she said one woman was the same as another to a man.

"And how is Rilla? Is she as hard on you as she used to be?"

"Oh, Rilla was never hard on me. She is quite well, thank you. You're coming up to the house to make us a call and take tea, aren't you?"

"I thought I would."

Infant looked anxiously at the westering sun. She hoped Rilla would have the cold soap cut into cakes and boxed, and herself bather, clothed, and in her right mind, before the Honorable Truman Condit rode up to their door.

"I want to have a talk with you first, though," he added. "And my way is to go right to the point. Why did you never marry?"

"Come to that," retorted Infant, a sparkle breaking through her face, "why did you marry?"

"In the first place, because you wouldn't have me, and in the second place, because I found a very good wife where I went. I've been a widower now several years, and the boys are settled. I'm loose from business for almost the first time in my life, and back here to look at the old neighborhood before spending some years abroad. your never marrying has revived certain things. Maybe you've forgotten."

Among her other thoughts, Infant was conscious of recollecting how often she had wished to go abroad if only some happy friend could go along as a cushion betwixt Rilla and her. She unfastened with a furtive hand the rose rope wound about her, but unwilling to let so many precious roses go, gathered it into loops on her arm.

"Did you ever know," pursued the Honorable Truman, "that Rilla told me you were going to marry one of the Pierson boys?"

"No!" Infant cried out so suddenly that the horse started.

"She did," said the Honorable Truman.

"Why," stammered Infant, "how could you believe it?"

"I was a hot-headed boy with more pride than sense. I wouldn't say anything to you about it."

"I remember your quarreling with the Piersons."

"Weren't you engaged to one of them?"

"No; which one?"

"Abner."

"I never was engaged to anybody except you," she retorted, burning hotly in the face, "and I did not admire that experience when you dropped me and went off. And I don't yet, though you do lay the blame on poor Rilla."

Plenty of time had Rilla for all the domestic countermarching she wished to perform before that conference by the fence ended. Unusually stirring were her tactics too, for all the Robbs were haled up from the tenant-house—Mrs. Robb to cook a supper, and the young Robbs not actually farming to run on errands.

It was six o'clock when Enos came riding his plough-horses to the great barn. He had turned off early on purpose to intercept Miss Infant and find out what changes were to be made. Infant hastened up the orchard, while the Honorable Truman hastened to the same destination by the road. She saw him leading his horse up the avenue, and felt impatient at Enos Robb's interruption.

"Sudden doin's up to the house," said Enos, wiping his forehead with the back of his hand. "'Pears like Miss Rill's made up her mind about Brother Sanderson at last."

"Is Brother Sanderson at the house?" inquired Infant.

"He is, for a fact, and the license and the preacher with him. Now what I want to know, and what I ought to been consulted, Miss Infant, seeing how long I been here, is this—what's you and me going to do afterward? Is it an interference?"

"Enos," said Infant, with a gasp, "this is almost as sudden to me as it is to you. But considering Rilla's firm character, do you think she would let any new person interfere with her established plans?"

"No, I don't," replied Enos, grinning.

Rilla was standing before the dresser in her room arrayed in her stiffest silk. She looked with composure upon her twin, who shut the bedroom door, and hurried up to embrace her.

"It was the best boiling of soap I ever had," said Rilla, warding the fading roses away from her silk.

"Rilla dear, you might have told me what you meant to do this evening. But I am so glad! I couldn't bear the thoughts of leaving you before, but now I can."

"I saw Truman Condit come into the yard with you," said Rilla. "He's grown fat. It must have agreed with him to go west."

"This has been a great rose day," said her twin, undoing all traces of the day's festival, and piling them carefully in a wastebasket where they could make no litter. "Won't you let me kiss you, Rilla?"

The acquiescent nip which Rilla gave Infant took up a world of forgiveness which Rilla never felt.

"And do you think dear," Infant ventured, "we'll ever wish we hadn't? We've lived so long with each other. Truman Condit and Brother Sanderson are really strangers to our ways."

"I think," replied Rilla, with decision, "that Brother Sanderson will never have a rose day while he lives on my farm; and when I say it is soap-boiling day it will be soap-boiling day, and Brother Sanderson will stir the soap."

Bibliography

Catherwood, Mary Hartwell. *A Woman in Armor*. New York: Carleton, 1895.

——. "Rose Day." *Harper's Bazar*, n.d. Rpt in *Queen of the Swamp and Other Plain Americans*. Boston: Houghton Mifflin, 1899. 55-76.

——. "Stirring Off." *Lippincott's Magazine* March 1883: 303-08. Rpt. in *Queen of the Swamp and Other Plain Americans*. Boston: Houghton Mifflin, 1899. 29-254.

James, Edward T., ed. *Notable American Women*. Boston: Belknap Press of Harvard University Press, 1971.

Kimbel, Bobbly Ellen, ed. *American Short Story Writers, 1880-1910*. Detroit: Edward, 1989.

"Mary Hartwell Catherwood." *Bibliography of American Literature*. Ed. Jacob Blanck. New Haven: Yale University Press, 1957: 107-16.

Pattee, Fred Lewis. *A History of American Literature Since 1870*. New York: Century, 1917.

Seaton, Beverly. "Mary Hartwell Catherwood." *American Women Writers 1*. Ed. Lina Mainero. New York: Ungar, 1979. 321-23.

Suckow, Ruth. "Middle Western Literature." *English Journal* 21.3 (March 1932): 175-81.

Constance Fenimore Woolson

1840-1894

Bred in New England, the grandniece of the romantic novelist James Fenimore Cooper, Constance Fenimore Woolson became the Western Reserve's most prominent nineteenth-century regional author. At the start of Woolson's life, a scarlet fever epidemic killed three of her siblings in Claremont, New Hampshire; her decimated family moved to Cleveland where both of her elder sisters later died, leaving Constance the eldest living child. Her family remained in Ohio's Western Reserve until her father died in 1869. Then Constance and her mother moved to New York City and later into the warmer South, living temporarily in such places as Asheville, North Carolina, and St. Augustine, Florida. After her invalided mother's death in 1879, Constance and her widowed sister, Clara Benedict, sailed for Europe, never to return to America.

Despite her peripatetic wanderings, or perhaps because of them, Constance Fenimore Woolson, was one of the nineteenth century's most interesting writers of regionalism. The perpetual outside observer, she wrote widely about American's regions, temperament, and character. Hers was a long and fruitful literary career that led a nineteenth-century Boston *Globe* critic to offer her the accolade of being America's "novelist laureate," a judgment seconded by such modern critics as Lyon Richardson.

She learned how to write during her early decades in Ohio. As the eldest daughter of an upper-class Cleveland industrialist, she enjoyed family vacations in such rustic places as the Great Lakes and the Tuscarawas Valley. Also, Woolson read widely, expressing indebtedness to George Sand, Charles Dickens, and George Eliot, and was well educated. She studied at Miss Hayden's School for Girls, the Cleveland Female Seminary, and graduated at the top of her class in 1858 from Madame Chegaray's school in New York City. She began her literary career by drawing upon the familiar, including her treasured Cleveland contacts with relatives like Samuel Mather and friends like her early teacher Lucinda Guilford. Woolson especially cherished the beloved setting of the Great Lakes and Ohio's interior farmlands where she used to holiday. Her life ended tragically in Europe as a sad expatriate who complained of her rootlessness and never finding a home.

Woolson was a prodigious writer who often used known locales for fiction. She commented in a letter to a relative that her writing consisted of each page being literally "thought about for years." Her first novel, *The Old Stone Church* (1872), was a children's story set in Cleveland, and five other American novels were published later: *Anne* (1882), *For the Major* (1883), *East Angels* (1886), *Jupiter Lights* (1889), and *Horace Chase* (1894). Her final stories were set in Europe, and all of Woolson's fiction reveals her continual interest in observing environment.

During the years between 1869 and 1875, Constance Fenimore Woolson's fiction drew upon Ohio's Lake Country and Tuscarawas County. Her local color sketches and stories were published in such established eastern magazines as *Harper's New Monthly Magazine, Atlantic Monthly, Scribner's,* and *Century.* In 1875 they were collected in *Castle Nowhere: Lake-Country Sketches,* which has been compared favorably to Sarah Orne Jewett's 1877 collection, *Deephaven.* Both mature writers employ realism and psychological analysis to alter the moralistic tradition of nineteenth-century women's writing. Among the influential New England and middle-western regionalists who Woolson enjoyed were such diverse practitioners as Harriet Beecher Stowe, Bret Harte, Edward Eggleston, Helen Hunt Jackson, and William Dean Howells.

Woolson's highly descriptive sketches study the differences between the surface of settlers' lives and their undercurrents; usually an objective narrator is indirectly characterized, too, but conveys the author's sympathy for social outcasts. Her regional sketches appeared first, among them "The Happy Valley," which chronicles a family visit to Zoar. Published in *Harper's New Monthly Magazine* in July 1870, this sketch provides a setting that later evolved into Woolson's mature 1873 regional stories "Solomon" and "Wilhelmina," which appeared in the *Atlantic Monthly,* respectively in October 1873 and January 1874. "The Happy Valley" is a personal essay, a descriptive, autobiographical sketch about the Tuscarawas Valley and was followed by two other 1873 regional essays; June saw publication of "The Wine Islands of Lake Erie" in *Harper's,* and in November "Lakeshore Relics" appeared in *Lippincott's Magazine.*

From "The Happy Valley" sketch about the Tuscarawas Valley, two stories are derived that reveal Woolson's interest in the community of Zoarite separatists who named themselves after the town to which Lot fled after the Biblical destruction of Sodom and Gomorrah. Ohio's Zoarites migrated from Germany in 1817 to find religious freedom in America, and their utopian commune endured for more than seven decades. Their social experiment failed in 1898, officially disbanding four years after Woolson died, perhaps a disintegration anticipated by the Civil War defections that Woolson documents.

"The Happy Valley" is particularly interesting because it shows readers how Woolson's narrative technique grows from autobiographical, first-person commentary into a clever fictional point of view. In "The Happy Valley," Woolson describes how she, her sister Sadie, and father take a two-day train "pilgrimage" to the "region of the great barns." The sketch praises the innocent Zoarite immigrants, while the narrator ponders over how this static "New Eden" may deal with such threats as social change and passion.

Three years later "Solomon" reintroduces the fictionalized Zoar setting. The story's action is conveyed by Cleveland cousins Dora and Erminia who visit Zoar to "play" at being "shepherdesses" (239). There they twice meet Solomon, a native of Painesville in Lake County, who has fallen in love with a beautiful Zoarite separatist named Dorcas. He is an untrained artist who must suppress his talent in a pragmatic religious community. Solomon labors as a coal-miner by day; by night he is a clandestine primitive artist who sketches Dorcas. The visiting shepherdesses admire his work but remain voyeurs. The falsity of their pastoral vision is inadequately masked by their tutorial in "perspective," and the artist must die without a nurturing environment.

"The Happy Valley" sketch also introduces relevant motifs to Woolson's second Tuscarawas Valley local color story, "Wilhelmina." For example, there is an "ancient hostler" named Jacob in "The Happy Valley"; he is converted into a minor character in the story. Also the theme of a frustrated romance grows from the courtship of actual Zoarites Salome and Louis who in the story become Wilhelmina and Gustav. Another interesting relationship between the sketch and story is found in the expanded role of the two narrators. In "The Happy Valley" the female narrator, presumably Woolson, asks a Zoarite girl if she "would not like to go with them" to Cleveland. The girl smiles and replies: "'Oh no! I'se better here.'" In "Wilhelmina," the Zoar maiden's frustrated love is subtly paralleled by the narrator's unusual interest and thwarted affection for the innocent Zoarite maid who not only refuses to move to the city but prefers death to life without Gustav. These parallel stories of thwarted affection, miscommunication, and human isolation reveal this story's keen, psychological artistry.

"Wilhelmina" has a simple plot: girl loves and loses boy. Similar in theme to "Solomon's" concern with social misfits, "Wilhelmina" shows how a conformist community can destroy those who are different, even if superior. The visiting narrator watches the Civil War soldier, Gustav, rejoin his fiance, Wilhelmina, at the close of the war. But the outside world has introduced him to other women and a desire to escape the Separatists. Gustav breaks with Wilhelmina, refuses to sign the articles of the Community, and departs. She is hastily married off to a stolid baker and promptly withers away.

These two stories both view rural village life from the perspective of urban outsiders. Woolson's Cleveland-based narrators, Dora, Erminia, and the nameless chronicler of Wilhelmina's decline, may question Zoar's picturesque but sterile culture, but each woman is an unself-conscious and condescending intruder. This dual focus was a precocious development in Woolson's local color style and renders them a unique achievement.

Deaths in these local color stories are viewed by Zoarites as journeys to the "next country," an appropriate metaphor for a regional writer who spent her life travelling and recording the cultures of other countries until her Italian suicide. The surface of her American stories incarnates a memorial to a vanishing kind of American life (Van Bergen 87), the utopian idealists of the nineteenth century. Constance Fenimore Woolson's regional stories and European fiction were admired by her friend Henry James and were compared to the work of Alice James and Edith Wharton. Other old friends, like William Dean Howells, ceased praising Woolson when she turned away from regional American fiction.

Woolson's contribution was diverse and uneven, but as a writer fascinated by human behavior, she contributed minute recordings of the psychology behind a facade. Woolson was committed to portraying what she once called the "not so beautiful truth." Her short stories delve deeply into minds distorted by frustration. In Lyon Richardson's terms, Woolson had "extraordinary power to fuse period, place and character"; he sees her as "one of the most authentic and perhaps the most versatile woman writer of regional literature" (18). Many critics concur; John Dwight Kern praises Woolson's ability to fix scenes in the reader's mind as a background for events.

In retrospect, Woolson's stories leave behind early American regional nostalgia and forge a new style by viewing subjects with an ironic eye so that the human condition is shown as transcending conventional social roles. She is a transitional figure, as Cheryl B. Torsney notes, between early regionalists and realistic, turn-of-the-century "New Woman" writers.

Woolson's themes include small-town life and the effects of human isolation which are set against northeastern and central Ohio regional landscapes. She exists as a leader among the realists of her day (Boren 456) in local color realism, disparate in subject matter, but unique for her keen presentation of human psychology.

As she explained her aims in a notebook:

The plot must be a riddle, so as to excite curiosity. My idea is that there should be a riddle and exciting adventure. And *growth* of at least several of the characters. . . . An intense realism of description and dramatic action. *And there shall be nobility.*

Solomon

Constance Fenimore Woolson

Midway in the eastern part of Ohio lies the coal country; round-topped hills there begin to show themselves in the level plain, trending back from Lake Erie; afterwards rising higher and higher, they stretch away into Pennsylvania and are dignified by the name of Alleghany Mountains. But no names have they in their Ohio birthplace, and little do the people care for them, save as storehouses for fuel. The roads lie along the slow-moving streams, and the farmers ride slowly over them in their broad-wheeled wagons, now and then passing dark holes in the bank from whence come little carts into the sunshine, and men, like silhouettes, walking behind them, with glow-worm lamps fastened in their hat-bands. Neither farmers nor miners glance up towards the hill-tops; no doubt they consider them useless mounds, and, were it not for the coal, they would envy their neighbors of the grain-country, whose broad, level fields stretch unbroken through Central Ohio's; as, however, the canal-boats go away full, and long lines of coal-cars go away full, and every man's coal-shed is full, and money comes back from the great iron-mills of Pittsburgh, Cincinnati and Cleveland, the coal country, though unknown in a picturesque point of view, continues to grow rich and prosperous.

Yet picturesque it is, and no part more so than the valley where stands the village of the quaint German Community on the banks of the slow-moving Tuscarawas River. One October day we left the lake behind us and journeyed inland, following the water-courses and looking forward for the first glimpse of rising ground; blue are the waters of Erie on a summer day, red and golden are its autumn sunsets, but so level, so deadly level are its shores that, at times, there comes a longing for the fight of distant hills. Hence our journey. Night found us still in the "Western Reserve": Ohio has some queer names of her own for portions of her territory, the "Fire Lands," the "Donation Grant," the "Salt Section," the "Refugee's Tract," and the "Western Reserve" are names well known, although not found on the maps. Two days more and we come into the coal country; near by were the "Moravian Lands," and at the end of the last day's ride we crossed a yellow bridge over a stream called the "One-Leg Creek."

"I have tried in vain to discover the origin of this name," I said, as we leaned out of the carriage to watch the red leaves float down the slow tide.

"Create one, then. A one-legged soldier, a farmer's pretty daughter, an elopement in a flat-bottomed boat, and a home upon this stream which yields its stores of catfish for their support," suggested Erminia.

"The original legend would be better than that if we could only find it, for real life is always better than fiction," I answered.

"In real life we are all masked; but in fiction the author shows the faces as they are, Dora."

"I do not believe we are all masked, Erminia. I can read my friends like a printed page."

"O, the wonderful faith of youth!" said Erminia, retiring upon her seniority.

Presently the little church on the hill came into view through a vista in the trees. We passed the mill and its flowing race, the blacksmith's shop, the great grass meadow, and drew up in front of the quaint hotel where the trustees allowed the world's people, if uninquisitive and decorous, to remain in the Community for short periods of time, on the payment of three dollars per week for each person. This village was our favorite retreat, our little hiding-place in the hill-country; at that time it was almost as isolated as a solitary island, for the Community owned thousands of outlying acres and held no intercourse with the surrounding townships. Content with their own, unmindful of the rest of the world, these Germans grew steadily richer and richer, solving quietly the problem of co-operative labor, while the French and Americans worked at it in vain with newspapers, orators, and even cannon to aid them. The members of the Community were no ascetic anchorites; each tiled roof covered a home with a thrifty mother and train of grave little children, the girls in shortwaisted gowns, kerchiefs, and frilled caps and the boys in tailed coats, long-flapped vests, and trousers, as soon as they were able to totter. We liked them all, we liked the life; we liked the mountain-high beds, the coarse, snowy linen, and the remarkable counterpanes; we liked the cream-stewed chicken, the käse-lab, the fresh butter, but, best of all, the hot bretzels for breakfast. And let not the hasty city imagination turn to the hard, salty, sawdust cake in the shape of broken-down figure eight which is served with lager-beer in saloons and gardens. The Community bretzel was a delicate flaky white in the inside, shading away into a golden-brown crust of crisp involutions, light as a feather, and flanked by little pats of fresh, unsalted butter and a deep-blue cup wherein the coffee was hot, the cream yellow, and the sugar broken lumps from the old-fashioned loaf, now alas! obsolete.

We stayed among the simple people and played at shepherdesses and pastorellas; we adopted the hours of the birds, we went to church on Sunday and sang German chorals as old as Luther. We even played at work to the extent of helping gather apples, eating the best, and riding home on top of the loaded four-horse wains. But one day we heard of a new diversion, a sulphur-spring over the hills about two miles from the hotel on land belonging to the Community; and obeying the fascination which earth's native medicines exercise over all earth's children, we immediately started in search of the nauseous spring. The road wound over the hill, past one of the apple orchards, where the girls were gathering the red fruit, and then down a little declivity where the track branched off to the Community coal-mine; then a solitary stretch through the thick woods, a long hill was a curve, and at the foot a little dell with a patch of meadow, a brook, and a log-house with overhanging roof, a forlorn house unpainted and desolate. There was not even the blue door which enlivened many of the Community dwellings. "This looks like the huts of the Black Forest," said Erminia. "Who would have supposed that we should find such an antique in Ohio!"

"I am confident it was built by the M.B.'s," I replied. "They tramped, you know, extensively through the State, burying axes and leaving every now and then a mastodon behind them."

"Well, if the Mound-Builders selected this site they showed good taste," said Erminia, refusing, in her afternoon indolence, the argumentum nonsensicum with which we were accustomed to enliven our conversation. It was, indeed, a lovely spot—the little meadow, smooth and bright as green velvet, the brook shattering over the pebbles, and the hills, gay in red and yellow foliage, rising abruptly on all sides. After some labor we swung open the great gate and entered the yard, crossed the brook on a mossy plank, and followed the path through the grass toward the lonely house. An old shepherd-dog lay at the door of a dilapidated shed like a block-house which had once been a stable; he did not bark, but, rising slowly, came along beside us—a large, gaunt animal that looked at us with such melancholy eyes that Erminia stooped to pat him. Erminia had a weakness for dogs; she herself owned a wild beast of the dog kind that went by the name of the "Emperor Trajan," and, accompanied by this dignitary, she was accustomed to stroll up the avenues of C——, lost in maiden meditations.

We drew near the house and stepped up on the sunken piazza, but no signs of life appeared. The little loophole windows were pasted over with paper, and the plank door had no latch or handle. I knocked, but no one came. "Apparently it is a haunted house, and that dog is the spectre," I said, stepping back.

"Knock three times," suggested Erminia; "that is what they always do in ghost-stories."

"Try it yourself. My knuckles are not cast-iron."

Erminia picked up a stone and began tapping on the door. "Open sesame," she said, and it opened.

Instantly the dog slunk away to his block-house and a woman confronted us, her dull face lighting up as her eyes ran rapidly over our attire from head to foot. "Is there a sulphur spring here?" I asked. "We would like to try the water."

"Yes, it's here fast enough in the back hall. Come in, ladies; I'm right proud to see you. From the city, I suppose?"

"From C——," I answered; "we are spending a few days in the Community."

Our hostess led the way through the little hall, and throwing open a back door pulled up a trap in the floor, and there we saw the spring—a shallow well set in stones, with a jar of butter cooling in its white water. She brought a cup, and we drank. "Delicious," said Erminia. "The true, spoiled-egg flavor! Four cups is the minimum allowance, Dora."

"I reckon it's good for the insides," said the woman, standing with arms akimbo and staring at us. She was a singular creature, with large black eyes, Roman nose, and a mass of black hair tightly knotted on the top of her head, but thin, pinched, and gaunt; her yellow forehead was wrinkled with a fixed frown, and her thin lips drawn down in permanent discontent. Her dress was a shapeless linsey-woolsey gown, and homemade list slippers covered her long, lank feet. "Be that the fashion?" she asked, pointing to her short, closely-fitting walking-dress.

"Yes," I answered; "do you like it?"

"Well, it does for you, sis, because you're so little and peaked-like, but it wouldn't do for me. The other lady, now, don't wear nothing like that; is she even with the style, too?"

"There is such a thing as being above the style, madam," replied Erminia, bending to dip up glass number two.

"Our figgers is a good deal alike," pursued the woman; "I reckon that fashion 'ud suit me best."

Willowy Erminia glanced at the stick-like hostess. "You do me honor," she said suavely. "I shall consider myself fortunate, madam, if you will allow me to send you patterns from C——. What are we if not well dressed?"

"You have a fine dog," I began hastily, fearing lest the great, black eyes should penetrate the sarcasm; "what is his name?"

"A stupid beast! He's none of mine; belongs to my man."

"Your husband?"

"Yes, my man. He works in the coal-mine over the hill."

"You have no children?"

"Not a brat. Glad of it, too."

"You must be lonely," I said, glancing around the desolate house. To my surprise, suddenly the woman burst into a flood of tears, and sinking down on the floor she rocked from side to side, sobbing, and covering her face with her bony hands.

"What can be the matter with her?" I said in alarm, and, in my agitation, I dipped up some sulphur-water and held it to her lips.

"Take away the smelling stuff,—I hate it!" she cried, pushing the cup angrily from her.

Ermine looked on in silence for a moment or two, then she took off her neck-tie, a bright-colored Roman scarf, and threw it across the trap into the woman's lap. "Do me a favor to accept that trifle, madam," she said, in her soft voice.

The woman's sobs, ceased as she saw the ribbon; she fingered it with one hand in silent admiration, wiped her wet face with the skirt of her gown, and then suddenly disappeared into an adjoining room, closing the door behind her.

"Do you think she is crazy?" I whispered.

"O, no; merely pensive."

"Nonsense, Ermine! But why did you give her that ribbon?"

To develop her aesthetic taste," replied my cousin, finishing her last glass, and beginning to draw on her delicate gloves.

Immediately I began gulping down my neglected dose; but so vile was the odor that some time was required for the operation, and in the midst of my struggles our hostess reappeared. She had thrown on an old dress of plaid delaine, a faded red ribbon was tied over her head, and around her sinewed throat reposed the Roman scarf pinned with a glass brooch.

"Really, madam, you honor us," said Ermine gravely.

"Thankee, marm. It's so long since I've had on anything but that old bag, and so long since I've seen anything but them Dutch girls over to the Community, with their wooden shapes and wooden shoes, that it sorter come over me all't oncet what a miserable life I've had. You see, I ain't what I looked like; now I've dressed up a bit I feel more like telling you that I come from good Ohio stock, without a drop of Dutch blood. My father, he kep' a store in Sandy, and I had everything I wanted until I must needs get crazy over painting Sol at the Community. Father, he wouldn't hear to it, and so I ran away; Sol, he turned out for nothing to work, and so here I am, yer see, in spite of all his pictures making me out the Queen of Sheby."

"Is your husband an artist?" I asked.

"No, miss, he's a coal-miner, he is. But he used to like to paint me all sorts of ways. Wait, I'll show yer." Going up the rough stairs that led into the attic, the woman came back after a moment with a number of sheets of drawing-paper which she hung up along the walls with pins for our inspection. They were all portraits of the same face, with brick-red cheeks, enormous black eyes, and a profusion of shining black hair hanging down over plump white shoulders; the costumes were various, but the faces were the same. I gazed in silence, seeing to likeness to anything earthly. Erminia took out her glasses and scanned the pictures slowly.

"Yourself, madam, I perceive," she said, much to my surprise.

"Yes, 'm, that's me," replied our hostess, complacently. "I never was like those yellow-haired girls over to the Community. Sol allers said my face was real rental ."

"Rental?" I repeated, inquiringly.

"Oriental, of course," said Ermine. Mr.—Mr. Solomon is quite right. May I ask the names of these characters, Madam?"

"Queen of Sheby, Judy, Ruth, Esthy, Po-co-hon-tus, Goddessaliberty, Sunset, and eight Octobers, them with the grapes. Sunset's the one with the red paint behind it like clouds."

"Truly, a remarkable collection," said Ermine. "Does Mr. Solomon devote much time to his art?

"No, not now. He couldn't make a cent out of it, so he's took to digging coal. He painted all them when we was first married, and he went a journey all the way to Cincinnati to sell 'em. First, he was going to buy me a silk dress and some ear-rings, and after that, a farm. But pretty soon, home he come on a canal-boat, without a shilling, and a bringing all the pictures back with him! Well, then he tried most everything, but he never could keep to any one trade, for he'd just as lief quit work in the middle of the forenoon and go to painting; no boss'll stand that, you know. We kep' a going down, and I had to see the few things my father give me when he found I was married whether or no,—my chany, my feather-beds, and my nice clothes, piece by piece. I held on to the big looking-glass for four years, but at last it had to go, and I just gave up and put on a linsey-woolsey gown. When a girl's spirit's once broke, she don't care for nothing, you know; so when the Community offered to take Sol back as coal-digger, I just said, 'Go,' and we come." Here she tried to smear the tears away with her bony hands, and gave a low groan.

"Groaning probably relieves you," observed Ermine.

"Yes'm. It's kinder company like, when I'm all alone. But you see it's hard on the prettiest girl in Sandy to have to live in this lone lorn place. Why, ladies, you mightn't believe it, but I had open-work stock-ings, and feathers in my winter bunnets before I was marked!" And the tears broke forth afresh.

"Accept my handkerchief," said Ermine; "it will serve your purpose better than fingers."

The woman took the dainty cambric and surveyed it curiously, held at arm's length. "reg'lar thistle-down, now, ain't it?" she said; and smells like a locust-tree blossom."

"Mr. Solomon, then, belonged to the Community?" I asked, trying to gather up the threads of the story.

"No, he didn't either; he's no Dutchman. I reckon, he's a Lake County man, born near Painesville, he is."

"I thought you spoke as though he had been in the Community."

"So he had; he didn't belong, but he worked for 'em since he was a boy, did middling well, in spite of the painting, until one day, when he come over to Sandy on a load of wood and seen me standing at the door. That was the end of him," continued the woman, with an air of girlish pride; "he couldn't work no more for thinking of me."

"*Où la vanité va-t-elle se nicher?*" murmured Ermine, rising. "Come, Dora; it is time to return."

As I hastily finished my last cup of sulphur-water, our hostess fol-lowed Ermine toward the door. "Will you have your handkercher back, marm?" she said, holding it out reluctantly.

"It was a free gift, madam," replied my cousin; "I wish you a good afternoon."

"Say, will yer be coming again tomorrow?" asked the woman as I took my departure.

"Very likely; good by."

The door closed, and then, but not till then, the melancholy dog joined us and stalked behind until we had crossed the meadow and reached the gate. We passed out and turned up the hill, but looking back we saw the outline of the woman's head at the upper window, and the dog's head at the bars, both watching us out of sight.

In the evening there came a cold wind down from the north, and the parlor, with its primitive ventilators, square openings in the side of the house, grew chilly. So a great fire of soft coal was built in the broad Franklin stove, and before its blaze we made good cheer, nor needed the one candle which flickered on the table behind us. Cider fresh from the mill, carded gingerbread, and new cheese crowned the scene, and during the evening came a band of singers, the young people of the Community, and sang for us the song of the Lorelei, accompanied by home-made vio-lins and flageolets. At length we were left alone, the candle had burned out, the house door was barred, and the peaceful Community was asleep; still we two sat together with our feet upon the hearth, looking down into the glowing coals.

> "Ich weisz nicht was soll es bedeuten
> Dasz ich so traurig bin,"

I said, repeating the opening lines of the Lorelei; "I feel absolutely blue tonight."

"The memory of the sulphur-woman," suggested Ermine.

"Sulphur-woman! What a name!"

"Entirely appropriate, in my opinion."

"Poor thing! How she longed with a great longing for the finery of her youth in Sandy."

"I suppose from those barbarous pictures that she was originally in the flesh," mused Ermine; "at present she is but a bony outline."

"Such as she is, however, she has had her romance," I answered. "She is quite sure that there was one to love her; then let come what may, she has had her day."

"Misquoting Tennyson on such a subject!" said Ermine, with disdain.

"A man's a man for all that, and a woman's a woman too," I retorted. "You are blind, cousin, blinded with pride. That woman has had her tragedy, as real and bitter as any that can come to us."

"What have you to say for the poor man, then?" exclaimed Ermine, rousing to the contest. "If there is a tragedy at the sulphur-house, it belongs to the sulphur-man, not to the sulphur-woman."

"He is not a sulphur-man, he is a coal-man; keep to your bearings, Ermine."

"I tell you," pursued my cousin earnestly, "that I pitied that unknown man with inward tears all the while I sat by the trap-door. Depend upon it, he had his dream, his ideal; and this country girl with her great eyes and wealth of her hair represented the beautiful to his hungry soul. He gave his whole life and hope into her hands, and woke to find his goddess a common wooden image."

"Waste sympathy upon a coal-miner!" I said, imitating my cousin's former tone.

"If any one is blind, it is you," she answered, with gleaming eyes. "That man's whole history stood revealed in the selfish complainings of that creature. He had been in the Community from boyhood, therefore of course he had no chance to learn life, to see its art-treasures. He has been shipwrecked, poor soul, hopelessly ship-wrecked."

"She too, Ermine."

"She!"

"Yes. If he loved pictures, she loved her chany and her feather-beds, not to speak of the big looking-glass. No doubt she had other lovers, and might have lived in a red brick farm-house with ten unopened front windows and blistered front door. The wives of men of genius are always to be pitied; they do not soar into the crowd of feminine admirers who circle round the husband, and they are therefore called 'grubs,' 'worms of the earth,' 'drudges,' and other sweet titles."

"Nonsense," said Ermine, tumbling the arched coals into chaos with the poker; "it's after midnight, let us go up stairs." I knew very well that my beautiful cousin enjoyed the society of several poets, painters, musicians, and others of that ilk, without concerning herself about their stay-at-home wives.

The next day the winds were out in battle array, howling over the Strasburg hills, raging up and down the river, and whirling the colored leaves wildly along the lovely road to the One-Leg Creek. Evidently there could be no rambling in the painted woods that day, so we went over to old Fritz's shop, played on his home-made piano, inspected the woolly horse who turned his crank patiently in an underground den, and set in motion all the curious little images which the carpenter's deft fingers had wrought. Fritz belonged to the Community, and knew nothing of the outside world; he had a taste for mechanism, which showed itself in many labor-saving devices, and with it all he was the roundest, kindest little man, with bright eyes like a canary-bird.

"Do you know Solomon, the coal-miner?" asked Ermine, in her correct, well-learned German.

"Sol Bangs? Yes, I know him," replied Fritz, in his Würtemberg dialect.

"What kind of man is he?"

"Good for nothing," replied Fritz placidly.

"Why?"

"Wrong here," tapping his forehead.

"Do you know his wife?" I asked.

"Yes."

"What kind of a woman is she?"

"Too much tongue. Women must not talk much."

"Old Fritz touched us both there," I said, as we ran back laughing to the hotel through the blustering wind. "In his opinion, I suppose, we have the popular verdict of the township upon our two proteges, the sulphur woman and her husband."

The next day opened calm, hazy, and warm, the perfection of Indian summer; the breezy hill was outlined in purple, and the trees glowed in rich colors. In the afternoon we started for the sulphur-spring without shawls or wraps, for the heat was almost oppressive; we loitered on the way through the still woods, gathering the tinted leaves, and wondering why no poet has yet arisen to celebrate in fit words the glories of the American autumn. At last we reached the turn whence the lonely house came into view, and at the bars we saw the dog awaiting us.

"Evidently the sulphur-woman does not like that melancholy animal," I said, as we applied our united strength to the gate.

"Did you ever know a woman of limited mind who liked a large dog?" replied Ermine. "Occasionally such a woman will fancy a small cur; but to appreciate a large, noble dog requires a large, noble mind."

"Nonsense with your dogs and minds," I said, laughing. "Wonderful! There is a curtain."

It was true. The paper had been removed from one of the windows, and in its place hung some white drapery, probably part of a sheet rigged as a curtain.

Before we reached the piazza the door opened, and our hostess appeared. "Glad to see yer, ladies," she said. "Walk right in this way to the keeping-room."

The dog went away to his block-house, and we followed the woman into a room on the right of the hall; there were three rooms, beside the attic above. An Old-World German stove of brick-work occupied a large portion of the space, and over it hung a few tins, and a clock whose pendulum swung outside; a table, a settle, and some stools completed the furniture; but on the plastered walls were two rude brackets, one holding a cup and saucer of figured china, and the other surmounted by a large bunch of autumn leaves, so beautiful in themselves and so exquisitely arranged that we crossed the room to admire them.

"Sol fixed 'em, he did," said the sulphur-woman; "he seen me setting things to rights, and he would do it. I told him they was trash, but he made me promise to leave 'em alone in case you should call again."

"Madam Bangs, they would adorn a palace," said Ermine severely.

"The cup is pretty too," I observed, seeing the woman's eyes turn that way.

"It's the last of my chany," she answered, with pathos in her voice,—"the very last piece."

As we took our places on the settle we noticed the brave attire of our hostess. The delaine was there; but how altered! Flounces it had, skimped, but still flounces, and at the top was a collar of crochet cotton reaching nearly to the shoulders; the hair too was braided in imitation of Ermine's sunny coronet, and the Roman scarf did duty as a belt around the large flat waist.

"You see she tries to improve," I whispered, as Mrs. Bangs went into the hall to get some sulphur-water for us.

"Vanity," answered Ermine.

We drank our dose slowly, and our hostess talked on and on. Even I, her champion, began to weary of her complainings. "How dark it is!" said Ermine at last, rising and drawing aside the curtain. "See, Dora, a storm is close upon us."

We hurried to the door, but one look at the black cloud was enough to convince us that we could not reach the Community hotel before it would break, and somewhat drearily we returned to the keeping-room, which grew darker and darker, until our hostess was obliged to light a candle. "Reckon you'll have to stay all night; I'd like to have you, ladies," she said. The Community ain't got nothing covered to send after you, except the old king's coach, and I misdoubt they won't let that out in such a storm, steps and all. When it beginning to rain in this valley, it do rain, I can tell you; and from the way it's begun, 't won't stop 'fore morning. You just let me send the Roarer over to the mine, he'll tell Sol; Sol can tell the Community folks, so they'll know where you be."

I looked somewhat aghast at this proposal, but Ermine listened to the rain upon the roof a moment, and then quietly accepted; she remembered the long hills of tenacious red clay, and her kid boots were dear to her."

"The Roarer, I presume, is some faithful kobold who bears your message to and from the mine," she said, making herself as comfortable as the wooden settle would allow.

The sulphur-woman stared. "Roarer's Sol's old dog," she answered, opening toe door; "perhaps one of you will write a bit of a note for him to carry in his basket.—Roarer, Roarer!"

The melancholy dog came slowly in, and stood still while she tied a small covered basket around his neck.

Ermine took a leaf form her tablets and wrote a line or two with the gold pencil attached to her watch-chain.

"Well now, you do have everything handy, I do declare," said the woman admiringly.

I glanced at the paper.

"Mr. Solomon Bangs:—My cousin Theodora Wentworth and myself have accepted the hospitality of your house for the night. Will you be so good as to send tidings of our safety to the Community, and oblige, "Erminia Stuart."

The Roarer started obediently out into the rain-storm with his little basket; he did not run, but walked slowly, as if the storm was nothing compared to his settled melancholy.

"What a note to send to a coalminer!" I said, during a momentary absence of our hostess.

"Never fear; it will be appreciated," replied Ermine.

"What is this king's carriage of which you spoke?" I asked, during the next hour's conversation.

"O, when they first come over from Germany, they had a sort of a king; he knew more than the rest, and he lived in that big brick house with the dorniel winders and a cuperler, that stands next the garden. The carriage was his'n and it had steps to let down, and curtains and all; they don't use it much now he's dead. They're a queer set anyhow! The women look like meal-sacks. After Sol seen me, he couldn't abide to look at 'em."

Soon after six we heard the great gate creak.

"That's Sol," said the woman, "and now of course Roarer'll come in and track all over my floor." The door opened and a shadow passed into the opposite room, two shadows,—a man and a dog.

"He's going to wash himself now," continued the wife; "he's always washing himself, just like a horse."

"New fact in natural history, Dora love," observed Ermine.

After some moments the miner appeared,—a tall, stooping figure with high forehead, large blue eyes, and long, thin, yellow hair; there was a singularly lifeless expression in his face, and a far-off look in his eyes. He gazed about the room in an absent way, as though he scarcely saw us. Behind him stalked the Roarer, wagging his tail slowly from side to side.

"Now then, don't yer see the ladies, Sol? Where's yer manners?" said his wife sharply.

"Ah,—yes,—good evening," he said vaguely. Then his wandering eyes fell upon Ermine's beautiful face, and fixed themselves there with strange intentness.

"You received my note, Mr. Bangs," said my cousin in her soft voice.

"Yes, surely. You are Erminia," replied the man, still standing in the center of the room with fixed eyes. The Roarer laid himself down behind his master, and his tail, still wagging, sounded upon the floor with a regular tap.

"Now then, Sol, since you've come home, perhaps you'll entertain the ladies while I get supper," quoth Mrs. Bangs; and forthwith began a clatter of pans.

The man passed his long hand abstractedly over his forehead. "Eh," he said with long-drawn utterance,—'eh-h? Yes, my rose of Sharon, certainly, certainly."

"Then why don't you do it?" said the woman, lighting the fire in the brick stove.

"And what will the ladies please to do?" he answered, his eyes going back to Ermine.

"We will look over your pictures, sir," said my cousin, rising; "they are in the upper room, I believe."

A great flush rose to the painter's thin cheeks. "Will you," he said eagerly,—"will you? Come!"

"It's a broken-down old hole, ladies; Sol will never let me sweep it out. Reckon you'll be more comfortable here," said Mrs. Bangs, with her arms in the flour.

"No, no, my lily of the valley. The ladies will come with me; they will not scorn the poor room."

"A studio is always interesting," said Ermine, sweeping up the rough stairs behind Solomon's candle. The dog followed us, and laid himself down on an old mat, as though well accustomed to the place. "Eh-h, boy, you came bravely through the storm with the lady's note," said his master, beginning to light candle after candle. "See him laugh!"

"Can a dog laugh?" I asked.

"Certainly; look at him now. What is that but a grin of happy contentment? Don't the Bible say, 'grin like a dog'?"

"You seem much attached to the Roarer!"

"Tuscarora, lady, Tuscarora. Yes, I love him well. He has been with me through all, and he has watched the making of all my pictures; he always lies there when I paint."

By this time a dozen candles were burning on shelves and brackets, and we could see all parts of the attic studio. It was but a poor place, unfloored in the corners where the roof slanted down, and having no ceiling but the dark beams and thatch; hung upon the walls were the pictures we had seen, and many others, all crude and highly colored, and all representing the same face,—the sulphur-woman in her youth, the poor artist's only ideal. He showed us these one by one, handling them tenderly, and telling us, in his quaint language, all they symbolized. "This is Ruth, and denoteth the power of hope," he said. "Behold Judith, the queen of revenge. And this dear one is Rachel, for whom Jacob served seven years, and it seemed unto him but a day, so well he loved her." The light shone on his pale face, and we noticed the far-off look in his eyes, and the long, tapering fingers coming out from the hard-worked, broad palm. To me it was a melancholy scene, the poor artist with his daubs and the dreary attic.

But Ermine seemed eagerly interested; she looked at the staring pictures, listened to the explanations, and at last she said gently, "Let me show you something of perspective, and the part that shadows play in a pictured face. Have you any crayons?"

No; the man had only his coarse paints and lumps of charcoal; taking a piece of the coal in her delicate hand my cousin began to work upon a sheet of drawing-paper attached to the rough easel. Solomon watched her intently, as she explained and demonstrated some of the rules of drawing, the lights and shades, and the manner of representing the different features and curves. All his pictures were full faces, flat and unshaded; Ermine showed him the power of the profile and the three-quarter view. I grew weary of watching them, and pressing my face against the little window gazed out into the night; steadily the rain came down and the hills shut us in like a well. I thought of our home in C——, and its bright lights, warmth, company, and life. Why should we come masquerading out among the Ohio hills at this late season? And then I remembered that it was because Ermine would come; she liked such expeditions, and from childhood I had always followed her lead. "Dux nascitur, etc. etc." Turning away from the gloomy night I looked toward the easel again; Solomon's cheeks were deeply flushed, and his eyes shone like stars. The lesson went on, the merely mechanical hand explaining its art to the ignorant fingers of genius. Ermine had taken lessons all her life, but she had never produced an original pictures, only copies.

At last the lesson was interrupted by a voice from below, "Sol, Sol, supper's ready!" No one stirred until, feeling some sympathy for the amount of work which my ears told me had been going on below, I woke up the two enthusiasts and took them away from the easel down stairs into the keeping-room, where a loaded table and a scarlet hostess bore witness to the truth of my surmise. Strange things we ate that night, dishes unheard of in towns, but not unpalatable. Ermine had the one china cup and her corn-coffee: her grand airs always secured her such favors. Tuscarora was there and ate of the best, now and then laying his shaggy head on the table, and as his master said, "smiling at us"; evidently the evening was his gala time. It was nearly nine when the feast was ended, and I immediately proposed retiring to bed, for, having but little art enthusiasm, I dreaded a vigil in that dreary attic. Solomon looked disappointed, but I ruthlessly carried off Ermine to the opposite room, which we afterwards suspected was the apartment of our hosts, freshened and set in order in our honor. The sound of the rain on the piazza roof lulled us soon to sleep, in spite of the strange surroundings; but more than once I woke and wondered where I was, suddenly remembering the lonely house in its lonely valley with a shiver of discomfort. The next morning we woke at our usual hour, but some time after the miner's departure; breakfast was awaiting us in the keeping-room and our hostess said that an ox-team from the Community would come for us before nine. She seemed sorry to part with us, and refused any remuneration for our stay; but none the less did we promise ourselves to send some dresses and even ornaments from C——, to feed that poor, starving love of finery. As we rode away in the ox-cart, the Roarer looked wistfully after us through the bars; but his melancholy mood was upon him again, and he had not the heart even to wag his tail.

As we were sitting in the hotel parlor, in front of our soft coal fire in the evening of the following day, and discussing whether or no we should return to the city within the week, the old landlord entered without his broad brimmed hat,—an unusual attention, since he was a trustee and a man of note in the Community, and removed his hat for no one nor nothing; we even suspected he slept in it.

"You know Zolomon Barngs," he said slowly.

"Yes," we answered.

"Well, he's dead. Kilt in de mine." And putting on his hat, removed, we now saw, in respect for death, he left the room as suddenly as he had entered it. As it happened, we had been discussing the couple, I as usual, contending for the wife, and Ermine, as usual, advocating the cause of the husband.

"Let us go out there immediately to see her, poor woman!" I said, rising.

"Yes, poor man, we will go to him!" said Ermine.

"But the man is dead, cousin."

"Then he shall at least have one kind, friendly glance before he is carried to his grave," answered Ermine quietly.

In a short time we set out in the darkness, and dearly did we have to pay for the night ride; no one could understand the motive of our going, but money was money, and we could pay for all peculiarities. It was a dark night, and the ride seemed endless as the oxen moved slowly on through the red clay mire. At last we reached the turn and saw the little lonely house with its upper room brightly lighted.

"He is in the studio," said Ermine; and so it proved. He was not dead, but dying; not maimed, but poisoned by the gas of the mine, and rescued too late for recovery. They had placed him upon the floor on a couch of blankets, and the dull-eyed Community doctor stood at his side. "No good, no good," he said; "he must die." And then, hearing the returning cart, he left us, and we could hear the tramp of the oxen over the little bridge on their way back to the village.

The dying man's head lay upon his wife's breast, and her arms supported him; she did not speak, but gazed at us with a dumb agony in her large eyes. Ermine knelt down and took the lifeless hand streaked with coal-dust in both her own. "Solomon," she said, in her soft, clear voice, "do you know me?"

The closed eyes opened slowly, and fixed themselves upon her face a moment; then they turned toward the window, as if seeking something.

"It's the picter he means," said the wife. "He sat up most all last night a doing it."

I lighted all the candles, and Ermine brought forward the easel; upon it stood a sketch in charcoal wonderful to behold,—the same face, the face of the faded wife, but so noble in its idealized beauty that it might have been a portrait of her glorified face in Paradise. it was a profile, with the eyes upturned,—a mere outline, but grand in conception and expression. I gazed in silent astonishment.

Ermine said, "Yes, I knew you could do it, Solomon. It is perfect of its kind." The shadow of a smile stole over the pallid face, and then the husband's fading gaze turned upward to meet the wild, dark, eyes of the wife.

"It's you, Dorcas," he murmured; "that's how you looked to me, but I never could get it right before." She bent over him, and silently we watched the coming of the shadow of death; he spoke only once, "My rose of Sharon,"—and then in a moment he was gone, the poor artist was dead.

Wild, wild was the grief of the ungoverned heart left behind; she was like a mad-woman, and our united strength was needed to keep her form injuring herself in her frenzy. I was frightened, but Ermine's strong little hands and lithe arms kept her down until, exhausted, she lay motionless near her dead husband. Then we carried her down stairs and I watched by the bedside, while my cousin went back to the studio. she was absent some time, and then she came back to keep the vigil with me through the long, still night. At dawn the woman woke, and her face looked aged in the gray light. She was quiet, and took without a word the food we had prepared, awkwardly enough, in the keeping-room.

"I must go to him, I must go to him," she murmured, as we led her back.

"Yes, said Ermine, "but first let me make you tidy. He loved to see you neat." And with deft, gentle touch she dressed the poor creature, arranging the heavy hair so artistically that, for the first time, I saw that she might have been, and understood the husband's dream.

"What is that?" I said, as a peculiar sound startled us.

"It's Roarer. He was tied up last night, but I suppose he's gnawed the rope," said the woman. I opened the hall door, and in stalked the great dog, smelling his way directly up the stairs.

"O, he must not go!" I exclaimed.

"Yes, let him go, he loved his master," said Ermine; "we will go too." So silently we all went up into the chamber of death.

The pictures had been taken down from the walls, but the wonderful sketch remained on the easel, which had been moved to the head of the couch where Solomon lay. His long, light hair was smooth, his face peacefully quiet, and on his breast lay the beautiful bunch of autumn leaves which he had arranged in our honor. It was a striking picture,— the noble face of the sketch above, and the dead face of the artist below. It brought to my mind a design I had once seen, where Fame with her laurels came at last to the door of the poor artist and gently knocked; but he had died the night before!

The dog lay at his master's feet, nor stirred until Solomon was carried out to his grave.

The Community buried the miner in one corner of the lonely little meadow. No service had they and no mound was raised to mark the spot, for such was their custom; but in the early spring we went down again into the valley, and placed a block of granite over the grave. It fore the inscription:

SOLOMON.
He will finish his work in Heaven.

Strange as it may seem, the wife pined for her artist husband. We found her in the Community trying to work, but so aged and bent that we hardly knew her. Her large eyes had lost their peevish discontent, and a great sadness had taken the place.

"Seems like I couldn't get on without Sol," she said, sitting with us in the hotel parlor after work hours. "I kinder miss his voice, and all them names he used to call me; he got 'em out of the Bible, so they must have been good, you know. He always thought everything I did was right, and he thought no end of my good looks, too; I suppose I've lose 'em now. He was might fond of me; nobody in all the world cares a straw for me now. Even Roarer wouldn't stay with me, for all I petted him; he kep' a going out to that meader and a lying by Sol, until, one day, we found him there dead. He just died of sheer loneliness, I reckon. I sha'n't have to stop long I know, because I keep a dreaming of Sol, and he always looks at me like he did when I first knew him. He was a beautiful boy when I first saw him on that load of wood coming into Sandy. Well, ladies, I must go. Thank you kindly for all you've done for me. And say, Miss Stuart, when I die you shall have that coal picter; no one else 'ud vally it so much."

Three months after, while we were at the sea-shore, Ermine received a long tin case, directed in a peculiar handwriting; it had been forwarded from C——, and contained the sketch and a note from the Community.

E. STUART—The woman Dorcas Bangs died this day. She will be put away by the side of her husband, Solomon Bangs. She left the enclosed picture, which we hereby send and which please acknowledge by return of mail. JACOB BOLL Trustee.

I unfolded the wrappings and looked at the sketch. "It is indeed striking," I said. "She must have been beautiful once, poor woman!"

"Let us hope that at least she is beautiful now, for her husband's sake, poor man!" replied Ermine.

Even then we could not give up our preferences.

Wilhelmina

Constance Fenimore Woolson

"And so, Mina, you will not marry the baker?"

"No; I waits for Gustav."

"How long is it since you have seen him?"

"Three year; it was a three-year regi-ment."

"Then he will be home soon?"

"I not know," answered the girl, with a wistful look in her dark eyes, as if asking information from the superior being who sat in the skiff,—a being from the outside world where newspapers, the modern Tree of Knowledge, were not forbidden.

"Perhaps he will re-enlist, and stay three years longer," I said.

"Ah, lady,—six year! It breaks the heart," answered Wilhelmina.

She was the gardener's daughter, a member of the Community of German Separatists who live secluded in one of Ohio's rich valleys, separated by their own broad acres and orchard-covered hills from the busy world outside; down the valley flows the tranquil Tuscarawas on its way to Muskingum, its slow tide rolling through the fertile bottom-lands between stone dikes, and utilized to the utmost extent of carefulness by the thrifty brothers, now working a sawmill on the bank, now sending a tributary to the flour-mill across the canal, and now branching off in a sparkling race across the valley to turn wheels for two or three factories, watering the great grass-meadow on the way. We were floating on this river in a skiff named by myself Der Fliegende Hollander, much to the slow wonder of the Zoarites, who did not understand how a Dutchman could, not why he should, fly. Wilhelmina sat before me, her oars idly trailing in the water. She showed a Nubian head above her white kerchief: large-lidded soft brown eyes, heavy braids of dark hair, a creamy skin with purple tints in the lips and brown shadows under the eyes, and a far-off dreamy expression which even the steady, monotonous toil of Community life had not been able to efface. She wore the blue dress and white kerchief of the society, the quaint little calico bonnet lying beside her; she was a small maiden; her slender form swayed in the stiff, short-waisted gown, her feet slipped about in the broad shoes, and her hands, roughened and browned with garden-work, were narrow and graceful. From the first we felt sure she was grafted, and not a shoot from the

198

Community stalk. But we could learn nothing of her origin; the Zoarites are not communicative; they fill each day with twelve good hours of labor, and look neither forward nor back. "She is a daughter," said the old gardener in answer to our questions. "Adopted?" I suggested; but he vouchsafed no answer. I liked the little daughter's dreamy face, but she was pale and underdeveloped, like a Southern flower growing in Northern soil; the rosy-cheeked, flaxen-haired Rosines, Salonies, and Dorotys, with their broad shoulders and ponderous tread, thought this brown changeling ugly, and pitied her in their slow, good-natured way.

"It breaks the heart," said Wilhelmina again, softly, as if to herself.

I repented me of my thoughtlessness. "In any case he can come back for a few days," I hastened to say. "What regiment was it?"

"The One Hundred and Seventh, lady."

I had a Cleveland paper in my basket and taking it out I glanced over the war-news column, carelessly, as one who does not expect to find what he seeks. But chance was with us, and gave this item: "The One Hundred and Seventh Regiment, O.V.L., is expected home next week. The men will be paid off at Camp Close."

"Ah!" said Wilhelmina, catching her breath with a half-sob under her tightly drawn kerchief,—"ah, mein Gustav!"

"Yes, you will soon see him," I answered, bending forward to take the rough little hand in mine; for I was a romantic wife, and my heart went out to all lovers. But the girl did not notice my words or my touch; silently she sat, absorbed in her own emotion, her eyes fixed on the hilltops far away, as though she saw the regiment marching home through the blue June sky.

I took the oars and rowed up as far as the island, letting the skiff float back with the current. Other boats were out, filled with fresh-faced boys in their high-crowned hats, long-waisted, wide-flapped vests of calico, and funny little swallow-tailed coats with buttons up under the shoulder blades; they appeared unaccountably long in front and short behind, these young Zoar brethren. On the vine-covered dike were groups of mothers and grave little children, and up in the hill-orchards were moving figures, young and old; the whole village was abroad in the lovely afternoon, according to their Sunday custom, which gave the morning to chorals and a long sermon in the little church, and the afternoon to nature, even old Christian, the pastor, taking his imposing white fur hat and tasselled cane for a walk through the Community fields, with the remark, "Thus is cheered the heart of man, and his countenance refreshed."

As the sun sank in the warm western sky, homeward came the villagers from the river, the orchards, and the meadows, men, women, and children, a hardy, simple-minded band, whose fathers, for religion's sake, had taken the long journey from Würtemberg for across the ocean to this distant valley, and made it a garden of rest in the wilderness. We, too, landed, and walked up the apple-tree lane towards the hotel.

"The cows come," said Wilhelmina as we heard a distant tinkling; "I must go." But still she lingered. "Der regi-ment, it come soon, you say?" she asked in a low voice, as though she wanted to hear the good news again and again.

"They will be paid on next week; they cannot be later than ten days from now."

"Ten day! Ah, mein Gustav," murmured the little maiden; she turned away and tied on her stiff bonnet, furtively wiping off a tear with her prim handkerchief folded in a square.

"Why, my child," I said, following her and stooping to look in her face, "what is this?"

"It is nothing; it is for glad,—for very glad," said Wilhelmina. Away she ran as the first solemn cow came into view, heading the long procession meandering slowly toward the stalls. They knew nothing of haste, these dignified Community cows; from stall to pasture, from pasture to stall, in a plethora of comfort, this was their life. The silver-haired shepherd came last with his staff and scrip, and the nervous shepherd-dog run hither and thither in the hope of finding some cow to bark at; but the comfortable cows moved on in orderly ranks, and he was obliged to dart off on a tangent every now and then, and bark at nothing, to relieve his feelings. Reaching the paved court-yard each cow walked into her own stall, and the milking began. All the girls took part in this work, sitting on little stools and singing together as the milk frothed up in the tin pails; the pails were emptied into tubs, and when the tubs were full the girls bore them on their heads to the dairy, where the milk was poured into a huge strainer, a constant procession of girls with tubs above and the old milk-mother ladling out as fast as she could below. With the bee-hives near by, it was a realization of the Scriptural phrase, "A land flowing with milk and honey."

The next morning, after breakfast, I strolled up the still street, leaving the Wirthshaus with its pointed roof behind me. On the right were some ancient cottages built of crossed timbers filled in with plaster; sundials hung on the walls, and each house had its piazza, where, when the work of the day was over, the families assembled, often singing folk-songs to the music of their home-made flutes and pipes. On the left stood the residence of the first pastor, the reverend man who had led these sheep to their refuge in the wilds of the New World. It was a wide-spreading brick mansion, with a broadside of white-curtained windows, an enclosed glass porch, iron railings, and gilded eaves; a building so stately among the surrounding cottages that it had gained from outsiders the name of the King's Palace, although the good man whose grave remains unmarked in the quiet God's Acre, according to the Separatist custom, was a father to his people, not a king.

Beyond the palace began the Community garden, a large square in the centre of the village filled with flowers and fruit, adorned with arbors and cedar-trees clipped in the form of birds, and enriched with an old-style greenhouse whose sliding glasses were viewed with admiration by the visitors of thirty years ago, who sent their choice plants thither from far and near to be tended through the long, cold lake-country winters. The garden, the cedars, and the greenhouse were all antiquated, but to me none the less charming. The spring that gushed up in one corner the old-fashioned flowers in their box-bordered beds, larkspur, lady slippers, bachelor's buttons, peonies, aromatic pinks, and all varieties of roses, the arbors with red honeysuckle overhead and tan bark under foot, were all delightful; and I knew, also, that I should find the gardener's daughter at her never-ending task of weeding. This time it was the strawberry bed. "I have come to sit in your pleasant garden, Mina," I said, taking a seat on a shaded bench near the bending figure.

"So?" said Wilhelmina in long-drawn interrogation, glancing up shyly with a smile. She was a child of the sun, this little maiden, and while her blond companions wore always their bonnets or broad-brimmed hats over their precise caps, Wilhelmina, as now, constantly discarded these coverings and sat in the sun basking like a bird of the tropics. In truth, it did not redden her; she was one of those whose coloring comes not from without, but within.

"Do you like this work, Mina?"

"O—so. Good as any."

"Do you like work?"

"Folks must work." This was said gravely, as part of the Community creed.

"Would n't you like to go with me to the city?"

"No; I's better here."

"But you can see the great world, Mina. You need not work, I will take care of you. You shall have pretty dresses; would n't you like that?" I asked, curious to discover the secret of the Separatist indifference to everything outside.

"Nein," answered the little maiden, tranquilly; "nein, fraulein. Ich bin zufreidein."

Those three words were the key. "I am contented." So were they taught from childhood, and—I was about to say—they knew no better; but, after all, is there anything better to know?

We talked on, for Mina understood English, although many of her mates could chatter only in their Würtemberg dialect, whose provincialisms confused my carefully learned German; I was grounded in Goethe, well-read in Schiller, and struggling with Jean Paul, who, fortunately, is "der Einzige," the only; another such would destroy life. At length a bell sounded, and forthwith work was laid aside in the fields, the workshops, and the houses, while all partook of a light repast, one of the five meals with which the long summer day of toil is broken. Flagons of beer had the men afield, with bread and cheese; the women took bread and apple-butter. But Mina did not care for the thick slice which the thrifty house-mother had provided; she had not the steady unfanciful appetite of the Community which eats the same food day after day, as the cow eats its grass, desiring no change.

"And the gardener really wishes you to marry Jacob?" I said as she sat on the grass near me, enjoying the rest.

"Yes. Jacob is good,—always the same."

"And Gustav?"

"Ah, mein Gustav! Lady, *he* is young, tall,—so tall as tree; he run, he sing, his eyes like veilchen there, his hair like gold. If I see him not soon, lady, I die! The year so long,—so long they are. Three years without Gustav!" The brown eyes grew dim, and out came the square-folded handkerchief, of colored calico for week-days.

"But it will not be long now, Mina."

"Yes; I hope."

"He writes to you, I suppose?"

"No. Gustav knows not to write, he not like school. But he speak through the other boys, Ernst the verliebta of Rosine, and Peter of Doroty."

"The Zoar soldiers were all young men?"

"Yes; all verliebta. Some are not; they have gone to the Next Country" (died).

"Killed in battle?"

"Yes; on the berge that looks,—what you call, I not know—"

"Lookout Mountain?"

"Yes."

"Were the boys volunteers?" I asked, remembering the Community theory of non-resistance.

"O yes; they volunteer, Gustav the first. *They* not drafted," said Wilhelmina, proudly. For these two words, so prominent during the war, had penetrated even into the quiet valley.

"But did the trustees approve?"

"Apperouve?"

"I mean, did they like it?"

"Ah! they like it not. They talk, they preach in church, they say 'No.' Zoar must give soldiers? So. Then they take money and pay for der substitute; but the boys, they must not go."

"But they went in spite of the trustees?"

"Yes; Gustav first. They go in night, they walk in woods, over the hills to Brownsville, where is der recruiter. The morning come, they gone!"

"They have been away three years, you say? They have seen the world in that time," I remarked half to myself, as I thought of the strange mind-opening and knowledge-gaining of those years to youths brought up in the strict seclusion of the Community.

"Yes; Gustav have seen the wide," answered Wilhelmina with pride.

"But will they be content to step back into the dull routine of Zoar life?" I thought; and a doubt came that made me scan more closely the face of the girl at my side. To me it was attractive because of its possibilities; I was always fancying some excitement that would bring the color to the cheeks and full lips, and light up the heavy-lidded eyes with soft brilliancy. But would this Gustav see these might-be beauties? And how far would the singularly ugly costume offend eyes accustomed to fanciful finery and gay colors?

"You fully expect to marry Gustav?" I asked.

"We are verlobt," answered Mina, not without a little air of dignity.

"Yes, I know. But that was a long time ago."

"Verlobt once, verlobt always," said the little maiden, confidently.

"But why, then, does the gardener speak of Jacob, if you are engaged to Gustav?"

"O, fader he like the old, and Jacob is old, thirty year! His wife is gone to the Next Country. Jacob is a brother, too; he write his name in the book. But Gustav he not do so; he is free."

"You mean that the baker has signed the articles, and is a member of the Community?"

"Yes; but the baker is old, very old; thirty year! Gustav not twenty and three yet; he come home, then he sign."

"And have you signed these articles, Wilhelmina?"

"Yes; all the women signs."

"What does the paper say?"

"Da ich Unterzeichneter,"—began the girl.

"I cannot understand that. Tell me in English."

"Well; you wants to join the Zoar Community of Separatists; you writes your name and says, 'Give me house, victual, and clothes for my work and I join; and I never ferner Forderung an besagte Gesellschaft machen kann, oder will.'"

"Will never make further demand upon said society," I repeated, translating slowly.

"Yes; that is it."

"But who takes charge of all the money?"

"The trustees."

"Don't they give you any?"

"No; for what? It's no good," answered Wilhelmina.

I knew that all the necessaries of life were dealt out to the members of the Community according to their need, and, as they never went outside of their valley, they could scarcely have spent money even if they had possessed it. But, nevertheless, it was startling in this nineteenth century to come upon a sincere belief in the worthlessness of the green-tinted paper we cherish so fondly. "Gustav will have learned its value,"I thought, as Mina, having finished the strawberry-bed, started away towards the dairy to assist in the butter-making.

I strolled on up the little hill, past the picturesque bakery, where through the open window I caught a glimpse of the "old, very old Jacob," a serious young man of thirty, drawing out his large loaves of bread from the brick oven with a long-handled rake. It was gingerbread-day also, and a spicy odor met me at the window; so I put in my head and asked for a piece, receiving a card about a foot square, laid on fresh grape-leaves.

"But I cannot eat all this," I said, breaking off a corner.

"O, dat's noding!" answered Jacob, beginning to knead fresh dough in a long white trough, the village supply for the next day.

"I have been sitting with Wilhelmina," I remarked, as I leaned on the casement, impelled by a desire to see the effect of the name.

"So?" said Jacob, interrogatively.

"Yes; she is a sweet girl."

"So?" (doubtfully.)

"Don't you think so, Jacob?"

"Ye-es. So-so. A leetle black," answered the impassive lover.

"But you wish to marry her?"

"O, ye-es. She young and strong; her fader say she good to work. I have children five; I must have some one in the house."

"O Jacob! Is that the way to talk?" I exclaimed.

"Warum nicht?" replied the baker, pausing in his kneading and regarding me with wide-open, candid eyes.

"Why not, indeed?" I thought, as I turned away from the window. "He is at least honest, and no doubt in his way he would be a kind husband to little Mina. But what a way!"

I walked on up the street, passing the pleasant house where all the infirm old women of the Community were lodged together, carefully tended by appointed nurses. The aged sisters were out on the piazza sunning themselves, like so many old cats. They were bent with hard, outdoor labor, for they belonged to the early days when the wild forest covered the fields now so rich, and only a few log-cabins stood on the site of the tidy cottages and gardens of the present village. Some of them had taken the long journey on foot from Philadelphia westward, four hundred and fifty miles, in the depths of winter. Well might they rest from their labors and sit in the sunshine, poor old souls!

A few days later, my friendly newspaper mentioned the arrival of the German regiment at Camp Chase. "They will probably be paid off in a day or two," I thought, "and another day may bring them here." Eager to be the first to tell the good news to my little favorite, I hastened up to the garden, and found her engaged, as usual, in weeding.

"Mina," I said, "I have something to tell you. The regiment is at Camp Chase; you will see Gustav soon, perhaps this week."

And there, before my eyes, the transformation I had often fancied took place; the color rushed to the brown surface, the cheeks and lips glowed in a vivid red, and the heavy eyes opened wide and shone like stars, with a brilliancy that astonished and even disturbed me. The statue had a soul at last; the beauty dormant had awakened. But for the fire of that soul would this expected Pygmalion suffice? Would the real prince fill his place in the long-cherished dreams of this beauty of the wood?

The girl had risen as I spoke, and now she stood erect, trembling with excitement, her hands clasped on her breast, breathing quickly and heavily as though and overweight of joy was pressing down her heart; her eyes were fixed upon my face, but she saw me not. Strange was her gaze, like the gaze of one walking in sleep. Her sloping shoulders seemed to expand and chafe against the stiff gown as though they would burst their bonds; the blood glowed in her face and throat, and her lips quivered, not as though tears were coming, but from the fulness of unuttered speech. Her emotion resembled the intensest fire of fever, and yet it seemed natural; like noon in the tropics when the gorgeous flowers flame in the white, shadowless heat. Thus stood Wilhelmina, looking up into the sky with eyes that challenged the sun.

"Come here child," I said; "come here and sit by me. We will talk about it."

But she neither saw nor heard me. I drew her down on the bench at my side; she yielded unconsciously; her slender form throbbed, and pulses were beating under my hands wherever I touched her. "Mina!" I said again. But she did not answer. Like an unfolding rose, she revealed her hidden, beautiful heart, as though a spirit had breathed upon the bud; silenced in the presence of this great love, I ceased speaking, and left her to herself. After a time single words fell from her lips, broken utterances of happiness. I was as nothing; she was absorbed in the One. "Gustav! Mein Gustav!" It was like the bird's note, oft repeated, ever the same. So isolated, so intense was her joy, that, as often happens, my mind took reference in the opposite extreme of commonplace, and I found myself wondering whether she would be able to eat boiled beef and cabbage for dinner, or fill the soft-soap barrel for the laundry-women, later in the day.

All the morning I sat under the trees with Wilhelmina, who had forgotten her life-long tasks as completely as though they had never existed. I hated to leave her to the leather-colored wife of the old gardener, and lingered until the sharp voice came out from the distant house-door, calling, "Veel-hel-*meeny*," as the twelve-o'clock bell summoned the Community to dinner. But as Mina rose and swept back the heavy braids that had fallen from the little ivory stick which confined them, I saw that she was armed *cap-i-pie* in that full happiness from which all weapons glance off harmless.

All the rest of the day she was like a thing possessed. I followed her to the hill- pasture, whither she had gone to mind the cows, and found her coiled up on the grass in the blaze of the afternoon sun, like a little salamander. She was lost in day-dreams, and the decorous cows had a holiday for once in their sober lives, wandering beyond bounds at will, and even tasting the dissipations of the marsh, standing unheeded in the bog up to their sleek knees. Wilhelmina had not many words to give me; her English vocabulary was limited; she had never read a line of romance nor a verse of poetry. The nearest approach to either was the Community hymn-book, containing the Separatist hymns, of which the following lines are a specimen.

> "Ruhe ist das besta Gut
> Dasz man haben kann,"—
>
> "Best is the best good
> That man can have,"—

and which embody the religious doctrine of the Zoar Brethren, although they think, apparently, that the labor of twelve hours each day is necessary to its enjoyment. The "Ruhe," however, refers more especially to their quiet seclusion away from the turmoil of the wicked world outside.

The second morning after this it was evident that an unusual excitement was abroad in the phlegmatic village. All the daily duties were fulfilled as usual at the Wirthshaus; Pauline went up to the bakery with her board, and returned with her load of bread and bretzels balanced on her head; Jacobina served our coffee with her slow precision; and the broad-shouldered, young-faced Lydia patted and puffed up our mountain-high feather-beds with due care. The men went afield at the blast of the horn, the workshops were full and the mills running. But, nevertheless, all was not the same; the air seemed full of mystery; there were whisperings when two met, furtive signals, and an inward excitement glowing in the faces of men, women, and children, hitherto placid as their own sheep. "They have heard the news," I said, after watching the tailor's Gretchen and the blacksmith's Barbara stop to exchange a whisper behind the wool-house. Later in the day we learned that several letters from the absent soldier-boys had been received that morning, announcing their arrival on the evening train. The news had flown form one end of the village to the other; and although the well-drilled hands were all at work, hearts were stirring with the greatest excitement of a lifetime, since there was hardly a house where there was not one expected. Each large house often held a number of families, stowed away in little sets of chambers, with one dining-room in common.

Several times during the day we saw the three trustees conferring apart with anxious faces. The war had been a sore trouble to them, owing to their conscientious scruples against rendering military service. They had hoped to remain non-combatants. But the country was on fire with patriotism, and nothing less than a *bona fide* Separatists in United States uniform would quiet the surrounding towns, long jealous of the wealth of this foreign community, misunderstanding its tenets, and glowing with that zeal against "sympathizers" which kept star-spangled banners flying over every suspected house. "Hang out the flag!" was their cry, and they demanded that Zoar should hang out its soldiers, giving them to understand that if not voluntarily hung out, they would soon be involuntarily hung up! A draft was ordered, and then the young men of the society, who had long chafed against their bonds, broke loose, volunteered, and marched away, principles or no principles, trustees or no trustees. Those bold hearts once gone, the village sank into quietude again. Their letters, however, were a source of anxiety, coming as they did from the vain outside world; and the old postmaster, autocrat though he was, hardly dared to suppress them. But he said, shaking his head, that they "had fallen upon troublous times," and handed each dangerous envelope out with a groan. But the soldiers were not skilled penmen; their letters, few and far between, at length stopped entirely. Time passed, and the very existence of the runaways had become a far-off problem to the wise men of the Community, absorbed in their slow calculations and cautious agriculture, when now, suddenly, it forced itself upon them face to face, and they were required to solve it in the twinkling of an eye. The bold hearts were coming back, full of knowledge of the outside world; almost every house would hold one, and the bands of law and order would be broken. Before this prospect the trustees quailed. Twenty years before they would have forbidden the entrance of these unruly sons within their borders; but now they dared not, since even into Zoar had penetrated the knowledge that America was a free country. The younger generation were not as their fathers were; objections had been openly made to the cut of the Sunday coats, and the girls had spoken together of ribbons!

The shadows of twilight seemed very long in falling that night, but at last there was no further excuse for delaying the evening bell, and home came the laborers to their evening meal. There was no moon, a soft mist obscured the stars, and the night was darkened with the excess of richness which rose from the ripening valley-fields and fat bottom-lands along the river. The Community store opposite the Wirthshaus was closed early in the evening, the houses of the trustees were dark, and indeed the village was almost unlighted, as if to hide its own excitement. The entire population was abroad in the night, and one by one the men and boys stole away down the station road, a lovely, winding track on the hillside, following the river on its way down the valley to the little station on the grass-grown railroad, a branch form the main track. As ten o'clock came, the women and girls, grown bold with excitement, gathered in the open space in front of the Wirthshaus, where the lights from the windows illumined their faces. There I saw the broad-shouldered Lydia, Rosine, Doroty, and all the rest, in their Sunday clothes, flushed, laughing, and chattering; but no Wilhelmina.

"Where can she be?" I said.

If she was there, the larger girls concealed her with their buxom breadth; I looked for the slender little maiden in vain.

"Shu!" cried the girls, "de bugle!"

Far down the station road we heard the bugle and saw the glimmering of lights among the trees. On it came, a will-o'-the-wisp procession: first a detachment of village boys each with a lantern or torch, next the returned soldiers winding their bugles,—for, German-like, they all had musical instruments,—then an excited crowd of brothers and cousins loaded with knapsacks, guns, and military accoutrements of all kinds; each man had something, were it only a tin cup, and proudly they marched in the footsteps of their glorious relatives, bearing the spoils of war. The girls set up a shrill cry of welcome as the procession approached, but the ranks continued unbroken until the open space in front of the Wirthshaus was reached; then, at a signal, the soldiers gave three cheers, the villagers joining in with all their hearts and lungs, but wildly and out of time, like the scattering fire of an awkward squad. The sound had never been heard in Zoar before. The soldiers gave a final "Tiger-r-r!" and then broke ranks, mingling with the excited crowd, exchanging greetings and embraces. All talked at once; some wept, some laughed; and through it all silently stood the three trustees on the dark porch in front of the store, looking down upon their wild flock, their sober faces visible in the glare of the torches and lanterns below. The entire population was present; even the babies were held up on the out-skirts of the crowd, stolid and staring.

"Where can Wilhelmina be?" I said again.

"Here, under the window; I saw her long ago," replied one of the women.

Leaning against a piazza-pillar, close under my eyes, stood the little maiden, pale and still. I could not disguise from myself that she looked almost ugly among those florid, laughing girls, for her color was gone, and her eyes so fixed that they looked unnaturally large; her somewhat heavy Egyptian features stood out in the bright light, but her small form was lost among the group of broad, white-kerchiefed shoulders, adorned with breast-knots of gay flowers. And had Wilhelmina no flower? She, so fond of blossoms? I looked again; yes, a little white rose, drooping and pale as herself.

But where was Gustav? The soldiers came and went in the crowd, and all spoke to Mina; but where was the One? I caught the landlord's little son as he passed, and asked the question.

"Gustav? Dat's him," he answered, pointing out a tall, rollicking soldier who seemed to be embracing the whole population in his gleeful welcome. That very soldier had passed Mina a dozen times, flinging a gay greeting to her each time; but nothing more.

After half an hour of general rejoicing, the crowd dispersed, each household bearing off in triumph the hero that fell to its lot. Then the tiled domiciles, where usually all were asleep an hour after twilight, blazed forth with unaccustomed light form every little window; and within we could see the circles, with flagons of beer and various dain-ties manufactured in secret during the day, sitting and talking together in a manner which, for Zoar, was a wild ravel, since it was nearly eleven o'clock! We were not the only outside spectators to this unwonted gayety; several times we met the three trustees stealing along in the shadow from house to house, like anxious spectators in broad-brimmed hats. No doubt they said to each other, "How, how will this end!"

The merry Gustav had gone off by Mina's side, which gave me some comfort; but when in our rounds we came to the gardener's house and gazed through the open door, the little maiden sat apart, and the soldier, in the centre of an admiring circle, was telling stories of the war.

I felt a foreboding of sorrow as I gazed out through the little window before climbing up into my high bed. Lights still twinkled in some of the houses, but a white mist was rising from the river, and the drowsy, long-drawn chant of the summer night invited me to dreamless sleep.

The next morning I could not resist questioning Jacobina, who also had her lover among the soldiers, if all was well.

"O yes. They stay,—all but two. We's married next mont."

"And the two?"

"Karl and Gustav."

"And Wilhelmina!" I exclaimed.

"O, she let him go," answered Jacobina, bringing fresh coffee.

"Poor child! How does she bear it?"

"O, so. She cannot help. She say noding."

"But the trustees, will they allow these young men to leave the Community?"

"They cannot help," said Jacobina. "Gustav and Karl write not in the book; they free to go. Wilhelmina marry Jacob; it's joost the same; all r-r-ight," added Jacobina, who prided herself upon her English, caught from visitors at the Wirthshaus table.

"Ah! but it is not just the same," I thought as I went up to the garden to find my little maiden. She was not there; the leathery mother said she was out on the hills with the cows.

"So Gustav is going to leave the Community," I said in German.

"Yes, better so. He is an idle, wild boy. Now, Veelhelmeeny can marry the baker, a good steady man.:

"But Mina does not like him," I suggested.

"Das macht nichts," answered the leathery mother.

Wilhelmina was not in the pasture; I sought for her everywhere, and called her name. The poor child had hidden herself, and whether she heard me or not, she did not respond. All day she kept herself aloof; I almost feared she would never return; but in the late twilight a little figure slipped through the garden-gate and took refuge in the house before I could speak; for I was watching for the child, apparently the only one, though a stranger, to care for her sorrow.

"Can I not see her?" I said to the leathery mother, following to the door.

"Eh, no; she's foolish; she will not speak a word; she has gone off to bed," was the answer.

For three days I did not see Mina, so early did she flee away to the hills and so late return. I followed her to the pasture once or twice, but she would not show herself, and I could not discover her hiding-place. The fourth day I learned that Gustav and Karl were to leave the village in the afternoon, probably forever. The other soldiers had signed the articles presented by the anxious trustees, and settled down into the old routine, going afield with the rest, although still heroes of the hour; they were all to be married in August. No doubt the hardships of their campaigns among the Tennessee mountains had taught them that the rich valley was a home not to be despised; nevertheless, it was evident that the flowers of the flock were those who were about departing, and that in Gustav and Karl the Community lost its brightest spirits. Evident to us; but, possibly, the Community cared not for bright spirits.

I had made several attempts to speak to Gustav; this morning I at last succeeded. I found him polishing his bugle on the garden bench.

"Why are you going away, Gustav?" I asked. "Zoar is a pleasant little village."

"Too slow for me, miss."

"The life is easy, however; you will find the world a hard place."

"I don't mind work, ma'am, but I do like to be me. I feel all cramped up here, with these rules and bells; and, besides, I could n't stand those trustees; they never let a fellow alone."

"And Wilhelmina? If you do go, I hope you will take her with you, or come for her when you have found work."

"O no, miss. All that was long ago. It's all over now."

"But you like her, Gustav?"

"O, so. She's a good little thing, but too quiet for me."

"But she likes you," I said desperately, for I saw no other way to loosen this Gordian knot.

"O no, miss. She got used to it, and has thought of it all three years; that's all. She'll forget about it, and marry the baker."

"But she does not like the baker."

"Why not? He's a good fellow enough. She'll like him in time. It's all the same. I declare it's too bad to see all these girls going on in the same old way, in their ugly gowns and big shoes! Why, ma'am, I could n't take Mina outside, even if I wanted to; she's too old to learn new ways, and everybody would laugh at her. She could n't get along a day. Besides," said the young soldier, coloring up to his eyes, "I don't mind telling you that—that there's some one else. Look here, ma'am." And he put into my hand a card photograph representing a pretty girl, over-dressed, and adorned with curls and gilt jewelry. "That's Miss Martin," said Gustav with pride; "Miss Emmeline Martin, of Cincinnati. I'm going to marry Miss Martin."

As I held the pretty, flashy picture in my hand, all my castles fell to the ground. My plan for taking Mina home with me, accustoming her gradually to other clothes and ways, teaching her enough of the world to enable her to hold her place without pain, my hope that my husband might find a situation for Gustav in some of the iron-mills near Cleveland, in short, all the idyl I had woven, was destroyed. If it had not been for this red-cheeked Miss Martin in her gilt beads! "Why is it that men will by such fools?" I thought. Up sprung a memory of the curls and ponderous jet necklace I sported at a certain period of my existence, when John—I was silenced, gave Gustav his picture, and walked away without a word.

At once the villagers, on their way back to work, paused at the Wirthshaus to say good by; Karl and Gustav were there, and the old woolly horse had already gone to the station with their boxes. Among the others came Christine, Karl's former affianced, heart-whole and smiling, already betrothed to a new lover; but no Wilhelmina. Good wishes and farewells were exchanged, and at last two soldiers started away, falling into the marching step, and watched with furtive satisfaction by the three trustees, who stood together in the shadow of the smithy, apparently deeply absorbed in a broken-down cask.

It was a lovely afternoon, and I, too, strolled down the station road empowered in shade. The two soldiers were not far in advance. I had passed the flour-mill on the outskirts of the village and was approaching the old quarry, when a sound startled me; out from the rocks in front rushed a little figure, and crying, "Gustav, mein Gustav!" fell at the sol-dier's feet. It was Wilhelmina.

I ran forward and took her form the young men; she lay in my arms as if dead. The poor child was sadly changed; always slender and sway-ing, she now looked thin and shrunken, her skin had a strange, dark pallor, and her lips were drawn in as if from pain. I could see her eyes through the large-orbed thin lids, and the brown shadows beneath extended down into the cheeks.

"Was ist's?" said Gustav, looking bewildered. "Is she sick?"

I answered "Yes," but nothing more. I could see that he had no sus-picion of the truth, believing as had he did that the "good fellow" of a baker would do very well for this "good little thing" who was "too quiet" for him. The memory of Miss Martin sealed my lips. But if it had not been for that pretty, flashy picture, I would not have spoken!

"You must go; you will miss the train," I said, after a few minutes. "I will see to Mina."

But Gustav lingered. Perhaps he was really troubled to see the little sweetheart of his boyhood in such desolate plight; perhaps a touch of the old feeling came back; and perhaps, also, it was nothing of the kind, and, as usual, my romantic imagination was carrying me away. At any rate, whatever it was, he stooped over the fainted girl.

"She looks bad," he said, "very bad. I wish—But she'll get well and marry the baker. Good by, Mina." And bending his tall form, he kissed her colorless cheek, and then hastened away to join the impatient Karl; a curve in the road soon hid them from view.

Wilhelmina had stirred at his touch; after a moment her large eyes opened slowly; she looked around as if dazed, but all at once memory came back, and she started up with the same cry, "Gustav, mein Gustav!" I drew her head down on my shoulder to stifle the sound; it was better the soldier should not hear it, and its anguish thrilled my own heart also. She had not the strength to resist me, and in a few minutes I knew that the young men were out of hearing as they strode on towards the station and out into the wide world.

The forest was solitary, we were beyond the village; all the afternoon I sat under the trees with the stricken girl. Again, as in her joy, her words were few; again, as in her joy, her whole being was involved. Her little rough hands were cold, a film had gathered over her eyes; she did not weep, but moaned to herself, and all her senses seemed blunted. At nightfall I took her home, and the leathery mother received her with a frown; but the child was beyond caring, and crept away, dumbly, to her room.

The next morning she was off to the hills again, nor could I find her for several days. Evidently, in spite of my sympathy, I was no more to her than I should have been to a wounded fawn. She was a mixture of the wild, shy creature of the woods and the deep-loving woman of the tropics; in either case I could be but small comfort. When at last I did see her, she was apathetic and dull; her feelings, her senses, and her intelligence seemed to have gone within, as if preying upon her heart. She scarcely listened to my proposal to take her with me; for, in my pity, I had suggested it, in spite of its difficulties.

"No," she said, mechanically, "I's better here"; and fell into silence again.

A month later a friend went down to spend a few days in the valley, and upon her return described to us the weddings of the whilom soldiers. "It was really a pretty sight," she said, "the quaint peasant dresses and the flowers. Afterwards, the band went round the village playing their odd tunes and all had a holiday. There were two civilians married also; I mean two young men who had not been to the war. It seems that two of the soldiers turned their backs upon the Community and their allotted brides, and marched away; but the Zoar maidens are not romantic, I fancy, for these two deserted ones were betrothed again and married, all in the short space of four weeks."

"Was not one Wilhelmina, the gardener's daughter, a short, dark girl?" I asked.

"Yes."

"And she married Jacob the baker?"

"Yes."

The next year, weary of the cold lake-winds, we left the icy shore and went down to the valley to meet the coming spring, finding her already there, decked with vines and flowers. A new waitress brought us our coffee.

"How is Wilhelmina?" I asked.

"Eh,—Wilhelmina?, she not here now; she gone to the Next Country," answered the girl in a matter-o-fact way. "She die last October, and Jacob he haf anoder wife now."

In the late afternoon I asked a little girl to show me Wilhelmina's grave in the quiet God's Acre on the hill. Innovation was creeping in, even here; the later graves had mounds raised over them, and one had a little headboard with an inscription in ink.

Wilhelmina lay apart, and some one, probably the old gardener, who had loved the little maiden in his silent way, had planted a rose-bush at the head of the mound. I dismissed my guide and sat there alone in the sunset, thinking of many things, but chiefly of this: "Why should this great wealth of love have been allowed to waste itself? Why is it that the greatest power, unquestionably, of this mortal life should so often seem a useless gift?"

No answer came from the sunset clouds, and as twilight sank down on the earth I rose to go. "I fully believe," I said, as though repeating a creed, "that this poor, loving heart, whose earthly body lies under this mound, is happy now in its own loving way. It has not been changed, but the happiness it longed for has come. How, we know not; but the God who made Wilhelmina understands her. He has given unto her not rest, not peace, but an active, living joy."

I walked away through the wild meadow, under whose turf, unmarked by stone or mound, lay the first pioneers of the Community, and out into the forest road, untravelled save when the dead passed over it to their last earthly home. The evening was still and breathless, and the shadows lay thick on the grass as I looked back. But I could still distinguish the little mound with the rose-bush at its head, and, not without tears, I said, "Farewell, poor Welhelmina; farewell."

Bibliography

Auerbach, Nina. Rev. of *Rediscovered Fiction by American Women: A Personal Selection*. Ed. Elizabeth Hardwick. *Nineteenth Century Fiction* 33 (Mar. 1979): 475-83.

Kelley, Mary. *Private Woman, Public Stage: Literary Domesticity in Nineteenth Century America*. New York: Oxford UP, 1984.

Kern, John D. *Constance Fenimore Woolson: Literary Pioneer*. Philadelphia: University of Pennsylvania Press, 1934.

Moore, Rayburn S. *Constance Fenimore Woolson*. New York: Twayne, 1963.

Torsney, Cheryl B. *Constance Fenimore Woolson: The Grief of Artistry*. Athens: University of Georgia Press, 1989.

Wood, Ann Douglas. "The Literature of Impoverishment: The Women Local Colorists in America, 1865-1914." *Women's Studies* 1 (1972): 3-45.

Woolson, Constance Fenimore. "Solomon." *Atlantic Monthly* 32 (Oct. 1873): 413-24. Rpt. in *Castle Nowhere: Lake-Country Sketches*. Boston: Osgood, 1875. New York: Garnett, 1969. 236-69.

——. "Wilhelmina." *Atlantic Monthly* 35 (Jan. 1875): 44-55. Rpt. in *Castle Nowhere: Lake-Country Sketches*. Boston: Osgood, 1875. New York: Garnett, 1969. 270-303.

Jessie Brown Pounds

1861-1921

Ohio's last woman writer of nineteenth-century local color region-alism was raised in the greater Cleveland area. Her New England ances-try goes back to the Mayflower and a Minuteman in the Revolutionary War. Holland Brown, her father, migrated to Wadsworth in 1824 and later moved to a number of small communities in northeastern Ohio. This was an area purchased in 1706 by Connecticut to serve as its "Fire-lands" or "Western Reserve"; Moses Cleavland's surveyors in 1803 urged New Englanders like Holland Brown to westward migration. It was his conversion by the charismatic Scotsman Alexander Campbell, leader of the Disciples of Christ, that moved Brown's life away from farming, toward itinerant preaching, and, eventually, church pastorship.

Jessie Brown's mother was a country school teacher and her daughter was born in Hiram in 1861, the eve of the Civil War, in an abolitionist home where Sojourner Truth was entertained; six decades later, Jessie Brown Pounds also died in this village. And though born in the country-side, Jessie Brown Pounds spent most of her adult life in urban Cleve-land's environs. She grew up amid ardent conversations between local, Hiram College-based intellectuals like James A. Garfield and Burke Aaron Hinsdale. Hearing their stories of the Western's Reserve's pioneer days and debates about religion and politics, Jessie Brown's informal education led the precocious youngster to first-hand consideration of the region's tra-ditions. Her juvenalia reveals the girl's precocious commitment to being a professional writer who would carry on her family's heritage.

During the early 1880s, she attended Hiram College but withdrew because of medical problems. After that she trained as an editorial assis-tant with Isaac Errett, distinguished regional editor of the Disciples' *Christian Standard*, and her career was launched. During four creative decades, Jessie Brown Pounds wrote eight novels, over eighty sketches and stories, and scores of poems and lyrics. Her wide reading and family's intellectual culture led her to work in several genres but pre-dominantly in women's domestic traditions of moral entertainment; like Alice Cary, Mary Hartwell Catherwood, and Constance Fenimore Wool-son, her short fiction often celebrated Ohio's rural milieu and the mixed virtues of Protestant village life.

Unlike many other regionalists, however, Jessie Brown never desired to leave the land of her upbringing. She cared for her parents, and after her father's death, married another Disciples' minister, John Pounds, who supported her intellectual endeavors. Her editorships and work with charitable activities led Pounds to conferences and business outside the Western Reserve, but she was a shy and frail person who preferred to remain home in northeast Ohio.

Jessie Brown Pounds never achieved a broad national reputation as a regionalist because her career was limited by several factors: staying in Ohio, not courting the eastern literary establishment, and restricting her submissions to publications of the region's indigenous religion, the Disciples of Christ. In one sense, though, Pounds did claim a national reputation, and that was as a Protestant hymn writer; her compositions include over 800 lyrics, including the famous hymns, "The Touch of His Hand on Mine," "Beautiful Isle," and "The Way of the Cross Leads Home." In her maturity, she distanced herself from this genre and said that its conventionalized limits were restrictive. Another kind of national reputation was tantalizingly near in 1920 when Charles Clayton Morrison, the editor of the influential, nondenominational *Christian Century*, published at the University of Chicago, asked her to be a contributing editor. This new career phase created a national forum for her thoughtful essays, but in little over a year her career was tragically halted by sudden death at her Hiram home.

Like other nineteenth-century women writers, such as Harriet Beecher Stowe and Louisa May Alcott, Jessie Brown Pounds wrote in many genres including poems and didactic material for children. Her polemical writings for young people within the Disciples of Christ encouraged interdenominational activities like the Young Peoples' Society of Christian Endeavor. And often her moral viewpoints were embedded within a narrative that was located in an actualized Western Reserve village-city setting. One regional novel, for example, *The Young Man from Middlefield* (1901), concerns a village lad's visit with enervated Cleveland relatives; *The Popular Idol* (1901) offers a realistic analysis of failed urban pastorship. The most interesting extended use of regional subject matter is found in her historical novel, *Rachael Sylvestre* (1904), in which an old man recalls Portage County's Blue Brook during the days of Alexander Campbell's fiery leadership of the Disciples of Christ when Jessie Brown Pounds' father, Holland, was a teenager.

As well as writing polemical regional novels, in the 1880s Pounds wrote local color fiction in which she self-consciously adapted New England and middle-western regional traditions, such as the village literature of Harriet Beecher Stowe and Alice Cary. No other writer created village sketches about the Western Reserve pioneers, and in 1911 Jessie Brown Pounds published a traditional series of village-based character sketches drawn from the towns of the Western Reserve where she had lived as a child. The models were probably such towns as Hiram, Wadsworth, and Brooklyn. *Hillsbury Folks* is a series of local character sketches that includes dialect and rustic themes. She recreates a credible Firelands village replete with stores, post office, churches and a "graded school of brick," which was later swallowed by Cleveland's growth, leaving only a graveyard to signify its one-time booming status as a community.

Jessie Brown Pounds' Hillsbury characters include two village school ma'ams, the doctor, two parsons, a drunkard, and a scalawag with a "loafer's seat," a town institution. The town's professional leaders are vividly recreated: the two school marms are respectively saintly and vicious; the men are incompetent—the doctor is misguided, and the Methodist and Congregationalist ministers are inept; the village's drunk-ard is a fallen Methodist preacher who has become afraid of his devoted Scotch terrier's moral reproaches. The final character, "The Scalawag" is a corrupt clown, unique among the eight portraits of Hillsbury's remem-bered Western Reserve denizens. This 1880s sketch is of a post-Civil War character, Bolingbroke Hedding. He is a New England immigrant to the Firelands who claims to have been a fisherman, miner, and hunter; he also spent ninety days with the Grand Army of the Potomac, and Bully's military pension allows him to dabble in "the pursoot of your livin' by the means of your wits," by selling spoiled butter to the unsus-pecting housewives of nearby Cleveland. Mostly, Bully rules as Hills-bury's village philosopher in the general store, a "clown with a purpose," Pounds says, who combines humor and petty villainy. But his "gift of talk" which "usedter kinder hanker" for an audience is vitiated by chang-ing times and alcoholism. With the demise of his "loafer's seat" at the Hillsbury general store, the village, too, disappears.

Jessie Brown Pounds wrote dozens of local color stories during this era; two of her most mature stories are undated; they were found among her papers at the time of her death and published posthumously in 1921. Pounds creates a quintessential 1870s Western Reserve village she calls Craydock's Corners. In "Trouble at Craydock's Corners," the author asks the compelling question: will women's millinery standards expel the minister and his wife? This story effectively fuses two significant regional preoccupations of Pounds: how do Christian values operate in a rural community and what is women's social leadership role?

The story concerns Reverend Paul Reid's bride, who is victimized by village women's conformist standards. Pounds dramatizes Craydock

Corner's social dynamics; the women learn to embrace the minister and his hatless wife after their infant dies. The tragedy leads to village tolerance and the relinquishing of self-righteous social control by regional matriarchs. Jessie Brown Pounds thus affectionately endorses the Western Reserve village matrix, but comically upbraids the silliness of regional gatekeeping. The disappearing rural heritage of the Western Reserve is embodied in women like the Craydocks Corners' matriarch, Mrs. Seakin, and patriarchs, like Bijah Morrison. Their characterization is Pounds's greatest strength: keen verisimilitude in story line and dialect reveals how environment affects character. In the words of her editor, Charles Clayton Morrison, Jessie Brown Pounds' characters "seem not only like acquaintances of ours, but like kinfolks" (6). "Trouble at Craydock's Corners" represent her typical local color style that affectionately but unsentimentally develops the microcosm of provincial village life. Unlike Alice Cary, Harriet Beecher Stowe, or Constance Fenimore Woolson, Pounds does not often demonstrate Ann Douglas's contention that local color writers present "impoverishment."

In her professional life as an essayist and editor, Jessie Brown Pounds provides an unsentimental critique of late nineteenth-century regional culture. It was late in her career as a writer and editor that Pounds became involved with the intellectuals at the University of Chicago who were the progressive wing of the Disciples of Christ. She outspokenly defended women's right to promote liberal social viewpoints. Among her commitments were the advancement of the "New Woman," temperance, and the franchise. For three decades Jessie Brown Pounds gained editorial experience working for conservative denominational papers like the *Christian Standard*. Then in 1920 she joined the liberal editorial staff of the *Christian Century*, finding a new audience and the opportunity to promote her strong political and artistic credo. In this liberal, nondenominational publication, for example, Pounds expresses her dislike of naturalism and decadence, the new cultural currents in America. She also rebuts regional diatribes like Theodore Roosevelt's attack on the futile "Western school of art" (198-99). And Pounds evaluates, illustrates, and defends local color realism, ironically fighting a rear-guard action in an aesthetic war that was already lost.

Jessie Brown Pounds celebrates "the beautiful and gallant soul, conquering environment through sheer goodness and courage" ("Life" 9). She recognizes that the "romance of isolated Americanism" is disappearing, as was its keystone, regional dialect. She placed the blame on "the railroad, the rural mail delivery, the centralized school, the telephone, and the flivver." Gone, Pounds laments, is the unself-conscious culture of provincial life, "small-town stuff," which once created isola tion that might lead to "heroism, or self-satisfied bigotry and complacency."

Born during the Civil War and surviving World War I, this committed regionalist never stopped endorsing human nobility in characters who conquer "environment through sheer goodness and courage." Jessie Brown Pounds was the last nineteenth-century regional woman writer to depict Ohio's localities and characters as based upon her direct experience and memories.

Hillsbury Folks—The Scalawag

Jessie Brown Pounds

It is strange, when one really comes to think of it, the direction that local pride will sometimes take. I know of more than one village whose vanity centers in its cemetery vault.

We Hillsbury folks have two objects of pride—our Graded School and our Scalawag. We regarded these as, respectively, the best and the worst of their kinds.

The name of our Scalawag was *Bolingbroke Hedding,* but he was generally known as "Bully." I believe he had himself adopted this name, probably for advertising purposes.

"Bully" Hedding has seen the world. He had scoured the deck of a manofwar, he had fished off the coasts of Newfoundland, he had mined in Colorado, he had hunted in Maine, he had marched in the war with the Army of the Potomac. At least, he said he had done all these things. To this day I do not know whether he was an experienced traveler or merely a born novelist.

To the Hillsbury mind, Bully represented irresistible humor blended with accomplished villainy. He was more than an ordinary village clown. He was a clown whose antics had a sustained purpose. It was for this reason that the small boys admired him and that the preachers held him up as an awful example.

Bully had many trades, none of which seemed to interfere with his daily occupation. This was to sit on a pork-barrel at Wetzel's executing lies of all sorts with great originality of construction and freedom of expression, or else entertaining his present audience with accounts of the tremendous effect produced by his romancing on former audiences. It was thus delicately that he flattered a Hillsbury crowd with the belief that they were less gullible than other people.

That Bully and his family did not starve was due to this habit of mental inventiveness and the trustfulness of the public upon which he preyed. His wife, when judged by Hillsbury standards, was a perfectly incomprehensible person. The story of their marriage was still current. On one of Bully's periodical visits to his old home in New England he had chanced, at a neighborhood picnic, to fall in with a quiet little woman who was a "preceptress" in the village academy. By what arts of the tongue he had worked upon her sympathy it would be impossible to say; perhaps the poor creature had never been wooed before, and for this reason the woman within her was unable to resist. At any rate, he prevailed upon her to marry him within a month from the time of their first meeting, and to come with him to his miserable little cabin on the outskirts of Hillsbury. If she repented of her bargain she certainly made no sign. We of Hillsbury felt a certain awe-stricken pride in her learning, which we considered prodigious, and a few boys who were ambitious for a college education employed her to tutor them in higher mathematics. This was almost her only means of contact with her neighbors. What her lonely life was like, and whether or not she really admired her Scalawag, none of us ever knew.

Bully drew a pension. Seated on her favorite pork-barrel and expectorating tobacco juice with wonderful precision of aim, he told how this remarkable piece of luck had come to him:

"It's certainly true," he began, "in these days of criticism and suspicion, when a feller can't mix in enough bad eggs with the good ones to make sure of a decent profit, that a stiddy income from Uncle Sam is a mighty pleasant sort of incident. I usedter kinder hanker after a pension for it did seem to me that a feller who had served his country for ninety days, and helped to end a bloody and turrible war, deserved some sorter financial recognition at the hands of his country. There was old Capt. Farnsworth, now—he ain't half as deservin' as I be, an' he got his pension all right. Sure, he had four years' service an' permanent disability, but I maintain the country owes more tome than it does to him. 'cause why? 'Cause that old fire-eater hain't got one mite of objection to war. He'd have gone on fightin' till the crack o'doom, an' liked it. But I didn't. I was down on the fightin' from the first smell o' powder, an' you see I brought things to a double-quick stand-still. So I thought something was due me, but I didn't know how to get my hand on it, till the Old Doctor put a notion in my head. Says he, one day, when I'd been spinning a little yarn about the way I done old Shailey Roberts out of his gray horse, 'Bully,' says Old Doc, 'you're crazy as a loon,' says he. He meant this for a kind of compliment to my gift of talk, you understand.

'Doc,' says I, 'would you have any objection to makin' affidavit to that?'

'What for?' says he.

"'To git me a pension,' says I. 'I was in a tent once when a shell went whizzin' by takin' a piece right out of the canvas. I b'lieve it made me loony, an' I want a pension,' says I. The Old Doc was game, an' he stood by me. He was an old soldier himself, and not the feller to desert an old comrade. So he signed my papers an' I got my pension. It ain't much, but to a feller of simple tastes an' the soul of a philosopher I own it comes handy."

If Bully had been asked to name his calling, he probably would have said that he was in the butter and egg business. He was wont to declare that earlier in his career he had found this business profitable and interesting. But of late he was meeting difficulties.

"The human mind seems to delight in harborin' mean suspicions of its feller human minds," he was accustomed to say, "which makes the pursoot of your livin' by means of your wits more complicated every year. Now, time as when my business was easy an' pleasant. I could pick up all the stale butter an' eggs for forty miles round, an' be sure of findin' grateful and appreciative buyers. But times is sadly changed. For years it has been my cheerful custom to buy up the soap-grease butter of our friend Wetzel, here."

The storekeeper pretended to occupy himself with folding a bolt of calico, but Bully would not let him escape: "Sho, Joe, don't blush, the butter smelt to heaven, an' you know it. But I couldn't refuse the stuff, at ten cents a pound, for I calc'lated there was a way to combine rancid butter with genius in such a way as to make it sell. I packed it in tidy little crocks, with a skinny layer of Mother Bauder's best home-churnin' on top—twenty-five cents a pound I had to pay the old lady for it, but it brought the returns, all right. Then I put on my oldest clothes—which is sayin' a good deal—splashed a little extry mud on 'em, harnessed Dobbin to the green spring wagon, an' drove into the city. There I hitched my horse before the most select houses on the bullyvard, rung the front doorbell, an' insisted in seein' the lady of the house. Sometimes I struck a man in buttons, an' got an exodustin. But if 'twas a girl that opened the door I al'lays stuck to it till I got her to call her missus. Then I told my story, about my leetle farm, an' my cows that was treated as members of the family, an' my nice old woman, and the springhouse where we kept our milk, jest like the one her grandmother must have kept her milk in. Then I begged her to git a spoon an' taste the real country article. She'd do it, an' of course she'd buy, for nobody could resist Mother Bauder's best. She'd pay me an extry price for it, too, smilin' while she counted out the change, to show she wasn't above an ignorant old farmer an' callin' after me to come to the back door next time. But there wasn't no next time, that was the one drawback. I had to spot that house an' give it a polite margin in the future. But wors'n that has come. Last week two of them mean-heartin', suspicionin' females jabbed their spoons right down through the layer of Mother Bauder, an' brought up a taste of Wetzel's soap-grease! One of 'em even threatened to have the police after me. I'm afraid there's nothin' ahead of me but ruined fortunes an' a seat on this pork-barrel for the rest of my life.

This was indeed our Scalawag's fate. As he grew old, he became less inventive and more garrulous. Where the boys of one generation had admired and imitated him, those of the next played jokes upon him. In his old age he was indeed a sorry figure. Even Wetzel grew tired of him, and the Scalawag bid in vain for an audience to whom he could tell his old stories over. He drank still more more heavily and the wit upon which he had prided himself was stolen, long before he died, by the enemy he had put into his mouth.

His son, as dishonest as his father and less shrewd, went to the penitentiary for stealing horses. His daughter ran away with a circus rider. His wife died—of grief, no doubt, though no one ever really knew, for her long reserve was unbroken.

And so, deserted and unmourned, Bully himself died, to be speedily forgotten. I should not have remembered him now, save for two items which I read in today's paper. One was a paragraph concerning the inspection of dairy products under the pure food law of the state. The other was an account of the effort being made by a group of women's clubs to abolish the loafers' seats from village stores.

The world does move!

Trouble at Craydock's Corners

Jessie Brown Pounds

Those who went to meeting in the little church at Craydock's Corners were obliged to go in "facing." That is to say, the little pulpit known in the pious vernacular of the Corners as "the stand," was between the doors, and late comers were obliged to climb the slanting floor to the rear seats in full view of curious eyes. The men sat on one side and the women on the other. The babies were on the fence, so to speak. They began the service on the mother's side, but presently became restless and insisted upon being passed over the high seat partitions to their respective fathers. This was the beginnings of a series of "boostings," which continued with more or less regularity to the end of the sermon.

The rear seat of all, a mere bench against the wall, had no partition, and belonged to the choir. Thus it will be seen that the disadvantages belonging to the divided state of the congregation might be largely overcome by enterprising young persons who had their wits about them. For instance, Lon Bassett, who pitched the tunes, and Maretta Lummis, who carried them safely over the high places, were said to have come to an understanding through the gallantry with which he found the hymns in his fair neighbor's book and her graceful recognition of these delicate attentions. Youth is nothing if not ingenious, and ingenuity will always find a way.

The chief event in the social life of the Corners was when a newly-married couple "made their appearance." The wedding itself, however imposing it might be, was tame in comparison with this subsequent ceremony, which was enjoyed not only by relatives and friends, but by the citizens of surrounding townships. On this day of all days the bridegroom not only attended his wife to a seat, but sat with her during the entire service, in the awful and joyful discomfort of knowing that they were arrayed in their best, and the center of more attention than they would again receive in life. The only events which eclipsed these first appearances in importance were the funerals; and after the first glory had been attained life settled down to a sober, steady routine, apparently without other strong ambition than to have a long "procession" at one's funeral.

The preacher at Craydock's Corners was Paul Reid, a good-looking young man of four and twenty, who had been graduated from college the previous June, and had come to the Corners rich in the possession of a brand new Prince Albert coat and four sermons. He was surprised to find how soon one's stock of sermons is exhausted, but the suit remained fresh, he had a pleasant smile and a way of getting on with people, and so he stayed on. During the fall and winter he demolished the Higher Critics and preached a series of discourses on Jonah's gourd, and early in the spring he confessed that he was going to be married.

He was absent from the pulpit one Sunday, his place being filled by a colporteur who had offered to preach for the collection, and near the close of the following week it was announced that on Sunday the preacher and his bride would make their appearance.

It was the first time a preacher had ever married while in actual charge of the congregation at the Corners. Old Brother Hiland had, after betaking himself to fresh pastures, returned to carry off Miss Silena Grue as the consoler of a third—and brief—widowerhood; but this had scarcely seemed to call for an official demonstration. In Mr. Reid's case it was different. Something was expected of the Corners and the Corners was equal to the public expectation.

On Sunday morning vehicles of every kind and description, from 'Squire Seakin's great carry-all to Lon Bassett's dapper little sulky, were drawn up about the meeting house. Even the burying ground which was in the rear of the church, had been invaded, and horses were tied to the fence along the untenanted side. There had not been such a demonstration since that Fourth of July, when four townships united in the celebration and 'Squire Seakin's nephew spoke on "The Spirit of Liberty and the Future of the Republic."

Mr. Reid came late. This was according to the code, and not a word of censure was heard. He assisted his wife to alight, and then Lon Bassett, eager for a nearer view of the central attraction, came forward and offered to take the preacher's horse.

The bride was very small, and very, very young. She had big violet eyes, which seemed to be full of childish wonder. Lon decided that she was not nearly so handsome as Maretta Lummis, but that she looked like "a nice little thing."

Mr. Reid showed her to a seat, and then left her to begin the already belated service. The sisters craned their necks to get a view of her clothes, and their verdict was not favorable.

"Look at her hat!" whispered Mrs. Seakin to Mrs. Lummis. "I should have thought, bein' a preacher's wife, she'd have had a bunnet."

Sure enough, why had she not had a bonnet? The girl-wife asked herself this question many times in the weary months that followed. Perhaps the best which can be said for her is that she had never heard of a nineteen-year-old bride, even the bride of a preacher, who wore a bonnet; and being of a simple habit of mind, with no foresight for a crisis, she followed in the way of her limited experience.

The offending hat was not itself especially dangerous looking. It was a cheap little white chip, trimmed with a wreath of corn flowers and daisies, and with a knot of blue ribbon under the brim. Mrs. Seakin took it from the bed and looked at it that afternoon. Mr. Reid and his bride had come home to dinner with the Seakins, and were now taking a stroll in the orchard. "I wouldn't have minded so much if there hadn't been so many outsiders there," the Squire's wife murmured, with a heavy sigh. "I can't bear to see the preacher's wife set down before them—that's all."

During the week little Lucy Reid flitted about the cottage which was to be her home, in happy ignorance of the anxiety she was causing. And the preacher's ignorance was as complete. He put down carpets, hung up curtains, arranged his few books on their shelves, and told his wife that he had never really begun to live until now. And she enjoyed his saying it quite as much as if it had never been said before in the history of the world.

It was not until after another Sunday that the storm broke.

"Maybe she's got a bunnet," Mrs. Lummis had pleaded. "You can't blame her for wanting to be a little mite fixey when she made her appearance. I shouldn't wonder if she'd come out different another time."

But she had not. The little chip hat had been at church again, and had seemed to perch upon the wearer's head a little more airily than before.

On Monday afternoon Mrs. Seakin called at the cottage. She was a large and solemn woman, with a tremendous sense of her responsibilities. She was fond of saying that she would rather go through a stone wall than to go around it, and I am not sure but she would have preferred the stone wall to the open path.

Mrs. Reid was alone, for which she was thankful. Mr. Reid was one of those good natured fellows with whom serious conversation is difficult.

"I s'pose bein' a preacher's wife comes hard at your age," she said.

Lucy flushed. "I have hardly found out what it is like, yet," she said.

"U-um! You look dretful young. No wonder you need some one that's had experience to advise with. I always try to be an adviser to the preacher and his family. I want to see 'em set a good example before them that's without, and adorn the cause. I know they're only human, you see, and liable to make mistakes."

Poor little Lucy! Crushed and sick at heart, she nevertheless looked up quite bravely, as she said, tremblingly, "If you see anything in me that you don't like, I certainly hope you'll tell me so."

"O, no, I wasn't thinkin' of faultin' you or anyone. I was only sayin' you need some one that's had experience to help you along. Now, Brother Hiland's wife—the third one—she often says to me, "Sister Seakin,' she says, 'I never see any one in the pulpit or out, that's had as much experience with preachers as what you've had.' I was only thinkin' about that hat you wear. I ain't got nothin' at all against the hat, but we've never had a preacher's wife as young as you be, and we've always been on the habit of havin' 'em wear bunnets."

Lucy laughed—a hysterical little laugh. "I think a bonnet would look funny on me," she said.

Mrs. Seakin gathered herself up with as much dignity. "It ain't a matter of looks," she said. "A preacher's wife ought to adorn herself with a meek and quiet spirit, and not think about the vanities of this present world."

"I never thought it was any vanity," Mrs. Reid protested. "You have to wear something on your head, and I never thought it made any difference." She spoke in a mild tone, and Mrs. Seakin was encouraged.

"She's young and light-minded," she told Mrs. Lummis afterwards. "But I've got my plans, and they'll be carried out."

A week later the Seakin carry-all again stood before the cottage. This time the little bride seemed much stiffer and more reserved than before. The truth was, she had told her husband of the former interview, and he had keenly resented what he called "the abominable interference of that woman."

She melted somewhat, however, when Mrs. Seakin asked her to "take a ride," and accepted a place in the carry-all with real gratitude.

They drove to Miss Hortense Smith's milliner shop, which was kept in the front room of a small house opposite from the church. Miss Hortense seemed to expect them, and came forward, smoothing her white apron with an air of nervous eagerness.

"I want to fit you out with a bunnet," Mrs. Seakin told Lucy. "I told Mrs. Lummis it wasn't reasonable to ask you to buy a new one when you'd just been to the expense of your wedding things. So I says to Hortense she mustn't tax too high for a shape, now most of us have got our spring bonnets, and she won't have much chance to sell out what she's got. I guess we can make it up amongst us. Mis' Lummis had this bunch of berries that was on Maretta's last year's hat. You see, they ain't hurt a mite. And I bought a whole bolt of this striped ribbin when I was in town last fall. They was sellin' it out at half price, and I knew I'd come around to need it. I trimmed Lucy May's spring hat with some of it, but there's plenty to put all you want on the bunnet. I don't want you to be one mite stingy with it, Hortense—just use a plenty. And, now then, I want to see you try on your shapes."

The "shape" selected by Mrs. Seakin was a prim little capote of black straw, under which the childish face looked like that of a little masquerader. It was a very set face now, for Lucy's humiliation had gone deep.

When the new bonnet was shown to Mr. Reid his indignation rose to a fever heat. Like many persons who bear well the pain which comes to themselves, he was quick to resent a hurt to the one he loved.

"Give the thing to me!" he told his wife. He caught the prim little bonnet and would have flung it into the fire had not her quick hand saved it.

"Don't dear!" she begged. "They don't know what they are doing. They don't know how it hurts. O, don't let's mind it more than we have to!"

"Mind it! It's the grossest impertinence! My poor little girl, to think I have brought you to this!"

She insisted on wearing the bonnet, and for a few weeks the parish was calm. But it was evident that the preacher had lost much of his hold upon the people. He avoided meeting them in their homes, and his preaching no longer appealed to them as it had done.

As for his wife, she grew more shy and quiet every day, and the look of homesickness in her violet eyes was something pitiful to see.

In July a college friend of Mr. Reid's came to spend Sunday, and was invited to preach. On Sunday morning, as Mrs. Reid entered the sitting room dressed for church, her husband rose and came forward.

"You shall not wear that hideous thing today!" he said, untying the strings of the little black bonnet. "What will Littleton take us for? Go and get your hat and try to look like yourself."

Lucy knew full well that in this case obedience would not be a wifely virtue, and yet she obeyed. It is sweet to be told to do what you would like to do if you dared.

The metaphorical red flag could not have caused more excitement than did the little chip hat on the occasion of its reappearance. The 'Squire edged close to the seat partition to get a full view of his wife's face, and Maretta Lummis nudged Lon Basset's elbow when he handed her the hymn book.

"Well, I do allow!" was all that Mrs. Seakin condescended to say. She did not allow, though, and everybody at the Corners was aware of the fact.

Mrs. Lummis, not having the same sense of responsibility, expressed herself freely. "A bunnet ain't fixey enough for her city friends," she said. "She's awful light-headed and onrealizin' Sister Seakin."

From this time there was a chill over the church. Poor little Mrs. Myler, who had a soft heart and was accused of a head to match, did indeed display her weakness by sending the preacher a chicken at Thanksgiving. Some of the boys and girls who had been attracted at the first by Lucy Reid's gentle friendliness persisted in saying that she was "a nice little thing." But otherwise there was a studied coldness in the manner of the people toward the preacher and his wife. The general impression was that the latter was childish and worldly, and that the minister, though undoubtedly capable of better things, was inclined to minister to her foolish vanities.

With the return of spring a baby girl came into the preacher's home—a tiny, wrinkled, old-faced baby, with a look something strangely like homesickness in its violet eyes.

For the first time since the second week of her married life the girl-wife seemed completely happy. All the imprisoned life within her seemed to be set free. Into her face there came a look which was not quite the old expression of childish wonder, but was rather the pure, deep yearning of motherhood—the expression the masters have tried in vain to give to the purest of their Madonna faces.

Her mother, who was with her, wondered what the history of the year had been, but she learned nothing. When the iron has really entered our souls we do not talk of our wounds.

"Why don't you go to the meeting today?" her mother asked one Sunday morning. "Better slip away while I am here to look after Baby."

Lucy looked up quickly, in an anxious, almost frightened way. Her mother had seen the same look when Mrs. Seakin came in solemn fashion to inspect the baby. But she went at once to make ready for church.

Mr. Reid was away, fulfilling his monthly appointment in an adjoining town, and the brethren held a "social" meeting. There was nothing very social about it except the name. After this—why of course! How silly of her not to have remembered that this was the time for the annual business meeting.

'Squire Seakin presided. He was a short man, who had been stout and grown thin, and had accumulated amazing wrinkles in the latter process. He had a fringe of whiskers under his chin, and a rasping voice which made Lucy think of the sound caused by scraping a piece of ribbon with the finger nail.

"Brethren," he said, "we hev before us some solemn and important dooties." Here he cleared his throat, and Lucy thought he tried to look over her head. "The first one is, the withdrawin' of fellowship from them that's been walkin' disorderly. It's my painful dooty to say that one sech case has been reported. Sister Lowizy Benslow, she that was Lowiszy Betts, is the name to be considered."

Old Brother Grue arose. "What charge is brought agin sister Benslow?" he inquired.

'Squire Seakin was unflinching. "She has absented herself from the assemblin' of ourselves ever sence last summer," he said, sadly, but firmly. "An' worse than that, I am informed by some of the sisters that hev visited her that her house is redickelously dirty."

Lucy gave a little convulsive movement. She would have laughed, only that she was so strongly tempted to cry. Poor Lowizy Benslow, with her five babies and her shiftless husband—Lowizy, who was raise "on the town," and had married into pauperism and hopelessness! Must the last door be closed against her?

The preacher's wife voted "No!" on the question of the withdrawal of fellowship, but perhaps no one heard the timid little voice. At all events Lowizy Benslow was withdrawn from in proper form, and Lon Bassett laboriously noted the fact in the clerk's book.

"We now hev another dooty to perform," the 'Squire began again. "We hev come to the time when we must think of hirin' a new preacher for the comin' year. We can get Brother Reid agin, I understand, if it's thought best."

This time Brother Lummis arose: "I hear Brother Thornberry's to be hed for three-quarters of his time," he said. "He's a older man than Brother Reid, and hez had more experience. His wife"—he, too, seemed to make an effort to look over Lucy's head—"his wife is a powerful sight to help him, managin' the Ladies' Aid Society, and sech like."

"How high does he tax?" queried old Brother Grue, who was notoriously careful of his dollars.

"I understand he'll hire with us three-quarters of his time for four hundred dollars," 'Squire Seakin informed him, with amazing readiness. "That's the same we've been payin' Brother Reid."

There was an awkward pause. Lucy longed to fly, but she felt certain that she could not move.

"I'd like to git an expression of opinion," 'Squire Seakin resumed. "All them that's in favor of hirin' Brother Reid for another year say 'aye.'"

There was a feeble response, coming from young people and from those inconsiderate persons who always vote on any question whenever they were asked to do so.

"Now, them that's in favor of Brother Thornberry," the 'Squire suggested.

The chorus was quite general. No one seemed to know just what to say. Lon Bassett toyed absently with his tuning fork for a moment, and then started up, through force of habit, "Praise God from Whom All Blessings Flow."

Ten minutes later the preacher's wife, with the face of one who has been hurt beyond all healing, slipped into the door of her little home and covered her baby's face with kisses and tears.

The Aid Society had been in session in Mrs. Seakin's best parlor. It had been the time for the annual elections of officers, which accounted for the fact that the best parlor was in use. Ordinary quilting meetings were held in the big family room across the hall.

Mrs. Seakin had been president of the Aid Society since its organization, so the formality of an annual election might have seemed useless to one unaccustomed to the social forms of Craydock's Corners. In point of fact this annual meeting was a great occasion, for the brethren were invited in to supper, and each of the sisters contributed some culinary marvel in the way of pyramid cakes or lemon cream pies. These feats often left their memories for weeks and months in the way of impaired digestions and housewifely jealousies. Indeed it was said that Mrs. Lummis and Mrs. Hayete had had their back door neighborliness permanently impaired by Mrs. Hayte's cool affirmation that she liked to put a little more into the inside of her cakes than some folks did, and not quite so much foolishness on top.

The brethren had been served, the second table had been filled with weary and triumphant women, the dishes had finally been disposed of, and the company, having gone through the conventionalities with credit, settled themselves into easy attitudes and made ready to enjoy themselves. Lon Basset asked 'Squire Seakin how many acres he had put into corn, and what he thought of the chances for a rise in wheat. Mrs. Seakin told little Mrs. Myler that she had put up seventy-two quarts of strawberries, and Mrs. Myler, sadly overawed, confessed that she would be obliged to get along with half that number. Then, the conversational machinery having been oiled, everybody felt easy and comfortable, and began to talk about the preacher and his wife.

"Brother Reid's folks ain't out this evenin', I see," Brother Lummis remarked, boldly. "I s'pose he's heard what action the church took Sunday."

"Pretty likely he has," said Mrs. Lummis, briskly, "when his own wife was there and heard every word of it. I should have thought," she whispered to Maretta, "that Sister Reid would have managed to get out this afternoon, seein' there wasn't no quiltin' to be done. She's a dretful poor quilter and I suspicion, she don't like to come when there's a quilt on."

"They say that sister Thornberry is a prime one at quiltin's," old Brother Grue suggested. "I guess she'll run things all right."

This suggestion was a most unfortunate one. Mrs. Seakin was proud of her ability to manage an Aid Society single-handed, and the hint that Mrs. Thornberry might take matters into her own hands was not relished.

"I guess the women at the Corners know how to put on and take off a quilt without any help," she remarked to Mrs. Myler in a cold aside. "I showed Sister Thornberry that quilt we took off last month—the one we put nine spools of thread into—and she allowed herself she never laid eyes onto anything handsomer."

The conversation flagged, but 'Squire Seakin took the matter up in a semi-official tone. "I s'pose Brother Thornberry had better be notified right off," he said. "The Blue Point folks hain't paid him up very prompt, and he's anxious to hire with us, so I guess there won't be any trouble."

"I feel kind of sorry for Brother and Sister Reid," said Mrs. Myler, shyly. "They'll feel awful cut up, I'm afraid."

Mrs. Myler's position was clearly unpopular, and no one supported her in it.

"Wal, Brother Reid couldn't noways expect to hold his own with Brother Thornberry," 'Squire Seakin resumed, still speaking officially. "He ain't no such Scriptorian as Brother Thornberry is. Brother Thornberry, you know, he gives us chapter an' verse straight through, from Genesis to Revelation. An' he's powerful strong at argyin'. He has nine debates with the Seventh Day Advents, an' Brother Cloverhill, over to Blue Point, says he has beat 'em every time."

"Brother Reid is awful easy on the denominations," said Brother Grue, with an air of one making the most damaging statement possible. "For my part, I believe in comin' out from among 'em an' being separit an' able to give a reason for the hope thet's in ye."

"I guess Brother Reid will have a pretty hard time to git another place," Brother Lummis ventured.

"Brother Reid has some hendrances," observed Mrs. Seakin, in a tone which suggested unutterable things in the way of white chip hats and worldly vanities. All were silent for a moment. Presently she herself took up the thread. I do say that them that's set over the Lord's vineyard ought to be examples, and not put stumbling-blocks in the way of them that's without."

All nodded assent except Mrs. Myler, who was always on the soft side of a question.

"Sister Reid is real young," she pleaded, "and she's got an awful kind heart. I see her over to Lowizy Benslow's day before yesterday, with her baby. I think jest as like as not she was laboring with that poor creature."

Mrs. Seakin withered her with a glance. "I ain't a-faultin' sister Reid or any one," she said. "It's jest as I've always said—she's onrealizin' an' took up with vanities. She's more fit to be a seekin' counsel for herself than she is to be guidin' them that's gone out of the way."

A bustle at the door interrupted the conversation. Dr. Caskey had come in. Dr. Caskey was the village doctor, a shrewd old man, of whom Paul Reid had once said that he never loved people until he found them sick and dependent upon him, and never ceased to love them afterward.

There was a chorus of welcomes, for every home about the Corners was more or less indebted to the Doctor's skill.

"You ought to have been here before," said Maretta Lummis, with the agreeable pertness of a girl who knows that she is pretty and knows that other people know it. "Ma brought one of the black fruit cakes that you always say are going to be the death of us, so you can expect to have at least twenty cases within the next week."

"Good thing I didn't come, then," was the doctor's comment. "More profitable to stay away."

He seemed downcast, however, and would not sit down.

"No," he said, "I won't stop. The truth is, I'm in no mind for it. I've just come from Brother Reid's, and I'm afraid they're going to lose their baby."

"Don't tell me!" cried a dozen women at once. There was a sudden commotion, as they hastily gathered together their baskets and tied on their bonnets. At the corners, sick people were common property.

"I wouldn't all go over there at once," was the Doctor's advice. "They need you, but one or two at a time will be better."

"I'm goin' over an' set up there tonight," said Mrs. Seakin, with the face of a soldier ready for battle. Everybody about the Corners knew that Mrs. Seakin was "good in sickness."

"Im goin' with you," said Mrs. Myler, tearfully. "Poor little lamb—I guess it would be glad to go, if it knew what kind of world it's got into." Mrs. Myler, like many other soft-hearted persons, could give a thrust on her own part, now and then.

The two women found that one visitor had already arrived at the cottage. It was poor Lowizy Benslow, who sat on the back step, with her head buried in a corner of her ragged shawl, and crying as if her heart were broken.

"O lawsy, she's a-goin' to die!" she moaned. "She's got them awful spasms. An' she's going to die, an'—an'—I'd ruther 'twas one of my own, Mis' Myler—the Lord knows I'd ruther 'twas one of my own. Why, she brung it to see me, herself, she did, when everybody else was set agin me, an' wouldn't look at me noways, she brung that darlin' little baby right into my house for me to see. She says, "I thought you'd like to see my little girl, an' I know you don't ever git time to go nowheres,' she says. An' now she's a-goin to lose it, an' the Lord knows I'd ruther it was own of my own—an' me not fit to bring em up like that angel would." She rocked to and fro in her misery, and Mrs. Myler gave her neighbor a look of awful significance.

All night the two women worked over the dying baby. There was little indeed that really needed to be done, except to comfort the father and mother; and for this duty, unfortunately, Mrs. Seakin felt herself peculiarly well qualified.

"It's a real blessin' to have her took," she told Lucy, soothingly. "They ain't hardly ever right after havin' spasms, an' you couldn't ask to have the poor thing grow up an idiot. I thought they was something wrong with her the first time I ever see her. I says to Sister Lummis at meeting, the very next Sunday, I says, "There's something wrong with that baby, Sister Lummis, an' it'll be a mercy if she's took early."

Lucy bore all this with singular patience, but her husband tramped the floor with a savage face and a leaden heart. Now and then he paused in this weary march to lay his hand for a moment upon his wife's head. If he could have borne it for her—but, alas! he did not know how to bear it for himself.

Just at dawn the tiny limbs grew quiet, the wrinkled little face settled into peace, and the violet eyes were closed, nevermore to open, with their look of homesickness, upon this world.

When Mrs. Myler said softly, "It's all over," Lowizy Benslow, sitting at the foot of the bed, broke into a piteous wail.

"Hush, Lowizy," the girl mother whispered tenderly, between her quiet sobs. "She will be happy—my poor little baby."

Mrs. Seakin tried to speak some appropriate word of philosophy, but, to her own surprise, the lump in her throat had deprived her of utterance. Mechanically she took the dainty little garments which Lucy brought, and began to prepare the little one for her last sleeping place.

As she wrought at her lonely task, the years seemed to slip away from her, and she was herself a young wife, sitting dry-eyed beside the body of her first born. She could hear 'Siah saying—'Siah's voice had not been so rasping in those earlier days—"I s'pose, Mirandy, the baby's better off," and she could hear her own sharp answer, "Better off! Don't tell me that! The Lord gave her to me, an' now He knew what He was doin'. I don't b'lieve nothin' about it's bein' His will that she should be took." Somehow Mrs. Seakin had always felt that she was peculiarly privileged in understanding the Lord's will.

That was twenty years ago, but the old pain was still there. The children who had come since had not filled the vacant place in her heart. "Jason an' Lury May favor their pa," she said softly, as she smoothed the cold baby face before her. "But my first one—she was featured like the Summerses. Seems, somehow, as if this one looked like her."

She heard voices in the adjoining room, and rose to close the door. As she did so, she heard the preacher's wife saying, softly:

"But it is so sweet to have had her, Paul—no one can ever take that away from us. And we shall have her again—I know we shall. She is so safe for all the years to come, and then we shall have her again, and feel that, even though she is so much better and wiser than we are, she is still our very own."

"O, darling," groaned her husband, if I could feel that way. But you are right, and O! so brave, and I will try."

Mrs. Seakin had never been accused of possessing less than the average share of feminine curiosity, but she nevertheless closed the door and went away. The front room was full of women by this time, but she waved them back majestically. "I promised sister Reid that I would lay out the baby with my own hands," she said.

* * *

Never, since the burial of old Major Craydock, when all the Masonic lodges in the country had attended the remains, had the Corners seen such a funeral.

"Did you ever hear of the like?" questioned Mrs. Lummis of Maretta, as they came in sight of the church. "The Bassett girls have always had a lot to say about the long procession their mas had, but I don't believe they was more than two-thirds as many buggies. I doubt if it was more than half."

Brother Thornberry conducted the funeral service. He was a spare man, with a high voice and amazing fluency of utterance. In his prayer he dwelt at length on the mysterious dispensations of Providence, and expressed the hope that sinners would be warned and fall in with the divine overtures of mercy, since such sudden visitations were possible and might come at any moment. "For we know not," he said, "how many of us may be laying upon our cooling boards before the dawn of another morning." His sermon, too, was severely doctrinal, and was aimed particularly at the friendly outsiders who came seldom to hear preaching except on funeral occasions. His peroration was what Sister Lummis afterward described as "awfully solemizin," and was followed by the good old hymn beginning:

> "O, lovely appearance of death!
>   What sight on earth is so fair?
> Not all the pageants that move
>   Can with a dead body compare!"

Then the great moment came, and Craydock's Corners "viewed the remains." Slowly and decorously the long march went on, as the heads of old and young in turn were bent over the tiny casket. Like a bit of Parian marble seemed the sleeping babe, lying in its bed of white roses. There had been roses and to spare, for every garden yielded its choicest blossoms.

The march ended, the father and mother were bidden to take their last look. The people viewed the scene with undisguised interest. Their hearts were full of real sympathy, but they would not have missed this part of the service for the world.

There was one person at the funeral who had not been in the church for a long, long time before. Lowizy Benslow had slipped in, and sat in one of the short seats near the door, with a forlorn-looking baby on her lap. When Lucy Reid laid her face against that of her baby, she almost mechanically took a half-blown rose from the casket; and she held it in her hand, when pale and brave, she walked out beside her husband, between the long rows of curious eyes. Lowizy, standing in the shadow of the church porch, gave a little sob at the sight. Lucy looked up and saw her, and, with something like a smile, she placed the white rose in the toilworn hand.

Mrs. Seakin and Mrs. Lummis were standing together when Mrs. Reid entered the carriage, after the sad little service in the graveyard. Both noticed at he same moment that she wore a small black straw bonnet, with a fold of black crepe in it. It was the prim little capote.

The two women rode home together. "Sister Reid looks bad," Mrs. Lummis said, when the silence had been unbroken for a long time. "Seems to me she's fallen off like everything the last few days. I believe she looks older in a bunnet than she does in a hat—don't you think so?"

Mrs. Lummis had been burning with desire to mention the bonnet, and felt that she had done so with an adroitness and decorum which benefitted the occasion. But she received no encouragement.

"May be she does," Mrs. Seakin agreed, absently.

"I never see a baby laid out so pretty," Mrs. Lummis went on, well knowing Mrs. Seakin's weakness. "I told Maretta I thought you never done quite so nice before—bein' the time of roses, an' all."

"May be not," was the forced response. Then, as if with a determined effort, she rallied herself and changed the subject. "I s'pose it's so," she said, interrogatively, "that Lon and Maretta are goin' to make their appearance next Sunday?"

*   *   *

The following evening the preacher and his wife sat in the June twilight, hand in hand, trying to think about the future. The last year had been full of heartaches, yet now that the time had come they shrank from leaving the place. The new grave of their child was here, and in the past week the people had been full of unexpected kindness.

They were roused by a knock at the door. To knock, at the Corners, implied that a call was formal, if not official, and the preacher hastened to open the door.

"Good evenin,' Brother Reid," said 'Squire Seakin, "would you mind steppin' outside?"

Mr. Reid stepped outside at once, anxious to save his wife from any new pain.

"I jest came over," said the 'Squire, trying hard to modulate his rasping voice, "to tell you that we ain't hired Brother Thornberry yit, an' we don't want to, unless we're obleeged to. The fact is, I guess our women folks hain't jest understood each other—an'—an' if you ain't spoke for, we hope you'll stay at Craydock's Corners for a considerable spell yit."

He reached out his hand, and Mr. Reid took it without a word. The trouble at Craydock's corners had been buried in the grave of a little child.

Bibliography

Bailey, Fred A. "Disciples Images of Victorian Womanhood." *Discipliana* 40.1 (Spring 1980): 7-12.

Kingsley, Ruth Reynard. "A Great Little Lady." *Western Reserve Magazine* Jan.-Feb. 1983: 7-8.

Morrison, Charles Clayton. "Jessie Brown Pounds, An Appreciation." *Jessie Brown Pounds: Memorial Selections.* Ed. John E. Pounds. Chicago: Disciples Publication Society, 1921. 5-11.

Parker, Sandra. "An Enduring Prophet." *The Disciple* 16.11 (Nov. 1989): 25-26.

——. "Separating Apples, Potatoes and Peaches: Jessie Brown Pounds, Advocate of the Social Gospel in Cleveland, 1880-1920." *Western Reserve Studies Symposium. The Cleveland Western Reserve Historical Society* (Nov. 1989): 1-13.

——. "A Yankee with Crust: Ohio Writer Jessie Brown Pounds." *Ohioana Quarterly* 33.1 (Spring 1990): 2-7.

Pounds, Jessie Brown. "Life and Modern Fiction." *Christian Century* 24 Feb. 1921: 8.

——. "The Scalawag." *Christian Evangelist* 7 Sept. 1911: 1271-72. Rpt. in *Memorial Selections*. Ed. John E. Pounds. Chicago: Disciples Publication Society. 1921: 251-56.

——. "The Trouble at Craydock's Corners." *Memorial Selections*. Ed. John E. Pounds. Chicago: Disciples Publication Society, 1921. 188-211.

Roosevelt, Theodore. "What Americanism Means." *Forum* 17 (April 1984): 198-99.